The Unexpected

The Unexpected

Donal Myrick

Library of Congress Control Number:		2019913804
ISBN:	Hardcover	978-1-7960-5881-9
	Softcover	978-1-7960-5880-2
	eBook	978-1-7960-5879-6

Print information available on the last page.

Rev. date: 09/12/2019

To order additional copies of this book, contact:
Xlibris
1-888-795-4274
www.Xlibris.com
Orders@Xlibris.com
796529

CHAPTER 1

It wasn't a really large earthquake as earthquakes go, but at 6.9 on the Richter Scale it gave a good shaking to the area. It was centered just off of the coast of Venezuela and about six miles deep. While all eyes were focused looking north in anticipation of a possible tsunami hitting the coast of Venezuela or washing over the ABC islands, the real action was occurring to the south where the Churum River, which normally spilled from the top of the high table mountain Auyán tepui creating the world's highest waterfall, suddenly dried up. Angel Falls located in Venezuela's Canaima National Park suddenly was no more.

Atop the Auyán tepui a giant crack in the normally impervious sandstone cap had opened up swallowing the Churum River. This new chasm was about a half mile long and roughly fifty to one hundred feet wide. The river cascaded down several hundred foot high waterfalls and finally disappeared into the mouth of a large dark cave. The remainder of the Churum's river bed leading to the edge of the escarpment was completely dry.

Miguel Santos, a Park Ranger with the Parque Nacional Canaima, was among the first to witness the demise of Angel Falls which he immediately brought to the attention of his superiors in the Venezuelan Department of Parks. Needless to say, the Venezuelan government and especially the personnel in the Department of Parks experienced an immediate and massive panic attack with the apparent loss of their crown jewel of natural wonders. This was a potentially devastating and irreplaceable loss to the country both in terms of international tourism and national prestige.

The Venezuelan Department of Parks immediately dispatched a photo recon team to investigate and document the event. Angel Falls often dries up during the dry season, but this event occurred during the middle of the wettest rainy season on record. Obviously something catastrophic had just occurred, and no one was prepared for what they would soon discover.

While similar earthquakes have occurred in the past off of the coast of neighboring Columbia to the west without causing any major damage or tsunamis, the fault where this earthquake occurred was completely unknown. No seismic activity had ever been recorded this far to the east. Further, since the Table Mountains of Venezuela are some of the most remote and difficult to access areas on the planet, the geology of the area has not been fully explored nor well described. So, other than the fact that the two events occurred basically at the same time, it was hard to definitively connect the two events. This lack of information made it impossible for the government officials to proffer more than mere speculations about what had happened and what was the likely impact on the Venezuelan economy.

News of this event stirred both shock and excitement throughout the scientific community. So when the Venezuelan government asked for assistance, scientific institutions across the planet were eager to come, investigate the event and recommend a course of action to restore the world's highest waterfall. The response from the scientific community was swift and massive. Unfortunately, the region was quickly overwhelmed by the teams of people flocking the region. It is a very remote region, and had a very limited capacity to accommodate their needs for lodging, food, transportation, and communication as well as other basic necessities. Despite the fact the Venezuela is a major oil producing country, petrol in the quantities required by all the vehicles, boats, and aircraft converging in the area, was simply not available. This in turn put a serious damper on the accomplishment of any really useful scientific investigations. After months of fumbling about, talking heads recording sound bites for their home networks, excessive complaining about the lack of support from the Venezuelan government, and massive environmental impact on the local environs, most of the teams returned to their home countries without accomplishing much of anything.

There were a few exceptions. The Venezuelan equivalent of the U.S. Corp of Engineers did establish a primitive runway near Jimmy Angel's original landing site that was capable of handling light aircraft, and they cleared several landing pads for helicopters. One of the teams from one of the nature magazines did a drone video survey of the narrow gorge and several hundred feet back into the gaping cave at the end of the gorge.

This gave the world at large a view as to what a massive event this was. A geological team from a major U.S. university, also using drones, developed a high resolution laser map of the gorge and about a thousand feet of the cave back to where the Churum River disappeared into a dark deep chasm.

In terms of how to fix the problem, a few big international construction firms concluded that the only way to restore the flow to the falls would to build a large aqua duct over the gorge re-connecting the river to the now dry river bed beyond the gorge thus returning the Churum River flow to the falls. They also noted that this would be a massive, expensive, and extremely challenging engineering effort considering the remoteness of the area. No actual proposals were offered, and that in turn begged the question as to who would step up to do the project, and who would pay for it.

Those were the only tangible real results produced during the few months following the earthquake. Everyone came and then everyone left. News interest waned, and soon only a few entities in the government and those directly connected to the Canaima National Park continued to have a concern. All that were left were the massive environmental impacts, huge piles of trash, many unanswered questions, and little continuing international interest.

That is until a group of spelunkers from a caving club, also known as a Grotto, near Austin, Texas acquired access to the laser map of the Churum River Cave. The notion that the entire Churum River disappeared into a dark deep chasm got their attention big time. Exploring deep dark complicated caves is what they lived for. This is what they did. This was the most exciting deep pit prospect that they had heard about in years. Many members of this group had spent the better part of their adult lives exploring deep pit caves in Northern Alabama and Georgia and the thousand foot deep pits in the Yucatan area of Mexico. The possibility of exploring a potential two thousand foot deep pit was just something they could not pass up.

It began when Ted Baldridge, PhD, a consultant to the oil industry and an adjunct professor of geology at a local Texas state college received a copy of the laser map of the Churum River Cave. He was also a caver, and he had been following the Angel Falls saga with some professional interest. Ted was highly intrigued with the obvious relationship between the earthquake and the opening of the Churum River Gorge. When Ted brought up the digital map, it didn't take him two minutes to note the identification of a pit at the terminus of the laser mapped portion of the cave. When he noted that the river disappeared into this pit, he immediately recognized the potential for a pit with a record setting depth. He knew his caver friend Max Meccum needed to see this and needed to see it quick.

Ted got on the phone and called Max. "Yo, Max."

"Hey Ted", Max replied, "What's up?"

Ted said, "Max, I've got something that you've got to see. How quickly can you get over to my place?"

"I can leave right now. I'll be there in fifteen minutes. What do you have that is so important? Are you okay, you sound upset."

"No, I'm okay. I'm definitely not upset, I'm just excited. Get over here quick as you can, and I'll fill you in when you get here."

"Okay, I'm on my way."

Sure enough, when Ted showed the Churum River Cave map to Max, Max was immediately frothing at the bit to go and check it out. Ted brought Max up to speed on what he knew of the recent history of the event and all that had transpired since.

Max said, "Ted, I fully understand why you have an interest in this cave, but really, how did you come by this information? And, given that you have it, others must have it also. How come there isn't a caravan of cavers trekking to Venezuela to check this out? I remember seeing something about this on television a couple of months ago, but there was never a mention of a deep pit back in the cave."

Ted said, "It is true that I have a professional interest in the event. I've been following everything that has been published on this event ever since it occurred. One of my colleagues made me aware that this map was available to anyone who had an interest. So, I immediately downloaded it. When I saw the pit, I called you. I knew you would have an interest."

They both speculated as to why there was no significant follow up interest in this incredible geological event from the geological community or in the cave with its potentially deep pit from any caving organizations. Max concluded that, "Well, speaking for the caving community, it must have had something to do with the fact that there was little or no mention of a potentially deep, deep pit. Or, perhaps the logistics and likely cost of conducting a massive expedition in such a remote region, and the probable extreme difficulty in actually successfully exploring the pit was a deterrent."

"Or maybe the right cavers were simply not aware of it yet", said Ted.

Max Meccum was now aware of it, and he was not to be deterred by the potential difficulties. This was now at the top of his to do list, and he knew that it definitely would be worth pursuing.

Max was a real estate lawyer, who fortunately had just recently completed the closing of a forty million dollar land development deal. So, not only would it be possible for him to take time away from his professional job, he was looking for an excuse to get away from the stresses of his high pressure job for a while. This was the perfect excuse. The opportunity to explore this new cave with its potential world record pit was just exactly what he needed. Ted, on the other hand, stated that his interest in the cave was primarily professional, but deep down, he knew that he was just as eager as Max was to bounce that pit. As an adjunct professor, he had a very flexible teaching schedule, so it would not be difficult for him to take professional time away from his teaching duties to pursue the exploration. His consulting business would just have to wait a bit.

They decided to contact a couple of members of the local Grotto whom they knew very well and had shared extensive caving experiences while exploring some of the deep caves of the Yucatan. Max knew that when he and Ted told them about the cave what their answer would be even before he asked the question, "Are you guys interested in checking out the Churum River Cave?." Their answer would of course be an enthusiastic "YES".

Both of the people that Max initially contacted were self-employed or else worked in an industry that permitted them to take considerable time off from their jobs for personal reasons. The first person Max contacted was Peggy Allen. Peggy was a very attractive tall and slender woman. She was athletic and adventurous. She had not only caved with Max but she had also worked professionally with him. She also kinda liked Max. Peggy was an expert drone pilot and photographer. She worked primarily in the real estate industry supporting the marketing of high end properties with her photography. Her skills were in high demand, and she was able to set her own hours. She often lent her skills to law enforcement to photograph crime scenes, and sometimes for the surveillance of persons of interest. Her real passion however was cave photography, and her drone photography skills had earned her numerous awards. Basically, she was able to pick and choose when she worked, and that generally was whenever she needed money for the pursuit of something of personal interest.

When Max called, he said, "Peggy, I hope you don't have any plans for the near future."

This got Peggy's attention, and she replied jokingly, "Oh Max, is this a proposal? I know we have been friends for a long time and I really like you, but this is kinda sudden."

Max said, "Oh, cut it out. I've got a proposal alright. Do you want to go caving?"

With a more serious tone, Peggy said, "When the infamous Max Meccum calls and asks if I want to go caving, my answer is of course yes. I assume you will tell me when and where later."

Max said, "Our friend Ted has come up with a lead that we absolutely must check out before others get wind of it. Do you know if Jim Ralston is in town?"

"Yes, as far as I know. I haven't talked with him since the last grotto meeting."

"I think I'll ping him now," Max said, "and if he is around, we will need to get together as soon as possible."

Peggy asked, "Aren't you going to at least tell me a little something about this incredible lead before you call Jim?"

Apologizing, Max said, "Oh sorry, I'm so excited about this prospect that I'm getting ahead of myself." Max proceeded to fill Peggy in on the details of the Churum River event, after which Peggy was beside herself with excitement and anticipation.

After Max finished filling Peggy in on the Churum River Cave prospect, he contacted Jim Ralston. Jim was an electrician who worked in the HVAC construction industry, so his work was often seasonal. Jim was also an experienced vertical caver. Jim had a couple of other skills which would later prove useful to the expedition: he was a licensed ham radio operator and most importantly, he was bi-lingual. Jim's mother was Columbian, so Spanish was his second language.

"Jim, are you busy these days?" Max asked when he called.

"Not really. I'm just messing around waiting for my next job opportunity. I'm not working at the moment. What's on your mind?" As with Peggy, after Max explained, Jim was immediately on board.

Ted suggested that they all meet soon at the La Ventana Cantina to toss some ideas around and begin planning the expedition. This group often met at the La Ventana for burgers and beers, and they had their own semi-reserved table near the back.

When the group got together, Ted brought out his laptop and displayed the laser map of the gorge and the cave. Ted said, "This map was made by a group from MSU using a drone laser mapper. It is not the best map in the world, and Peggy, I'll bet you could do a much better job. The MSU folks were among the original group of scientist that went to Venezuela to research the post-earthquake event at Angel Falls. Apparently not a lot of people are paying attention to this map, because if they did, I'll bet there would be a lot more interest. When we look at the end of the map, it clearly shows a large pit where the river disappears. No other information is available, but considering the topography of the region, and the fact that no resurgence of the river has been reported, this pit could be as much as twenty five hundred feet deep."

"That is what got my attention", said Max. He went on to say, "This is an opportunity like no other we have ever had."

Jim said, "Bouncing that pit will certainly be a first, but what do we know about the waterfall?"

Ted answered, "We know little to nothing about both the pit and the waterfall. All we know comes from this map, a bunch of pictures that have been published, and what we know about the geology of the region."

Max opined, "That it is actually a twenty five hundred foot deep pit is our speculation, but it has real potential."

This high resolution scan, while lacking in many ways, was very helpful in that it provided answers to many questions that otherwise would have required a preliminary visit to the site. As talk centered about equipment that would be needed, how much they already had, logistic issues, costs, and the like, one really important issue emerged. The scan revealed that the walls of the gorge and cave appeared to be essentially sheer and smooth. There were few ledges, cracks or other discontinuities that would have made the climbing entry into the cave less daunting. Ted, Max, and Jim had plenty of experience climbing around and rigging deep vertical pits, however, entry into Churum River Cave was going to be a highly technical horizontal assault along and down a very smooth cliff face. It was going to involve a lot of hole drilling and setting of expansion bolts to provide safe and secure anchor points for safety lines, belay points, climbing aids and the like. The advent of light weight cordless hammer drills powered by long lasting lithium batteries made this type of assault feasible. Both Max and Jim had plenty of experience bolting their way to the top of several dome pits to explore what lay beyond, but they never faced a challenge anything like what the walls of the Churum River Cave appeared to be presenting. It was agreed that this might involve a skill that was above and beyond what any of them had. For a moment, this looked like it might be a show stopper, but Max had an idea.

A year previously out in Utah, he met a couple, 'couple' loosely speaking, of awesome rock climbers. Lilly Lawson and her climbing partner, Bufford Ellis, had a reputation of being able to scale the most seemingly impossible rock spires and boulder challenges found throughout the mountain west. Lilly's prowess had earned her the nick name of "Spider Woman". Her friends called her Spider for short. She was a five foot one inch, hundred and five pound bundle of muscle and guts who seemed to have the magical ability to scramble across, up or down vertical faces with ease where there appeared to be no visible means of support. This ability enabled her to conquer some exceptionally difficult climbs. Also, because she was apparently completely without fear, she would not hesitate to attempt to execute some insanely difficult moves. As a consequence, she was often seen dangling in space at the end of her belay line, hence the nick name "Spider Woman". This is where Bufford came in. Bufford was the muscle on the other end of her belay line, and she had total confidence in his ability to catch her whenever she fell. Together they formed an awesome rock climbing duo. As a bonus, they both had some fairly extensive caving experience.

Max posited that if he could get them to join the team, they could lead the horizontal assault along the vertical wall of the cave back to where the river plunged into the black abyss. From there, Max, Ted, and Jim could take the lead. When Max put in the call, he called Bufford, because Bufford's number was the only one he could find.

"Is this Bufford Ellis?" Max asked.

"Yeah, this is Bufford. Whom may I say is calling?"

Max said, "This is Max Meccum. We met about a year ago at an event down on the Green River."

Bufford's ears perked up because he remembered some of the tales about Max Meccum. "Yeah, I remember you. What's up? You in town?"

Max replied, "No, I'm still in Austin, but I've got a proposition for you and Lilly, that is if you two are still climbing together."

"Well, Spider and I still do a bit of climbing whenever we get a chance. I'm on my way over to her place right now. How about I call you back when I get there and you can tell us about your proposition then. Besides, I don't make any decisions without the boss's okay anyway. I'll be there in about ten minutes. Can I call you back on this number?"

Max said, "That would be great. Talk with you in a bit."

When Bufford and Spider called back, Max explained the reason for his call. It took only a moment for Max to be rewarded with an enthusiastic "Yes, indeed we would be delighted to be part of the team."

And that is how the initial team composition was set.

The next several months were spent working out details. It was thought that the initial foray would require about three weeks to execute. Equipment lists were formulated, camping supplies specified, travel visas were applied for, coordination with the Canaima Park personnel was initiated, travel itineraries were worked out, and actual acquisition of some of the extensive list of supplies and equipment was begun. It was then that the obvious became apparent: this was going to be both a difficult and very expensive undertaking. Unlike previous expeditions in which they had participated, where you could drive to within a few miles of the objective and then hike in, and if necessary hire a bunch of locals to help, the top of the Auyán tepui was extremely remote. There were no real roads in the area, and the only road that led to the top was very primitive and would require several days using four wheel drive vehicles to cover, that is if it wasn't washed out or over grown. It was decided that most likely everything would have to be flown into Venezuela on a commercial flight, and then ferried on to the top of top of the Auyán tepui on a small chartered plane. Several round trips on a chartered plane would be necessary, making the logistic support even more expensive. Bottom line was that this expedition was going to cost much more than this small group could afford out their own pocket. Hence a sponsor was going to be needed.

Across the U.S. there numerous grottos of the National Speleological Society, and within these grotto's membership are thousands of diverse and talented cavers. But Max had in mind one specific caver that he thought might be able to help them out.

Scott Mueller was the grandson of one of Dr. Werner Von Braun's scientist who back in the early nineteen sixties was a principal in the formation of a very successful aerospace/engineering company in Huntsville, Alabama. That company has provided technical services to NASA and the Army at the Redstone Arsenal for many decades. Scott's grandfather retired as a very wealthy man. Scott had both an engineering and an accounting degree from one of Alabama's premier universities, and his grandfather appointed him to manage a foundation that he had established to provide endowments to worthy scientific and environmental efforts.

From this foundation, Scott had already provided generous endowments to both national caving organizations and to regional cave conservation and preservation groups.

When Max briefed Scott on their plan to explore the Churan River Cave and laid out the complexities, difficulties, and expense of the proposed effort, Scott was deeply intrigued. He agreed that this was indeed the type of effort that the foundation was chartered to support.

Scott told Max, "Max, I am absolutely fascinated with your proposal. I am sure that I can justify the Mueller Foundation funding the effort, but I have a couple of conditions."

Max thought to himself, "Whatever the conditions are, I'll agree to them." Then Max said, "Okay, just what are your conditions, I'm sure we can agree to them."

Scott said, "My conditions are that you keep me totally informed on a near real time basis of the progress and findings of the expedition, and that you allow the foundation to publish a post expedition report."

Without hesitation Max said, "Oh, that's easy. However, I can do better than that. Why don't you join the expedition team? And in particular, why don't you become the Chief Financial Officer and Purchasing Agent for the group? In that capacity and by being an active member of the exploration team, you not only can be constantly informed of our progress, but you can also be assured that the foundation's money is being appropriately spent." Scott was flattered with the offer and graciously accepted.

With Scott on the team, things began again to progress very quickly. Scott leaped into his new job with relish. Over a mile of special NMI caving rope was quickly ordered, as were several hundred pounds of technical climbing equipment along with every other item on the group's shopping list. Scott was like a kid in a candy store buying up every item he thought might be useful on the expedition. He made arrangements to ship the gear and supplies to Canaima Camp in Venezuela, and to have it stowed there awaiting the arrival of the team. He also negotiated a contract for the requisite charter aircraft and a pilot to ferry everything and everybody to the landing strip atop Auyán tepui.

Scott was an excellent manager, and before long it was time to depart.

CHAPTER 2

The caving team arrived in Caracas where they were met by Félix Ruiz, Director of the Canaima National Park and Carlos Ortega, the pilot of the Cessna 205 which they had chartered. The Director was excited that the group had taken up the challenge to fully explore the Churum River Cave and perhaps shed some light on the mystery. He explained that, because no resurgence of the river had yet been detected, there was a growing concern with the locals in the area that the mountain was hollow and was filling up with water and would soon burst forth flooding the entire area. Everyone couldn't help themselves, and they laughed out loud. Max said, "You've got to be kidding!"

Ruiz responded, "I'm not joking. This is more than just a growing local rumor, but the truth be told, there is of course no real scientific basis for the concern." But then he added, there was no good verifiable scientific explanation for what had occurred either.

Max assured him that he had been in many a deep cave with big waterfalls, and never ever was there a hollow mountain filling up with water. If there was no resurgence of the river, it simply meant that it was draining directly into an aquafer beneath the ground level of the valley below. Senor Ruiz agreed that of course that was the thinking of the educated minds in the area. The Director also stated that the government wanted Miguel Santos, a ranger with the park, to join the group as an observer and liaison, and to assure that the group received all of the assistance that they might need from the Venezuelan Government. Max agreed that Miguel would be a welcomed addition to the expedition.

Carlos, the owner/pilot of the chartered Cessna 205, indicated that it would take two trips to shuttle the team and their luggage from Caracas to Canaima Camp. Since it was getting late in the day, and since he opined that he really did not like making night landings in the park, it was agreed to continue the venture early the next day.

The next day, that leg of the excursion went uneventfully. Upon their arrival at Canaima Camp, they were met by Miguel. Miguel was happy to report, "The equipment that you all sent ahead arrived several weeks ago, and I have it in storage waiting for you. I have been very anxious to meet you. Welcome to Canaima Camp."

It took five round trips in the little Cessna 205 to shuttle all of the caving equipment and supplies for the eight team members from Canaima Camp to the crude air strip on top of Auyán tepui. The list of caving equipment that Scott had assembled was quite extensive and included over five thousand feet of caving rope, mechanical equipment and hardware for technical climbing, camping gear, communications gear, food and miscellaneous supplies to support a two week assault of the Churum River Cave. Also included in this list of equipment were Peggy's drones. The pilot was instructed to return in two weeks unless otherwise contacted to return earlier. It was expected that the assault would take the entire two weeks and perhaps a bit longer. It would turn out that would not be the only thing they grossly under estimated.

From the air strip, the cavers backpacked all of their equipment to the preselected camp site area which they had scouted out using Google Earth and the vast array of pictures that had recently been published. As a result of the activities of the many recent visitors to the area, numerous potential camp sites were available, so they selected one near the end of the chasm just above the cave entrance. By the time all the supplies and equipment were packed in and camp set up, it was quite late at night and everyone was more interested in hitting the sack than eating. Thus ended their second day in Venezuela.

Early the next day they were up and about. After a quick breakfast, they began scouting the edge of the chasm to find the most appropriate point to rig the ropes for the initial descent into the chasm. The walls of the chasm were sheer and slightly overhanging. There was a small ledge about two hundred and thirty feet down and about a hundred feet above the river. This appeared to be the best place from which to stage entering the cave. The only problem was that, due to the inward slant of the chasm walls, it would be impossible to rappel directly onto the ledge. Not to be deterred, a scheme was devised so that the first person down would stop his rappel and pendulum over to the ledge. This might sound easy, but it would be anything but easy. This would be like sitting in a two hundred and thirty foot high swing and trying to pump like when you were a kid on the school playground trying to get your swing going. Unfortunately, as they all knew, you can hang on the end of a long rope and wiggle all you want, but not much is going to happen. So, their scheme was to have the first person down to take the end of a second rope down with him. The others would walk the other end around to the opposite side of the chasm. Then, when he reached the stopping point, they would give a tug to get him started to swing. Because of the very small angle between the two ropes, a big tug wouldn't result in much of a push, so the tug had to be repeated over and over at just the right interval to generate a large swing. The period of a two hundred and thirty foot pendulum is about seventeen seconds, so the tugs had to be precisely timed to be effective.

Max elected to be the first down. He quickly rappelled down the two hundred and thirty feet so that he was at the same level as the ledge, and then he tied off his rappel rack. Then they began the tricky process of penduluming over to the ledge. After about thirty minutes of trial and error, they had him swinging wildly back and forth. The first time he tried to step gingerly onto the narrow ledge he lost his balance and fell backwards out over the chasm again. But as he fell backward, he gave a big push off the ledge which increased the amplitude of his swing. After several repetitions of this he finally was able to get a foothold on the ledge sufficient to retain his balance. This was not easy since there was a dearth of handholds of any kind to be had.

While carefully balancing on the narrow ledge, his first task was to quickly establish a secure anchor. He was thinking that maybe Spider Woman should have been the first down because she seemed to be magically able to find handholds and footholds where there appeared to be none. Max stood plastered as close to the vertical wall as he could while running his hand up and down the wall seeking a crack or indentation on the wall that he could grasp to steady himself better. After a minute or so he found a small crack about two feet to his right and above his head. He quickly slipped a small jamb nut into the crack, pulled down sharply to securely set it, and then he clipped in. Now securely tethered to the wall, he set about placing a really secure bolt anchor from which the conquest of the ledge could proceed.

The ledge was about thirty feet long and widened a bit as it extended to the east and into the mouth of the cave. Max pulled about fifteen feet of slack through his rappel rack, flipped a bowline in it, and secured it to the anchor. Then beyond the anchor, he clipped a Jumar Ascender onto the rope, pulled more slack through his rack and began to self-belay himself carefully along the ledge. As he moved slowly down the ledge, he placed several more jamb nuts in small cracks which unfortunately were few and far between. When he reached the end of the ledge, he set another bolt anchor and secured the end of the rappel line to it. This established a fixed safety line running the entire length of the ledge. He then clipped the end of the line that was used to get him swinging to that anchor thus establishing a second rappel line to the ledge. Now the process of bringing equipment and supplies down to the ledge and securing them to more anchors could begin. For the next week or so, this ledge would be the starting point for the assault into the cave.

Next down were Spider and Bufford. Spider, because of her exceptional rock climbing skills, would lead the technical climb effort into the cave along the cave's vertical wall. Bufford, her rock climbing partner, would belay her as she moved along the wall setting temporary anchors as she went. The plan was for Bufford to follow her and replace her temporary anchors with secure bolts and establish the route with fixed ropes so the others could follow. Because there were few cracks and other discontinuities in the near featureless two hundred foot high and at least thousand foot long wall, progress was going to be slow and very tedious.

Spider was anxious to get started. Bufford secured himself safely to the anchor at the end of the ledge and to a freshly placed bolt anchor. He was now prepared to belay Spider as she seemingly oozed off of the ledge onto the cave wall, he said "Belay on". She responded, "On belay." Somehow she always managed to find handholds and toe holds adequate to support her lithe hundred and five pound frame. She carried with her an array of jamb nuts, carabiners, a pair of trusty jumars with stirrups attached, and a supply of chalk. In her mouth she always carried a small knife thin wedge with sling which in emergencies she could quickly jam into even the smallest crack for support. This small aid had saved her from vicious falls on numerous occasions.

She quickly discovered that this was not going to be a typical technical rock climb. Even for her there were few hand and footholds. She had barely gone twelve feet before she found herself dangling in space a dozen feet below the ledge where Bufford was securely tied in. This was certainly an auspicious start for the assault, and portended the level of difficulties they would be facing. Bufford hauled her back up, and the assault began again. This time she opted for a slightly higher route which appeared to offer a few more hand holds and small cracks for not particularly secure jam nuts. After about twenty feet of tedious progress, she found a decent crack and slipped in a secure jam nut. She clipped into the anchor and relaxed. This twenty feet of progress took almost forty minutes.

She called back to Bufford and remarked, "I am climbing basically by braille. I can't see ahead for any handholds so I am just feeling my way along searching for anything I can cling to."

Bufford quipped, "Well, back in the cave it is going to be really dark, so maybe braille is good."

Spider shot back, "Not funny."

Meanwhile back up top, Peggy had been busy setting up her squadron of drones. She set a unique GPS coordinate for each of her four drones to takeoff from and to return to for recovery. The problem of course was that once the drone entered the cave, the GPS signal would be lost, and all flying and maneuvering would have to be accomplished manually. Fortunately with the aid of Scott's financial input, each of the drones was also outfitted with a rudimentary inertial navigation system that would help flying and recovery after the GPS signal was lost. Another problem was that the radio and video signals do not propagate through rock, so line-of-sight had to be maintained for control. If line-of-sight was lost, recovery of the drone would have to rely on its inertial navigation system to return. Unfortunately, line-of-sight could not be maintained from ground level where Peggy had her control station setup. This was an anticipated problem for which the solution required the placement of a multi-channel relay near the mouth of the cave with a clear line-of-sight view that went far back into the cave. So, once the relay was setup down on the ledge, Peggy was in business. She quickly set about photographing the process of lowering equipment and securing it on the ledge.

After clipping her belay line into the newly set anchor, Spider ventured out once again onto the sheer wall. After several minutes and tedious little progress, Spider yelled back to Bufford, "This is not working; I absolutely can't find a damn thing to hold onto. This rock is crazy slick, it is like glass almost." And with that she was again dangling in midair ten feet below her last anchor. Spider clipped in a Jumar with a stirrup and quickly made her way back up the belay line to her last anchor and then back to the ledge where Bufford was waiting.

"We have got to rethink our plan. Clearly we aren't going to make it very far, very fast or very safe doing it like this. If I keep falling every five feet or so, I'm going to get beat up pretty bad. And, that is not what I signed up for."

Spider continued, "Have you noticed how smooth this rock is? You can't get a friction hold, a toe hold, or anything. It doesn't seem natural."

Bufford remarked, "Yeah, I noticed. Standing here watching the difficulty you are having just trying to find a handhold of any kind has made me very aware that this is not like any climb we have ever attempted before. And you are right, this is really weird rock."

Spider said, "The further you go in, the worse it gets because you can't see. Where I quit, there was nothing above, below, or in front of me to glom onto. We need a new plan. Let's get the group together and powwow over this."

By the time everyone got top side, everyone pretty well understood the problem. Ted pointed out, what they all also knew, that this cave was not a solution cave formed in limestone but rather a fault cave formed in very hard and very ancient crystalline rock that was later capped with sandstone. Ted was especially intrigued with the glassy nature of the cavern walls. Volcanism was not a geologic process associated with the region. Despite this fact, he postulated that there must have been at some time a volcanic fissure here and the earthquake had caused the rift to form along the boundary of the fissure. Obviously something unusual had happened here, so perhaps volcanism could have played a part. Maybe yes, maybe no.

At any rate, what this group knew in the here and now was that these glassy walls were going to make normal technical climbing techniques and skills null and void. This was not good news and was a potential show stopper bringing the expedition to an end before they even really got started. A lot of ideas were tossed about, none of which appeared workable of feasible.

Then Peggy offered an idea. "Spider, how many of those little razor thin chocks do you have?"

Spider said, "Two, the one I carry in my mouth and a spare."

Scott chimed in "Actually, we have about a dozen. I put an order in for some of them too. What do you have in mind?"

Peggy said "I've been taking pictures of everything we have been doing.

The cameras on my drones are very good. I think I can scout ahead of Spider with my drone and locate any small cracks that might exist. I can use the robotic arm on my big drone to place one of the small chocks into the cracks and clip in a hand line. Spider could then clip onto the hand line and Bufford could lower her so she could do a pendulum traverse over until she was below the chock. Then she could climb up, set an anchor and repeat. This way we could make ten, fifteen, twenty, or maybe even thirty feet at a time."

Everyone agreed that, even though doing a pendulum traverse from a chock placed by a drone sounded a bit sporty, it appeared feasible and they needed a plan. The mood of the group began to change from gloomy to enthusiastic. Bufford suggested that best way to proceed would be to seek places for chock anchors well above the planned route for two reasons. First, the small razor chocks don't take lateral loads well at all. They need to be loaded vertically to be safe. Secondly, the higher the anchor point, the larger the pendulum steps that could be made safely. This looked like the way to go. Preparations were made try this process first thing in the morning. Rock climbing history was going to be made.

After breakfast the next day, Spider, Bufford, Max and Jim rappelled down to the ledge to begin the assault. Ted opted to stay top side. He wanted to see everything that Peggy's drone saw. While Bufford and Spider made their way out to the last secure anchor, Peggy began her survey. She started out about thirty feet above Bufford and Spider. She began a slow up/down survey of the cavern wall staying about three feet from the wall. As expected, cracks were few and far between. Peggy searched a zone about ten feet high and twenty five feet wide before spotting a promising looking crack. It was small but appeared to be several inches deep. Peggy carefully maneuvered the robotic arm and expertly placed the small chock snuggly into the crack. Then she gave the small attached cable loop a downward tug, and the chock was set. Peggy then flew back down to Spider, retrieved the hand line, and flew back up to the chock. She clipped the hand line into the chock and then flew back towards the center of the chasm to photograph Spider as she began her pendulum swing. Spider took up the slack in the hand line; put her weight on the line and Bufford slowly payed out the belay line to allow her to swing gently forward for over twenty five feet. After getting stable, Spider quickly pulled out her hammer drill and set a new anchor. And just like that, twenty five feet of progress was made; safely and with comparatively little effort.

Peggy flew up to retrieve the razor chock. The retrieval was a bit more difficult than was anticipated, but with some tugging, wiggling and whipping with the attached hand line, the chock finally popped loose. With success under their belt, everyone was ready to make the next leap. One problem, in the excitement of the night before, Peggy had forgotten to put the drone on charge and consequently, the drone's battery had dropped to below fifty percent. So Peggy had to make a swift retreat to switch out batteries.

This process was repeated an additional six times over the next nine hours with a cumulative result of almost two hundred feet of progress. Max remarked, "With this kind of progress, in another four days they will be at the pit." Although progress was relatively rapid, it was not without difficulties and severe hazards. On two of the six traverses, Peggy was left hanging below Bufford because twice the razor chock pulled loose as Peggy began her pendulum swing. On two other swings, the razor chocks were so tightly wedged that Peggy's drone could not retrieve them.

At camp that evening, Jim remarked that, "You know, we probably shouldn't have Peggy retrieving the razor chocks at all, but rather we should make them into permanent hanging lines. It would certainly make moving equipment back and forth and our coming and going in and out much easier. We could just clip into the fixed line and clip onto the hanging line and 'Tarzan' into the cave."

Bufford and Spider both chimed in with an enthusiastic "Yeah, I agree, I think that might definitely be the way to go."

Spider said "I think that is a good idea also because really, I don't relish the thought of having to meticulously climb along the fixed line each time we go in or out."

Bufford pointed out that, "If the hanging line doesn't work out well, then we need to rig a lower fixed rope for our feet so that we can kind of skinny along because so far there are zero foot holds along the route."

Jim chimed in and said, "Regardless, I think foot lines are going to be necessary, so let's just plan to do them as well."

Scott said, "Well, we do have plenty of rope, so we might as well use it. And, besides, rigging those extra lines will give Jim, Ted and Max something to do while Bufford and Spider are forging ahead." Scott went on to say, "Miguel that leaves you and me to stay topside and guard the home front."

So far Miguel's role had just been that of observer and camp cook, a job he filled surprisingly well, but you could tell he was itching to become a real member of the team. Miguel said, "When are you guys going to teach me how to rappel and do that technical rope stuff? It looks like a lot of fun."

Max said, "Miguel, when do you think you will be ready? You aren't afraid of heights are you? How do you feel about dangling on the end of a rope in the dark a hundred feet above a roaring river?"

Miguel replied, "Si, si amigo, no tengo miedo. Mañana I'll be ready."

Max said, "I'll bet you will be. We will start your training soon."

The next day the plan that was agreed to the previous evening was put into motion. Bufford and Spider moved into the cave first and made their way to the last permanent anchor. Peggy's drone was already ahead of them searching for a crack for the next razor chock. Jim, Ted and Max followed behind, climbing the lines hanging from the razor chocks, and replacing the chocks with a secure permanent anchor. While this process seemed quite simple, it was actually quite dangerous. The razor chocks were not really suitable for sustaining the jerking load associated with a hundred and eighty pound guy with all of his gear climbing up the rope, and as such, they were susceptible to being dislodged. Consequently, the climber had to pause every eight to ten feet and set a bolt to limit his exposure. This was very time consuming, but it paid great dividends in terms of safety.

This plan was executed flawlessly over and over, and as predicted earlier, in a mere five days they were at the brink of the abyss where the Churum River disappeared with a deafening roar down the deep dark abyss.

The large crack which had formed the cave up to this point appeared to terminate at here. It was like the crack had been forced apart and then slammed back together sealing up the floor of the cave except here at the end where a hole remained open. The Churum River flowed along the narrow floor and cascaded into the open hole. The group gathered around the abyss, each hanging from a secure anchor, and gaped in awe at the frightening scene that lay before them. Although all of their helmets were fitted with open-mike communications gear, the roar of the water drowned out any attempt to carry on any kind of meaningful conversation. The roar of the river was deafening, and each of them sat in their personal silence wondering the same thing. . . "how in the heck are we going to conquer this hole?" "This looks like a death trap." "Looks like we aren't going any further, at least not on this trip." After pondering this awesome scene for thirty minutes or so, the group began their slow and rather solemn retreat back to the base camp.

Around the campfire that evening, the mood was a mixed bag. On one hand there was some euphoria for having successfully forged a route back to the pit, but on the other hand there was abject concern and depression about the possibility that it might be impossible to safely rig and descend the pit with all that water flowing in. There was no way to divert it; not the least little bit, and probably not even in the dry season.

Max, sensing the dismal mood of the group thought he better get a conversation going. He said, "Okay, everyone, anyone got any bright ideas?"

Ted said, "Well for one thing, it is obvious that we will have to plan the descent during the dry season."

"No shit" remarked Jim, "I felt for sure that there would be a place on the far side of the pit where we could rig away from at least some of the waterfall. Unfortunately, I didn't see a place. Did any of you see a possible spot?" No one answered in the affirmative.

Ted went on to point out that the flow of the river in the canyon in the cave was noticeably greater than the flow of the river into the canyon where the rift began. That probably meant that the river was being augmented by some subsurface source, most likely from a shallow aquifer. That also meant that even in the dry season, there probably would still be substantial flow to be contended with. Max said, "Well, I'm not going to be deterred. We will just have to engineer a way. After all, we have already advanced the art of brute force assault of sheer cliff faces by our Avant guarde use of drones. I don't think what we have done has ever been done before. Thank you Peggy for your contribution to rock climbing history. So tomorrow, let's get a good measure of what we are actually contending with and go from there. First of all, we need to figure out how deep this pit is." With that, everyone was both in agreement and in a better mood. They proceeded to scarf down a couple of six packs of beer, which further lightened the mood, and then they hit the sacks.

The next day back at the pit, ropes were rigged across the top of the abyss in ever which direction. Over fifty anchors were set.

The mood of the group was much better today thanks to the fact that the communication gear in their helmets were now equipped with noise cancelling headsets. All of this was courtesy of Scott who had a thing for high tech gadgetry and also the foresight to anticipate the potential need for such equipment. Spider remarked, "Why haven't we been using these headsets all along? Without the roar of the cascade, this place doesn't seem near so intimidating."

Everyone was in full agreement. Scott remarked, "Well, at first, it didn't seem like we really needed them. We all did just fine without them, so I sort of forgot about having bought them. But when we got back to the pit yesterday, and we were right there at the drop where the noise was so loud, I remembered them."

The top of the pit was thoroughly scouted to determine the best place to rig for the descent. What was meant was a possible future descent, because obviously no descent was going to be made on this trip. Special anchors were set to hold the wire reel that would be used to measure the depth of the pit. There appeared no way to avoid at some point being inundated in the cascade. The question was, for how long would the exposure be, and what would the dynamic pressure be of the falling water on the ascending/descending climber? And, was this descent even going to be possible?

Jim and Ted muscled in the heavy wire reel with the depth counter and a digital recording tension meter attached. Scott had sprung for this expensive high tech automated device because no one believed that use of a less capable manual device could be properly controlled nor would anything less provide adequate information to plan the assault of such a monumentally difficult descent. The tension meter was very important device to have in order to ascertain how severe the load from the falling water would be on the climber and how long it would have to be endured.

Positioning the wire reel was very tedious. It was an awkward balancing act accomplished by standing and walking on a network of fixed ropes while clipped into various safety ropes all the while also being belayed from twenty or so feet away. Once it was finally emplaced and secure, everyone was anxious to begin probing what lay below. The special five pound spherical plumb bob probe was affixed to the wire, the five small internal video cameras were activated, and the plumb bob began its slow descent into the cascading torrent. A descent rate of twenty feet per minute was selected to ensure adequate data acquisition. If the pit turned out to be the anticipated twenty five hundred feet deep, the probe would take right at two hours to reach the bottom. That is assuming no problems were encountered. The four circumferential cameras would provide a full 360 degree lateral view, and the fifth camera would provide a continuous downward view. As the probe descended, all eyes were on the depth counter and the digital readout on the tension meter. Initially, the dynamic load from the falling water was brutal and constant, but after a while it began to lessen and become more variable. One thing was unfortunately obvious. The flow maintained its continuous laminar flow for several hundred feet before it began to breakup into very turbulent streams. Dealing with this the first few hundred feet was going to be an extremely challenging technical task.

The falling water in the confined space of the pit generated vicious upward and downward winds that buffeted the probe unmercifully and broke the water flow into a gale like maelstrom. At this point it was apparent that the probe was too light to survive this type of beating for very long. So, probe was reeled back in.

Ted checked the onboard specs for the reel and noted that the wire had a working tensile strength of 1000 pounds, so the question was how to attach additional weight to the plumb bob probe to stabilize it through the maelstrom. This was not an anticipated problem, although it should have been.

Back at camp, a full court press was initiated to find something that would make a suitable weight. Finally, a nice round river rock was located which appeared to properly fit the bill. Actually finding a suitable river rock wasn't the real problem, but how to attach the rock securely to the plumb bob was an issue. A variety of slings and knots were tried, but none of them passed the "I'm sure this will work" test.

Then it was Spider's chance to shine. She said, "I think I know how to do this one. We have a roll of para-cord somewhere, don't we?" she asked.

Scott assured her that we had a couple hundred feet somewhere.

Spider said, "I won't need near that much. One of my non-climbing hobbies is Macramé. I love knots, and the fancier the better. I can tie an encapsulating Macramé net around the plumb bob and then another around the rock." She went on to explain that "The net will keep the plumb bob and the rock securely and symmetrically attached and should allow it to survive the level of buffeting we observed."

Bufford said, "Wow, that sounds like the perfect solution. How long have I known you? I didn't know you knew that kind of stuff."

Spider quipped, "That's because you are an unobservant oaf. Have you not noticed all of the hanging pots all around my porch? They don't just happen to come that way from the nursery. I made all of the macramé hangers myself."

"Well, I guess I do recall them, I just didn't pay that much attention to them. They were kind of a girly thing you know."

"Oaf!!", was Spider's repeated response. Everyone had a good chuckle over their quibbling.

Scott found the roll of para-cord, and Spider set about plying her art. The result was indeed a work of art, but also a very robust work of art, one that would serve a very rugged purpose. The only problem with Spider's net was that it would block the view of the probe's downward facing camera. It was agreed this was a small price to pay for such an elegant solution. This project consumed the remainder of the day, so the group dined once again on some of Miguel's fine Caracas Style cuisine and a couple of six packs of local beer before preparing for the next day's attempt.

By nine o'clock the next morning they were again atop the pit ready to affix Spider's work of art to the wire. Once that was done the sounding of the pit began anew. This time, the vicious winds and buffeting streams of falling water had only a minimal effect on the probe, so the sounding of the pit continued unabated. By five hundred feet down, most of the water had been blasted into large raindrops falling at raindrop terminal speed. As such they no longer posed a grave danger, but they did severely obscure the view. The probe finally bottomed out at twenty four hundred and ninety five feet. The probe was retracted about twenty feet and the wire pulled to one side of the pit. When lowered again, the pit depth was measured to be twenty five hundred and two feet. When the process was repeated from the opposite side, the measurement was twenty four hundred and eighty nine feet. So, it was concluded that this was very likely the bottom or at least very near the bottom. The probe was then reeled back up, a process that required a little over two hours.

Three hours later (it should be noted that it typically took the group about three hours each way to traverse between the camp and the top of the pit), back again at camp, everyone was anxious to see the downloads from the probe's cameras. The ten terabyte solid state memory devices (SSD's) were plugged into a laptop computer, and video from the four cameras were displayed simultaneously. Initially there was nothing to see but water streaming rapidly past the camera lenses, so Ted fast forwarded the video to about the three hundred foot level. Here the torrent began to break up a bit, and soon glimpses of the cavern wall could be seen. A hundred feet lower, it appeared that the cavern walls were suddenly becoming further and further away. The glimpses were so tenuous that it was not certain that this was indeed the case. However, another three hundred feet down, the walls appeared to be back close again, and remained roughly the same for the remainder of the descent. This portion of the video was reviewed several times, and the first impressions were reinforced. This apparent geometry of the pit was certainly unanticipated and equally inexplicable.

Ted said, "Guys, we have got to explore this in much greater detail. This is just plain weird. I know of no geologic reason why this should or even could exist. Something big time not natural has occurred here. Understanding this could be the most important finding of this whole expedition."

Little did he know just how true this would turn out to be. Ted went on to say, "Somehow we need to get a more accurate profile measurement of the pit. It won't be possible to use a standard laser mapper because first of all, we don't have one, and secondly, if we did, it wouldn't begin to survive the trouncing it would get while being lowered. Also, we need to do it now while we are here. We might not get another chance."

Scott said, "So what you are really saying is that 'now is the time for some good old fashioned Alabama MacGyver engineering', right?"

Ted said, "Absolutely. It's time for some serious brainstorming."

Scott figured that it was about time he put his fancy Alabama University engineering degree to use. He said, "The first thing we are going to need is some kind of a durable container for our 'device'."

Fortunately, there were piles of garbage, trash, abandoned equipment, and miscellaneous junk left from the earlier visitors at the site that provided lots of potential resources. Miguel, the de-facto camp cook came up with an idea. He used propane to fuel the camp stove. He suggested that an empty propane tank might fill the bill for what Scott described as to what was needed.

Within the next twenty minutes, five suitable empty tanks were scavenged. Scott busily sketched out a design for a makeshift laser mapper. With the list of supplies and tools he needed for the task complete, he raised Carlos on the radio and gave him his list and implored him to expedite its delivery to the camp as soon as possible. Carlos assured him that his list was fairly easy and everything could be procured from one of the building supply stores in Caracas. He would have the supplies to the camp by late the next afternoon. Miguel sensed an opportunity, now being the de facto camp cook, he also submitted to Carlos a list of consumable supplies.

Scott's design was simple. He would fill the bottom of one of the propane tanks with fast setting cement. This would give the device the requisite weight to remain reasonably stable during descent. On top of the cement platform, he would mount eight small laser levels, each projecting out through small ports around the circumference of the tank. The plumb bob probe would be suspended below the tank. The probe's cameras would video the laser beams which, although would be considerably attenuated, should be reasonably visible through the torrential rain. The laser beam lengths could be measured to get rough cross section estimates of the pit's profile. One problem that would complicate the data interpretation was that the probe would likely twist back and forth, so no good directional reference could be established. The resulting pit profile most likely would appear to be twisting back and forth. However, despite this, useful information could certainly still be gleaned.

Once again, Spider plied her macramé skills, and soon the laser mapper was ready for deployment.

The time frame that the group had allocated for this expedition was soon coming to an end, so everyone felt a great deal of pressure to get some resolution regarding the extent and characterization of the pit, and the magnitude of the effort that was going to be required to continue the exploration of the cave. So early the next day, Max, Ted, Scott, and Bufford made their way back to the pit. Spider, Peggy, Jim and Miguel remained behind at the camp to monitor their progress via real time video courtesy of one of Peggy's drones. By mid-morning, Scott's laser mapper was activated and ready for lowering. Slowly the device was lowered, and all appeared to go quite well. One thing was noticed that was very interesting. The rounded dome of the propane tank acted like an umbrella, and formed a tunnel in the falling water. This was an excellent happening because it allowed the laser beams to pierce through the water much more effectively than had been anticipated. This gave hope that the resulting map of the pit would yield some additional detail and a greater level of useful information.

Just as the mapper was about to touch down at the bottom of the pit, Jim informed the folks in the cave that a group of people had shown up and announced that they were also going to begin an independent exploration of the cave.

This was totally unexpected. Miguel confronted them and in his most official voice stated in Spanish, "No puedes simplemente aparecer aquí e interferir con nuestros esfuerzos en curso."

Noting that the leader's English was excellent but that he apparently did not understand Spanish, Miguel repeated in English, "You can't just show up here and interfere with our ongoing efforts. You need to have permission from the government, and you must coordinate any proposed activities with the Director of the Canaima National Park. I am the liaison between the Director and this expedition, and I have heard nothing about another authorized group."

The leader of the group introduced himself as Sergei Vassilov, and although he was totally fluent in Spanish he acted as though he didn't understand a word. He responded to Miguel in English that indeed they had coordinated their expedition with the Venezuelan government, though not with the Director of the Canaima National Park, but rather with the Department of Commerce and Foreign Affairs. All arrangements had been coordinated through the Russian Embassy in Caracas with the appropriate top Venezuelan officials, and he apologized if the local Director had not been informed of their proposed expedition. He also pointed out that the Venezuelan military had agreed to provide his expedition with logistic support, and that shortly their equipment would be arriving. This announcement absolutely stunned Max and Scott. Even though Miguel was supposedly authorized to request whatever government support was needed, no such support had been offered or suggested for their expedition, so immediately everyone was highly suspicious and a bit jealous of what was transpiring.

Jim told Max that Sergei and his associates were very curious about our setup. They wanted to see Peggy's video, but she quickly shut down the live stream. Some of the Russians were viewing how the rappel lines were rigged down to the entrance ledge and were asking lots of questions about how the rigging was established in the cave. Max warned Jim to be very cautious about revealing anything about our activities. Jim and Miguel started speaking Spanish so that the Russians couldn't easily follow their conversations, and that turned out to be a total mistake in that it alerted Sergei to the fact that he was not to be trusted. Jim told Miguel that he was very uncomfortable with telling these people anything.

After Sergei made his announcement, Miguel got on the radio and called the Director. The Director immediately went absolutely ballistic and told Miguel to inform Sergei that his group was to cease and desist all activities until he, the Director, received a complete briefing and issued authorization to allow them to proceed. When Miguel informed

Sergei of the Director's decision, Sergei informed Miguel that, while he had no intention of interfering with the activities currently authorized here, he believed that he had all of the necessary permissions for the conduct of his expedition. Sergei was a polished diplomat so he didn't just bluntly say it, but he left no doubt about the fact that he didn't need the Director's permission to conduct his groups' investigations. He made it clear by way of implication that he had authorization from government officials way above the Director's pay grade. He further offered that at some future date he would be happy to brief the director on his expedition's mission and objectives. However, for the moment they would be proceeding with their current plan and schedule. It was obvious to both Miguel and Sergei that this initial encounter had started off bad, and if the conversations were continued in this vein, that it was only going to get rapidly worse.

So, in order to avoid escalating tensions and distrust, Sergei and his associates departed back to the landing field where equipment and supplies for their expedition were already arriving and being unloaded from the military helicopters.

By this time Ted and Scott had retrieved the mapper. Scott said, "This does not bode well for us. Obviously someone in the upper echelons of the Venezuelan government thinks we are onto something and they intend to know or own whatever it is they think we have."

Ted pointed out that there might be another explanation. "Perhaps the Russians and the Venezuelan government had some ongoing secret activities in the area, and their presence here was just part of that activity. There are still some very corrupt people in positions of power left over from previous defunct socialists regimes, and I know that some of them had been courting a relationship with Russia."

Max said, "Well that would explain why the Russians are here." Ted added, "I'll bet there are some Russian activities around here somewhere that they don't want us to see."

Scott, who was always suspicious of the Russians said, "Well, we don't need to make it easy for them. For starters, I think we need to protect all of our stuff. Let them figure out how to get back here. We don't need to be overly cooperative. We cannot let them have what we have just recorded. I think we need to take the memory module with all of the data and drop the mapper and wire sounder back down this hole."

"I definitely agree", Max replied. "Also, as we leave, let's clean our route down to bare rock. I'll bet they don't have a 'Spider' or a Peggy on their team, which means they will be going through hell to get back here."

Ted said, "While I was doing some of my solo exploring trying to figure out the geology of this cavern, I found a high lead that led to a small dead end alcove high up above anchor point 720 where we can stow the stuff which is too heavy for us to carry out in a hurry. I doubt seriously that anyone else will ever find it. It is really hidden away. We can leave our long ropes there. I left a fixed line leading up to it tied to the anchor for the pendulum line for 720." Max radioed back to Jim and told him that he and Spider were needed asap to help with ferrying equipment out of the cave. He didn't mention anything about cleaning their route or concealing their data just in case their conversations were being monitored. He sent Scott back to tell Peggy what they had done, and to help her compile all of the important expedition data and video onto a high capacity solid state drive.

Jim and Spider 'Tarzaned' into the cave as quickly as they could in order to render help with the removal all unnecessary bolts, hangers and ropes. On his way out Scott met them as they were on the way in. He filled them in on the plan, rudimentary as it was, and cautioned them about saying too much over the radio.

They worked all night, and all that they left behind at each anchor point was the expansion sleeve in the drilled hole into which the anchor bolts were screwed. The small holes would be very difficult for anyone unfamiliar with the route to find or use, especially considering the difficulty of the route. Max made a bet that even if the Russians did find some of the anchor points, that they would screw them up because they would be using metric threads, and ours were English. Incompatibility is a bitch. The safety lines and pendulum ropes were coiled, transported, and most stashed in the secret alcove, and the salvaged hardware was ferried out of the cave by Peggy's heavy drone.

In between ferrying hardware out of the cave by Peggy's heavy drone, she and Scott were busy copying files. Scott suggested that they copy a bunch of miscellaneous survey video onto the spare SSD, encrypt several files with data headers, and then label the decoy SSD as "Expedition data archive." Scott thought this decoy SSD would be a good idea in case the government or the Russians attempted to seize their data either overtly or covertly. Objections could be vigorously made, and then this disc could be reluctantly handed over. The real data hopefully could be concealed and protected until it was safely removed from the country.

Max was concerned that their every move was likely being monitored, and there was nothing that he could do about it. So they schemed up a little ruse for the benefit of any eyes that might be watching. None of the ropes or hardware that were used to rig the first several hundred feet into the cave were particularly valuable, so they packed those items loosely in the remaining duffle bags that they had. All of this was ferried to the entrance ledge as they cleaned the final stages of their route. After they finally assembled all of the bags on the entrance ledge, Bufford and Spider began the two hundred foot climb up the two rappel lines. When they were about half way up, Max and Jim staged their catastrophe.

They had all of the bags secured together on a single line tied to a single anchor, an anchor they had rigged to fail. Clipped to that anchor was a carabiner into which the rope linking all of the equipment bags was attached. The rope was attached in a manner so that when a sudden load was placed on the rope, the carabiner gate would fail and release the load. Hopefully, the anchor would fail also, lending additional credence to it being an authentic accident. Jim was on the end of the ledge nearest to the cave entrance. Spider was half way up the rappel line whose lower end was secured near this point. Max was on the other end of the ledge where the lower end of the first rappel line was tied off. Bufford was half way up this line. Between Max and Jim was the fixed safety line that ran the length of the ledge, and the bags full of ropes and miscellaneous hardware. They made a big to-do about all the problems they were having managing the equipment bags. This to-do was to make sure that any watching eyes were indeed watching. After a bit, Max gave a tug to the line attached to all the bags, and off the ledge they went. The hanger to which the line securing all the bags was attached popped off the anchor bolt and the carabiner failed, just as planned, and the entire assemblage plunged into the Churum River below where it would soon be flushed down the pit never to be seen again.

In unison Max and Jim shouted, "Oh NO!."

This was followed by lots of expletives, and shouts that everyone was ok but that all of the equipment was lost. After an appropriate amount of time was spent fumbling around, they retrieved the ledge safety line along with the remaining bolts and hangers, and then they began the long climb out. By dawn, the cave was clean and the entire crew was back at camp, exhausted and ready for some well-deserved rest.

CHAPTER 3

Later that day, Sergei and some of his associates made the expected visit to the camp. Everyone except Miguel was still sacked out. Miguel was busy preparing a large mid-afternoon lunch in anticipation that the crew would be famished after the herculean effort they had made the previous night. Sergei announced that he would like to pick the crews' brains and get some tips on how best to proceed with their effort. Miguel claimed that he didn't understand Sergei very well, so he went to rouse Max.

Miguel shook Max awake and said, "We've got visitors, and they want to talk."

Max replied, "That figures, they got here sooner than I expected. Go wake up the others while I get dressed. Then I'll go talk with them."

While everyone was getting up and dressed, Sergei and his guys were prowling around seeing whatever there was to see. The only things that they saw were the things that were intended for them to see. Peggy had disassembled and packed her drones, so they were out of sight. Lots of miscellaneous caving and climbing gear was lying about. The tent with the remainder of Scott's purchases was open and its contents visible, and Miguel's kitchen was smelling good. The communications tent was also still set up. Inside several laptops were visible, cameras were lying around, and the radio was turned on but silent at the moment. And most importantly, the prominently labeled decoy SSD was attached to one of the laptops. It did not go unnoticed.

It was also noted with some real and feigned displeasure that the rappel lines had been removed and apparently so had the safety lines down on the ledge. Sergei had been hoping to make an offer to use or acquire those lines for his troop's use. He of course already knew that they had been removed, but he didn't want to admit that he had monitored their exit or had witnessed their catastrophe. Actually, he was quite interested in hearing their version of just what had happened.

As the others began to appear from their tents, Max joined Sergei and exchanged pleasantries. Noting that Miguel had a large sumptuous meal nearly prepared, Max invited Sergei and his crew to dine with them following the philosophy of keeping your friends close and your enemies closer. Max and his crew were as anxious to learn about why the Russians were here as the Russians were to learn everything that they could about the American expedition. Unsurprisingly, the Russian accepted the invitation to dine.

Sergei was a smooth operator. He exuded openness and trust. Sergei complimented Miguel on his cooking skills, and thanked Max for the opportunity to talk. Sergei related that scientists in his country had received a video, Max noted to himself that it was probably the same video that Ted had received, and that they noted that the cave had some very, very unusual geology associated with it. He said that they thought it was so unusual that they contacted the Venezuelan Government and arranged for their expedition to come study the cave's geology. He made no mention of the fact that for many years Russia already had a presence in Venezuela, and that they already had considerable assets located all across the country.

He asked Max if he would share just what was their interest in the cave. Max stated very truthfully that they were just a bunch of cavers whose sole interest was the exploration of very deep and difficult caves. That was what they did, and it was what they lived for. Sergei found that a bit hard to believe.

He said, "Are you telling me that you arranged this obviously very expensive trip just to rappel down a deep hole?"

Max replied, "Yes, we did."

Sergei asked, "How are you, a bunch of individuals like you able to afford a venture like this? You all don't look like a bunch of rich gad abouts."

Max said with a chuckle, "No, definitely none of us are rich."

Max had to explain how it was Ted who first received the video. How it led to the formation of this group of cavers, and how they had to solicit the support of Scott's grandfather's foundation to finance the expedition. Max explained that being the first to descend a major pit, like this one promised to be, carried with it a huge amount of prestige in caving circles. And, they were determined to be the first.

Max asked, "What specifically drew your scientists attention to this cave?"

Sergei said, "Surely you found the cave walls unusual didn't you?"

"God yes!" exclaimed everyone in unison.

Ted interjected that he didn't understand how the walls could be so glassy slick. He said, "I know of no natural process that could have caused it. I considered volcanism, but there is no evidence to suggest that. It may be from some kind of chemical surface wash. I simply don't know. I sent some samples back to my university for further analysis, but I am skeptical of finding actual causation from analysis of so few samples."

Sergei said, "I agree totally with you on that."

Ted thought to himself, "Why would he agree so quickly to my skepticism? What are we missing?"

Max pointed out that "From a climbing and caving perspective, we have never encountered anything like this before. If it weren't for Spider's exceptional climbing skills, we could never have made it back to the pit."

Scott added, "Even with Spider's exceptional skills, it was an extremely difficult assault. When we finally made it to the pit, there was so much water flowing, that it was impossible to go further. We tried to plumb the depth of the pit, but we couldn't manage the force of the water on our rope and the weight that we tied on the end of the rope proved to be too much. We probably should have used a smaller weight and been more careful. We ended up losing it and the camera we had tied on as well. We got into much too big of a rush."

Max said, "That was an expensive rope we lost. We weren't expecting such a brutal jolt when the full force of the water hit it. We want to come back during the dry season, and hopefully be better prepared. We have to get a depth measurement before we can do much more."

Sergei took all of this in, and it was obvious that he was more than a little bit skeptical. Never-the-less, he didn't pursue the issue any further. "One last question, why, if you all are planning on returning, did you remove all of your ropes from the cave?"

Spider explained, "We try to leave nothing behind. That is part of our caving credo. 'We take nothing but pictures and leave nothing but footprints'. At least that is what we try to do."

At this, Sergei scoffed in disbelief. You could tell what he was thinking.

Sergei politely thanked Max once again for inviting him and his crew to dine with him and his caving associates. He apologized for appearing so abrupt at their first meeting, and indicated that he looked forward to seeing them again. Max and Scott were thinking the same thing. . . this Sergei was a slick operator and any interaction with him warranted extreme care. Max asked Sergei that since he had so much support from the Venezuelan military if perhaps he could get some of the soldiers to help carry some of their equipment back to the airfield. They were planning to depart tomorrow, and a bit of help would be greatly appreciated. This request caught Sergei by surprise, but after a short pause, he recognized an opportunity when he saw it. He replied, "Of course I will be glad to help. I will send some troops over this afternoon. That is the least I can do in return for such a delightful meal."

After Sergei left, Peggy and Scott packed the laptop computers, com gear, and all the support gear into cases for transport. The decoy SSD, digital cameras, and several smaller memory devices with lots of drone video were also prepared for transport. None of the selected video showed the use of Peggy's drone searching for and placing the razor chocks in cracks, or video of the crew "Tarzaning' along the route. There was lots of video scanning the wall looking for cracks, and video showing Ted rappelling hither and yon collecting samples of the cave wall. The important data however were carefully packaged so that it could be distributed among the group and carefully concealed on their person.

As promised, that afternoon, a dozen soldiers showed up, and in a single trip moved everything to the airstrip. Max thought how nice it was to have the support of a lot of military muscle to do the heavy lifting. Max's group found a nice place to camp overnight not too far away from where the residual supplies and equipment were piled by the runway. Miguel once again did his thing. There was no use in taking any food or beer back, so virtually every consumable item was either eaten or drunk that evening. What beer there was remaining was shared with the soldiers that had helped with the heavy lifting that afternoon. After the beer was gone, the party ended, and everyone sacked out for the night. Sometime later on, probably in the early morning, one of Sergei's tech gurus managed to sneak over and copy all of the data on the decoy SSD and other memory devices that Peggy and Scott had carefully stored in the transport cases.

Early the next morning Carlos arrived in the Cessna and they began the exodus from the top of Auyán tepui.

The first stop was at Canaima Camp where all of the remaining expedition gear was stashed for use on the next trip. Miguel promised to look after it and assure that no one pilfered any of it. Then it was on to Caracas. Once back in Caracas, the group rented a large van, loaded their personal gear, and made the obligatory trip to the American Embassy where they debriefed the ambassador on their last couple of weeks and their recent encounter with the Russian expedition. The ambassador was very interested in the Russians, much more interested in them than in the objectives of the American expedition. He wanted all of the details down to the very last thing they could remember. Everyone regurgitated everything they could remember, leaving out of course details of what they had found. After the debrief was concluded, they asked if they could have access to a high speed secure internet connection. Scott indicated that they would like to up load their data to his foundations' servers as a precaution to possibly losing their data in transit or having it confiscated at the airport. The ambassador thought if there was a possibility that the Russians would want their data for whatever reason, then he would do everything he could to thwart their efforts to get it. So he agreed and a high speed secure internet access was granted. Several hours later, all of the data was secured on Scott's servers. A quick phone call to his secretary confirmed that the data had been received. Scott directed her to duplicate the data, and place all copies in his safe and then to remove the files from the server. No hacking of this data was going to occur on his watch if he could help it. It was then decided to destroy all of the data in their possession. That way it could not be confiscated nor compromised as they were leaving the country. When they got back in country, they figured that they could construct a reasonably accurate profile of the pit, plan the next assault, and then maybe shed some light on the origin of the cave with its mysterious walls.

Max thanked the Ambassador for his help and promised to keep him in the loop as things developed. The group gathered their things together, loaded into their van and departed to their motel for the evening. The next morning they boarded their flight back to the states without incident. For this they were grateful and a bit surprised.

Several hours later, they landed in Houston. They deplaned and headed as a group towards Customs and Security. As they approached Customs, they were met by a couple of uniformed TSA agents and greeted by name. That caught everyone's attention, and they thought correctly, "well, here it begins." They were escorted through the Customs check point and down a long corridor to a private and secure conference room. Once in the room, they were greeted by three individuals who introduced themselves as agents for the Department of Homeland Security and the FBI. After they were all seated around the conference table, the lead FBI agent told them that normally they would interview them each individually, but considering the likelihood that they had all already coordinated their stories that they might as well listen to them all at once. He explained that the Ambassador had informed the FBI of their meeting with the Russians. He noted that such meetings are unusual and that the U.S. Government needed to know every detail of their meeting as well as any observation they may have made. He asked if anyone had a notion as to what the Russian's interests were. He also pointed out that they, meaning the FBI, must be informed of any future contacts that any member of the group might have with the Russians. With that, the group spilled their guts, elaborating in great detail about the things which the agents already knew, but omitting any mention of the fact that they had successfully plumbed the pit and had a cursory view of its geometry. Ted also didn't mention his real theory as to what he thought had caused the geologic anomaly.

The meeting with the government agents lasted for about an hour and a half, and was terminated only because the group needed to catch their flights to Austin. Everyone planned to spend a day or two in Austin before heading back to their respective home bases.

CHAPTER 4

The first thing that Ted did after arriving home was to pack up some of his samples and overnight express mail them to his friend and mentor Dr. Fred Schillinger. Dr. Schillinger was Ted's major professor while he was in graduate school at a major university up in the Texas panhandle, and the two had remained good friends and colleagues ever since. Dr. Schillinger was quick to respond to Ted's request for his opinion.

He called Ted up the next day. He said, "Ted, I know exactly what these samples are. Now, I've got a question for you. Why have you been mucking around on the Antioch Site, and how did you get permission to collect these samples?"

Without actually acknowledging what they both were thinking, Ted responded, "I was thinking the same thing, and it wasn't the Antioch Site."

"Oh, really? Can you tell me where or is that classified?"

"Sure, it's not classified, but keep it under your hat anyway. Venezuela."

"Venezuela! What the heck, you've got to tell me more."

Ted said, "I'll be glad to, but not over the phone. Could you possibly pop down here, like tomorrow, and I will fill you in. You won't believe what we've been up to lately."

Dr. Fred said, "I've got a few things I need to do first, but I can be down there for the weekend. I'll leave here Friday afternoon."

Ted said, "Great, you can crash at my place."

Dr. Schillinger couldn't wait for the weekend to come. However, he didn't just idle his time away wondering what Ted had become involved with. He got busy with a little bit of research on his own. The first thing he did was to go online and research current events in Venezuela. It didn't take him five minutes to figure out that it had something to do with the recent demise of Angel Falls. He knew Ted was an avid caver, so the samples must have come from the Churum River Cave. In his lab, he took a closer look at Ted's samples. He was surprised that the samples did not exhibit any significant evidence of radioactivity. He thought, how could that be? The Table Mountains of Venezuela are all composed of very ancient rock, so maybe the event that caused the glassifying of the rock samples was also an ancient event. Since the event in question was postulated to be an underground nuclear explosion of some sort, he wondered, what in the world sort of nuclear explosion could possibly have happened millions if not billions of years ago inside of Auyán tepui. It absolutely made no sense what-so-ever. The more he thought about it, the more mysterious it became. When Friday arrived, immediately after his last class, Dr. Fred was on the road tearing away at the four hundred miles of Texas highway that lay ahead of him.

Around ten o'clock that evening he rolled into Austin and pulled into Ted's driveway. Ted and Max were anxiously awaiting and greeted him on his arrival. Ted had prepared a generous batch of cheese and jalapeño nachos and a large pitcher of margaritas which they consumed as they sat around Ted's kitchen table. Over the next several hours, Max and Ted filled Dr. Fred in on all the details of their recent adventure. Dr. Fred filled them in on his recent findings, and pointed out that this could be the most important geological discovery in recent history, and possibly ever. There were many lingering questions and much was yet to be explained. Max related that their initial plumbing of the pit had revealed what appeared to be a large spherical cavity several hundred feet down the pit, and that would be consistent with that region being the epicenter of a large explosion. The actual dimension of the cavity was yet to be determined as the mapping technique they employed was rather crude. It would require another expedition with appropriate equipment to accurately map the pit and confirm the nature of the cavity. Dr. Fred could see years and years of field work ahead and research to fully explain the event. Max emphasized that only his crew and now Dr. Fred knew that they had successfully plumbed the pit and had speculated on the origin of the glassy walls. Dr. Fred said that he would like very much to be included on the next expedition even though he had relatively little caving experience. Max and Ted both agreed that he would be a welcome addition to the team.

Discussions went on through the night. If the event truly was a nuclear event, how, why and when did it occur? If it was an ancient event, were there more occurrences elsewhere around the globe? If it was a recent event, how recent would be considered recent? If it happened within the past few thousand years, would there be any record of the event in the lore of the indigenous people. What if this was a really recent event, like some experiment being conducted by the Russians that went wrong. That would explain their presence and interest in what we had discovered.

Max said, "Now that you mention it, when Sergei showed up, he did seem a bit surprised with our presence there."

Ted remarked, "It seemed obvious that he hadn't been briefed on our mission, and he didn't know what to do with us."

"Yes, and I think he was relieved when we told him that we were just spelunkers, although, I think he had reservations with our stories." Max continued, "I'll bet he is having background checks made on all of us as we speak. I think we will need to be very careful."

Dr. Fred said, "If there is a possibility of what we are speculating is true, then we need to keep our findings totally to ourselves, or else we may find ourselves in the middle of something which we won't want any part of, and our knowledge could become a danger to all of us."

Max suggested that if Ted could spare the additional time off, he should go to Huntsville and bring Scott up to date regarding their latest speculations and concerns. Ted accepted this assignment and said he couldn't go immediately but that he would make it happen soon.

CHAPTER 5

Back in Huntsville, it took Scott a couple of weeks to reestablish his routine. Although Connie, his secretary at the foundation, had handled his affairs with exceptional competence, there were numerous ongoing projects that he felt needed his personal input and attention. So he was quite busy doing catch up work. He welcomed the fact that Ted was coming to Huntsville soon, because he was going to need some help in unravelling the mapper data. So far, the data was still sitting untouched in Scott's safe. He knew that programming of some new algorithms was going to be needed, and some additional human intelligence would be most appreciated in the accomplishment of these tasks. He also knew that Ted would want to be the first to view the results as they emerged.

When Scott began sketching out the flow for the algorithms to process the mapper data, he was thinking that it was about time that he really put his engineering degree to use. Being the manager of the foundation was rewarding and had its own perks, but in reality, nothing is as satisfying to an engineer as getting down in the nitty-gritty of solving a difficult technical problem. Processing of the mapper data in a manner that would yield useful results was going to be a difficult problem. The lack of data fidelity, the gaps in the data due to obscuring of the images, coupled with a lack of a rotational orientation reference for the data was going to make data processing a challenge. So he thought that we will just look at all possible orientations of the data and see which ones make the most sense. After all, that is what computers are best at, i.e. number crunching, so looking at all possible orientations of the pit cross section slices would certainly be a rational approach.

When Ted arrived in Huntsville, he was grateful that Scott had already made arrangements for him for a place to hang his hat. After he was settled in, he and Scott got down to business. Ted told Scott about his mentor and major professor, and the fact that Dr. Schillinger confirmed his suspicions about the cave walls. He pointed out that Dr. Fred also noted that this could be the greatest geologic find of all times or it could be that we just embroiled ourselves in a major international illegal nuclear test or maybe even some kind of nuclear accident. At this point we don't know which. The presence of the Russians and their interest in us suggests the later. The interest of our own government in us also lends credence to the later. But in either case we need to keep our findings and intents to ourselves and closely guarded. Ted also told Scott that Dr. Fred wanted to join our group, and that Max concurred. Scott said that he also concurred, and thought Dr. Fred would be an invaluable addition to the team.

Scott then brought Ted up to speed on what he was pursuing, and that he needed Ted's input on refining, testing, validating, and interpreting the output of the computer code he was developing.

Ted said, "Absolutely, that is the second reason I was anxious to get over here."

Scott also showed Ted some sketches for a potential design for a shield that would protect them during the rappel into the pit through the waterfall and what was obviously going to be a tortuous climb out. After reviewing Scott's sketches, Ted said, "I have a few suggestions. If we put a small bowhead prow on the top, like on an ocean going ship, it will reduce the drag on the shield and if we properly shape the shield, we can make the water to flow off of the trailing edge in a smooth laminar sheet. This should create a dry tunnel around and beneath the climber."

Scott agreed, "If we could do that, it would be a tremendous achievement, and might actually make a descent possible."

Scott remarked further that he had some contacts in the boat manufacturing business, and that they could very quickly make prototypes for testing. We will get them made using carbon fiber so they will be light weight and super strong. Also, there is a pit not far from here with a substantial waterfall where we can test the designs.

Ted was thinking out loud, "We need to get Jim over here to do the testing. He has lots of wet cave experience, so he can be the guinea pig on the rope."

"That's a good idea", Scott said. "We need to give him a heads up so he can plan some time and get his gear ready."

"And there is another thing I have been thinking about", Scott continued. "Communications. Conventional modes of communications won't work in the extreme environment posed by the torrential waterfall. I am betting that, based on the amount of rope we have already bought and are going to buy, that we can get NMI to make a special rope for us, one with embedded conductors in the middle. We can make a magnetic transducer and send and receive signals anywhere along the line. This would be rather simple to implement, but it is something we need to start working on immediately."

Ted said, "Wow, another good idea from the aggie engineer."

Scott said, "I resent that, you must have me confused with one of your associates from Texas. The problem I see here is that we need more people that we can trust. We need someone to honcho this project."

Ted said, "Jim is a big time ham radio enthusiast, he understands this communications stuff."

"Jim is going to have his hands full testing the shield. He won't have time to honcho communications as well. However, he might know someone we could enlist."

And, it turned out that Jim did know somebody. One of his ham friends, Sam Holbrook, was an electronics engineer who worked for one of the big electronics manufacturers in Dallas. So, when Jim was assigned to recruit someone for this particular job, he immediately thought of Sam Holbrook. Sam was the kind of nerd that liked to putter around the lab ten or twelve hours a day inventing stuff. He held over twenty patents, so it was evident that he was pretty good at what he did. Unfortunately, Sam was no caver. Nor was he athletic or much of an outdoors person. Other than that, he was a good guy, very bright, and perfect for the job. But, he also had his own pursuits, so when Jim approached him about managing this unconventional communications project, he was not particularly interested, especially when learned that there was no money involved. He would be expected to volunteer his time. It took some real arm twisting on Jim's part to convince Sam to take the job. Jim had to stroke his ego a bit. Jim pointed out that he would become a member of a highly elite exploration team that was involved in an equally high clandestine mission. He said that the Russians and the CIA, FBI, and Homeland Security were all involved, but that he couldn't tell him more until he was fully committed to the team. Jim described the extreme environment that they were dealing with, and pointed out that an additional challenge was that they needed to keep their communications secure form eavesdropping by the above mentioned entities. It was this last little tidbit that hooked him in. He could not pass up the opportunity to snark both the Russians and the CIA/FBI/DHS at the same time. He agreed, and he was in. They shook hands to seal the deal, and Jim proceeded to brief Sam on the details of what was needed. Sam thought that it shouldn't take more than a month or so to develop and test a prototype, work out the bugs, and then make a couple of full up systems. The next day, Sam let his company know that he needed to take a short leave of absence. They were not in the least happy with this sudden request, but Sam was a very marketable commodity and they did not want to lose him to one of their competitors. In the end they reluctantly agreed to a six month leave.

Over the next several weeks, the projects progressed smoothly. NMI produced six thousand feet of the special rope with the embedded wire strands. The boat manufacturer produced two beautiful shields, which when tested in the waterfall cave, performed better than could have been expected.

Sam was in his own element. His system would take all audio signals and encode them using a secure algorithm before transmitting them. The key for the encoding algorithm could be changed daily thus making the system near impossible to hack in real time. He outfitted all in helmet transceivers with his device. His primary system interacted inductively with the wires in the rope and with a transceiver mounted in each shield. This system allowed any helmet within a hundred feet or so from the primary system or the transceiver in the shields to communicate securely without fear of unfriendly eavesdropping.

While all of these projects were on going and planning was being finalized for the next in-country expedition, things were not going as smoothly for the Russians atop Auyán tepui. However for Miguel Santos, life was good. Miguel had been assigned to monitor the activities of the Russian expedition. The Park Service built him a very nice "temporary" ranger station, and he was the onsite permanent park ranger. His accommodations were not nearly as Spartan as they were when he camped with Max's crew. His home was a nice sized tent erected on a newly built platform. His office was a similar facility. He had a screened in tent next to his kitchen that served as both a dining facility and a meeting room. He had a solar array to provide power, he had a refrigerator, an adequate kitchen, an ATV, and most importantly, he had satellite internet. Miguel also had a new toy. He had a drone, and when he wasn't busy watching the Russians, he was busy honing his drone piloting skills.

Miguel communicated daily with Scott. It was with some glee that he reported that the Russians were having a bit of difficulty. He said that it was absolutely comical watching them trying to rappel down to the ledge. They spent over a week trying to pendulum over to the ledge. Miguel didn't give them any information as to how Max did it. After about a week, they came up with a simple but effective solution. They used a long bamboo pole. The pole was light weight and long enough to reach the wall. They used it to push off from the wall and start swinging. And, after just a few minutes the Russian climber was on the ledge struggling to find a hand hold. He found a hole where one of the American's secure anchors had been affixed. He tried to screw in one of his bolts only to discover the incompatibility of English and metric threads. With great disgust and a few choice Russian expletives, he set about drilling a new hole for his own anchor. Miguel reported that that event had pretty well set the theme for the remainder of the time he had been observing the Russian activity.

Miguel reported that when the Russians began their assault into the cave, things got very interesting. Most notably, they didn't have Lilly Lawson. The crew they had assembled for the assault were woefully unprepared. They lacked the skill sets required to tackle climbing challenges of such great difficulty. Of course the Americans' skills were also a bit lacking at first, but the Americans had both Spider and Peggy with her drones. Miguel reported that the Russians had opted for a lower route which they thought might be easier. He said that during the first three weeks the Russian climbers experienced several near catastrophic falls and twice climbers had to be fished out of the river. He also reported that after the first three weeks, there was a noticeable change in personnel. New climbers were brought in all of whom seemed to have some serious alpine skills. The new personnel were able to make progress much faster and without any new serious incidents. However, they were still using brute force assault methods. That is to say, hang on your anchor, lean over thirty inches or so, drill a new hole, set a new anchor, rig the new anchor, shift your lines, move over, and repeat. The lead climbers were followed by another team that added more ropes and structure to their route. Then with all this infrastructure in place, the Russians began building what looked like a two meter wide hanging bridge all the way back to the pit.

Sometime between the fifth and sixth week, Miguel reported that they had made it all the way back to the abyss with their hanging bridge. He flew his drone in and out of the cave on a daily basis taking high resolution video of the Russians' progress. He up loaded his video each day to Scott's server. Max's group was both amused and amazed with the Russians' effort. Amused with the enormous effort they were making, and amazed with what they accomplished. From the video, it appeared that the narrow suspended rope walkway or bridge that they had constructed all of the way back to the abyss was indeed an excellent piece of engineering. It was amazing what you could do with an unlimited budget and man-power, and this structure certainly made moving equipment in and out relatively easy.

Miguel reported that they were moving some substantial pieces of equipment back to the pit area. The equipment appeared to be some sort of winch apparatus, so it was apparent that they were in the process of plumbing the pit. Everyone was wondering if they would discover the same cavernous anomaly some four to five hundred feet down, and if they did, how they would interpret their findings. Max and Jim were also concerned that they would descend the pit first, upstaging their own personal caving objectives. This was not good, and the possibility spurred the team to finish their development projects as quickly as possible.

When Max and Jim saw the Russian winches, they thought maybe they should consider using winches to lower and raise the shield and climber rather than rappelling in and climbing the rope back up. It would be hugely easier, but Max thought it would require some new and untried technology.

They posed the idea to the group. Scott said, "I think it is a good idea, and frankly, the technology is neither new nor untried. All we have to do is buy it and adapt it to our needs."

Max questioned, "Oh really? Just what is and where do we just go and buy this technology?"

Scott replied, "Large sail boats have been using electric powered winches for at least a century to manage the sheets for their large sails and anchors. The winches are mature technology, extremely robust, and specifically designed for handling rope. Also, they are sealed for use in wet environments."

Max continued his query, "What sort of battery bank do you think we will need?"

Scott said, "Probably just a couple of batteries. What we will really need is a light weight heavy duty twenty four or maybe a forty eight volt dc generator, depending upon what size winch we choose. We can get it all within a week. We can get the boat guys to make us a carbon fiber frame that we can hang on the wall some place with a couple of carabiners, and we will be in business. We will need a frame for both the generator and the winches. Consider it done. In eight days we will test it out."

Jim interjected at this point directing his comments to Scott, "Scott, first of all, order two of everything, and second, let's keep our options open. If everything fails, we need to be able to climb up the rope like we would normally do from any other deep pit, and do it while pushing the shield ahead of us. A manual climb of this magnitude up through a waterfall with the shield, will be more difficult than running a marathon in a hurricane, so the thought of being winched up is very, very attractive. But we need the backup plan." Jim's comments were well taken and no one disagreed.

Scott contacted the marine equipment manufacturing company that was making the carbon fiber shields to discuss options for a winch. He explained that he thought a large sheet winch would meet their needs. However, after explaining how it would be used and the need for high reliability in harsh environments, it was brought to his attention that a variant of the winches used for towing parasails would be a much better choice. An electric version of the parasail wenches met all of Scott's criteria, and as a result, Scott ordered two.

D-day was set for eighteen days in the future. Everything had to be finalized on a frantic schedule. Every few days some equipment or supplies were readied for shipment and were airfreighted to Canaima Camp. The last things to be crated were the two Shields, Sam's communication gear, the winches and generator, and a long list of late arriving gear and supplies. At last they were ready to go.

CHAPTER 6

Meanwhile atop Auyán tepui, Sergei had caught wind of the Americans imminent return. It was not possible to keep their travel plans secret since they had to be coordinated with several branches of the Venezuelan government, so it was no surprise to Miguel when he received a visit from Sergei who just wanted to confirm the American's planned arrival time. Miguel gave him all that he knew, and that seemed to satisfy Sergei.

When the Cessna 205 touched down with Max and Scott aboard, guess who was at the runway to welcome them back to Auyán tepui, none other than Sergei and Miguel. "Welcome back Mr. Meccum and Mr. Mueller. I have been looking forward to your return. We have a lot to discuss", said Sergei.

Thanks, it's good to see you also, Sergei", replied Max wondering what all Sergei had discovered and with some dread as to exactly what Sergei wanted to discuss.

Sergei said, "Can I offer you some assistance with moving your supplies to your camp area, and possibly with helping you get set up again?"

It was obvious that there weren't going to be many secrets held back from Sergei on this trip, so Max said, "Yes, of course, any muscle you can lend will be most appreciated. That will help us get reestablished much quicker."

With a wave of Sergei's hand a military pickup truck came rumbling up, and a couple of beefy soldiers quickly loaded up things that Max and Scott had brought with them on the Cessna 205. Miguel, Max, Scott, and Sergei climbed into Miguel's new ATV and headed off to Miguel's new ranger station.

Max asked, "How did that truck get here?"

Miguel answered for Sergei, "You can actually drive up to here from Canaima Camp. Unfortunately, the road is unimproved, and it takes about two days to make the trip. Generally speaking, only military style vehicles are suitable."

Sergei remarked, "As you can see, there have been some changes made since you were here. For instance, we have some new roads; we can drive all of the way up to the rift." As they headed off down the newly graded dirt road, the pickup with their supplies fell in behind them.

Miguel was anxious to show off his new quarters. Upon arriving, Scott said, "Wow, you did get an upgrade. Did you get a pay raise also?"

"Si, si, it came with the territory." You could say that Miguel was a 'happy camper'. Miguel pointed to a nearby open area and suggested that Max set up their operations there.

After the soldiers unloaded the truck and returned to the Russian's base of operations, Miguel invited Max, Scott and Sergei to join him in his new dining tent for a few beers.

As they sat around Miguel's conference/dining table, Miguel passed out some cold beer's which he brought to everyone's attention that they were in fact, thanks to his new refrigerator, 'cold beers'.

Sergei opened the discussions with a statement, "Like you Americans like to say, let's put our cards on the table. While I believe that everything you have told me is true, I also believe that there is a lot that you haven't shared. I'm not blaming you or faulting you, I'm just stating the facts. I am sure that if I were in your position, I would be careful with what I shared as well. So, I'll tell you what we know, and what we suspect. We recently were able to successfully lower a camera down the pit. On the bottom we noted the bags of equipment that you lost as you were exiting the cave. We also noticed several other things on the bottom. One was a high tech wire reel which obviously was used to measure the depth of the pit and probably some other parameters as well. Another was a curious device enclosed in an interesting net. I am very curious as to how you just happened to have that obviously specialized net in your inventory, you must tell me all about that sometime. Some of our scientists have opined that this device was used to profile the pit. Are we correct? And, if you profiled the pit, you must be aware of the unusual anomalous structure that exists two hundred meters down. Since you have added Dr. Schillinger to your expedition personnel, I gather that you have formed a rather solid opinion as to what caused that anomaly. Am I correct again?"

Max nodded in agreement, and Scott said, "You are correct on all counts. Ted noted that the spherical anomaly was definitely not natural, and must have been caused by a very large explosion, and considering the glassy character of the walls of the cave, he almost immediately came to the conclusion that the explosion had to be nuclear. He spent most of his time collecting samples to support his thesis. So, yes, when you showed up, we were immediately suspicious that your government was somehow involved. By the way, if that is the case, we don't want to be involved. We know nothing, we've seen nothing. We just want to explore the pit. On the other hand, if as Ted and Dr. Schillinger believe, the explosion is ancient, and hence no modern government is involved. All they want to do is research the event. They believe that geologic history may be made at this site, and they want to write that history."

Sergei asked, "Why do they believe that it was an ancient event?"

Scott said, "No radiation, I'm sure that you noticed that as well."

"Yes, of course we did. We did not conclude that it was an ancient event, however. Now, the big question, will you share with me your government's opinions regarding this anomalous event?"

Max said, "Our government is totally clueless. They have no idea as to what is really going on here or as to what we have found or observed. As far as they know we are just a bunch of cavers that have somehow gotten involved with a bunch of Russians. What they really want to know is what are you Russians doing here, and specifically what are your interests in the area. They want to know about every conversation that we have with you. They are probably watching us from a satellite right now. If they thought nuclear anything was involved, they would be crawling all over this place like beetles on a pile of dung."

Scott also pointed out that, "If they had a clue or if they thought nuclear was involved, they wouldn't allow us to be here. You know, we need to continue these discussions, but the rest of our crew also needs to be involved, especially Dr. Baldridge and Dr. Schillinger."

Sergei said, "Let's reconvene tomorrow after you all get settled in. My scientists have a theory that they will share with you. They have an alternate theory to the nuclear supposition that I am sure you will find interesting."

By the following afternoon, with the help from Sergei's crew, Max's camp was set up and organized. It was however not nearly as opulent as Miguel's digs. It was about four in the afternoon as everyone was tapering down from a busy day's work when Sergei and some of his comrades showed up. These men did not appear to be military or political operative types but rather academics of some sort.

Sergei said, "I hope that we haven't come at an inconvenient time, but I was hoping to continue our discussions that we were having yesterday."

Max greeted them and said, "Not at all, we were just finishing up, and now is a good time for a break. Let's meet over there in Miguel's dining tent. Let me round up my crew, and we will meet you there."

Miguel's dining tent was a bit crowded, but somehow everyone managed to find a place to sit. Sergei began with introductions, "This is Dr. Pavel Ramanski, our lead scientist. Dr. Ramanski is a professor of physics at the University of Moscow. Dr. Dmitry Ormant and Dr. Yuri Kuznetsov are professors of geology with the Lenin Institute of Mining."

Max then introduced the members of his crew. After handshakes all around, Ted said, "I understand that you have a theory regarding the anomalous nature of this cave system. Is that correct?"

Sergei said, "We have a number of things that we would like to discuss, and yes, that is one of them."

Dr. Ramanski began, "I believe that you all discussed yesterday the possibility that the anomaly was caused by some sort of nuclear explosion. We agree that is a possibility, and we have not discounted it. Such an event would explain a lot of what we have observed. However, to be conclusive, we need much more information and rock samples. The lack of any residual radiation is a conundrum. Is it possible that this is such an ancient event that the radiation is completely dissipated? That does not seem to be possible, so we are forced to consider other possibilities."

Dr. Shillinger asked, "Do you have a plausible alternative theory?"

Dr. Ramanski replied, "Plausible, yes. But just how plausible is an open question. You are familiar with Nikola Tesla, yes."

Everyone nodded in the affirmative. Dr. Ramaski continued, "Tesla did extensive research on ball lightning and elucidated extensively on what he believed were its properties, yet to date still little is really known about the phenomena. As a possibility, we believe that a huge quantity of ball lightning may have somehow become encapsulated in the ancient rock of this mountain. How or why it might have been encapsulated, we have no idea, but an encapsulate plasma the size of the geologic anomaly observed two hundred meters down the pit would contain pent up energy comparable to a mid-sized nuclear bomb. If an earthquake occurred that caused a breach in the rock encapsulating the plasma, the release of energy would have been sufficient to cause the glassification of the rock which we all have observed. Now, this is just a theory, but we believe it is equally as plausible as the nuclear explosion theory. Both theories have giant holes that require explanation before either can be accepted as fact."

Dr. Schillinger remarked, "I congratulate you on your theory. It certainly seems plausible, and the idea never crossed any of our minds. You know, the Catatumbo Lightning of Lake Maracaibo may be a long term artifact of such an event like you are postulating. We obviously need a bunch of samples, especially from the spherical anomaly area."

Ted pointed out that getting samples from the spherical anomaly area might be difficult to the point of being impossible, but surely there would be debris on the bottom from the area which could be collected.

That brought up the next point that Sergei wanted to discuss. Sergei said, "I propose that we collaborate on this effort. We are not prepared to descend the pit, but you are. We have already set up an analytical laboratory where we can chemically and physically assay the samples. You collect, and we analyze. Drs. Ormant and Kuznetsov are prepared to do whatever analysis is appropriate, and Drs. Baldridge and Schillinger can participate in the analysis in whatever capacity they desire. This would be a win-win situation for both of our expeditions. You spelunkers would get credit for descending and exploring the pit, the 'pit from hell' as some of my men have described it. And, both of our science teams would get the data they need to validate/invalidate one or both of the theories. The scientist can jointly author papers on the findings. That is my proposition. I hope that you will give it serious consideration. Together we are more likely to succeed than if we work separately. By the way, for your information, I can assure you that our government is not currently conducting, and never has in the past conducted any type of nuclear activity in this area."

On the previous day when Sergei said that he had things he wanted to discuss, Max had expected to be dressed down for not being totally honest with him. What max did not expect was to receive an open arms proposition for cooperation and support. Max was over whelmed, so he thanked Sergei for the opportunity, but before he could give him an answer, the whole group would need to discuss the proposition and come to a consensus.

Max said, "How about we let you know in the morning. You have given us a lot to think about."

After that, the meeting broke up into informal one-on-one discussions. After an exchange of some pleasantries and small talk, most of Max's crew excused themselves to prepare for the next day's activities. Ted and Dr. Schillinger started talking with Drs. Ramanski, Ormant and Kuznetsov about the analytical capabilities they had in their field laboratory, and what level of technician support they had at their disposal. They wanted to know if the Russians had discovered anything of significance, and if they had formulated la list of specifics they were hoping to find or not find. Dr. Ramanski indicated that they would be looking specifically for any artifacts that would indicate a nuclear event had occurred. If they could find no artifacts, that would rule out a nuclear explosion. If they found some artifacts, they would be interested in accurately determining their age. They would be especially interested if they turned out to be recent. The implications of that would be huge. Dr. Schillinger said that the preliminary tests that he had made did not turn up any unexpected radiation related artifacts, and that in itself was unexpected. Ted was wondering what sort of physical evidence could they turn up that would support the theory of a ball lightning plasma explosion.

Dr. Kuznetsov said, "Well, if we find no fates of any known nuclear reaction, that finding would say look carefully at the next best theory, which at the moment is the ball lightning theory." That of course would not constitute proof, but would simply be evidence of plausibility.

On the other side of the tent, Max and Sergie were talking. Max told Sergie about their plans for descending the pit, the special equipment they had developed to make it possible, and what help they could use in transporting and setting the equipment up back at the pit. Max told Sergei that even if for some reason his crew decided that it would be inappropriate to work closely together, that he would still appreciate some help in getting the equipment back to the pit. Sergei was amused with the boldness of Max's request should they agree not to collaborate, but as noted before, Sergei was a smooth politician and he recognized opportunity when he saw it, so he promised his full support. Max agreed that the Russian's route would be the most expeditious for moving the heavy equipment back to the pit, and that he and Scott would oversee the effort. Max also explained that Jim, Bufford, Spider, and Peggy would be busy re-rigging the American's original route, because it would enable the most rapid means for personnel to travel to and from the pit. Max told Sergei that he would now get to see how they did it. He said, "We used drones and a Spider."

CHAPTER 7

Later that evening everyone gathered at Miguel's Diner for supper. Discussions centered around whether or not to accept Sergei's offer. Max stated that he was in favor of accepting because Sergei could provide a huge amount of support, and they had a field laboratory to analyze samples for Ted and Dr. Schillinger. That was a big plus. He said that we are going to be crawling all over each other anyway, so there is not going to be any secrets, at least not topside of the pit. Scott pointed out that there might be hell-to-pay if or when the CIA learns that we are collaborating with the Russians. However, there is probably nothing they can do about it. Collaborating for mutual benefit should be totally legal so long as there is no exchange of money. We aren't their agents and they aren't ours. We aren't contracting to provide them anything and vice-versa.

Ted said, "I say, let's go for it. After all, the CIA hasn't exactly fallen all over themselves to offer us any support."

Max said, "Let's see a show of hands for who is in favor of accepting Sergei's offer." All hands showed in favor.

The next morning, Max informed Sergei of the group's decision to accept his offer, but that it must be kept informal or else the CIA might later misconstrue our intentions. Sergei was elated with the news, and true to his word, a dozen men were put at Max's disposal to do whatever needed doing.

It turned out to be a very busy day and everything progressed successfully and without incident. By the end of the day, the route was re-rigged, the winch and generator were installed, the special NMI rope was carefully laid out ready for use, and the communications network was checked out and certified ready for use. The primary shield was attached to the NMI rope and positioned ready for lowering. The secondary shield and NMI rope was stowed in the attic out of sight but ready for use if necessary. All systems were checked and re-checked, and it was agreed that the next day would be a 'go for descent'.

It was decided that Max would be the first down, followed by Bufford, then Spider, and finally Jim. Everyone else would remain topside to monitor progress, and to respond to any requests or emergencies. Considering the time that would be required for both the descent and the ascent, the group planned to spend several days, perhaps even a week, on the bottom. This meant that the first items down would be supplies to support the crew for three to four days as they explored around the bottom of the pit and collected samples for the scientists.

When the time arrived for Max to begin his descent, every detail was checked and rechecked. In addition to his regular caving helmet, which was now outfitted with Sam's one-of-a-kind communications gear, and his regular caving boots, Max was wearing a special lightweight wetsuit and sporting a full face mask and a state-of-the-art rebreather. The rebreather would provide up to eight hours of breathable air should the shield or winches fail and leave him stranded in the middle of the falling torrent. Dangling beneath Max would be a pack containing his climbing gear. The idea for using the rebreather was to maximize his survival time if the shield failed thereby maximize the time for the topside crew to come up with solutions. Everywhere a single point failure possibility was identified, a redundancy was incorporated, and when redundancy was not possible, extra robustness was provided or a workaround was developed. As a consequence of all this preplanning, everyone held a high degree of confidence in the likely success of the plan.

Despite all this preparation, as Max began clipping onto the descent rope beneath the shield, there was an air of serious concern as well as excitement. Caving history was about to be made, or a gigantic disaster was about to unfold. Once Max was clipped in and snugged up tight beneath the shield, the slow descent began. As he descended into the torrent, he could feel the tremendous force of the water pounding down on top of the shield. The whole rig shuddered under the load. He couldn't help but think what a good idea it would have been to have added several additional layers of carbon fiber to the shield. Even with the noise cancelling earphones, the noise was deafening. The shield was doing its job, just as planned. The water struck the shield and then flowed along its curvature and down creating a tunnel around and beneath Max. Max remarked, "This is freaking awesome! I can see twenty to thirty feet below me, then the tunnel collapses." Scott queried, "How are you doing? Are you ok?" Max could barely hear him when he replied, "Yeah, I'm ok. I can barely hear you though, it is really noisy down here."

Topside Jim was controlling Max's descent. Since the spool of the parasail winch wouldn't hold three thousand feet of rope, several coils of rope were placed around the spool. For descent, the winch spool was used as a rappel device, no power needed. For ascent, the power feature of the winch was used. Jim was being helped by Boris Anatoly, one of the Russians, and by Ted and Bufford. When it came time for Jim to descend, Ted would be in charge of controlling their descent with Scott and the Russians helping. The way they were managing the descent was to use the winch drum as the primary rappel device backed up by a six bar rescue rappel rack. Five loops around the drum provided more than the requisite friction to control Max's descent. While Jim managed the descent, Ted managed the feed of the rope through the rappel rack ensuring that Jim had sufficient slack to smoothly control Max's descent. Should the five wraps around the spool prove to insufficient, Ted could squeeze a couple of brake bars together and completely halt the descent if necessary. The five wraps worked perfectly. Periodically, Peggy would pour some water over the winch drum to ensure that it didn't overheat and damage the rope.

When Max was down about seven hundred feet, the noise level had diminished substantially. Max said, "This is amazing, it is like descending through a thick rain. Occasionally I get a glimpse of what lies beyond the rain, but then it disappears again. You can lower me a little faster if you can. There is nothing to gain from lingering when you can't see anything."

With that, Jim loosened up a bit on the rope and the rate of descent increased considerably. Jim said, "Peggy, keep pouring water on the drum. I don't think it is getting too hot, but let's not take any chances."

Peggy poured another bucket of water on the winch drum and said, "I think we are doing okay. We aren't even generating any steam yet."

"Good, generating steam is exactly what we don't want to do." Scott said, "Max, are you still okay?"

"Yeah, I'm fine. We are really zipping along now. How far down am I now?"

Ted looked back at the coils of rope that were being fed through the brake bar rack and estimated, "It looks like you are eighteen hundred to nineteen hundred feet down. You should be able to see the bottom soon. There are several cyalume lights on top of the equipment package we lowered earlier."

Max peered into the darkness below and said, "I think I can see them faintly now. I can also see the walls fairly good now. They are pretty close. I can tell how fast I am actually going. You know, when you can't see anything but the water rushing past, you get the sensation that you are going up rather than down. It is a very strange feeling."

Scott cautioned, "You have to keep your mind in the game, because your eyes and ears are playing tricks on you. You can easily get vertigo under these circumstances."

"Yes, I know, and I have been thinking exactly that." Max replied. "Now that I can see the walls, that sensation has mostly disappeared. It is still easy to imagine that you are traveling up instead of down though." Max was getting close to the bottom now, so Jim slowed the rate of descent. Max shouted, "Slow me down, I'm nearly there. About twenty more feet to go." Jim put more tension on the rope and eased Max on down slowly, then Max said, "I'm down. Give me a little slack so I can get unclipped. It looks just like the pictures we took. And yes, tell Sergei it looks like the pictures he took as well."

The first thing Max did was to take out the sample bag he brought down with him and he filled it with a variety of small rock fragments that were plentiful all around. He attached the bag to the rope close up under the shield, and said, "The sample bag is ready for hoisting. I am signing off for now. I am going to go look for some shelter from falling objects while you are pulling the rope back up." Jim flipped on the winch, and began reeling the rope with the sample bag back up. As the rope was being retrieved, Scott and Peggy were busy coiling the rope in large hanks so it wouldn't become tangled.

Meanwhile Max moved down the massive boulder pile towards a high narrow canyon where the rain had recoalesced again into a noisy river and flowed off to the east. As he moved down the boulder pile he noted with some mirth the piles of now destroyed equipment that they had tossed down the pit on their previous trip. He paused and grabbed one of the rope bags thinking it might come in handy soon. Once in the canyon, there was little room to maneuver, but at least he would be safe here from falling debris from above. The river took up most of the space, but at least it was flowing much slower and much less menacing now. Max was searching for some place where they could establish their camp. It was agreed that he wouldn't stray too far downstream until the other members of the descent crew were safely down. There was just too much risk in going off alone down here, and besides he needed to remain close in case the next person down needed aid of some sort.

The next person to start down was Bufford. Once he was clipped in, Jim began to lower him into the torrent. The initial onslaught of the water was brutal, and Bufford just out of instinct snugged up tight under the shield. He too was amazed to see the tunnel formed by the shield form just below him as the water streamed rapidly past him. Bufford closed his eyes and he could sense the fact that he was going down, but just as Max had described, when he opened his eyes he had the immediate sensation that he was flying up like a rocket.

He said, "God this is a weird and awesome experience. This could easily make one sick in a hurry. I think it is better to keep my eyes closed."

Scott consoled him and said, "Go ahead and keep your eyes closed if it makes you feel better. We'll tell you when you are six hundred feet down, and you need to start looking around."

Bufford replied, "Ok, that's a deal."

The rest of Bufford's descent went as planned, and he was met at the bottom by Max. This time as they scurried down the boulder pile to the safety of the canyon, they pulled the rope with them. There, in safety, they filled a second bag with rock samples collected from inside the canyon, and then signed off communications with the top as the rope was being winched back up.

Max said, "We need start unpacking and moving our provisions down to here. There is not much room as you can see, so I think we will need to nail most of it to the wall somewhere."

Bufford said, "Let's do it."

With that they moved back up the boulder pile and started to unpack the provisions bundle. Bufford said, "This isn't that heavy, I think the two of us can muscle the whole thing down to the canyon without having to unpack it."

Max agreed. They untied it from the rope, and began lugging it down. After a bit of struggling, Bufford said, "This is tougher than I thought it would be. What does this damn thing weigh two hundred pounds?"

Max said grunting with effort, "Almost, I think. Remember this was your idea."

"I hope there is nothing breakable in here", said Bufford as they drug the oversized duffle bag down the boulder slope and into the mouth of the narrow canyon.

Back on top, Spider was readying herself for the descent. When the shield broke through the cascading torrent, Ted quickly unclipped the sample bag, and Spider moved into position to clip in. When all was ready, Spider took hold of the shield and swung out over the torrent and Jim began to lower her. As the torrent swallowed her, she screamed a stream of un-lady like expletives which included statements like "this is scarier than …" you know what. Spider continued to babble expletives as Jim lowered her down.

As Spider began to calm down, she rambled to no one in particular, "I don't like this at all. When I climb or rappel, I like to be in control, and I don't feel in control. And when I am not in control, it is usually when I am hanging on the end of a rope. Kind of like now. However, when I am hanging out in space on the end of a rope, I like for Bufford to be on the other end of the rope. No offense to you Jim, but that is just the way I feel. Bufford and I have been climbing together for a long time, and I just feel safe when he is on the other end of the rope."

Jim said, "No offense taken Spider, but don't worry, I am going to take good care of you."

"Yeah, I know you will, but never-the-less, get me down as quickly as you can. I should have been second down." With that, Jim loosened his grip on the rope, and Spider began to whiz rapidly down the pit.

Bufford moved up the boulder pile to meet Spider when she touched down. It was as though he knew Spider would be very uncomfortable with someone else belaying her. When Spider touched down, she immediately grabbed Bufford, and they hugged for several minutes.

Spider said, "I should have come down second."

Bufford replied, "That is what I thought when I was about half was down. I don't know what I was thinking when I went second. I know you aren't comfortable with someone else belaying you. I'm sorry. Are you okay now?"

"Yeah, I'm good", she said.

Max looked up at Spider and Bufford and thought to himself, "They are an odd couple but a sweet couple." It was obvious that Spider and Bufford did not like being real far from each other.

With Spider safely on the bottom, it was Jim's turn to prepare to make his descent. After hauling the rope and shield back to the top, Jim turned descent control over to Ted and said, "Ted, are you ready for this?"

Ted replied, "I was born ready. Get clipped in." By now Jim knew what to expect, so his descent was a little less dramatic than his team mates. Ted managed the descent control just as expertly as Jim, and without incident, Jim joined Max, Bufford and Spider on the bottom.

This time, the rope and shield were not retrieved to the top, but instead were tied off near the mouth of the canyon. Now the top and bottom could have continuous communication. Ted, with the help of several Russians, moved the provision rope over to the winch, and hauled it up in preparation to lower additional provisions to the bottom. Several of Sergei's men were kind enough to handle the task of muscling the second provisions pack from the surface back to the pit. The first provisions pack contained mostly camping gear and some food; basically, survival stuff. The second pack contained more food, two hammer drills, miscellaneous climbing hardware, spare batteries, two small water turbines for charging the batteries, a change of clothes for everyone, and some first aid supplies. This completed the basic supplies necessary to support the initial exploratory efforts on the bottom. More supplies would be needed, but they would be lowered later the next day.

The canyon that led off from the bottom of the pit was about forty feet high and twenty five feet wide. The river occupied most of the bottom. There were few ledges and many boulders along the edge of the river leading back into the canyon. Further back, the roof of the canyon rapidly became higher and higher. Six hundred feet or so down the canyon from the pit, the canyon terminated. Actually, the canyon continued, but it was jam packed full of boulders from the floor to as high as one could see. And at this point, the top of the canyon was at least four hundred feet up, and the river syphoned into the boulder jam. One might have thought that this was the end of the road except for the fact that there was air movement. In fact, there was considerable air movement, and that could mean only one thing. Beyond this boulder jam, there had to be lots more cave, and that cave would have to be massive.

With every one now on the bottom and the supplies moved into the canyon, the first task was to find places to stow all the stuff and to find somewhere to set up their camp. When Bufford was descending, Max took the opportunity to set a half dozen hangers about forty feet inside the canyon. He knew that due to the paucity of flat places, most of the equipment and supply bags would have to be hung from anchors placed in the walls. This was true for their sleeping hammocks as well. So the next several hours were spent drilling holes, setting anchors, and hanging stuff up.

Max said, "I don't know about all of you, but I am a sweaty mess. This high tech wet suit is nice, but I think I prefer my trusty coveralls."

"Amen to that", said Spider. "You all know that there is no way I can climb in this outfit. I'm changing, so close your eyes."

"No way", said Max, "get used to it. We are all going to be watching."

"Suit yourself, nothing to see here."

With that, everyone dove into the now sorted supply stashes, and dug out and donned their personal caving garments. Feeling much more comfortable now, Max, Bufford and Spider set off down the passage to do a little bit of exploring. Jim stayed behind to finish a couple of tasks. One was to haul the descent rope and shield closer to where they had set up their camp.

He said, "I haven't heard much from the top, are you guys listening?"

Peggy said, "We have been trying to listen, but you all have been too far from the shield for us to hear well. We could only get occasional snatches of what you all have been talking about."

"We have just been sorting things out and setting up camp, so you haven't missed anything. When I say camp, I am using that term rather loosely. We are scattered up and down one side of the river for about fifty feet or so. There no flat places, so we have stuff hung up just about everywhere. You should be able to hear us all now when we are in our camp."

Peggy said, "Keep talking, there are curious people up here who want to know everything that's going on down there."

Jim said, "I'll do it. Right now I am setting up the two water turbines so we can keep stuff charged up, then I am going to break out something to eat. No one down here has eaten anything since we left the top. I'm here by myself right now. Everyone else has gone on down the canyon to get a look-see. They should be coming back soon." About then, Jim could see down the passage some headlamps moving up and down as the others were slowly making their way back to camp. Jim remarked, "Looks like they are almost back now, I can see their headlamps."

As they made their way back into camp, Jim asked, "What did you find?"

Scott announced, "We can all hear each other now. Give us the details, we are all dying to know."

Max explained, "Well, the canyon is quite narrow and filled with boulders. The river is running through them, so it is quite dangerous scrambling over boulder after boulder to make you way down the passage. We managed to go four or five hundred feet on back before it all ended."

Bufford remarked, "It didn't really end; it just got a lot different."

Spider laughed, "Yeah, it didn't really didn't end, it just went straight up."

Max clarified, "The canyon gets wider and higher as you go until you get to this giant breakdown pile where the river disappears. The boulder pile slopes up steeply until it completely fills the canyon wall to wall. I couldn't tell how high the canyon is back there, but it is at least four hundred feet. We will know how high when we map this segment of the cave with the laser mapper. One thing though, there is passage beyond the breakdown block."

Spider said, "Another thing, we need to set our base camp up back there. It is a lot wider, and we won't have to be right next to the water."

Jim said with some disgust in his voice, "Geeze guys, we just spent several hours setting camp up here."

Max said, "Yeah, I know, but Spider is right. We will be a lot better off back there rather than here. Let's spend the night here, get some rest, and move on tomorrow. Also, we can survey the passage as we move back."

Jim asked to no one in particular, "Does anyone know how long the NMI rope is?"

Scott, who was listening said, "Yes, the rope is right at three thousand feet long."

Jim said, "That means that we should have about four hundred extra feet that we can pull back here in the canyon. That will determine where we should set up camp and still have communication with the top."

Bufford said, "I'll bet we can stretch that rope another hundred feet if we need to."

Jim agreed, "I'll bet you are right. Ted, are you listening?"

Ted replied, "I hear you loud and clear. We will tie off as short as we can and give you as much slack as possible."

Max said, "That sounds like a plan. Let's get a bite to eat and sack out so we can get an early start in the morning."

Spider said with a chuckle, "You know Max, morning is a relative term down here. It's always dark down here."

Before hitting the sack, Max dug out the laser mapper to make sure it would be ready for use in the morning. The laser mapper was probably the highest tech gizmo that they had with them. Simply point it at a spot, and it would give you the distance to the spot accurate to within a fraction of a centimeter, the altitude angle relative to the horizontal, which it sensed automatically, and the azimuth angle relative to magnetic north. It had a voice logger, a holographic keyboard for data entry, and a holographic display. It automatically logged all survey data onto a high capacity memory chip. Whenever a shot was made, it also made a three hundred and sixty degree cross section scan and a digital picture centered on the laser beam. This device made cave surveys easy and accurate. With the holographic keyboard, the user could also type in any notes that he thought relevant, or he could just voice record his remarks.

Max made two shots, one back towards the pit, and the other down the canyon passage. He spoke into the voice logger and said, "This is where we spent the first night at the bottom of the pit."

Early the next morning, as someone in the group remarked "at O'dark thirty", pun intended, they were up and about and preparing to move forward with the exploration. The first order of business was to move the base of operations back to the break down pile, and then pull the NMI rope back as far as possible and tie it off. Once camp was reestablished, Bufford and Spider set off climbing to the top of the sloping breakdown pile.

Spider remarked that, "These boulders don't look all that old."

Bufford said, "To me they look like they are the result of some kind of shattering. Notice how sharp the edges are."

Spider said, pointing to the near canyon wall, "Look at all of the cracks in the wall. Up top, you couldn't buy a crack when you needed it. Down here they are everywhere."

Bufford noted, "That's good actually. It'll make climbing easier and safer."

Spider added, "All those cracks also support your notion that all these boulders are a result of the canyon walls being shattered somehow. It's sort of like they were slammed together and bounced back letting all these boulders fall down. I hope they are stable."

"I'm not real sure that they are", commented Bufford. As they arrived at the top of the slope where the stack of boulders went strictly vertical, the movement of the air increased noticeably.

Looking up at the boulder jam, Spider remarked, "I don't think I have ever seen anything like this before."

"It is unique for sure", Bufford said as he poked his head into an opening between two boulders. "This whole pile of rocks seems really porous. The river is obviously running right through it without slowing down, and there is lots of air movement. I wonder if this hole goes anywhere?"

With that, Bufford squeezed through the crack and into a small void that led to another crack between more boulders. He could see that there was more space beyond this second narrowing. Continuing, crawling on his belly, Bufford moved further into the boulder jam. He yelled back at Spider, "You know that this is my least favorite type of passage to explore. I hate squeezing my body through these tight contorted passages where I could get stuck, and then what? You think you could pull me out?"

By now Spider had caught up with him, and she answered his question. "Naw, if you get stuck, I don't think we could pull you out. We would just have to leave you there, so you had better be careful."

"What a fine caving partner you are", grunted Bufford as he squeezed further down the passage. "You would just leave me there?", he asked sheepishly.

Spider quipped, "Well, we would probably take your boots. There wouldn't be any sense in leaving a perfectly good pair of boots down here to rot. Besides, you have really nice boots, and we would need something to remember you by."

Bufford said, "You are such a joy to cave with. You know, you have a really mean streak in you."

They squeezed and crawled, grunted and moaned their way on through the boulder maze for about a hundred feet before the passage terminated with the air whistling through a small crack much too small for either of them to squeeze through. Bufford said. "Well, so much for this lead. We can't go any further." With that they started inching their way backward. Bufford complained, "Is there any place back there where I can turn around? This belly crawling backwards is worse than backing up a long nosed Peterbilt with a fifty three foot rifer through a Wally World parking lot on black Friday."

Spider laughed, "I think there is a place about twenty feet back here. Think you can make it?"

"Well, I damn sure don't want you to leave me down here and let you take my boots." Bufford quipped back.

Spider laughed again trying not to make too much fun of Bufford's struggles, "You poor thing. I won't leave you. Besides, your boots are too big for me."

Bufford grunted, "You skinny broad, you know you are going to pay for your sick humor, I promise."

Spider said, "I'm so afraid."

About thirty minutes later, they emerged from that tortuous dead end passage. Bufford said, "That there is the reason I prefer rock climbing."

About then Max saw their lights emerge at the top of the breakdown pile, and he hollered up at them, "Get on down here, Ted has some news. Turn your helmet phones on so you can hear."

Bufford and Spider scrambled down the rock pile and met Max and Jim at the camp. "What's up?", Spider asked.

Ted, who could hear everyone now said, "Fred has been spending a lot of time over with the Russians in their lab. They have discovered something, but we don't know what it means yet."

"Tell us, tell us", said Spider excitedly.

Ted explained, "Well, they have been analyzing all the samples that we gathered plus a bunch more from the canyon and around the area. They are using a mass spectrometer to assay the elemental composition of all the stuff. First, they determined what the ancient rock that makes up this mountain was made out of, that is to say what elements are present in the vast majority of the unaffected rock samples. They also managed to get a good quantitative measure of proportions in which those elements appeared. There were no surprises there. They then performed the same analysis on the samples from the cave wall leading back to the pit and on the samples you all collected from the bottom of the pit. Then they subtracted the unaffected results from the affected results. The difference identified everything that shouldn't be there. That's where the plot thickens. There is a ton of stuff that shouldn't be there. There is stuff that probably shouldn't be on this planet, much less on this planet in the same place. Anyone got any ideas?"

Max quickly replied, "Aliens!"

Ted responded, "That would be the easy explanation. The Russians are speculating that most of the unusual elements showing up are generally associated with highly advanced electronic devices, but there are some elements that as far as anyone knows are not associated with any known integrated circuit, laser device, superconducting material, or anything else.

All this suggests that this was not a natural event, and that this Churum River event was due to the explosion of a highly sophisticated man made device. So, how did that stuff get here? Who is behind whatever occurred here? Those are the questions now. Sergei says that it definitely is not his government, and from their intelligence, he doesn't think the U.S is involved, at least not directly. He says that leaves China, Israel, or possibly one of the international mega-corporations. Actually, I got the feeling he was leaning towards the later. There are several dozen possible candidates if that is the case."

Jim, who had been listening silently chimed in, "Okay, what now? What are we supposed to do? The way I see it, we are in a rather precarious position down here. Whoever is behind all this probably doesn't want a lot of light shed on this event or on their activities. Which in turn probably means that they would rather we stay down here you know like forever."

Max said, "You may be right. Ted, what are your thoughts?"

After a brief pause, Ted opined, "I think that, if there are other players, we will be protected by the Russians. To get to us, they would have to contend with the Russians first, and I believe the Russians have the strongest position here of anyone. Our best strategy is probably to continue working closely with Sergei and stay in his favor."

Max said, "I think you are undoubtedly correct. I also think we need to finish up down here as quickly as possible and get our butts back top side."

Ted finished his report and said, "I'll keep you informed, so stay tuned."

Bufford said, "The day is early, so let's get started. Spider and I opt for not trying to push through this rock pile but rather, let's go over the top if possible."

Jim said, "I assume you didn't find much promise in following the air through the breakdown, right?"

Bufford said with emphasis, "You are so very, very right. Belly crawling through cracks and crevices, and ridiculously low passages is not what I call fun. I thought for a while I was going to be stuck in there, and I am not interested in going back."

Max asked, "What do you think are the chances of going over the top?" Spider said, "I think the climb to the top will be fairly easy. If there is passage up there, it has to be easier than what Bufford and I pushed earlier. From what I saw earlier, I think I can climb it fairly quickly. Bufford and

I can set up fixed ropes, and then we can all go up and down quickly and easily."

Max said, "Okay, let's do it."

Bufford said, "Someone grab that rope bag. It's got about four hundred feet of rope in it. We will need all of it. Spider, do you have your stuff?"

Spider said, "You all go on ahead and get the gear up to the top of the slope. I'm changing into some shorts. I don't climb in long pants very well."

Everyone grabbed their climbing gear, some spare hardware a couple of extra ropes, two spare batteries for the drills, some eats and water and began the trek up the break down boulder pile. Spider quickly changed and rejoined the group. Once at the top, Spider clipped in her belay line and said "On belay" as stuck her hand in a crack and up she went like a gecko chasing a fly.

CHAPTER 8

Back in Miguel's dining tent, Peggy was lamenting to Scott, "On the last trip, I was really involved. I had a lot to do. On this trip, I feel like a bump on a log. I'm not doing anything, I'm not contributing anything, I need to get involved."

"You know", Scott replied, "Ted was saying much the same thing. He told me he was just being the messenger between us and Dr. Fred and the Russian scientists. He said that he really needed to get down the pit and see the cave structure for himself."

Peggy said, "Do you see any reason why Ted and I shouldn't join the group on the bottom? I know I could be a lot more productive, and besides I really want to do that pit while we are here this time. I've done nearly as many deep pits as Max. Well, maybe not nearly as many, but I've done a lot."

Scott suggested, "Let's go talk with Ted and see what he thinks."

Thirty minutes later, Peggy and Scott were hanging on slings beside Ted atop the pit where Ted and Sam were perched listening for any conversation that might emanate from below.

Peggy said casually, "Ted, why don't you and I join the guys below?"

It took a second for Ted to understand what Peggy had said, then he responded, "Hell yeah, I think that's a great idea. I've been thinking along those lines all along. What do you think, Scott?"

Scott agreed, "I think you both need to get your stuff together and get down there and help. Look, Miguel, Sam and I can handle everything here on top, especially since Sergei has his troops helping us at every turn. Go on back there and get you stuff, and tell Miguel to start preparing a new provisions package to support the two of you. I think they are going to be moving away from the base camp soon, so you need to hurry. Hopefully one of them will check in soon. We can't haul the shield back up until they release it from below, and you can't descend until we get it back up here."

Ted said, "Understood."

Ted and Peggy started making their way back to the topside camp to get their gear ready. On the way back, Peggy said, "I'm going to take one of my drones down with me."

"And just how are you going to do that?" asked Ted. Peggy said confidently, "I'll just pack it up in its Pelican case, duct tape the fool out of it to ensure that can survive the waterfall, and hang it below me when I descend."

Ted said, "Sounds like a plan."

Peggy went on to say, "I can't imagine that it won't come in handy, especially if we get into some more high canyon passage."

Down below, Spider was making spectacular progress towards the top, alternating between climbing on and around the boulders that were jammed between the walls of the canyon, and climbing on the vertical canyon walls themselves. She periodically paused her climbing only to set secure anchors so that Bufford could climb up to join her and reset his belay for her next pitch.

As she approached the one hundred and fifty foot mark, she hollered down to Max, "I think we will reach the top in another two to three hours. I'm going to want to change back into my caving jeans then. Do you think you could get my jeans and bring them up when you and Jim climb up?"

"Max hollered back, "Sure, I'll be glad to. Anything else you need?"

"No, that's it." She replied. When Bufford joined her, they set about sinking two secure anchors for the first of the fixed ropes for this route.

Max and Jim had been sitting around watching Bufford and Spider do their thing. Max was getting a bit stiff from just setting down, so he was grateful to have a reason to get up and stir around. Jim opted to keep sitting where he was, so Max went by himself back down the breakdown pile to their base camp. As he neared the camp and came in range of the shield, his head phones became active. It was Sam pinging to see if anyone could hear him.

Max responded back, "I can hear you now, Sam, we've been a little out of range. Is everything okay?"

"Yeah", Sam said, "I just want to give you a heads up, Peggy and Ted will be on their way down there soon."

"Oh, really!" Max responded rather surprised. "What prompted this decision?"

Sam said, "They and Scott decided it would be a good idea. I think they were just getting bored with sitting around up here, and thought they could be more useful down there. I think they were jealous that you all were having all the fun. Anyway, they will be heading down soon, and we will be sending a provisions package for them shortly after."

Max said, "Actually, I think it's a good idea. We should all be pushing this together anyway. Anything else I need to know before I sign off? I'll have to untie the NMI rope so you can haul the shield up."

"No that's it." Sam said. "Okay, let me know when you are ready to start hauling up. I have to walk the shield back to the pit when you begin. Right now we have it tied off a long way from the bottom of the pit."

Sam said, "Understood. Give me about ten minutes to get organized up here before we begin hauling."

Max shouted up to Jim, "Jim, come on down here. We've got work to do. Tell Bufford that we will be busy down here for a while." Jim, wondering what was going on, did as he was told, and started down the breakdown pile back to base camp to join Max.

When Jim told Spider and Bufford that he was heading back down to base camp and would be busy for a while, both of them couldn't help but wonder what was going on and whether they should be concerned or not. They concluded that since Jim didn't seem concerned, maybe they shouldn't be either.

After they got the first fixed rope secured, Spider began climbing once again. Spider remarked that, "You know, this rock has plenty of cracks, but they are all mostly very small which makes finding useful handholds very tedious. I thought I was going to be able to climb much faster."

Bufford suggested that she make more frequent use of her razor chock instead of trying to muscle her way up as she so often did on their rock climbing ventures.

Spider agreed saying, "Yes, you are right. It is probably more important that we make progress than it is how we make progress." With that she slipped her razor in a small little crack, clipped in and relaxed as she fished out her spare razor chock and stirrup. Using the two chocks in tandem on the cave wall, up she went. She started going so fast that to the uneducated eye, one might have thought she was climbing a ladder.

Bufford shouted up to her, "Don't go so far without setting a safety anchor. With this much rope out, if you fall, you could get hurt."

"Yes, you are right", she replied, then she paused to hammer in a wedge and then clip the belay line into its carabiner.

As Jim clambered over the last boulder into base camp, Max was just about to finish untying the shield and NMI rope from its secure tie down point. Max said, "Peggy and Ted will be coming down as soon as we can get this shield back up."

"Great" replied Jim, "What prompted their decision to join us?" he asked.

"I'm not sure, but I'm happy that they are coming down. I think it is only appropriate that the six of us explore cave together. Grab hold of this with me, this rope has a lot of tension on it. When I cut it loose, it's going to have a mind of its own." said Max as he loosened the last loop on the tie down. As the three thousand foot rope recoiled from being stretched a couple of hundred extra feet, Jim and Max practically had to run with it back to the bottom of the pit.

"That was awkward", Jim said as they were finally able to slow down.

Max commented, "Well, you have to remember that it took all four of us to stretch it back to the base camp, so it had a bunch of stored up energy. Hey, Sam, you all can start hauling the rope up whenever you are ready."

Sam said, "Starting the retrieval now. Stand by, in an hour or so, Peggy will start down. After both Ted and Peggy are down, we will be lowering a provisions package, so stand by for that as well. Signing off till then."

Max said to Jim, "I'll hang around here until Peggy gets down. Why don't you go back and let Bufford and Spider know what is going on. By the time you get back here, Peggy will probably be down, and you can show her back to base camp."

"Okay" Jim replied, "And while I'm at it, I think I'll haul another one of these rope bags back with me. See you in an hour or so."

While he was waiting for Peggy's arrival, Max started poking around the area on the bottom of the pit. Previously, they had quickly picked up any small loose rocks that were lying around and sent them back up for assessment. This time Max took the time to dig down a bit and to turn over some of the boulders to see what might lie beneath. His efforts did not go unrewarded. Almost immediately he found some glassy rocks with some unusual colors, much more colorful than any they had seen before. Then, with considerable effort, he pushed over a sizeable boulder, and underneath was his most interesting find. "What the heck is this?" he thought out loud to himself. "This looks like something metallic, but what the heck is it doing here? Ted really needs to see this." He looked around and spotted a rope bag that had ripped open during impact. Inside was a smaller bag that was undamaged. He dumped out the contents, ripped off a piece of the ripped up bag, and carefully wrapped and stowed his new finds in the small bag. He knew that these new finds would be much more interesting than the previously collected samples. About then he could hear Peggy descending so he scrambled back to the top of the breakdown pile to meet Peggy as she touched down with her gear and drone case which were dangled below her on the way down.

"How was your ride?" he asked. Peggy was beside herself with excitement.

"That was absolutely incredible!" she exclaimed. "It was a lot more exciting than how you described it. I listened to you when you first went down, and you didn't say anything about how it felt like flying!"

"I did too. I told everyone that it felt like I was going up instead of down." Max said in his defense.

"Maybe you did, but you didn't say it with enthusiasm, you didn't shout it out to let us know how incredible it felt. I remember that you sounded rather calm", Peggy lamented.

Max said, "That's probably because I was scared out of my gourd."

Peggy exclaimed, "What, the infamous Max Meccum scared? I can't believe I just heard that."

"Well, don't tell anyone." Max said.

Sam chimed in, "Too late, I heard every word. I'm posting it to the internet right now."

Max replied, "Eavesdropping again, Sam? You are bluffing, you know there is no internet service down here, besides, you have to haul this shield back up. So get to it."

Sam acknowledged with a "Roger that", and then began hauling the shield back up.

About then Jim arrived back at the pit, and they began shuttling Peggy and her gear back to the base camp. Max said, "It will be about an hour and a half before Ted can get down here, so that should be enough time to get Peggy set up and changed into some proper caving garb."

Peggy was quick to agree, "This wet suit was great for going through that torrent up top, but mine is a bit tight. I need to get out of it."

Jim quipped, “It was the first thing we all did once we got out of this pouring rain and into the canyon. I don’t mind wet coveralls, but that wet suit just didn’t feel right.”

As they were climbing down the breakdown on the bottom of the pit towards the entrance to the canyon, Peggy asked, “How far to the base camp?”

“Not far” Max said. “But it is a bit treacherous.”

CHAPTER 9

Miguel was busy putting together a provisions package for Peggy and Ted when he was visited by one of the friendly Russians that Sergei had assigned to help the Americans. The trooper was noticeably nervous as he told Miguel, "We just got a new boss. Not good, I think. Comrade Vassilov has been recalled to Moscow, and this new guy is bad news. He gave immediate orders to cease working with you all, so I won't be hanging around here anymore. I don't know what it is all about, none of us suspected anything. So, I'm warning you to take care and watch your back."

Just about then, Dr. Schillinger showed up. He had run practically all of the way from the Russian's lab to Miguel's tent. "Guess what", he said, "I just got kicked out of the lab and was told by Dr. Kuznetsov that I was no longer permitted to be there."

Miguel said, "Anatoly here just told me there is a new person in charge and that he is terminating the agreement that we had with Sergei immediately. Also, Sergei is being recalled to Moscow."

Anatoly corrected, "He has already left. He is no longer here. Someone said he left in a hurry early this morning."

Dr. Schillinger said with concern, "This is definitely not good."

Miguel agreed, "This is definitely not good. We need to get this information back to Scott immediately. Ted is fixing to head to the bottom of the pit to join in the exploration of the cave beyond the pit. He needs to know. They all need to know. This changes everything."

Schillinger asked, "Can we still talk directly with Scott back at the top of the Pit?"

Miguel replied, "I think so. I can't from here. All the com gear is over in Peggy's tent. She handled all the communication and video feeds. Surely the link is still active." With that said, Miguel and Dr. Schillinger hustled over to Peggy's tent. Once inside, a quick look around located a couple of headsets plugged into the communications controller.

They donned the headsets, and Dr. Schillinger said, "Can anyone hear me?"

Scott and Sam replied simultaneously, "Yeah, I can hear you." Sam went on to say, "What's up Doc?"

Schillinger asked, "Is this line secure?"

Scott replied sensing the seriousness in Schillinger's voice, "Yes, this line is very secure. Only people directly connected to the system can hear us. Why?"

Miguel said, "Things have changed."

Schillinger added, "Drastically."

Miguel and Dr. Schillinger went on to explain everything that had just transpired, emphasizing that they no longer had the Russian's support or access to the assay laboratory, and probably no longer access to the Russian's bridge back to the pit.

Scott said, "Ted is about seven hundred feet down right now, so he probably couldn't hear any of what you just said." Then he asked, "Ted, can you hear me yet?"

Ted replied, "It is still quite noisy, but I can hear somewhat. I caught a bit of what Fred was saying, but not enough. Repeat now that I can hear better."

Miguel gave a quick rundown of what they had just said. Ted asked, "Scott, how do you suspect that this is going to affect our operations?"

After a moment, Scott replied, "Well, actually, I don't think it will affect us much at all if they will just leave us alone. Basically, we are back to Plan A. This is how we planned to proceed in the first place. We have benefited from the extra muscle they provided. We really don't need it any more. We have the results of the lab analysis, so we know as much as they do, and we are in a better position than they are in regard to acquiring more data. So, I think we proceed as per Plan A. What do you think, Ted?"

Ted said, "I think you are dead right. Let's rock and roll and steer clear of the Russians for now."

Scott said, "Miguel, how are the provisions packages coming along?"

Miguel replied, "I'm just about done. I'll have them ready within the hour."

Scott asked, "Do you think you can sneak them back here along the Russian's bridge before they shut us down?"

Miguel, just realizing how dependent they had become on the bridge, replied, "I hope so. I'm not real comfortable with that 'Tarzaning' yet. I've done it only twice."

Scott said, "Well, you said you wanted to learn the ropes. Looks like you are going to get your wish. As soon as we get Ted situated, you need to let Director Ruiz know what's going on."

Miguel said, "Definitely. By-the-way, Sam, how are your rope skills?"

Sam said sheepishly, "Just about non-existent. I'm sitting here thinking, 'what the hell am I doing here?'."

Scott said, "What you are going to be doing is learning some new tricks. I hope you are a quick learner."

Ted interjected, "Scott, slow me down, I'm just about to the bottom!"

Scott put the brakes on Ted's descent, and gently landed him on the bottom where he was greeted by Max and Jim. Max said as Ted touched down, "You came in com range about a hundred feet up. What is with Sam being a quick learner?"

As Ted was getting unrigged, Scott began to fill Max and Jim in on the new developments. Max said without any prompting from Scott, "Well, it looks like it is back to Plan A. Scott, secure your end of this rope. We have to pull real hard on it in order to stretch it all the way back to our camp."

"Roger that" replied Scott. "Let me know when we can start pulling" Max said.

Jim said, "Ted, grab some slack and let's start hauling the shield down this pile and get out of this rain."

Peggy finished unpacking the gear that she brought down with her, and began to prepare her heavy drone for its maiden flight. All flying down here would have to be controlled manually with some inertial assists. Peggy found a nice flat and almost level boulder for Charlie to take off from and to land on. Peggy had recently named her heavy drone, Charlie. Charlie's battery was fully charged, and it was almost as if he was eager to take flight. Peggy situated herself nearby and donned her control visor. Through this visor, Peggy saw what Charlie saw, in all directions. Because of this omnidirectional multi-view, it required a high level of skill to fly Charlie manually. And, Peggy was a highly skilled drone operator, so Charlie just became an extension of Peggy's reality. In an instant Charlie leaped into flight. If anyone watched Peggy as she flew Charlie, they surely would be amused. What they would see would be this person sitting with something covering her face while her hands would be waving back and forth at some imaginary object in front of her. In reality what was happening was that the hand waving was actually Peggy operating the virtual controls that were displayed on her visor. When Peggy turned her head, she saw the view in that direction as seen from the drone. If for some reason, Peggy lost connection with Charlie, Charlie would simply return to his landing site following the reverse of the exact path he had followed since takeoff. Peggy flew up a little ways, then slowly rotated to get a feel for the flight environment. Looking upward, Peggy could see Bufford and Spider's lights four hundred feet above her and the fixed ropes that they had emplace during their ascent. It was time to pay a visit, and Charlie zoomed upward following the fixed lines.

As Charlie slowed and hovered fifteen feet from the duo, Spider said, "Hello Peggy, so glad to see you."

Peggy responded, "You two look cozy just sitting up there. Glad to see you all too."

Bufford asked, "When did you get down here?"

"About an hour ago", Peggy responded. "Can I be of some help?"

Spider said, "We were just about ready to rappel back down when we saw your drone's lights come on. We were just waiting for you to find us. However, now that you are here, maybe you can help. As you can see we are temporarily stymied by this overhang. I can't climb this one, so it looks like we will have to bolt our way around. Question, will it be worth the effort? Is there any passage above us? We can't tell from here."

Peggy said, "Just a moment; I'll check." With that, Peggy flew Charlie around then up and over the overhang. Peggy said, "Oh yeah. It looks like there is lots of passage up here. It is a breakdown slope that goes up at a very steep angle. It doesn't look particularly stable, and might be really dangerous climbing. I'll shoot some high res video. You can analyze an attack when you get down."

"Sounds good. It's great to have your help once again. We'll see you down at base camp in a bit. Good to see you again too, Charlie."

Back at base camp, Max, Jim, and Ted were struggling to stretch the rope back towards the base camp. Max lamented as the pulled on the rope, "Dang, it didn't seem this hard when stretched before."

Ted asked, "How much further do we need to go?"

"About twenty five feet. We have a good anchor set for it that is close enough to our camp for the com pickup to work", replied Max.

After struggling for a few more minutes, Jim said, "Forget this crap. We're not getting anywhere. Let's tie off here and wait till Bufford get back down. He's the one with the brawn."

Max opined, "For some reason, I think this is going to require more than just brawn. We are going to need to rig up a pulley to get some additional leverage. Hold tight and I'll try to get a loop around this boulder. There, I got it. Put a couple of half hitches on it then we can wait for Bufford."

Scott had been listening to all their effort with a mixture of concern and amusement. He chimed in, "Sounds like you need an engineer down there. Have you got it under control yet?" "Just about", replied Max.

Scott said, "In about an hour, be prepared to receive the provisions packages. Miguel said he just about has them ready. I want to get them down there as soon as possible before the Russians cut off our access to their bridge. I'm the only one up here with experience with our Tarzan method, so I want to minimize the transport of heavy loads that way. I want to get Sam back topside because he has practically no rope experience, and I don't want his first experience to be under adverse circumstances. So, while we can still use the bridge, he is going back." Everyone agreed that would be a good idea.

While Max and Jim were figuring out how to rig a pulley to help stretch the NMI rope back nearer to the base camp, Charlie landed gracefully on his hew landing pad and shut down. Peggy stowed her control visor and made her way down the passage to rejoin with the men. Bufford and Spider were still about three hundred feet up slowly rappelling their way down.

There were limited places to sit comfortably in the base camp area. The canyon was not very wide, and the Churum River took up most of the width. Finding sitting places for six people was not easy. But, as everyone got situated, Peggy began to describe what she had seen above the overhang where Bufford and Spider had paused their climb.

Peggy said, "As I told Spider and Bufford, the passage continues above the overhang. The canyon walls are about twenty feet apart and slopes steeply upward at about forty five degrees. The space between the walls is filled with loose rocks. It reminds me of the talus filled slot that leads to the top of the Middle Teton in Wyoming for those of you who have climbed there. It looked very dangerous to me. I've been thinking, and I don't believe we can have anyone climbing up that slot while we have a base camp down here. Whoever or whatever is left down here will literally get bombed with falling rocks."

"That's a problem," said Max, "this is the best place we've seen so far to set up camp."

Peggy said, "It looked like the passage goes up steeply for about two hundred feet. I didn't fly up to check out the passage, but I'll bet there are many better places to camp up there than there are down here."

"Well then, we will have to find a way to get our stuff up there. Ideas, anyone?" asked Max.

Spider said, "That overhang where Bufford and I stopped is huge. That's the reason we stopped. I couldn't climb around it. We could haul everything up to there. I wouldn't want to camp there for long, but we would be sheltered while we worked our way up the slot." Peggy said, "I can fly up and set a jam nut anchor and clip in a rope. Then, Spider can climb up and set a bolt anchor. That way she won't have to bolt her way up. It'll be a lot quicker and safer." Max said, "Yes, that sounds like a plan, and if you make sure to set the anchor high enough, Bufford will be out of the line-of-fire while he belays Spider. The rest of us will sit under the overhang and watch the rocks fall. Spider, after you get a fixed line set up all the way to the top, the rest of us can come up one at a time carrying some of our gear. Actually, some of us may have to make several trips. We have a lot of stuff, and more is coming down soon."

Ted said, "Well, let's start packing stuff up. How much spare rope do we have down here?"

Max and Jim looked at each other with a smile and simultaneously said, "Oh, we've got lots of rope, but some of it is still in bags back at the bottom of the pit."

Scott and Sam had been busy at the top of the pit preparing to lower provisions for Ted and Peggy. Scott, who had been listening, entered the conversation and told them, "Looks like Miguel has packed up everything he had that's edible from his kitchen as well as from our stash. I think you have enough here to last for over a week. I'm beginning to wonder what is left up here for us to eat. I hope he made a call to Carlos to fly in more provisions. Get ready, we will start lowering in a few minutes. Also, it looks like it is going to take at least two drops. There is a lot of stuff here. We have three full duffle bags and two large Pelican cases. I hope you have a knife down there to open these packages. It looks like Miguel must have used two complete rolls of duct tape sealing this stuff up."

Max said, "We'll manage, send it on down."

Almost two hours later, the five provision packages were safely on the bottom. Earlier, Jim and Bufford grabbed a bag of rope and anchor gear and began the climb up the ropes to the bottom of the overhang. There they began setting a bunch of anchors from which to hang all of their gear. When Bufford and Spider set the fixed ropes, they did so in three separate pitches. This was fine for climbing up and rappelling down. It just meant that the climber had to change ropes three times each way. This was not okay for hauling a lot of gear up four hundred or so feet. For that purpose, they rigged a single four hundred and fifty foot rope through a pulley. That way, using their rope walking ascender rigs, they could haul a load approximately equal to their weight up the four hundred foot climb with no more effort than was required to make the actual climb.

The easy part of relocating the base camp was packing up the gear and hauling it up to the top of the breakdown slope where Bufford and Jim would take turns hauling it the rest of the way up to the overhang. Ted asked Max, "What do you want to do about tying off the NMI rope and shield. Since we are relocating there is no sense in expending the effort to stretch it on back to where you originally had it tied. I vote that we finish tying it off where it is since once we move we will be out of communications range anyway."

"I think you are completely right. Let's get that done." Max also said, "Scott, are you still listening?"

Scott replied, "I'm listening, but I don't have anything to contribute from up here."

Max said, "When we move up to the top of the canyon, we won't be able to communicate, and I don't know how long we will be out of touch. If the passage goes, we will follow it as far as we can. If it takes a couple of days, then we will be gone at least that long. If it peters out, we will be back sooner. So, if you don't hear from us for a while, don't panic. If there turns up a reason to panic, you will be the first to know. So, as soon as we finish tying off the shield, we are signing off for a while."

Peggy had a question, "Am I right in assuming that once all this is hauled up, that we are going to be sleeping hanging from a couple of anchors four hundred feet up there?"

Spider said, "Yep, I believe that is the plan. I take it that you have never done that before."

"Nope, never done that. And, I'm not sure I'll be sleeping either."

Spider chuckled, "After we get all situated up there you will be so tired that I guarantee that you will sleep."

Max was mumbling as he struggled to get a particularly heavy bag tied to the haul rope, "I've been on a lot of long cave expeditions, and I can't ever remember hauling this much stuff into the cave. This is ridiculous."

Ted remarked with admiration, "You know, Jim and Bufford are doing a yeoman's job hauling all this gear up. It's got to be like doing a couple of tandem fifteen hundred foot rope ascents. You talk about a couple of guys that are going to be worn out; I'll bet they are going to sleep well tonight."

Max suggested to the girls, "Spider, why don't you and Peggy head on up. I'm sure they could use some help setting anchors and stashing these bags. Ted and I will head up when we finish securing the shield."

Spider agreed, "We're not being much help down here. I think we are done with all that we can do. Is there any loose stuff I can carry up with me?"

"No, I don't think so. Get on up there and figure out just how you are going to get around that overhang."

When it came to rope climbing, the two girls couldn't have been different. Peggy preferred the standard rope walking system that let her legs do most of the work. Spider on the other hand preferred a two Jumar system that allowed her to take giant steps and climb really fast. Her system required a lot of upper body and arm strength, both of which Spider had in abundance. Spider arrived at the overhang in about fifteen minutes which was a scorching climbing pace considering that she had two rope changes on the way up. Peggy took a more leisurely pace and took about forty minutes to complete her climb. Max and Ted were about twenty minutes behind Peggy. They pulled the fixed ropes up behind them to ensure that they didn't get damaged by falling rocks when they began the assault on the slot.

It was really tight all huddled together under the overhang with all of the gear bags hanging down, the hammocks bumping together, and the safety lanyards all entwined. To an outside observer, it would have looked like a bunch bats hunkered down hanging from the ceiling trying to stay warm. It was not cold; it was just that the accommodations were very tight.

Max said, "I hope everyone is comfortable."

Bufford quipped, "I'm so tired, I could be comfortable on a bed of nails."

Ted remarked while rummaging through his pack digging something out to eat, "Bufford, you and Jim did a fantastic job hauling all this gear up here."

"No thanks necessary, it's all part of the job", Jim replied. "But, you know what I'm really going to miss on this trek is Miguel's cooking."

"Don't remind us of that, please", said Peggy as she chowed down on a couple of protein bars.

"Ted, are you still awake?" asked Max.

"Yeah, I'm not asleep yet."

"I haven't had a chance to tell you what I found on the bottom of the pit while I was waiting for Peggy to come down."

"Oh, what did you come up with?"

"I was already soaking wet, but rather than retreating back into the canyon, I started poking around. When we collected our original samples, we just picked up any loose rocks we found lying around, and hoped for the best. I'm actually surprised that we found anything useful. Anyway, I started turning over some of the breakdown that were small enough for me to move. Underneath several of the boulders, I found some very interesting rocks, glassified like the other rocks we collected, but very colorful, unlike anything we had seen before."

"No crap! What did you do with the rocks?" "I packed them away in a little sack. They are in one of these bags here. You can look at them later. But that's not all. I also found something that looks like a piece of metal. Again something like I've never seen before."

"Oh, the plot thickens! That kind of stuff lends more and more credence to the illegal secret Russian nuclear experiment gone bad theory."

"Exactly, that's what I thought. Couple that with the fact that Sergei is out, a new guy is in, and we are no longer partners with them certainly points to the fact that they are somehow deeply involved in all this."

Peggy joined the conversation and pointed out, "Max, I recall your saying something to the effect that if this is some kind of a Russian operation, then we don't want to be involved. Is that still your feeling?"

"Yes, but like it or not, it looks like we are right in the middle of it anyway."

Ted added, "If this is a Russian operation gone bad, then Kuznetsov already knows what is down here, and he probably would rather we not tell the outside world anything."

Max said, "And, that makes our situation down here rather precarious, doesn't it?"

"Yes it does", Ted agreed. "Remember, we speculated about that possibility before, but now it seems a lot more realistic."

Max said, "Do you all think we should turn back now and get out of here as quick as possible, or shall we press ahead?"

Ted offered his opinion, "I think that if we bail, the Russians will think we found something and will probably do whatever they can to prevent us from revealing it. I vote that we push on. We may never have another chance to get down here again. However, if we spend several days down here and then bail, the Russians will be sure we found something. So we are screwed no matter what. So, let's push on."

"How does everyone else feel?" asked Max. Everyone was in general agreement to push on except Jim and Bufford. They were both sound asleep.

CHAPTER 10

Early the next morning Sam, Scott, and Dr. Schillinger joined Miguel in Miguel's kitchen to mooch another of Miguel's gourmet breakfasts. The Americans had brought with them more than adequate supplies to feed themselves, however, they much preferred Miguel's cooking to their own. Besides, they would claim that they had sent most of their reserve down the pit to support the team on the bottom. That would be a bit of a stretch, but that was their story and they were sticking to it. This was all okay with Miguel because he enjoyed cooking, and it made him feel more as a part of the team.

Scott opened the morning's conversation with a rhetorical question, "I wonder what crisis is going to rear its ugly head today?"

Sam remarked back, "Well, aren't you in an optimistic mood today. I take it that you slept well."

"Well, you take wrong", snarled Scott as he watched Dr. Schillinger filling his plate with a generous helping of eggs, sausage, hash brown potatoes, fresh fruit, and a couple of biscuits. "Dr. Fred, you look mighty pensive. What's weighing heavily on your mind?"

"Coffee, I need coffee."

"Coming right up", said Miguel much too cheerfully for this time of morning, "I've got a fresh pot right here. Where's your cup?"

"I don't know", mumbled Dr. Fred. "Do you have one I can borrow?"

"Yeah, sit down Doc, I'll take care of you." Scott said as he was filling his plate, "If you are bringing the pot, I could use a refill also."

Sam piped in and said, "Me too."

Dr. Fred, who obviously had been awake for most of the night thinking about their situation, looked at Scott and said between bites, "I think we are in a dangerous situation here, especially since the Russians have withdrawn their support. If we had known that they were going to do that then Ted and Peggy wouldn't have joined the team on the bottom. As it is now, Scott, you are the only one of us who has any competence in this kind of caving. If we have any kind of a problem, even a small one, then we are in big trouble." Scott nodded his head in total agreement. Dr. Fred went on to ask, "I was wondering if you had any experienced caving friends back in the States that you could get on short notice to come down here and bolster our capabilities? Do you know if Max has any friends we could contact?"

"As a matter of fact I do have a lot of friends in Huntsville I can call on, and I know a couple of Max's friends in Austin as well. I agree with you completely. We need some help on board down here fast."

"Can your foundation finance a couple more team members? I know that most of the cavers I know, especially the young ones won't be able to afford to drop whatever they are doing and to hop on an airplane and fly down here."

"That won't be a problem. After we finish breakfast, I'll get right on it."

Scott made a list of everyone that he could think of that had the right kind of experience and skills and that might be able to join the team on short notice. Then he added a couple of names that he knew Max respected. When the list was done, despite the fact he knew a lot of capable cavers, he noted that the list of cavers with what he considered the right stuff was a rather short list. He thought he might have to ask some of the people on the list if they had any recommendations. Scott was thinking that he would feel comfortable if they could add four more people to the team. He got on Miguel's satellite phone and called Connie, his secretary at the foundation.

"Hi Connie, this Scott. How are things going?"

"Hi Boss, things are going well here. How is your vacation going?"

"Vacation hell!! You know damn well I'm not on vacation! This is anything but a vacation. As a matter of fact and since you asked, things are not going well down here at all. That's why I'm calling. I need to contact several people and see if I can recruit them to join us down here. At the moment, we are seriously shorthanded. We need some serious help of the caver variety."

"Good Lord, are you in some kind of trouble?"

"No, at least not yet, but we could be. That's why we need some help. I have just emailed you a list of people. I need to know how and when best to call them. I would like for you to dig up phone numbers and make an initial call for me. Find out when is the best time for me to call them. I think you can find most of their phone numbers in the NSS Members Directory."

"Okay, can do. Is there anything I should tell them when I call?"

"No, not really. You can tell them where I am, but not what I am doing. Also, you need to be looking into the availability of flights from Huntsville and Austin to Caracas. I'll arrange transportation from Caracas to here. The foundation will be funding their expenses, but don't tell them that. I'll let them know that I'll cover their expenses when I find out if they can drop what they are doing and join us. Call me back as soon as you can."

"Okay, I'm on it. Can you tell me what is going on? Do I need to be concerned?"

"I'll fill you in later. No reason to be really concerned yet. I'd say on a scale of one to ten, level four concern would be about right. Be on guard, be careful, be attentive, and take note of anything unusual. I'll talk with you later. Bye for now."

"Bye."

CHAPTER 11

On the surface, the rising sun marks the dawn of a new day. Twenty five hundred feet below the surface, the sun doesn't shine. Max used the highly accurate digital clock on the laser survey instrument to keep track of time. On the previous evening, he set an alarm for six am. When six am arrived, he poked Peggy's hammock to wake her. Peggy's hammock was jam packed next to his, so he could feel her stirring. "Are you ready to get going again?" he asked.

"I guess so if you insist", she replied with a yawn.

"Hey everyone, time to wake up", Max said in a much louder voice.

"Max! We are all right here, you don't need to yell", Spider complained.

"Who is cooking breakfast today?" Jim asked jokingly.

"Well, if anyone is cooking this morning, it must be you, Jim. I doubt that any of us will be volunteering", said Max as he dug into his backpack for some cherry breakfast tarts, his favorite caving breakfast.

"Okay, I was just kidding. What's the plan? How do we want to attack this overhang? Spider, that's your bag. What do you need for us to do besides get out of your way?"

Before Spider could remind Jim that they already had a plan, Peggy said, "If I can get a little room, I can deploy Charlie. Just like we talked about yesterday, Charlie can fly up, find a crack, insert a jam nut, clip in a line, and Bufford can belay Spider up to set a bolt."

"Oh yeah, it's all coming back now. I just need a cup of coffee to get my brain going."

"Well, you need to get it going without coffee, because until we reestablish our base camp up there somewhere, we aren't going to be brewing any coffee."

Max's hammock was located closest to the open space of the canyon, so he and Peggy traded positions. Spider and Bufford took up positions a few feet away with climbing rope and gear ready. Peggy unpacked Charlie, donned her control visor, and held Charlie out in space to allow his inertial system to establish his flight origin point. That is the point to which Charlie would return to if Peggy lost contact with him. Then Charlie took flight, headlights blazing out, up, and around the overhang in search of a suitable crack for a jam nut. About thirty feet higher up and on the wall of the slot, Charlie spotted exactly what he was looking for. He returned autonomously to his origin, and Peggy placed to appropriate Jam nut in his claw. Up and away he flew again, and expertly placed the jam jut in the aforementioned crack. Charlie flew back down, took the end of the climbing rope from Spider, and flew back up and clipped the rope securely onto the Jam nut. With that, Charlie's work was done. While Peggy re-stowed Charlie, Spider clipped her Jumars onto the newly established fixed line, clipped on her belay line, and swung out into space. Spider quickly made her way up and around the overhang, and found a site to sink a secure bolt anchor. She then moved a little higher and set another anchor from which Bufford could belay her as she climbed the boulder strewn slot establishing fixed ropes as they went. Bufford soon joined her, and she carefully began the dangerous climb up the steep boulder pile. As soon as she could, she made her way across the slot to the far wall away from Bufford so that any rocks she might dislodge would not tumble directly towards Bufford. Sure enough, as soon as she started up the unstable rock pile, she shouted, "Rock!", as the first of many rocks to come, became dislodged and rattled down the slope and launched off into space. Seven seconds later, came a reverberating "boom" as the rock crashed onto the bottom some four hundred feet below.

Spider shouted down to everyone, "As predicted, this is going to be a tricky climb. Expect a lot of rocks so keep you heads down." Spider continued to carefully pick her way up the rocky slope, but no matter how careful she climbed, every ten feet or so, another rock loosened and fell. As she moved higher, every rock that came loose caused a mini-avalanche of other rocks. After Spider made her way up the first twenty feet, she paused and set a new bolt as high on the wall as she could reach. Then she belayed Bufford up to this position. Bufford clipped in, pulled the fixed rope up, and slipped it into the carabiner to which he was likewise attached. He called for Max to take up the slack so that the fixed line would hang about six feet above the rock slope and out of danger of being damaged by cascading rocks. Spider then traversed back across the slope to the opposite wall and began her ascent again. In this manner, Spider and Bufford zig-zagged their way up the slot. This was a tedious process, and required several hours to reach the top.

When Spider final made it safely to the top, she shouted back to Bufford, "You aren't going to believe this, but the passage actually opens up and goes horizontal as far as I can see."

"Halleluiah", came the relieved cry. "Let's get this rope fixed and head back down."

"Amen to that, I'll bet everyone is bored stiff by now."

"Naw, they've been entertained by the falling rock serenade!"

Spider laughed, "I'll bet you are right."

After the fixed rope was secured, they made their way back down the slope. They stayed very close to each other so that when one of them dislodged a rock, it would not endanger the other. Everyone was greatly relieved to hear that the passage opened up, and that a comfortable base camp could likely be had.

While Spider and Bufford took a highly deserved rest, the others began the process of transporting all the gear and supplies to the top of the passage. Even with the newly established fixed ropes, this was not an easy task. The bags were heavy, and for safety reasons, only two people could make the ascent at a time. And, again because of the falling rock hazard, they had to stay close to each other. Jim and Ted made up the first duo to make the climb, each with a heavy load. Upon their return, Max and Peggy began their assault. Max loaded himself down with an eighty pound load, and Peggy took Charlie. Next, Jim and Ted made their second trip up the slot, each carrying a huge load.

On his second trip up, Max wandered a little ways down the passage and proclaimed, "Hey guys, here looks like a great place to set up our new base camp. Let's make sure that all the gear gets brought all the way back to here so we don't have to handle it yet another time."

It took a dozen round trips and the rest of the day to transport everything up. With the new base camp set up, Jim said, "Let's cook something. I'm famished; I'm so hungry I could eat a fried rock." Everyone was in complete agreement. Jim dug out the little cook stove, and looked into one of the food bags and announced, "The choices are: beans and franks or franks and beans. That looks like that all that got stowed in this bag."

"Well, in that case, I vote for franks and beans", said Bufford. Ted was digging around in one of the clothing bags that Miguel had packed, and said, "Holy cow, look what I found!" With that he proceeded to fish out a dozen carefully packed cans of beer, much to the delight everyone. As they popped the tops, a unanimous cheer went up, "Here's to Miguel! Long will he be remembered!"

That evening the crew sacked out in reasonable comfort and with full and contented bellies.

CHAPTER 12

When Connie called back, she had three names for Scott. She was unable to make contact with the other names he had given her. With obvious tension in her voice, she said, "Boss, I tried to call everyone the list that you gave me, but so far I've only made contact with three. Also, Boss, I am very concerned now. Not thirty minutes ago, right after I finished talking with Glen, a man with a foreign accent came into the office. He said that he had a message for you. I told him that you were unavailable. He said that he knew that, but he also knew that I could get messages to you. He gave me an envelope with several wax seals securing it. Can you imagine that! Wax seals, who uses wax seals these days? He saw me looking at the seals, and he said, "Look carefully at those seals. Memorize what you see. After you give Mr. Mueller the message, destroy the message and the envelope, but remember the seals. You will be seeing them again." Then he left with no further explanation. Boss, what is going on?"

Now Scott was concerned. "Who is the message from?" he inquired.

"I don't know. I haven't opened it. I wouldn't dare open it until I told you."

"Open it. Let's see who it is from. Don't mess up the seals."

Connie fumbled around her desk looking for her letter opener. When she found it, she slit the envelope open and withdrew the contents. Looking at the bottom of the note, she said, "It is from a Mr. Sergei Vassilov."

"What does it say?"

Connie began reading the note to Scott.

"Mr. Mueller, I hope this note finds you and your comrades still in good health. I apologize for my hasty departure. I was ordered to return immediately to Moscow, and I did not have an opportunity to speak with you before I left. I did not leave under favorable circumstances, the details of which I cannot divulge, but I feel that it is of utmost importance that I give you this warning. My replacement as the head of the Russian/Venezuelan Cooperative Mission is Dr. Alexeev Kuznetsov. He is a very powerful, evil, and dangerous person. You must be very careful in dealing with this man. He will care nothing about you, your expedition, your people, or your purpose for being there. He views your presence there as an impediment to his mission. As such, he will do whatever he deems necessary to force your departure, and that includes creating very unfavorable circumstances for your continued presence. Russia and Venezuela have developed some close economic ties, and that gives Dr. Kuznetsov some powerful leverage with the Venezuelan Government. I know you have a very close relationship with the Director of the Canaima Park, but when a conflict arises, and it will, Mr. Ruiz will not be able to protect you. I urge you to exercise utmost caution, limit your interaction with Dr. Kuznetsov, and it is very important that you keep all of your findings to yourselves. Do not share any information with him. I will try to keep you appraised as much as possible; however, opportunities and lines for communication are very limited and monitored. Any communication to you in the future from me will be in writing and will bear my personal seal. Any communication not bearing this seal will not be from me. Note carefully the details of the seal. I wish you and your comrades the best of luck and safe passage. Sergei Vassilov"

"Well, that confirms my feelings. I knew instantly that I didn't like that Kuznetsov character, and we only partially trusted Sergei. However, I think I trust Sergei a whole lot more now"

"Scott, you have got to let me know what is going on. I'm scared to death now."

"Connie, there are some things I can't talk about over the phone. But the situation here is this: I've got six of my friends on the bottom of a never before descended twenty five hundred foot deep pit with a torrential waterfall pouring into it. I, we, thought we had the full cooperation and support of the Russians or else Ted and Peggy would never have joined the team on the bottom. Now I'm the only one left here on the top with any caving experience, and my experience is limited. If anything should go south, we are in big trouble. That's why I need some immediate experienced help. We have made some startling discoveries which we have partially shared with the Russians. There some things we have not shared, and Sergei's warning note confirms our intuition not to share some details was the correct decision. What we have found is what I cannot talk about over the phone."

"Oh my God! What are you going to do now?"

"Well, first, I need some back up help. Secondly, I need to talk with Max, but he and the team are off exploring and will be out of communications for several more days at least. Then we need to get them out of the pit, pack up our stuff and get the hell out of Dodge. Then we can figure out what to do next."

"What do you want me to do now?"

"Take a picture of Sergei's seals. Don't use your phone. Phones can be hacked. Use one of the high resolution cameras, and make sure you get several clear images. I think there may be more to his seals than meets the eye. Then store the camera's memory disc and the envelope somewhere safe and secure but in separate places. Then, let's contact Glen, and who else did you say you were able to contact?"

"Okay, but can I listen in?"

"Yes, as a matter of fact, set it up as a conference call, then you will hear everything."

"What are you going to tell them?"

"Everything I just told you except nothing about our discoveries."

By early that evening, Scott had recruited Thomas Mitchel, Jennifer Stoneman, and Glen Neely to join the expedition. Glen had a good suggestion. He pointed out that there was an active speleological organization in Venezuela, and surely some of the members could come to Scott's aid immediately. And certainly, a show of force in terms of bodies actively engaged in the expedition couldn't hurt. Glen said that he would handle making some contacts and get some local support asap.

True to his word, Glen put out a call to solicit support from several Venezuelan caving clubs, and by the following evening a dozen or more cavers of varying experience levels were headed to Canaima Park.

Scott put in a call to Carlos, "Hey Carlos, this is Scott Mueller."

"Buenos noches Mr. Scott. You are calling quite late in the evening. What's happening? It must be important. How can I be of help?"

"You are right, Carlos, it is important, and I do need your help. Can you possibly spend tomorrow flying people from Canaima Camp up to here? I know this is really short notice, but things are moving fast."

"I have a charter scheduled for tomorrow, but I can put them off for a day or two. What time do I need to be at Canaima?"

"As soon as you can get there; people are starting to arrive there this evening. I don't know how many will be there, but I know it will require more than one trip. I'll fill you in on the latest when I see you. I appreciate your help. I know this is really short notice, and an inconvenience to you."

"For you guys, I'm glad that I can be of service. I'll see you tomorrow."

Scott said to Miguel, "I like Glen Neely; he is a guy that can get things done. By the way, have you told Mr. Ruiz to expect visitors this evening?"

"No, I'm learning about them at the same time as you. I'll alert him now. I've been talking with the Director several times a day, so he is very aware that things are unsettled here. He probably won't be surprised, and I don't want him to be surprised."

"Tell him that Carlos will be flying in in the morning also."

Carlos, despite his best efforts, was unable to make it to Canaima Park as early as he would have liked. He finally touched down just before eleven am, and already ten cavers had arrived at Canaima loaded with all their personal caving gear. By noon, the first five were in the air headed to the top of Auyán tepui. Soon thereafter, the trouble began.

Miguel headed over to the runway to meet the incoming flight. One of the new Russians who claimed that he was in charge of the runway and that he must approve all incoming traffic said to Miguel, "I haven't been informed of any incoming flights for today, and Dr. Kuznetsov said that he must be informed ahead of time of any flights so they can be properly scheduled. You must inform your flight not to land until they have proper clearances!"

Miguel replied in his most official 'I'm in charge here' voice', "There shouldn't be any problems. As you just said, there aren't any other flights expected today. So, my flight will be landing in a few minutes. And by the way, this is Park property, and I am the designated Park Representative responsible for this area. I don't need your permission to authorize flights in and out of here. This is my runway, not yours. As far as scheduling flights, please be informed that I have scheduled several flights in and out of here today, and they all have proper clearances."

That was obviously not what the Russian expected to hear, and he left in a huff to report to Dr. Kuznetsov. Shortly thereafter, Miguel could hear the engine rumble of Carlos's Cessna 205 as they neared the runway. Carlos landed with an uncharacteristic heavy bounce and taxied up to where Miguel was waiting.

Miguel said jokingly to Carlos after he stopped, "That was a pretty good bounce for a beginner. Did you stay up late last night partying with the girls?"

Carlos was in no mood for humor. He replied, "You wouldn't believe how much stuff these guys brought with them. I needed an extra five hundred feet to get airborne, and I thought I was going to clip off a couple of treetops just getting clear."

"How many folks did you bring?"

"I've got five now, and at least five more back at the camp. I'll probably need to make two more trips today to get them all up here."

"You need to be aware, we are having a bit of a power struggle up here in regard to whom is in charge of who gets to fly in and out of here. Up until today, everyone has come and gone as they pleased, but the Russians decided they should decide who comes and goes. I just disputed that, and told them that this was my runway and that I would schedule flights in and out as I needed."

"Why would Sergei do that? I thought that you all had good relations with the Russians."

"We did. Sergei is no longer here, and the new guy is a butthole."

"When did all this take place?"

"Just a couple of days ago. It is going to take me a couple of trips to haul all these guys over to my camp. Can you hang around and watch what is left until I get back?"

"Sure", replied Carlos.

Miguel loaded three of the newcomers and their gear and headed off. Thirty minutes later when he returned, he was met by Dr. Kuznetsov himself. "Mr. Santos, I gather that we have a misunderstanding regarding the operation of this runway."

Miguel replied, "I wasn't aware that there was a problem. Everyone has been operating in and out of here using standard visual operating rules without incident for months. Then a short while ago, your man informed me that he was in charge of this runway and that he had to approve of all incoming flights. I informed him that that was not the case, that this was my runway, and that if anyone was going to start approving flights in and out of here, then that approval was going to come from me."

"I apologize for my man's abruptness and improper assumption of your authority, but surely you understand that we have the vast majority of air traffic using this runway. I am concerned with the safety of operations here, so I directed him to ensure that safe operating conditions are maintained.

He is an experienced air traffic controller, so he assumed he had complete authority."

Miguel sensed that this situation could be resolved amicably, but that ground rules for dual usage had better be resolved now or else later things could become adversarial. Miguel said, "I completely agree that safe operating conditions must be maintained, and I have no problem requiring all users to cooperate and coordinate. What I do have a problem with is your man telling me that my flight cannot land here without his permission and that I must tell my incoming flight that they must turn around and not come back until they have proper clearances."

"I understand and that will be corrected."

"Since you have personnel with air traffic control experience, I have no problem with them coordinating flights in and out providing that they don't abuse that authority."

Miguel went on to explain that Carlos would be making several more flights in and out over the next few days, and that between them they could work out the appropriate and mutually agreeable procedures. Miguel was surprised at how amenable Dr. Kuznetsov was with this arrangement. His demeanor was disarming, and it made Miguel very suspicious.

Carlos made two more round trips bringing a total eight cavers and their gear. When he left Canaima Camp on his last trip for the day, there were still seven more cavers awaiting their turn. Scott was gratified by the turn out, and his sense of eminent doom was slightly abated. That evening after the newcomers had settled in and had a bite to eat, Scott assembled them around a roaring campfire.

"I want to welcome all of you to Angel Falls. I appreciate your willingness to come bolster our situation on such short notice. As you all have been told, we have six cavers on the bottom of a twenty six hundred foot deep pit. The pit has the entirety of the Churum River flowing into it. Until recently, we had a mutual support agreement with our comrades which many of you met back at the airstrip. However, they recently withdrew their support and are no longer cooperating with us. Without their support, we find ourselves completely unable to provide logistic or any other type of support to the team on the bottom. That's why we put out a desperate plea to the caving community here in Venezuela for help."

One of the group replied, "We are more than delighted to help. We all are excited about participating in an exploratory adventure of this magnitude. This is history making for caving in our country."

Scott thanked them again, and explained, "In order to best utilize your talents, I need to understand what kinds of caving skills each of you have. First of all, how many of you have experience exploring vertical caves?" Four cavers raised their hands. "Okay, how many of you have experience in technical rock climbing?" The same four raised their hands. "How many of you have done rappels of over two hundred feet?" This time only two hands went up. Scott asked those two to tell about their experience.

The first individual explained that he was a former Army Special Ops guy, and that he had served a Joint Operations Tour in the U.S. with the U.S. Army in Huntsville. He said his name was Geraldo Ortega, and he indicated that he had extensive experience in rappelling, climbing and rigging ropes. He said that he had caved both in Venezuela and in the United States. It was in the U.S. where he had gained most of his vertical caving experience, and it was there that he had made his acquaintance with Glen Neely. Geraldo went on to point out that he was parachute qualified, and that he had loadmaster experience.

Scott said, "I am really happy to have you on our team. Your background is perfect." Scott pointed to the other individual that said he had experience rappelling over two hundred feet. "How about you, what is your background?"

He replied, "Mi nombre es Félix y hablo poco inglés."

Geraldo jumped in to say, "Felix doesn't speak much English, but he understands pretty good. He has caved with me for a couple of years. I have trained him in vertical techniques, and he is competent. He and his two buddies are special ops types and are also parachute qualified, not that that qualification has any relevance here. Basically what it does say is that they are all capable individuals and have skills that are widely applicable. Most of the others here don't speak much English either, but they also can understand pretty well. There are four others that will come up tomorrow that are competent in vertical techniques, but don't have a lot of caving experience. They have some, but not a lot. They do have a good bit of mountaineering experience though. They have climbed extensively in the Andes."

Scott explained that everyone's help would be appreciated, and that by the time this adventure was over, they would be seasoned beyond their wildest dreams. Scott went on to brief them on the layout of the cave, the techniques that they had developed to quickly traverse back to the pit, how every step they made would be made on belay, that they would be spending a lot of time transporting stuff back to the pit, and hanging suspended from an anchor above the pit from hell with a torrent of water pouring into it. Scott went on to explain how they would also be preparing provisions packages to be lowered to the bottom of the pit. These packages would be carefully wrapped in plastic and duct taped thoroughly to ensure that they would be water proof. They would then put the provisions in heavy duty duffle bags, and then they would transport the bags back near to the pit area. There the bags would be stowed awaiting communications from the team that they were ready to receive them. That brought up the third task that they would be helping with, and that would be 24/7 monitoring of the communications line. Sam explained how that needed to be done. He explained that while the team was away from their base camp, they would be out of communications range. But since we had no idea as to when they would be returning to the base camp, we had to monitor the line constantly. As Geraldo translated what Scott and Sam were saying, you could see in their faces some apprehension and perhaps some were wondering as what exactly they had gotten themselves into.

CHAPTER 13

When the arrival of the morning was announced by the alarm that Max had set on the Laser Surveyor, everyone was already awake and stirring. There was an air of anticipation of discovery of big passage ahead, and everyone was eager to begin the push. Jim was the first one up, and as usual, he was hungry. He fired up the little camp stove, and began to brew the morning's batch of coffee. As the aroma began to fill the area, the pace of activity increased significantly.

"Okay Jim, what's for breakfast?" Peggy asked as though she actually expected for Jim to know.

"I don't know. I kinda expect every meal is going to be a surprise."

Jim began digging through one of the ration bags, and noticed "Most of the stuff in here has 'Freeze Dried' on the label. Did anyone remember to bring lots of water? How about we have eggs and biscuits for breakfast?"

"Sounds good" said Bufford, "Cook them up, I'm all for it."

Unfortunately, on the little camp stove only one thig at a time could be heated. So after the coffee finished brewing, Jim reconstituted a large batch of eggs and began heating them on the stove. Eggs, biscuits, jam, and coffee is how they started the day.

Max observed, "Jim, a moment ago, you asked a very important question."

"I did? About what?" Jim asked.

"Water. We don't have a lot of water. Everything we have done so far on this expedition has been close, actually uncomfortably close to water. Now, it's like we are in a desert. Water is hours away from where we are, not in distance but in time. It is a critical resource that we have overlooked.

We have on hand now what, three maybe four gallons. That won't last us more than a day."

Everyone sat for a moment in stunned silence, for indeed they had overlooked their need for water. Everyone instantly had the same dreaded thought, "Someone is going to have to climb all the way back down to the bottom, collect three to four gallons of water, and climb all the way back up, and do it each day."

Jim said aloud, "Crud, we're screwed!"

Peggy said rhetorically, "A gallon of water weighs what, about eight pounds? Don't fret, Jim. I think Charlie and I can handle the water detail. He can take a small container or two down, dip into that quiet eddy pool where the current is fairly quiet, fill the containers, and fly back up here with eight to nine pounds of water. He can make a round trip every ten minutes or so. I can replenish our water supply each evening while we are getting supper ready."

"Lordy, Lordy, Peggy", Max exclaimed, "Once again it looks like you may have saved our collective butts if you can pull that off. You and Charlie are miracle workers."

"I didn't just suddenly think about how to solve our water problem. It is a natural extension of something else I've been thinking about. Our batteries; they will need to be recharged every couple of days. Our recharging stations are down there in the river. I've been thinking that I could take a set of batteries down every day, set them on the recharge platform, pick up a charged set, and return. Since all of our batteries are inductively charged, there is nothing complicated with doing this."

Ted said, "I vote for Peggy being promoted to 'Logistics Guru'. All in favor say aye."

"Thanks guys, but remember, it's not just me coming up with ideas. Remember Spider is the one with all the special knots skills, and she is the one doing all the heavy lifting when it comes to the extreme rock climbs", said Peggy.

"You are right", Max said. "You girls are leading the way, and I for one am extremely grateful. We wouldn't have made it this far without you both. Thank you girls."

"Three cheers for the girls", said Ted.

"Okay, let's get our day packs ready and see how far we can make it today. I'm feeling good about our chances of finding the big passage that all this air movement says lies ahead somewhere."

CHAPTER 14

Around ten in the morning, Scott received a phone call from Glen. "Morning Scott", Glen said cheerfully, "I thought I'd better let you know, the three of us are preparing to depart the States this afternoon and head your way. Connie arranged everything very efficiently; I'm very impressed with her competence."

"It's good to hear that you are on your way. By the way, thanks for rounding up some local help. That was remarkable that you were able to get so many local cavers to rally to our need on such short notice."

"It was a piece of cake, nothing to it. I just contacted my friend Geraldo, explained the situation, and he said he would handle it, 'consider it done' he said."

"Well, he did it. We have over a dozen locals here and on board. I am greatly relieved to have them here. Is Connie emailing me with your itinerary?"

"Yes, I am sure she is. She laid it out in great detail for us, so I am sure it is probably already in your inbox. By the way, is there any last minute things I can pick up for you?"

Scott thought for a moment and then said, "Yes, as a matter of fact there is. Do you have time to touch base with Connie before you depart?"

"Sure, no problem. What do you want me to do?"

"I'll have Connie explain it for you when you get there."

"Roger that. We will be seeing you sometime tomorrow. Take care."

"You too. Ciao."

As soon as Glen had hung up, Scott called Connie. "Morning Connie."

"Good morning to you too, Boss."

"I just hung up with Glen. He had good things to say about you."

"That's nice. He seemed to me to be a real competent individual. He was very intense though."

"That's basically what he said about you, and yes, he is a very intense type of person. He is very good though. You just have to get used to him. He will be coming by to see you shortly. I want you to prepare a package for him to bring to me. You know what to include in the package. Instruct him not to let anyone see or have the package. Instruct him that if it looks like it will be compromised that he must find a way to destroy it. Make sure he understands the sensitivity of what he is carrying, okay?"

"Understood Boss, and for your information, which I have emailed you already and which I am sure you haven't seen yet or you would have said something, they will be arriving at your place around noon tomorrow. Carlos will be meeting them in Caracas, and flying them directly to you."

"Excellent. I'll be in touch. Bye for now. Stay safe."

"You too."

Scott was beginning to feel a lot better about their situation. He had more than adequate support now, and things were progressing more smoothly than he had any right to expect. Little did he know that this was the lull before the storm. Things were about to go downhill quickly.

Scott left Sam in charge of the topside camp while he took Geraldo and Felix on a familiarization trip back to the pit.

Scott explained to Geraldo and Felix, "This is where we begin. We will rappel two hundred and thirty feet down to a narrow ledge. I will go down first, then you two follow. When you get down, we will move along the ledge to the cave entrance. We have a few fixed ropes in place there which we will use to get back to the first place where we start 'Tarzaning'. Understood?"

Geraldo and Felix nodded in the affirmative.

Geraldo then said, "By 'Tarzaning', I presume you mean doing pendulum traverses, right?"

"Yep", Scott said as he clipped the rappel line into his rack, pushed the bottom brake bar up to lock the rope, stepped to the edge of the canyon, loosed the brake bar, pushed off the edge and quickly rappelled down to the ledge. Standing on the narrow ledge, he clipped his self-belay line onto the fixed rope that ran the length of the ledge, unhooked from the rappel line and signaled for Geraldo to follow. As Geraldo neared the bottom, there was a moment of confusion because Geraldo didn't realize that he wouldn't actually land on the ledge. Instead, when he reached the bottom of his rappel, he was hanging out in space fifteen feet from the ledge. Scott grabbed the end of the rappel line and pulled Geraldo over to the ledge.

Scott said, "Sorry, I forgot to mention that little detail. When you get to the bottom of your rappel, you have to pull yourself over to the ledge. If you let yourself go too far down, it gets a little awkward pulling yourself up onto the ledge here."

"Yes, so I see."

"Clip into this line here and move over there a bit, and let's get Felix down."

Félix rappelled down without incident, and they moved along the ledge to the cave entrance. "From here, we move along on fixed ropes for about two hundred feet", Scott explained, "and then we will 'Tarzan' the rest of the way back to the pit gradually getting lower and lower. Here we are over a hundred feet above the river. Back at the pit, we will be only eight to ten feet above the water. It gets really loud back there. This is the dry season now, but the underground flow is still quite considerable, but at least we can talk above the roar of the waterfall. The first time we were here the water level was much higher, and the noise was so great that you couldn't carry on a conversation without our noise cancelling head gear."

"That sounds awesome, but it also sounds like it is going to be a lot of fun", remarked Geraldo.

As they progressed back into the cave, Scott was relieved to see that both Geraldo and Félix were actually more adept at doing pendulum traverses than he was. No training was going to be required for these two. A short distance before they arrived at the pit area, they were hailed by one of the new Russians that had arrived with Dr. Kuznetsov. He was standing on the Russian's bridge about twenty feet below.

"Is that you, Mr. Mueller?" he asked in perfect English.

"Yes, it is I."

"I was just headed back to the top to look for you. We have a serious problem!" he exclaimed with some alarm.

"What is the problem?" Scott asked, suddenly filled with concern.

"I'll meet you back there and explain."

The threesome quickly made their way on back to the pit where they were met by five Russians and one Venezuelan soldier whom Scott recognized. Scott immediately noticed that the NMI rope was missing. He yelled "What the hell is going on? Where is and what happened with our rope? Who messed with our equipment? My God, this is a disaster!"

Scott's wonder about what happened to the NMI rope quickly turned to anger. Scott directed his anger directly to the Russian who was obviously the leader of the group. "Are you responsible for this? Did you cut our rope?"

The Russian appeared visibly shaken by Scott's violent outburst and accusation. He assumed that he would be upset, but Scott's reaction was over the top. The Russian said, "Let me explain."

Scott said continuing with a loud and angry tone, "This had better be good! You realize that you may have just murdered six Americans?"

"No, we didn't cut your rope. What happened was an accident! We have been instructed to move our winch so we can handle the loads better. There isn't much room back here, and we need more room. Since you weren't using your equipment, we were just trying to move it over there temporarily. We tried to pull it up, but we couldn't. It must be tied off down below. I had two men hold it while I tried to retie it over where you are now. We didn't realize how heavy it was, and all three of us couldn't hold it. It went down."

"Jesus, you presumptuous idiots!" yelled Scott, not trying the least little bit to conceal his anger. "Don't you know that you never, ever, ever mess with other people's equipment, especially their rope riggings without their express consent?! Not ever! This is insane! This is completely unacceptable. You guys need to leave. You all need to vacate this area right now before you screw something else up. We need to figure out how to rectify this situation. You need to let Dr. Kuznetsov know we have a serious problem, immediately!" Scott made it clear that they needed to depart now without further delay.

As the Russians began their departure, the Venezuelan soldier made his way over close to Geraldo whom he recognized as being former military and quietly said, "No fue un accidente!" He then followed his Russian comrades out of the cave.

Scott still fuming, turned to Geraldo and Felix and said, "This is a hell of a way to introduce you to Churum River Cave. I apologize. You see why we need your help. It looks like things are going to get really complicated really quick."

Geraldo said, "No kidding, and you have no idea, do you?"

"What do you mean?" Scott asked.

Geraldo answered, "That Venezuelan soldier; I've seen him before, and he recognized me as well. He whispered to me as he was leaving that this was no accident. And, his tone was emphatic."

"You have got to be kidding! I was informed that we needed to be wary of these new Russians, but all this and especially that bit of information just confirms everything about which I was warned."

Geraldo asked, "What are you going to do now? What is next? How are we going to rescue the guys on the bottom?"

Scott was thinking out loud, "The situation maybe isn't as bad as it might seem, on the bottom they are going to go ape crazy, to put it mildly. Let's get back to camp and bring the others up to speed and do some planning."

"But how are we going to be able to help them?" persisted Geraldo.

"We have rope, lots of rope. That's how", Said Scott.

CHAPTER 15

With their day bags packed, the group was ready to push the new passage as far as they could. Max asked, "Bufford, are you bringing some rope?"

"Yes, I'm bringing a hundred and fifty foot length. We have this and a two hundred foot length left. We used the four-fifty to rig the slot. If we need the four-fifty, we can re-rig the slot with the two shorter lengths."

Max opined, "Well, with any luck we are going to need the four fifty."

The passage leading off to the east was a narrow canyon about ten feet wide and twenty feet high. The walls were sheer, and the floor was covered with breakdown. The passage continued for almost a mile and a half before narrowing down to four to five feet in width.

Bufford remarked, "Do you realize that Spider and I were trying to find a way through this god awful breakdown pile beneath our feet. I can't imagine a more miserable caving experience than belly crawling, twisting, turning, and squeezing through over a mile of breakdown. I for one am damn glad we found this route!"

Peggy chimed in and said, "I think I can speak for all of us when I say 'we are all damn glad'."

The floor of the passage smoothed out, no longer strewn with breakdown, but was back to bare rock with a small crack running roughly down the middle. The crack was only a few inches wide. It was not a clean crack, so one could only see a few feet down. But, as they proceeded down the passage, the passage gradually widened and so did the crack. After a few hundred yards, the crack was wide enough so that occasionally they could see all the way through into a dark abyss opening below.

Max said, "Be quiet for a moment."

And, sure enough, they could hear the rushing waters of the Churum River far below. "Someone grab a rock", Max said excitedly.

Jim went back up the passage to where the breakdown ended and found a baseball sized rock. He hurried back to the waiting group, and they dropped the rock through the crack and counted seconds as they listened.

"I didn't hear anything did you?" Max asked.

"Maybe, but I'm not sure", Jim replied.

"Get a bigger rock! This is probably a good four hundred and fifty feet deep, just like back there where we came from."

Jim scurried off back down the passage in quest of a larger rock. This time he returned with a thirty pound boulder. "This ought to do the trick", he said.

They pushed the boulder through the crack, and it rattled down a little ways before launching off into space. They counted off the seconds, thousand and one, thousand and two, . . ., thousand and seven, then Ka-boom came the reverberating sound as the boulder crashed on the floor far below.

"Yep, just like I said, it's a good four hundred plus feet down to the bottom." Bufford said with a sigh, "Well, Spider, let's go back and re-rig the slot. It looks like we are going to need the four-fifty after all, just like Max was hoping."

"He was hoping because he knew that he wasn't going to be the one re-rigging the slot", replied Spider. The crack at this point was not large enough to squeeze through, so they continued following the crack on down the narrow passage in hope of finding a spot large enough to rig and rappel through. The crack got bigger, then smaller, until finally they found a spot wide enough to comfortably rappel through. This was where they would make their descent.

On the way back to the base camp, Jim asked, "Max, where is the laser mapper?"

"It's back in camp, right where it doesn't need to be. I guess I was too anxious to get started checking out this passage that I forgot to bring it. I know what you are thinking. Yes, if I had brought it, we could have just measured the depth back there instead of dropping rocks." After a brief pause, Max continued, "However, on the other hand, I kinda like dropping rocks down deep holes. Somehow, it is really satisfying to hear them reverberate when they hit the bottom."

"You remind me of someone I used to know back home."

"Who? Is it anybody that I know?"

"I'm just saying, not telling."

CHAPTER 16

When Scott and his crew arrived back topside, he called everyone over to meet in Miguel's dining tent. Both Sam and Dr. Fred were concerned with the urgency in Scott's tone, but Miguel was the first to ask, as all the new crew began filing in, "What's going on? Has something happened?"

Sam said, "It is very quiet on the com; I can't hear anything."

Scott said, "The reason you can't hear anything is because the com is down, like down the pit."

"What!!" gasped Dr. Fred.

"Yes, down the pit. Actually, the com gear is still okay, but the NMI rope is down the pit. The Russians accidently dropped it, or at least that is what they claim. We have reasons to believe that it was no accident."

Dr, Fred said, "If the Russians had anything to do with it, I guarantee you it wasn't an accident."

Scott went on to explain, "When I saw what had happened, I went ballistic, and I read the new guy in charge back at the pit, the riot act. After I calmed down a bit, I told them to get out of the cave until we figured out how we were going to support our team and get them back up safely. I presume the new guy is Kuznetsov's number two man, so I am sure he will give Kuznetsov a full rundown on our reaction to their treachery. Although, I don't believe they think we think it was treachery on their part, but rather just stupidity. I think that is what they want us to think, and if we think that, it will serve their purpose, whatever that is. I think they are hoping that we will somehow retrieve our team and then vacate the area."

Miguel asked, "Why do you believe it wasn't an accident?"

"One of the guys back there was one of the Venezuelan soldiers that Sergei had assigned to help us. So I recognized him, and I could tell from his body language that he was very uncomfortable, and that he didn't want to be associated with this deed. He also apparently recognized Geraldo from some previous military encounter. Geraldo says that he remembers him also. He told Geraldo as they were leaving that it wasn't an accident. So, it is not just how I feel about the matter; my feelings are consistent with what he said."

"So, what now? Have you thought of a plan? Have you had time to think through things?" asked Dr. Fred.

"No, not really. I think we should examine our options immediately. I think our relations with the Russians are going to go from icey to frigid though. I also think we need to think through all this and try to understand what the Russian's game plan is. Exactly what do they expect to gain from dropping our rope? Now that I have kind of poisoned the well with my giving them a verbal whip lashing, what should our follow on response be? Miguel, update your boss asap. Fred, do you think we should let the American Embassy know what is going on?"

"Definitely. Of course you know that they can't keep their mouths shut. They will inform the CIA, and then the CIA will be messing with us. I guess that can't be avoided, and it might even be a good thing."

"I hope this doesn't get in the papers. All we need now is for both the CIA and a bunch of reporters to start poking around."

Scott looked around the tent at all the new faces and asked, "Well, what do you guys think? Are you still with us, or are you ready to bail and go home?"

Geraldo repeated Scott's questions and previous comments in Spanish to make sure everyone understood. Basically, their response was that they understood, and that they were excited to part of the unfolding drama. Geraldo said, "Please don't leave us out. This is the most exciting and probably the most important thing we have ever been involved with. We are all with you one hundred percent. Just let us know what we can do."

Miguel announced that, on his last trip, Carlos had resupplied his pantry, and that he had been cooking all afternoon. He said that it was his pleasure to invite the entire new crew to enjoy some of his Canaima Camp Cuisine and beer, and talk over the events of the day.

Dr. Fred had been trying to get his head around this whole Kuznetsov thing, and he couldn't come up with any concrete motives for his actions. He sat in the corner of Miguel's tent and mused to himself, "It is obvious that he doesn't want us here, and equally obvious that he can't just run us off. That would create an international incident with lots of publicity. For the same reason, he just can't kill us off either, which is a relief. But, it looks like his strategy is to make us very uncomfortable, and then see what we do."

Scott noticed that Dr. Fred was sitting alone and absorbed in his own thoughts. Scott went over and asked, "Okay Doc, I can tell that you are thinking of something. Share your thoughts?"

"I was just mulling over our situation. I suspect that Kuznetsov will be contacting us soon. We need to have out response ready. He is making our situation as untenable as possible without overtly threatening us. So, what does he expect to gain from this move? It should be obvious to him that we can't just pack-up, turn tail and run with our team still on the bottom. It should also be obvious to him that with all the new people coming to support us that we intend to continue our presence here. From his perspective, he doesn't want us here, but he can't run us off either. So what is he going to do? He could try to marginalize us somehow, but what he just did works to the opposite effect. It puts our activities front and center. I also don't think he wants a lot of publicity or to create an international crisis. So, again, I ask, what is he up to, and how do you plan to respond?"

"What if we just tell him basically what we are doing and what we are going to do, and that is contact the American Embassy, run it up the chain in the Venezuelan Park Service, and solicit help from our own government. All of that should get his attention, and if he doesn't want this situation to be on the front page news, he will realize that he needs to tone it down and not interfere with our operations."

"It should, but I doubt that it will. The Russians are way too invested in whatever they are doing here. And again I speculate that whatever the whatever is, they don't want our eyes on it."

"I believe you are a hundred percent right there. On another topic, I was talking to Geraldo about this very thing. When Max and his crew return to the bottom of the pit, they are going to see the rope in a pile down there. They are probably going to panic until they know we have a plan. So, we need a plan. We can still send stuff to the bottom, but we have no means of communication."

At this point, Geraldo and Sam came over to join the conversation. Scott took a few moments to bring them up to speed on what he and Dr. Fred had been discussing. Sam said, "We can write up a detailed description of what has occurred and lower it on the provisions rope."

"Yes, we probably need to do that, but the problem is that we don't know when they are going to get back to the pit. Things will probably change a time or two between now and then. We need the com system."

"Well, we have the back-up stashed in the attic." Sam said, "We can install it fairly quickly."

Scott said, "I'm reluctant to do that. If we should lose it, we would really be up a creek."

"I've got an idea" offered Geraldo. "Why don't we put messages in plastic bags, number them, place them in empty water bottles, and just toss them in the creek? I'm sure they would survive the fall without any problems. Max could pick them up, and because they would be numbered, he would know their currency. Also, the Russians would never know that we were in contact with the guys on the bottom."

Scott said, "That's brilliant. How did you come up with that idea?"

"Army survival training; we are taught to think like that."

"That solves one problem. Let's get some messages on the way. We probably ought to let them know that we will send messages down at particular times so they won't be standing in the middle of the pit and get clobbered by a water bottle. That would be ugly."

Sam was feeling a bit guilty about enjoying one of Miguel's sumptuous repasts knowing that the bottom team was probably eating canned beans and freeze dried ham said, "Maybe we should send the provisions rope down with some extra food and tell them to tie the NMI rope on so that we can get our regular communications reestablished."

"The food, yes, but the rope, no. It is probably a good idea to keep the Russians in the dark regarding our potential ability to communicate with them. As things unfold, we can make a decision to retrieve or not retrieve the NMI rope. Let's wait and see which action will benefit us best."

Sam agreed, "Good point. Let's not make any hasty decisions that we might later regret."

The remainder of the evening was spent writing out detailed notes, carefully sealing them in locking plastic baggies, then stuffing them into empty plastic water bottles, and carefully doubly sealing the bottles with duct tape. Then, after making sure that there were no unwanted observers watching, tossing the bottles into the Churum River where twenty minutes later they would be strewn across the rocky bottom of the pit waiting to be found.

Sure enough, early the next morning, a Venezuelan soldier from the

Russian compound arrived at Miguel's dining tent to deliver a message from Dr. Keznetsov to Scott. The brief message read, "I would like to apologize for the carelessness of my technicians who are responsible for the loss of your equipment. I propose that we meet later today, and discuss how we can help resolve the situation. If 10:00 am this morning would be convenient, I will meet with you then at the Park Ranger's compound. Let the messenger know if this is satisfactory."

Scott said, "Well, to say no would be rude and counterproductive. So yes, tell him yes. We will be here at 10:00 am."

At 10:00 am sharp Dr. Kuznetsov's jeep rolled up, and he was met by Miguel. Miguel escorted him and his Lieutenant into the dining tent where Scott, Dr. Fred, Sam, and Geraldo were waiting. After brief and icy introductions were made, they sat down to begin discussions. Kuznetsov began by reiterating his apology, and then said, "I think we are once again in a position where we can work together to help each other. We have examined our capabilities for placing some of our scientist on the bottom of the pit, and we feel that it will be highly risky for us to attempt to do so. On the other hand, you already have a party successfully located and functioning on the bottom. We have need for the collection of a substantial amount of rock and other debris if any from the bottom. I propose that if you would agree to collect the required samples, then we would make available our resources to aid you in the rescue of your team."

Scott thought for a moment before replying, "I appreciate your offer of help, and I am sure that we can use some help. However, we have not fully evaluated the situation sufficiently to formulate a course of action or to know what kind, if any, help we might need. Our team down there is in all likelihood unaware of their situation yet. They are pushing the passage as far as they can, and I don't expect them back to the bottom for at least two more days. We plan to lower a note later today with a provisions package to let them know what has happened. Obviously, they will see our main rope piled up down there and know something has happened, and be looking for some explanation. Until we get that rope back up, communications will be difficult."

Kuznetsov asked, "What does that rope have to do with communications?"

Scott explained, "That rope not only was our primary method for descending the pit, but it was also was our means of communication. It has a set of embedded wires that when used with our headsets and the transceiver to which it was connected enabled our two way communications. On the other end of the rope is a shield with a secondary transceiver, and the shield has been specifically designed to protect the caver during both the descent and ascent of the pit through the waterfall torrent. So you see, that rope is of paramount importance. If it was damaged during the fall, they will probably have to remain on the bottom until we can get a replacement."

Kuznetsov asked rather churlishly, "Why don't you have a backup?"

Scott answered, taking the opportunity to display a smidgen of annoyance, "We are a privately funded expedition. That rope is a very expensive item that was specially manufactured for this particular purpose. It is very strong with built in redundancies so it is unlikely to fail. We don't have an open checkbook from our government, so we could only afford one. We didn't anticipate that someone would just drop it down the pit. We weren't ready for that one."

"I understand, and again, I apologize. However, we do have our large winch system in place above the pit that we can make available to you to resupply your party until the rope can be retrieved. The winch proved satisfactory in lowering cameras to the bottom, although the resulting video and pictures haven't been of much use to our scientists. We really need a comprehensive set of samples from the bottom. I hope you will give consideration of our offer to help."

"I'm sure that we will." And with that the meeting came to an end.

After they left, Scott turned to the group and asked, "What do all of you think about what he just said? Do you think his apology was sincere?"

Geraldo asked, "Do you think they dropped the rope just to get us to do their sample collecting?"

"No, there has to be more to their motives than that", replied Dr. Fred. "Besides, they could have had our complete support in the collection of samples if they hadn't precipitously terminated our previous agreement and kicked us out of their lab."

"I think you are right on that. I also think he was being truthful when he admitted that they couldn't do their own collecting. Now they are back-tracking to make amends. I also, they think they are having second thoughts about cutting ties with us, because I don't believe they want us to involve our government in any way. Too late for that; I'm sure the embassy killed that possibility for them."

Geraldo pointed out that, "In order to take advantage of this situation, we need to come up with a reason not to be able to retrieve the rope immediately."

"You are right. Prepare to prepare another bottle!" commanded Scott jokingly.

CHAPTER 17

It was decided that scavenging the four-fifty from the slot and re-rigging the slot with the shorter ropes could wait till the morning. It was also decided that the three ropes that had been used to ascend up to the overhang should also be scavenged since useable lengths of rope were now in short supply. With these three lengths of rope they would have a backup for the four-fifty. Buford, Spider and Jim undertook the task of scavenging the ropes, and Max, Ted, and Peggy returned to the crack opening where they decided which was the best if not the only place to rig for rappelling to the bottom of the new abyss where they could hear once again the flow of the Churum River.

Max said, "As you all know, we are beyond help from the top. Down here we are totally on our own. Therefore, in the interest of safety and self-preservation, I think we should rig two ropes. It will be better to be safe than sorry. Besides, carrying those extra ropes with us to the bottom won't do us any good if the four-fifty should fail for any reason. We will rappel on the four-fifty, and if necessary climb the knotted rope if necessary,"

"I've climbed over knots before; it is no big deal." Ted said. With that said, they set about establishing two separate secure rig points, each with a backup bolt for redundancy. After finishing the rig points they waited for the others to join them with the ropes.

Peggy asked, "What in your wildest dreams do you expect that we will find down there?"

Max said, "Based on the air flow, I expect that we will find an incredibly large canyon passage with maybe side passages leading off to other equally incredible areas. But what I'm really hoping for is a lower entrance. What do you think?"

"Well, first off, I don't know what to expect, but what I do know is that I wish I had brought Charlie. Even though I couldn't fly him through that narrow slot there, I could carry him through, and once we are on the bottom, he could be very useful."

"I agree. Why don't you go back to camp and get him? We aren't accomplishing anything useful here, and it will be a while before they finish scavenging the ropes."

"I think I'll do just that. Ted, you want to go back with me?"

"Sure, why not. It's boring just sitting here."

Max said, "I think I'll just sit here and be bored and wait for everyone to get back."

The trek back the mile and a half to base camp was fairly easy and was accomplished in a little less than forty five minutes. On the way back they met Jim, Bufford and Spider with their load of ropes. They explained why they were headed back to camp, and that Max was waiting alone for them.

Ted said, "We will probably catch up with you about the time you get the ropes rigged."

"That will be just in time to draw straws to see who goes down first", said Spider.

"No", Jim remarked, "No need for straws, I'm sure Max will opt to go down first. And you know what? If we all go down and we find some extensive passage, we are not going to want to turn around and come back up here just to get something to eat. Ted, why don't you and Peggy pack up some extra provisions so we can stay down there for an extra day?"

Spider thought that that was a good idea, and she volunteered, "I can go back with you all and help with the provisions, that is, if I can get Bufford to carry this rope. Bufford, can you manage this with all the other stuff that you are carrying?"

"No problem", he replied.

While Jim and Bufford made their way back to the crack where Max was waiting, Ted, Peggy and Spider pushed on back to the base camp.

"How much food do we have left?" Ted asked with a bit of concern.

"Probably about three days' worth if we are careful." Peggy replied.

Ted did a little bit of logistics planning in his head before responding, "Let's take a full days' ration with us, and maybe a meal or two more. That will give us the rest of today, plus all day tomorrow, and then most of the next day to explore and get back here. From here it is only a day's effort to get back to the bottom of the pit where additional provisions should be waiting."

"That sounds like a plan. Let's get to packing."

When Jim and Bufford arrived back at the rig point, they found Max in the dark, sound asleep. As Max stirred awake, Jim said, "Well, I see that you have been busy."

"I thought getting a bit of shut-eye was the best use of my time. By the way, where is Spider?"

Bufford replied, "We met them back in the passage, and we discussed some ideas. We were thinking that we might be spending a good bit of time down this hole, and some extra provisions might be a really good idea. Spider went back to base camp with Ted and Peggy to help pack up an extra days' grub."

"Good thinking. So how much rope do we have?"

Jim said, "We have the four-fifty, two one-fifty's, and a two hundred. You said the drop here was about four hundred and twenty, so we should be good for two rigs."

"Okay, let's get to it."

Rigging the drop required less than an hour, and while they waited for the others to return, Max donned his rappel gear as he was eager to make the descent. Max said, "When they get back, I'm ready to go."

Thirty minutes later, the full team was together again at the top of the freshly rigged drop. The extra provisions were divided up between them to facilitate carrying everything down. Peggy's drone was packed securely in its carrying case along with two spare batteries, an array of spare parts including extra rotor blades, two memory sticks, the drone controller, and her virtual console visor.

Max asked, "Peggy, are you sure that you can navigate that case through this crack, or do you think that you might need to send it down piece meal?"

"I'm pretty sure that I can just suspend it below me when I rappel. The case will protect everything as I push it down through the crack. Once through the crack, no problem."

"Okay everyone, are we ready?"

"Affirmative!" was the reply.

Max rigged into the four-fifty and shouted "Geronimo!" as he slid through the narrow crack. About fifteen feet down, the crack opened up. Max stopped his rappel and shouted back up to the others, "It opens up into a huge room. I can't see the end of it. It has to be over five hundred feet long."

He then resumed his rappel and was soon on the bottom. He unrigged, and signaled the top that he was off rope so the next person could begin their descent. As Max explored around the area where he had just touched down, he made a discovery that shook him to his core. He found himself standing in the middle of what was obviously a path. Not a naturally occurring path, but what appeared to be a manmade path. He suddenly realized that he was not the first person to be in this area, but that obviously many others had preceded him here. He was beside himself with excitement, and he couldn't wait for the others to get down. He shouted up to the others, "HURRY ON DOWN! You're not going to believe what I just found!"

At the top, they could hear him shouting. They could tell that he was excited about something, but they could not understand a word that he said.

Peggy was the next person on rappel, and as anticipated, she had to struggle to get Charlie's case through the crack. But once through, she zoomed rapidly to the bottom where she was greeted by an absolutely giddy Max who couldn't wait another minute to tell her about his find. Peggy quickly unrigged from the rope, signaled the top that she was off rope, and followed Max over to where he found the path.

"Holy Cow!" she exclaimed, "This is totally unbelievable. Who do you think made this?" she asked.

"Some ancient pre-Incan culture maybe", he replied.

As they speculated, they could hear the 'zing' of Ted's rappel rack as he rapidly descended. Ted couldn't believe his eyes when he saw the path. "Surely this can't be manmade", he exclaimed, but if it is, you know what that means, right?"

Max answered, "It means that there is or was a lower entrance down here somewhere. Man!, I can't wait till the others get down here, and we can see where this leads."

Peggy said, "This could be the archeological find of the century."

"Couple that with the fact that this cave could be the geologic find of the century, together it's the find of the millennium", Ted asserted. Ted added, "Dr. Fred is going to have an epic fit of joy when he finds out about this discovery."

Soon, the others were on the bottom and marveling about the new discovery. "Max said, "Let's leave our extra stuff here, and go see where this path leads."

"Lead on, oh Leader", said Peggy, "we're right behind you."

They started off single file down the path which soon led out of the giant room into which they had just rappelled. The path went through a low tunnel like passage that stretched on for several hundred feet. As the neared the end of the tunnel, they could begin to see light ahead.

"It's the lower entrance!" shouted Ted, as they all hurried forward.

As they rounded a slight curve in the path, they all came to a screeching halt, for there in the middle of the path stood a figure silhouetted against the light in the background.

They looked at the figure and then looked at each other. Then they stared in disbelief at the figure again. They were stunned! After a few speechless moments, Max made what was probably the most profound statement of his entire life. He said, "I didn't expect that!"

If the figure had been a member of the Russian Army, that would not have been too unexpected. If the figure had been a member of an unknown indigenous tribe, an ancient Mayan or Incan descendent, that would have been exciting. If the figure had been an American or a CIA agent, that would have been surprising, but not totally beyond belief. If the figure had been a Russian soldier or a nuclear scientist in a white coat or radiation suit, that would have been consistent with recent events, and would have explained a number of things. But the figure standing in front of them was not any of these.

The figure standing in front of them was about four feet tall, slender with an oval shaped head and big bug eyes. It looked just like the pictures of the Roswell alien published in the old science fiction magazines. An Alien was totally and completely unexpected. It was so unexpected that it was totally beyond the pale. Such a possibility had never risen to the level of even a momentary conscious thought.

In a very quiet voice, Spider asked, "Is it real?"

Bufford whispered back, "I don't know."

Max raised his hand Indian style and managed a rather unsure, "Hello."

Then came the next surprise. The alien raised his four digit hand and replied, "Bonus dies. Quis es? Cur tu venisti? Quo modo huc venisti?"

Max and Jim looked quizzically at each other, and Max said, "I didn't expect that! Did I hear that right? It sounded like Latin to me. I didn't understand a word he said, but it sounded Latin."

Jim whispered, "I think it was Latin too. My Mom raised me Catholic and the priests were always saying stuff in Latin, but I never understood them either."

Max said, "I took Latin when I was in pre-law, but that was a long time ago."

Ted observed, "I think that thing hanging from his neck is what actually spoke. I don't see a mouth."

Max said facing his colleagues, "I don't think we can run. We could never climb the ropes fast enough to escape, so I think we are committed. Committed to what, I don't know. Let's introduce ourselves and see what happens next."

With that said, Max turned towards the alien and began introducing the team. "Hello, my name is Max Meccum." Then gesturing towards Peggy, he continued,

"This is Peggy Allen." He continued introducing each team member in turn. When he finished, he paused.

The alien remained silent for a moment then responded, "Salutatio. Te fuimus exspectatio."

"Did you get any of that?" Max asked Jim.

"I think he said, 'Salutations. You are expected.', or something like that. I could be completely wrong, and probably am."

"Say something to him in Spanish, it is sort of like Latin. Maybe he can understand Spanish."

Jim, who spoke fluent Spanish, said "Buenos días. ¿Cómo estás?"

After a brief pause, the alien responded, "Ego valeo, gratias ago tibi."

Jim said, "I think he sort of understands Spanish, but he didn't reply in Spanish. I think 'thank you' was in his reply somewhere."

The alien then said, "Tu Graeca loqui?"

"He said 'you Greek something.'"

Max said. "Tell him we don't speak Greek."

Jim repeated what Max said in Spanish, "No hablamos griego."

As they grappled with overcoming their language barriers, the alien turned towards the path behind him and waved his hand in the unmistakable universal language for 'follow me' and said, "Placere sequere me", and began walking away. After a few steps, he looked back and waved again for them to follow him.

Max turned to his fellow cavers with his hands up as if to say stop and said, "Guys, let's pause for a moment and try to get our heads around this situation. Obviously we can't turn around and run, nor should we. But, we need to think things through as much as possible. This may be the most important event in the history of mankind, or it may be our demise. We don't know if we have stepped into the Garden of Eden or into a hornets nest that poses unimaginable peril. We need to try quickly to figure out which it is."

Ted said, "You are right. If the myths are right, these entities are responsible for abductions of people and all kinds of other weird stuff. Supposedly they can neutralize your brains so you don't remember anything, and transport you up into their space ships. We need to be super cautious."

Spider sidled up a little closer to Bufford and let it be known that she was scared. Bufford said, "Well, since there is no going back at this point, let's go forward like we own the place. Maybe that will gain us a little bit of bargaining room." It was quickly agreed that that was probably their best strategy.

Max turned back to the alien who had been patiently waiting and boldly said, "Lead on."

A short distance later, they emerged into a large cavernous room. Light radiated from numerous points along the walls and from the very high ceiling of this gigantic room. It was an awesome sight for the cavers. One very important thing that they immediately observed was that this was not the lower entrance they had anticipated.

Max looked around awe struck and said, "I didn't expect this either!"

Spider said, "Max, quit saying that. None of us expected any of this. We are all thinking the same thing that all this is frigging unbelievable!"

Ted opined, "Folks, I think that we have just passed from Lil Abner land to Tomorrowland. Look at all these structures, and what kind of plants are these. We haven't ever seen anything like these plants topside."

As they approached a small open air structure that appeared to be a meeting place, the host alien was joined by several other aliens, who for all intents and purposes appeared identical to one another except for their clothing. The host alien stopped, turned around and the little device hanging around his neck said to the group in a voice that sounded a lot like Max's, "Hello, my name is Xyllio."

Max couldn't help himself as he said, "Whoa, I didn't expect that either!"

Spider gave him a little punch in the middle of his back as a reminder for him to stop saying that. "I'm sorry, but I'm dumbfounded by all this. Who is going to believe all this shit? We can't go back topside and say, 'Guess what we found? We found a bunch of aliens!' They would say, 'Yeah, right! Obviously what you really found was a bunch of mushrooms, and it sounds like you have been eating them.' Then they laugh in our faces and throw us in the looney bin. Of all the possible things I was expecting, this was not one of them."

He went on to say, "I also think that device must be learning from our conversations. That was the voice and words of how I introduced myself to them just a few minutes ago. Aren't you guys more than just a little bit astounded by all of this?"

Bufford piped in and said, "Yeah Max, I think we are all totally slack jawed, but you seem to be the only one able to express yourself. And yeah, this is beyond awesome."

The meeting place was a sunken circular structure about twenty feet in diameter with small seats arranged in circular rows. It was obvious that the seats would be too small for the humans, so Xyllio gestured for everyone to sit down where they were. The ground was not ground, nor was it concrete. It was rock like, obviously manufactured, and surprisingly comfortable to walk and sit upon. They sat down, took off their backpacks, and faced the aliens. It reminded Max of white men and Indians sitting down in a teepee preparing to smoke a peace pipe before starting negotiations. When they were comfortably seated, guestering to his right, Xyllio said, "This is Klarrio", then to each of the others in turn, "this is Allaria, this is Gharrizia, this is Tarbonio."

Spider remarked, "I think their names indicate their gender. Did anyone else get a sense of that?" she asked.

Jim agreed, "Yes, I think that is consistent with a lot of languages."

Ted offered his opinion, "I don't think those are their real names. I think they are Latinized names they have given to themselves."

Max pointed to the device hanging from Xyllio's neck and asked both verbally and with gestures towards his mouth, "Is that a language translator? Yes?"

After a short pause, Xyllio responded, "Yes."

Max turned to his associates and asked, "What should we talk about? This is such an incredibly momentous occasion, and we should talk about something important. I don't think we want to come across as being just stupid humans."

"Let's work on teaching them English", Spider suggested. "You know in real life when Bufford and I aren't off climbing something, I do substitute teaching in our middle school. I have a teaching degree with a major in English, so maybe I can be useful here. Let's assume that they already know a lot about humans, so let's begin teaching them by learning something about them."

"Good idea, go for it."

Spider began using both gestures and verbiage, "We came from up there. Where did you come from?" Not receiving any response, she continued with a series of questions, "How long have you been here? Did you make these lights? What do you eat? Where do you get your food? Where do you get your energy? What do you know about us? How many of you are here?" Spider paused and looked around trying to spot something that would prompt an intelligent question. She thought perhaps she should start with something that they must have in common. How about numbers she thought, after all, numbers should be universal. She held up one finger and said, "One." She continued with two, three, and so on through ten. Then she held up both hands with her fingers folded into fists and said, "Zero." She continued speaking and doing simple arithmetic using her fingers.

Spider said, "I know this is very simple stuff, but I am giving them vocabulary and context to go with the words. I assume that their translator is taking all of this in and developing a translation algorithm."

Max said, "I think you are doing a great job. Let's talk about things we have with us that we can show them and give them more context to work with."

Max began digging in his back pack and talking at the same time. "This is my backpack; this is some food, this is my water. We all drink water."

Then he pulled out the laser mapper, and when he turned it on, the aliens reacted with instant fear, and scrambled for cover. Max immediately turned it off and said in a reassuring voice, "It's okay, it's okay. This is not a weapon." He then turned it back on and pointed it at his hand, saying, "See, it doesn't hurt." He then pointed it at himself, then at the other cavers. After turning it off, he waved to the aliens to return, which they did with caution. When they were all reseated, Max offered it to Xyllio for his examination.

After Xyllio and his associates had examined the device, Max took it back and turned it on once again and activated the holographic display which showed a three dimensional rendering of the cave. When he did, although their facial expressions did not change, you could tell by their bodily motions that they were very excited.

Using his finger, Max pointed to a spot in the hologram and said, "We are here." Then he pointed to the top of the cave and said, "We came from here."

Klario pointed to the top of the cave and carefully traced with his finger the route all of the way from the top to the bottom where they were now. He indicated with his hands the question, "How far?"

Then max, using his virtual cursor, traced the route once again, and then queried the distance. The laser mapper displayed the distance digitally in feet. Max read the number out loud, "Fifteen thousand three hundred and twenty two feet."

He could tell that Klario wanted more information. Max realized that they needed context for the measure of distance. He pointed to the word feet in the display and said, "one foot", and indicated with his hands how much one foot was. Then he said, "two feet", and indicated how much two feet were. Then he pointed to the distance in the display. Surely, he thought to himself, these people must understand our numbering system, after all, they have been observing us for ages.

Klario once again tracing out the route on the display said very clearly, "Fifteen thousand three hundred and twenty two feet."

Max asked, "Do you understand our numbers?"

"Yes."

"Great, we are making rapid progress."

With the words out of Klario's translator, it was obvious that at least at a rudimentary level, they were beginning to communicate. Klario then asked, "Where did you get the laser mapper?" Max explained that this was a fairly standard piece of equipment used in the real estate industry and had been adapted for use in mapping caves. The technology relied on low energy lasers and fairly sophisticated computer algorithms. Max was unsure as to how much of his explanation was being understood by Klario.

Up to this point, Ted had said very little, but he was a keen observer. Ted asked quietly, "Is it me or does anyone else get the feeling that these folks haven't been in touch with the upper world for a very long time?"

Jim and Max both replied, "Yeah."

Max continued, "That feeling has been coming on me for several minutes. You would think they would know all of the world's major languages, and they shouldn't have been surprised by the laser mapper. And, of all the language choices they should have, why in the world do they speak Latin?"

Ted said, "I think they are trapped down here and we are the first humans they have seen in perhaps a thousand years."

Jim said, "Holy crap, I think you might be right, and if that is true, then it means that there is no lower entrance either. The way we came in is the only way in and out. That explains Klario's interest in the mapper."

Peggy opined, "Boy do we have a lot to talk about. We need to bring them up to speed on world history and current events."

"Not to mention, we need to understand how they got here, and what has happened to them since. I'll bet ten dollars that their being trapped here and that explosion back in the pit are related."

Peggy turned back towards Klario and Xyllio and asked, "How long have you been trapped down here?" Peggy asked her question just assuming the validity of Ted's speculation.

Klario answered, "Two thousand and twelve years."

Max started to say that he didn't expect that, but he caught himself just in time to avoid another punch in his ribs. Instead he said, "I can buy that, it makes sense."

Every time Xyllio or Klario spoke, their English was better, and they were able to express more complex thoughts. It was obvious that their translation devices were very excellent at parsing every word and sentence that was being spoken and inferring the appropriate meaning and grammar.

Gesturing back towards the direction from which they had come, Ted asked, "Does your being trapped down here have anything to do with a huge explosion back that direction?" Not knowing if they understood the word explosion, Ted gestured with his arms and said loudly, "KABOOM!"

Klario replied, "Yes!" The translator even applied emphasis to his response.

Max said speaking to Klario, "Okay, we have a lot to talk about. We need to give you a quick overview of what has transpired in the last two thousand years, and a bit about how the world is today. Then you need to tell us all about your selves. This may take a while. How many of you are here?"

"There are sixty of us, but only seven of us are awake now. Five are here, and two are inside."

Max asked, "What do you call your selves? "We refer to ourselves as 'Humans'."

Xyllio replied, "We are known as the 'Pollomarians'.

Max thought to himself, "I wonder if Pollomarian has anything to do with Apollo." Then he said aloud, "I suggest that we go one on one, and just start telling each other how things are now and what has happened. You know, a quick history lesson. Do your translators interconnect so that what one learns the others will know also?"

"Yes."

With that, Spider and Peggy squared off with Allaria and Gharrizia, and the four guys ganged up on Xyllio, Klario, and Tarbonio. They spent the next four hours talking about everything that came to mind. Peggy talked a lot about world geography, the countries that currently exist, their various governments, conflicts, different peoples, different religions, wars that had occurred, and something about world trade. Spider talked about different languages, different cultures, the weather, how we travel these days, and of course the way we educate our kids. Max and Ted talked about science, computers, engineering, technology, nuclear energy, space flight, communications, and of course politics.

Meanwhile, the alien translation devices were becoming more and more fluent in English.

About four hours later, everyone was mentally exhausted. Peggy suggested, "Why don't we take a break? I, for one, am famished!"

That brought up an interesting question, so Peggy asked, "What do you all eat?"

Allaria answered, "I think we metabolize much the same things as humans do. We have had to improvise somewhat down here. The river has always provided a variety of fish. If fish didn't get washed down here from the surface, I don't believe that we could have survived. That has been our main source for protein. There are other creatures in the water which we also consume, but they are not plentiful. We have modified the plants that were down here so that they are now edible, and that is what we have survived on for two thousand years."

"How come there were green plants down here in the first place? That doesn't seem possible."

"That is part of our story. This hasn't always been a cave. I'll let Xyllio explain."

As Xyllio began relating their history, Bufford unpacked a half dozen MRE's. Ted asked, "Would you like to share our food? I am sure it is a great departure from what you are used to."

The aliens looked at one another and one of them said, "Yes, we would like that. We will have to be careful to ensure that it won't harm us. We have tuned our bodies very carefully to use the meager food sources that are available to us here."

Bufford said, "I believe that all of these MRE's are the same. They can be ready in a few minutes. Ladies, why don't you take charge here? I am sure your hosting skills far exceed that of any of us guys."

Spider remarked, "Knowing you as I do, I am certain that you are right."

Off to one side of the meeting area was a long low table. Peggy and Spider arranged the MRE's on that table and began heating the food.

Peggy asked Gharrizia, "Do you all have plates and eating utensils?"

"Yes we do", Gharrizia replied simply as she disappeared into a nearby structure. Shortly later, she reappeared with an arm load of bowls, saucers, and a variety of small spoons.

"These will do nicely" Peggy said as she prepared to portion out the contents of the MRE's. "Let's make this a multicourse meal." She prepared several cheese and cracker hors d'oeuvres and passed them around for the aliens to sample.

The aliens all had rather small indistinct mouths, so when they ate, it seemed like they were just nibbling. Tarbonino was the first to try a bite. He nibbled away then paused and said, "This is incredible!" He then said something to his peers that didn't come through the translator, but it must have had the connotation of 'You must try this!' because they all reached for a cracker at the same time. The aliens obviously required much smaller portions than the humans, because they took very little and nibbled on it slowly. They tried all of the 'delicacies' contained in the MREs, and seemed to enjoy them far more than one could have expected.

Xyllio said, "Your food is very good. We have never eaten anything like this. Is this what you eat every day?"

"No, no" explained Peggy, "this is expedition style food. This food last for a long time without spoiling, it is easy to prepare, and has lots of energy. If you like this, then you are in for a real treat when we can share with you some real food like we eat every day."

When the cavers began to chow down on what was left of the MRE's, which was most of everything, Xyllio began to tell about their history, much of which he had already related. "We are a very old and long lived species. We come from a planet over twelve hundred and twenty light years from earth. It takes us over sixteen hundred of your years to make each trip. Our Kind has been watching and interacting with humans for over ten thousand years. We long ago recognized human's potential, and have sought to provide guidance to help you develop a moral basis and rules for living so that you wouldn't destroy yourselves long before you as a species reach your potential. From what you have just told us, we have not been very successful in this mission. Life is very common throughout the galaxy, but sentient species that develop high levels of technology are rare. And those that do, often self-destruct. That is why we chose to intervene on behalf of your species. About four thousand years ago, another old and long lived species discovered your planet. You would think of them as reptilian. They are known to us as the Maleoron. Unlike us, their evolution was stagnant and had been so for a hundred thousand years and maybe a lot longer. Their interest in you humans was not benign. They saw in humans a potential for rejuvenating their species. Their interest was in mining your DNA and the DNA of other earth species. You probably do not realize it, but this planet has the most diverse array of species of anywhere known to us in the galaxy. The Maleoron had no interest in the inalienable rights, feelings, or future of any of the denizens of this planet. They were only interested in exploiting the vast DNA resources found here. But, that is not all, they began conducting genetic modification experiments trying to see if certain components of your DNA could be incorporated into theirs. Apparently your DNA and theirs is not compatible, and the results of their experimentation were not very successful. This was very sloppy science and resulted in the creation of some very unearthly creatures, many of which are surely described in your world's mythology."

Spider said to Max, "Don't say it!"

Max replied, "I was just going to say that that explains a number of things that have confounded archeologist for ages."

Xyllio continued, "We felt that their actions were wholly unethical, morally wrong, evil, and could not be tolerated. We went to war with them in an attempt to drive them away from this earth. This war lasted for nearly a millennium before we were successful. We are sure that they retreated with a trove of stolen earth DNA, and what they are doing with that information, nobody knows other that it probably is not good. Within a few hundred years after they departed, we managed to eliminate all vestiges of the creatures that they had created except for one. That one was a genetically modified human. A little time bomb left just for us. As of the time when we became trapped down here, we were not able to detect which humans were modified and which were not. But these modified humans were enabled to detect our presence, to seek us out, and to kill us. That ability is built into their DNA as a natural instinct, and is passed from generation to generation. We suspect that they found us here and used a weapon left behind by the Maleoron to attack us. This area here was a deep rift valley, isolated from the upper surrounding jungle. There were ninety of us down here with two ships studying the unique biology of the area. One of our ships with thirty souls on board departed. Shortly after they rounded the corner into another part of the rift, there was a huge earthquake, and the walls of the rift collapsed inward. As the rift began to collapse, there was a tremendous explosion, and we know by the signature of the explosion that it was the ship that had just departed. We were shielded somehow from the explosive effects, and we found ourselves trapped here, and we have been here ever since. We don't know for sure that there was an Maleoron weapon or not or if it was used to cause the earthquake or not. That is our speculation. We do know that the explosion was caused by the ship's anti-matter reactor being compromised."

Ted said practically shouting, "Anti-matter! We didn't consider anti-matter. We considered every type of nuclear device we could think of, including neutron bombs, and the possible collision with a micro black hole, but not anti-matter. That is why there was no residual radiation. I can't wait to tell Dr. Fred. He is going to be amazed, just like the rest of us, maybe even more so."

Max asked, "So, you still have a space ship down here right?" Xyllio gestured off to his right, "Yes, we have our ship, but it isn't a space ship. It is a laboratory ship designed specifically to support terrestrial explorations. All of us are scientist, what you would call biologists. The resources that we have in that ship enabled us to genetically modify the plants native to the rift so as to make them edible to us. The ship also provides us power, power that will last for several thousand more years. However, the ship was not equipped with tools that would have enabled us to dig our way out of here."

"We would love to see your ship, will you show it to us?"

"Yes, in due time. It is right over there. We have built various structures around it to expand our living and working spaces."

Max's mind was buzzing now, and he persisted, "Are there more of your kind still here on earth watching us?"

"Yes, of course, if they are still here."

"And why did they not try to rescue you from down here?"

"I am sure that they did try, but without detecting any sign of our survival, I am sure they eventually gave up. We had no means of transmitting a signal through this dense rock, so we could not alert them to our presence."

Jim asked, "Did you try ultra-low frequency?"

"We would have liked to have tried that, but as I said, we had no means to generate such a signal. There was also the danger that had we been able to set up some sort of beacon, the wrong people could have detected it, and that would not have boded well for us. We felt that our best strategy was to simply wait and hope that someday someone friendly would find us."

Max continued exploring out loud an idea that was forming in his mind. "If those genetically modified humans were in fact responsible for your demise here, then the knowledge of that fact and this location will have been passed down through the generations to the present. That might explain the mission of the Russians. One or more of them might be descendants of the original modified humans. I'm going to refer to them as GMH's from now on. And you know what, I've got two candidates whom I think might be GMH's, Vassilov and Kuznetsov."

Ted remarked, "From the very beginning, they seemed to know a whole lot more than what they were sharing with us. It seemed to me that they were looking for something specific, and they didn't want us to find it before they did."

Klario asked, "Tell us more about these two individuals. From what part of the world do they come?"

"Well, they both are Russians. At first Sergei was very abrupt, and was dogmatic that he was in charge and that his mission should take precedence over ours. However, after we had mutual discussions, his attitude softened towards us, and we worked out a mutual cooperation and support agreement. I think he realized that we were not a threat to his mission, and that he thought he could exploit our skills. Shortly after we made our agreement, Kuznetsov arrived on the scene and replaced Sergei, and he abrogated our agreement. Since then our relations have been very frosty, so to speak. I think Kuznetsov would just as soon eliminate us, and he probably would do so if he thought it wouldn't create an international incident and draw a lot of unwanted attention to his activities. Sergie was immediately recalled to Moscow when Kuznetsov arrived on the scene."

After hearing this information, the aliens began buzzing intently among themselves with their translators muted. After a few moments, Xyllio said, "The Russians must not learn of our existence here. It is likely that they pose extreme danger to us, and by association to all of you as well. It is also possible that they are friendly, but it will be difficult to determine which they are. Most likely they are not friendly. You must find a way to shield all knowledge of our existence from them. Do you think this will be possible?"

"In the interest of self-preservation, we will dang sure do our best."

Max said, "Going forward, we need a plan. I see three things we need to do. First, we have forged a route down to here. If we could do it on our meager budget, others, who are much better financed than us, can do it as well. So, we need to block this route and find another one, or else secure it in some manner so that no one else can find or use it. Second, we need to find or generate justification for our continued exploration of this cave system. So far we have sold ourselves as being strictly spelunkers, and obviously we need to keep that appearance. And third, we need to convince the Russians that there is nothing more to see down here. They already know there was an explosion, and now I believe that they know what kind of explosion it was. They are seeking conformation. Some of them may also suspect exactly what we have found. We need to be able to convince the Russians and the world that the extension of the cave beyond the pit so far is just a maze of tortuous belly crawling passage through a massive pile of breakdown, and that so far it has led to nothing. We will need to conceal the detailed map we have generated thus far. We will need to make a convincing decoy in case our mapper gets confiscated or hacked."

Max asked, "Does anyone else have more ideas?"

Peggy said, "Let's make a really good map of this area to see if there is a possibility of finding or making an alternative entrance. I just have a funny feeling that we are not all that far from the cliff face on the north. Also, remember, I have Charlie with me. I think we need to take a good look at top of this huge room. It looks like it may be a thousand feet high in some places. Wouldn't it be cool if we could find a hole up there so that we could just rappel directly into here."

Jim agreed, "That would indeed be very cool." Jim continued, "Also, I need to remind everyone that we need to get back to the reality of the present. We have just about run through most of our supplies, so at least some of us need to go back to the pit and get another week or so of provisions sent down."

Max said, "You are right. It is easy to lose track of time down here and with all the flood of information and events which we are now in the middle of, it is easy to get distracted from what we need to be doing in the here and now. I suggest that us four guys go back to the pit and do the heavy lifting in regard to hauling more supplies back here. Peggy, can you take over the mapping chores?"

"Can do."

"And can you and Spider start work on faking up a decoy map that will obscure the existence of this part of the cave?"

"That part will be fun, faking is what we women do best", Peggy replied while doing a fist bump with Spider.

"Xyllio, I hope that you will be thinking of ways that we can best work together as we go forward. In particular, be thinking of ways that we can secure the route down to here."

"There is so much we need to tell you, and there is so much that we need to catch up on in regard to the past two millennia. I must also stress that I believe that we all are in extreme danger right now. We have some tools, but they are totally insufficient for creating a new entrance, however, they may be sufficient to help you in blocking a passage if the passage isn't too large. We used these tools to shape our structures that you see here"

"What else can you do with your tools?"

"We can move small boulders, and we can melt and mold rock."

"You can melt rocks?"

"Yes, but it takes some time. The device's main purpose is that of a portable energy source. It is very powerful and versatile in that role."

"How large are these tools? To be useful, we must be able to get them through a crack not much larger than my body. Will that be possible?"

"Yes, they are both smaller than you."

"That sounds great. We will need to position them in the upper passage and make some preliminary preparations, so that the passage can be closed on short notice. Also, we need to equip and teach you how to climb and descend using our ropes."

Jim said, "I'd like to see these tools in action so as to get an idea as to whether they are capable of doing what will need to be done."

Xyllio said, "Let's go over to one of our growing areas and I can demonstrate them."

The group quickly walked down one of the paths for about three hundred yards to a small garden area plush with a variety of plants. All around the plants were lights glowing brightly with a yellowish white light. The color of the light was obviously carefully tuned to the needs of the growing plants because the plants were flourishing with a vigor that would be the envy of the best of any terrestrial farmer. From a small shed, Xyllio pulled a small device that resembled a small wheelbarrow, except that it had no wheels, it hovered instead. Jim went over and pushed down on the bucket of the device and immediately felt it respond with an equal but opposite force.

"It is a 'hoverbarrow'. How cool is that? Exactly how much can it lift?"

Xyllio replied, "It should hold something your size."

To test that notion, Jim sat down in the bucket, and he felt it strain under the weight. "I believe that I'm right at its capacity. This little hoverbarrow, if I may call it that, may be useful in helping us block the passage somewhere, but we will need something much more powerful, like explosives to do the job."

Again, Ted, who had been quiet during this discussion pointed out, "Whatever blockage we put in place will need to look like it occurred accidentally; otherwise force will be brought to defeat the blockage. Back near our base camp is a narrowing and plenty of boulders are already strewn around that area. I believe that is the best place to block the passage."

Jim was thinking out loud, "What we really need is about five hundred pounds of ANFO. We could blast the passage shut, then Xyllio and his friends could, using this little tractor to finish the job in case the blast doesn't do the job."

Ted added, "I would also suggest that the rock melting device be used to weld some of the boulders together so they can't be easily moved. The welding would of course need to be discrete; otherwise it will be obvious that it is a non-natural construct."

Jim asked Xyllio, "Do you have the capability to manufacture ammonium nitrate?"

"Yes, but it takes time. We manufacture a variety of chemicals needed by our crops to grow."

"Time, unfortunately is not something we have. We will have to arrange to import the requisite ammonium nitrate and diesel to make this work. We will also need a cover story as to why we are blasting."

Peggy said, "The cover story is easy. We have all encountered situations where we would have liked to use dynamite to open up a passage. Only in this case we will have tried but failed miserably. Instead of opening a passage, we will end up inextricably closing the passage to further exploration."

"So, ladies it looks like you have an additional tasking. While we are gone, you need to teach our new friends how to climb and rappel. I think time is not in our favor now, hence we had better get to our tasks."

Bufford said, "Since Jim and I are about the same size, I can leave my climbing gear here, and Jim and I can share his. I'm sure they have the capability to modify it to fit their smaller bodies."

Jim agreed, "That should work."

The men left all of their supplies with the women so as to give them an extra day before they had to make a trip back to base camp. It took the men about six hours to make it back to base camp. Of necessity, they took with them the three ropes that were tied together to make the backup rope. While Jim and Bufford re-rigged the route back down to the original base camp near the bottom of the pit, Ted and Max began the process of ferrying the girl's personal gear and all the remaining provisions back to the crack so it could be lowered down to the girls. Max figured that this would save Spider and Peggy from having to make an unnecessary trip up to the base camp.

Jim and Bufford completed the re-rigging expeditiously. When they were both again on the bottom, they proceeded to the original base camp just a short distance from the pit. When they were in range of the shield, Jim flipped on the com system in his helmet and said, "Anybody up top listening?"

After a short pause, Bufford remarked with some concern, "I don't hear anything, not even any noise. Something is not right."

As they approached the shield which was securely tied down, they immediately noticed that the NMI rope was slack. It should have been very taut. "Oh crap!" muttered Jim as they both raced towards the bottom of the pit. They quickly grabbed and donned a poncho and entered the pit where they were greeted by a torrent of rain and a huge surprise. There before them lying in a pile were three thousand feet of NMI rope.

"What the HELL!!", exclaimed Bufford as he looked up into the falling water and darkness of the pit as though he expected to find an explanation emanating from above.

The only thing coming from Jim's mouth was a repetition of "Holy shits! This is not good!" After a moment of disbelief in what they were seeing, they spotted the bag hanging from the provisions rope. They quickly made their way over the breakdown to the bag, and observed along the way the large number of water bottles wrapped in duct tape with numbers written on them. They disconnected the bag and together dragged it down into the dryer passage. As Jim began to dig into the provisions bag, Bufford made his way back to the pit to retrieve some of the water bottles. After gathering up a half dozen numbered bottles, he returned to the dry passage where Jim had just found a written message enclosed in the provisions bag. Jim read out loud the message which detailed all of the events that had transpired on the surface. The message did not convey the impression that Scott and crew had regarding how the NMI rope ended up at the bottom of the pit.

Jim said, "Well this is certainly a fine can of worms. There is obviously a lot that they are not telling us."

"Maybe that's what all these bottles are about. They look like they have messages inside."

"Let's see what you have there."

"I've got numbers one, three, four, five, and seven."

The messages in the bottles explained the paucity of information that was in the provisions bag. The bottle messages explained that their every move was being watched very carefully, and that anything sent down or up via the provisions bag would likely be known to the Russians. Whereas, messages placed in a water bottle and tossed into the Churum River would remain secure and secret. They were warned to expect more bottles.

CHAPTER 18

At the top of the pit, both the Americans and Russians were keeping a 24/7 watch. At this particular moment, Félix was doing watch duty for the Americans. He sat hanging from the ceiling in his modified Swiss seat right next to the winch for the provisions rope. He whiled away the time listening to music on his pod as he watched the tell-tale that he had attached to the rope. When the tell-tale began bobbing up and down, it shook him back to the reality of the present.

He shouted excitedly into his com set using his best broken English, "Hola, hola, Sam, you here?"

Sam replied calmly, "Yes, Félix, what's up?"

"Go tell senor Scott we got bite on rope!"

"Okay, Félix, hang tight while I go and let Scott know."

The Russians noticed Félix's sudden surge in activity, but because of the noise of the cascade, they could not hear what he said. They did however let their superiors know that something was happening.

Scott, Geraldo, Dr. Fred, and Miguel were all sitting around a table in Miguel's diner tent along with several of the Venezuelan cavers when Sam came running over and said, "They are back."

Scott said, "Well, it's about time, I was beginning to wonder if something had happened. Leave it to Max to push it to the limit. I'm sure that they were blown away when they saw the rope on the bottom. Let's give them thirty minutes or so to read their messages before we send an update bottle. They will need some time to digest all that has happened and I am sure Max will have an opinion."

Sam said, "I'd like to be a fly on the wall down there now. I'll bet they are in a bit of a panic I don't care how cool Max normally is."

"Yes, we need for them to understand that things are not as bad as they might seem, and that we might be able to use this situation to our advantage. I am sure that they all understand that we have a strong backup plan. Prepare another bottle to let them know about Kuznetsov's proposal."

Geraldo cautioned, "It is still light; we probably should wait till after dark so our actions won't be observed. We don't want the Russians see us tossing bottles into the river."

Dr. Fred opined, "We need to think things through up here and try to anticipate all of our options so we can present them to Max and crew as choices since they will have limited ability to communicate their thoughts to us until we get the rope back."

"Obviously, we need to get the NMI rope back up, but until then, communications are basically one way. Tell them that when they are ready to send anything back up, they need to yank real hard on the rope five times."

Geraldo offered, "Maybe we should tell them to yank seven or eight times if they are including a message that is for our eyes only."

Scott agreed, "That is a good idea."

Sam suggested, "Also, maybe they should yank two, pause, three, pause then four times if their message is deceptive but for public consumption."

Scott said, "I think we are getting way ahead of ourselves. Let's keep it simple. Two signals should be enough. Geraldo, how about you and Sam relieve Félix. Actually, don't relieve him; keep Félix with you. That way he can help you and Sam manage the rope when you haul the NMI back up and reestablish our communications with the bottom. When we get the NMI rope re-connected, we won't need any secret signals."

"Can do, boss. We are on it. Let's do the bottle. I'll sneak it into the river when no one is looking."

CHAPTER 19

Back at the bottom, Jim and Bufford were mulling over the messages, wondering if anything important was in the two missing bottles. Jim said, "Looks like Max and Ted are about here, I see their lights coming down the breakdown pile."

As Max and Ted approached, they could not help but notice that things were amiss. Picking up his pace, Max hurried over to where Jim and Bufford were sorting through the messages.

"Okay, what is going on?", he asked. "What disaster has befallen us? What the hell has happened to the rope?"

"Well", Jim started off saying, "a lot has obviously happened. As to whether or not it is a disaster is yet to be seen. These are messages from Scott. He explains that Kuznetsov dumped our NMI rope. He says that they don't think it was an accident, and that relations with the Russians are now at an all-time low. Other than that, not much. They did send some more provisions down. Not a whole lot, we are going to need a lot more."

With a note of worry in his voice, Max asked, "Have you checked out the rope yet? Did you notice any damage?"

Bufford said, "I took a look at it, and fortunately I didn't see any damage. It should be okay; I'm sure that it had a soft landing."

"Good, let's find the end and send it back to the top."

Jim said, "Let's see if we can find any more message bottles." With that said, they set off towards the pit.

Max and Ted grabbed and donned their ponchos and joined Jim and Bufford at the end of the tunnel leading into the pit. Just then, another bottle came bouncing towards them. Jim managed to grab it before it disappeared into the re-coalescing Churum River. Bufford said, "That's probably what happened to two and six. They ended up in the creek." They all scurried back into the drier tunnel to see what was in the message.

"It looks like Kuznetsov has made us a proposal and we need to come up with a response. There is no way we can let them know what we have found down here. We need to buy some time so we can see what options we have and come up with a plan."

"Right", Bufford remarked. "We need to get com established, more provisions back to the girls, and a cover story worked up."

Max agreed, "And then, I need to get top side. However, before I go up, I need to talk with the girls to get their latest input from our new friends. I'm going to head back there and get briefed. Meanwhile, see if you can get the NMI headed back to the top, and by-the-way, send a message to drop more supplies and that I want to come up."

It took almost four hours to haul the three hundred plus pound wet NMI rope up, thread it into the communicator, secure it to its main and backup anchor, and get several friction loops around the winch drum. However, when all was done, they were rewarded with a grateful "Can you hear me yet?" from the bottom.

As everyone's com gear came online, a relieved "hooray" was heard by all who were tuned in.

Sam said, "Guys, I don't think you have met the latest additions to our team. Say hi to Geraldo and Félix. These guys are Venezuelan spelunkers, and they have more skills than we could have ever hoped for. When Glen Neely put out the word, these two highly experienced guys and about a dozen more like them showed up to help."

Jim said, "I don't think you can understand just how glad I am to meet you. We have all been worried about how we were going to manage with so few of us and so many tasks that have to be done. Welcome aboard. Sam, you need to get a full crew in there to help you, because as soon as Max gets back here, I'm sure that he is going to want for you to haul him up."

"Where is Max now?", Sam asked. Jim tried to ad lib a bit. He felt that he needed to buy some time. He also wanted everyone to be on stand-by for when Max returned, but he had no firm idea as to how long that would be. He also didn't want to tell too much about what they had been doing in case the Russians had found a way to eavesdrop.

"He is back in the passage where the girls are. And, that is a long way back. It will probably take him a good six hours to get back here. The passages are really nasty, almost all belly crawling. The girls have been leading the way because they are smaller and a lot more limber than us guys. Let's reconvene back here in six hours. Maybe you can get more supplies ready to send down, and in the meanwhile, we will ferry the stuff that you just sent back to our base camp. "

"Roger that. We are all interested in what if anything you all have found. Over and out." With that they turned off their communicators so that their conversations would remain confidential.

Jim whined, "Why does everything have to be so complicated? Why can't the Russians mind their own business? It seems that all of our plans are simply baselines from which to deviate."

Ted said, "It is a good thing that Max is a lawyer. He is going to have to do some fancy footwork in deciding whom to tell what, when, and how much."

CHAPTER 20

It took the better part of three days to establish the route with fixed ropes back to the crack leading down into the Alien's huge chamber, but Max, traveling alone with only his climbing gear made it back to the crack in a mere fifty minutes. He donned his Swiss seat, clipped in his rappel rack, slithered down through the narrow crevice, and began the four hundred foot rappel to the bottom. There he doffed his gear, and started down the path to meet the girls. He had not gone more than a few steps before he was greeted by Xyllio. "Welcome back Max, we were expecting you."

"I'm glad to be back, but there have been developments, and I don't think we have much time."

"What sort of developments?"

"The Russians have escalated the rift in our relations, and have interfered with our equipment. They dropped our ascent and descent rope to the bottom of the pit. That is something we can easily deal with, but what it did do was to cut our communications. Fortunately, as I left, we were in the process of restoring everything. Now, it also seems that the Russians want us to do their bidding down here, and I suspect that it will only be a matter of time before they send their own crew to the bottom. We are going to do our best to slow them down, but I don't know how much time we can buy."

"That is terrible news. We cannot let them discover us. They will with certainty destroy us."

"What if we could arrange for you to be protected under the aegis of our government?"

"How could we be certain that they wouldn't do the same? We must find a way to identify who may be our friends and also who has the power to protect us, and who are likely our enemies that were programmed a long time ago to hunt us down and kill us."

"I have no idea how to identify either. It will probably be easier to identify the GMO's than potential friendlies. The only thing I can think of to do is when we finally have to vacate from down here, that we seal the passage as permanently as possible to give us time to figure things out. Unfortunately, with today's technology, nothing we do will really be permanent."

"There are several things we will need for you to do. We have a device, a beacon if you will, that you can activate. If any of our kind is still present on this planet, they or their emissaries will come to check out the beacon. If they come, you can confide in them regarding our situation. If no one comes to the beacon, it will mean that all of our kind has either left the planet or they have been killed. If that is the case, then our only hope is to send a signal to our kind to come to our aid. Sending that signal will have its own set of complications, and also, unfortunately, that signal will require several hundred years to reach the closest of our bases. We are a very long lived species, so the time element is not a problem. Surviving discovery by our adversaries in the meanwhile is the problem. So, the more permanent the passage is sealed the better."

"There has to be a better solution than leaving you sealed up down here for another three or four hundred years. Like I said, we just need to buy some time to get this figured out."

Together they walked on to the central meeting area where they found Peggy and her companion Allaria. Peggy said, "You are back sooner than I had expected. Any news?"

"More news than you want to hear. Where is Spider?"

"She is over in that hovel over there." Peggy said pointing to a small domed building. "She has been holding class there ever since you left."

"Well, let's get her over here so I won't have to repeat myself too many times. I have a tendency to leave thing out when I go over and over the same thing."

"Before you give us your news, I've got some news for you that you are going to like."

"I could use some good news, tell me, tell me."

"Allaria and I have been surveying this cavern, and it is huge! It is over a mile long and for the most part, the ceiling is about four to five hundred feet up. Like I said, for the most part; about fifteen hundred feet to the east the ceiling opens up into a canyon that goes up for at least twelve hundred feet. It goes up further, but there are twists and turns that block the laser from seeing how far. I flew Charlie up to where it started getting narrow. I am baselining that flight now so if I lose contact with Charlie, he can find his way back. On my next flight, I'll see how high I can go." This got Max's attention. Another thing" Peggy added, "The air is really moving up there. That is where all of the air flow is going. There is no air moving on the east end of this room, it is all going up there. So, if we are going to find another entrance, it is going to be up there." Max's mind was racing. He could hardly control his excitement with this news. This was indeed good news.

Just as Peggy finished telling Max about the high lead, Spider joined the group and said, "Max, when you go back, tell Bufford to bring more rope and all the climbing hardware he can find. Peggy's high lead is the kind of thing that he and I do best; you know we both detest belly crawling passages. Also, ask him to bring over one of the chargers, our batteries are running low. Although I'm sure our friends here could find a way to give us a charge, it would be good to have our primary charger anyway."

"I'll tell them to bring over everything they have. However, we don't have any more rope. Every length we have is dedicated to some pitch. It will be at least another day, possibly two before we can get more dropped down."

"Dang!", Spider lamented. "I'd really like to get started sooner than that."

Max was thinking, "Well, there is a possibility, but it would require a lot of trust on your part."

"What possibility is that?"

"Bufford could come down here with all the gear that we have on hand. Then we could drop the four fifty. That would leave you all stranded until more rope could be brought down. Assuming everything goes okay, that would only be for a couple of days, but with our luck, it could be longer. But, the two of you could begin the assault, and get a three hundred foot or so head start. Jim and Ted would stay back and wait for more rope. I know we have plenty in store top side."

Without hesitation, Spider said, "Do it."

"That possibility dramatically changes our options. How cool would it be if we could find a secret passage and just rappel directly down into here." Turning to Xyllio, Max said, "Maybe, just maybe when we blow the passage, you guys won't be sealed up down here for another three of four hundred years. Actually, I don't see that as a real possibility anyway. We know you are here, and we won't abandon you."

Max went on to relate to the girls the details of situation in which they were now embroiled. He said, "I am going to go back topside and help Scott manage things there. As Xyllio said, we also need to find out who our friends are and who are our enemies, and that probably isn't going to be easy. While I am gone, you need to continue to learn as much about our new friends as you can, and they need to learn as much about the present as you can possibly convey. We don't know how much time we have before we have to exit, so be ready to go on a moment's notice. So, I guess it is good bye for a little while."

Peggy came over and gave Max a hug and said, "You be careful, stay safe, and make dang sure you come back, okay?"

Max gave her a hug back and said, "Don't worry. I'll be back. You can count on it."

As Max turned and started back towards the west end of the Alien's chamber to where the four fifty rope was rigged, Spider said to Peggy, "You kinda like Max, don't you?"

Peggy blushed briefly, then replied a little surprised, "Does it show? Well, of course I do, who wouldn't. He is a really cool guy, and we have done a lot of caving together. Besides, we have known each other for a long time."

Xyllio accompanied Max, and they chatted as they walked back to the four fifty. Xyllio reminded Max that he must be extremely careful not to reveal anything regarding their presence, and that he must be very mindful of his own safety. If the wrong people became suspicious, then he and his associates would be in peril even if he hadn't confided everything to them. Max assured Xyllio that he would exercise the utmost caution. Max then began the four hundred foot climb out of the chamber.

By this time, Max had been awake and going like crazy for about twenty hours, so he was starting to drag. His return trip to the pit was much more leisurely than his trip coming from the pit. He arrived back at the pit about two hours after Jim had said that they should reconvene in six hours.

Max told them about the tentative plan regarding Peggy's findings and Spider's desire to begin the assault as soon as possible if Bufford was also willing. Bufford indicated that he was game. Ted indicated that he would also like to return with Bufford to the alien's chamber and continue learning as much as he could.

Max announced, "I'm beat. I think I'm going to take this opportunity to get some rest before getting ready for them to winch me out of here."

A little over four hours later, Jim shook Max awake. He said, "They are ready at the top. They have run the Russians out and have a full crew ready to pull you up. Sam says all systems are go."

Max shook himself and stretched and said, "Let's do it. Man. I could use a cup of coffee."

Jim replied, "Yeah, I think we all could."

Together they walked over to the end of the tunnel leading out into the bottom of the pit. Max donned the wet suit, the re-breather, and his Swiss seat. He clipped his water proof travel bag, which contained his climbing gear which he would need later and the beacon that Xyllio had given him, to his Swiss seat. He then donned his hard hat again, switched on his com and said, "Get ready to beam me up Sam."

Sam replied, "Give me the word when you are ready."

He climbed to the top of the breakdown pile where Jim had the shield ready for him. Max snugged himself up tight under the shield knowing that a rough ride lay ahead of him. On the upward ride, the shield was going to be taking a much harsher pounding than it did on the way down. This ascent was would complete the first bounce of the world's deepest freefall pit. Max steeled himself for the ride and said, "Beam me up!"

As expected, the first thousand feet of the ascent went smoothly. But the higher he went, the more the rain coalesced into sheets of water which moment by moment became heavier and heavier. Then the sheets began to turn into steady streams which pounded on the shield and cause it to shake violently. The noise was intense, and while the noise cancelling feature of the com was helpful, it couldn't block out all of the noise. It did nothing to abate the violent shaking. Max shouted, his voice shaking in response to the pounding water, "This is a damn lot more scary than coming down was! I'm getting pounded and I can't see a thing."

Max closed his eyes and snugged up even tighter under the shield. The winch ground on inexorably pulling Max higher and higher, and with each foot gained, to Max it seemed like the pounding became harsher and harsher. Max thought that this was akin to running the gauntlet.

The twelve hundred feet of intense pounding lasted for about twenty minutes, but it seemed like a lifetime. As the shield slowly lurched and jerked its way through the spherical region of the pit, Max strained to see through the sheets of falling water. When Max descended the pit a week earlier, the falling water flowed smoothly around the shield forming a tunnel through which one could occasionally get a glimpse of the cavern walls. However, ascending through the torrent was a different story. The shield seemed to be struggling as though it was having to claw its way up through the torrent, and while a tunnel would start to form, the turbulence would cause it to immediately collapse. This made seeing anything impossible.

When Max finally emerged through the cascade at the top of the pit, he felt drained even though the ordeal had lasted for only a little over forty five minutes. While Scott and Geraldo helped Max unclip from beneath the shield and get secured to an anchor in the ceiling of the pit, Sam tossed a pre-prepared water bottle into the abyss. The bottle contained a message for the team on the bottom to let them know that Max had arrived safely at the top and that the NMI would soon be on the way back down.

Scott asked, "How was the ride?"

"It was hell! Going down was interesting and exciting, but coming back up was definitely not fun. I felt like I was being batted around like a piñata, and I couldn't help but wonder just how much abuse could this shield take."

Scott replied, "Well, it looks like it took the abuse with flying colors. It is not showing any visible damage, and you survived apparently intact. So, it did its job."

Sam said, "Welcome back topside. You are looking a little pale. Me thinks you could use a bit of sunshine."

"I think you are right. I wonder how long it will take for my eyes to adjust."

Since they had run the Russians out, they had the premises all to themselves. Actually, they hadn't run them out, but rather had politely requested that they yield their space at the top of the pit since Scott was going to have eight or nine people assisting in extracting Max from the bottom. Further, since no one was there to tell them no, they used the Russian's bridge to exit the cave. For such a large group, using the bridge was much easier and faster than Tarzaning out. Scott knew that Kuznetsov would somehow let them know that it was very presumptuous of them to use the bridge without permission. Scott figured that he would just take that hit. It is sometimes easier to beg forgiveness than to seek permission.

Miguel was waiting at the top of the canyon when the group finally emerged. "Welcome back Señor Meecum. A lot has happened since you left. Come over to my tent and let's have a beer. We can talk about everything that has happened. I need an update so I can keep my Director informed."

"Good to see you also, Miguel. Yes, we have a lot to talk about, and yes, I'd love a beer, but first let me get out of this wetsuit and into some clean clothes. By-the-way, you wouldn't just happen to have some of your famous nachos in the oven would you?"

"But of course."

"Okay. Sounds good. I'll see you shortly."

Max knew that he would have to be very careful about what he said. He knew that he would have to elaborate on the fake story that the girls were leading the way through a maze of belly crawls through the massive breakdown that filled the space between the canyon walls. In his mind, he had been working on a plan to have the Venezuelan cavers map the surface above what he would be claiming where the cave was leading. Hopefully that would also give the Russians a false flag to follow. He also knew that he needed to find a time to spend with Scott in some secure place so as to give him a full data dump. He knew it would be hard for Scott to swallow, but in anticipation of that he brought the memory stick from one of Peggy's cameras with him. Scott was going to be blown away. Further, he was going to need an excuse to return to the States for a week or two to activate the beacon. There was much to do, and too few trusted people in which he could confide.

Max dug around in his personal clothing stash and found a welcome change from the hot and sweaty wetsuit that he was still wearing. Although it was a high tech breathable suit, it was becoming very uncomfortable in this hot environment. After donning his change of clothes, he joined the group in the dining tent where the beer was already flowing in celebration of his successful and uneventful return. And most importantly, Miguel had just finished preparing a large batch of his famous four cheese jalapeño nachos.

Max reiterated how the girls were leading the assault, and how he, Jim and Ted spent most of their time exploring leads that so far had gone nowhere. He pointed out how Bufford didn't like exploring belly crawls, and that maybe he more than didn't like, he in fact hated belly crawls. So, as a consequence, Bufford spent most of his time either fixing meals for everyone, or else doing nothing.

"One thing", Max said, "the girls have been working along a high lead straddling a deep narrow crack. It is quite dangerous and very tiring. The need some more rope as soon as we can get it to them so they can rig some safety lines through that section, and if they can find a place where they can rappel down lower, they will need some rope for that."

Sam said, "I'll get right on that. I think we have two spools left. Hopefully twelve hundred feet will be enough. We will get it hanked up and sent down."

Dr. Fred asked if Ted had found anything that would shed further light on the mysterious explosion. Max related what Ted had expressed as his opinion. "Ted hasn't said anything about what he thinks caused the explosion other than it was obviously a massive event. He did say something about how he thought the shock wave had propagated to the bottom of the pit and some distance back into the canyon the ran off to the east from the bottom of the pit. He thinks the shock wave hit something solid and caused something like a hammer shock that shattered the walls of the canyon resulting in what we are observing. That is the structure of the cave appears to be a high canyon filled from wall to wall with massive breakdown."

"Interesting", remarked Dr. Fred, "it must have been one hell of a shock wave."

Max went on to explain that Ted also thought that, "The shock wave that propagated up through the top of the pit was basically unimpeded and that it resulted only in the glazing of the canyon walls instead of the massive damage we are seeing in the other direction."

"That is an interesting theory, and it makes some sense. Have you all collected any more samples from the bottom or poked around to see if you could find anything interesting and out or the ordinary, at least out of the ordinary considering that this isn't an ordinary cave? You know what I mean. Have you found anything you consider unusual?"

"I know what you mean, and yes we have poked around a good bit. But no, we haven't found anything that looks different from what we sent up initially. I would say that our main findings are what I just related regarding our observations, or actually Ted's observations. One other thing though, the reason we are continuing to push is the air flow. There is lots of air flow. It is going through the breakdown to somewhere, and that somewhere has to be large. Or else it is going to a lower entrance or another pit entrance somewhere."

Geraldo jumped in and said, "If there is another entrance, we ought to be able to find it."

"I agree, and that might be a good productive task for some of your guys to undertake. Why don't you assign a team to start mapping along the surface and keep on the lookout for any feature that might suggest a possible entrance. I can sketch out the general direction that the mapping should take."

Scott said, "I'll bet that will get the attention of Kuznetsov when he sees our guys surveying off through the jungle. He will know that we have found something important, and it will tear him up until he finds out what it is. Don't anyone tell any of your Russian acquaintances what we are looking for. Let's keep them wondering as long as we can."

Scott sensing that there was something that Max wasn't telling, conjured up an excuse to get Max off to the side to talk. Max was also looking for an excuse to get Scott off to the side to let him know that they needed to talk privately, so when Scott said openly to Max, "Max, when you get a moment, I need to talk with you about the finances of this operation." Max replied, "I understand. I know that this expedition must be becoming quite a drain on the Foundations resources. Let's take a walk where we can talk. We don't need to involve everyone else here in the administrative side of things. Let me get my camera, I want to show you something that I think you will find of interest. I think it will be of interest to the Foundation as well."

Max added further, "I'll be just a moment." Then he set off towards his tent to get his travel bag. On the way, he popped into Peggy's tent and picked up one of her spare cameras.

Geraldo observed this brief discourse between Scott and Max and quickly surmised there was more their wanting a private discussion than finances as they had openly announced. Geraldo quietly said to Scott, "I sense that there is a lot more that Max needs to talk about, and that it doesn't involve finances. If it is okay with the both of you, I'd like to hear what he has to say."

"You are right, I don't need to talk finances, and I too sensed he needed an excuse for a private off the record conversation. If it is okay with Max, it is okay with me for you listen in."

Max returned a few moments later and said, "Let's take a walk over towards the edge of the escarpment while we talk. I'd like to get a couple of pictures of the sunset."

Scott said to Max, "Geraldo would like to join us if that is okay with you."

Max paused for a second and then said, "Sure, why not. He just might have some good ideas on how to proceed."

Geraldo said jokingly, "Pictures of the sunset? I think that this is a symptom signaling that you have spent too much time underground."

Max laughed, "Very perceptive of you."

The edge of the escarpment was only a few hundred yards from the camp. When they found a suitable spot with a good view of the valley below and sufficiently out in the open so that they could see that there were no unwelcome ears listening to their conversation, Max sat down and took out the camera and installed the memory stick.

Max began, "I presume that I am correct in that the two of you have figured out that there is more going on than what I have told you."

Scott said, "You are absolutely correct. Spill it."

"Well, for starters, most of what I have told you so far is a lie. Most of it is a total fabrication to cover what we have really found, and hopefully buy us time to continue what we are doing."

"Why am I not shocked?" Scott remarked.

Geraldo said, "I sense that this is going to be really interesting."

"I am concerned that you are not going to believe what I am going to tell you. I think you might think that we have discovered a trove of mushrooms down there, and that we have been tripping out for the past week."

Max had their undivided attention. "I think what I told you about Ted's theory is correct. Everything else is bunk. What we do know now is what caused the explosion, what kind of explosion it was, and when it occurred."

"How could you possibly know all of that?" asked Geraldo.

"Well, that's a good question. The reason we know is because we talked with the people that were directly involved, and they told us everything. We are continuing our discussions with them, and there is so much more to learn."

"What do you mean, you talked with THEM? Who the hell is Them?" Scott said practically shouting. Both Scott and Geraldo were dumb struck with what Max just said.

Max said, "Shhh, keep your voice down, and don't express any surprise at what I am going to tell you. I am going to preface what I am going to say by telling you that it is unimaginable, unbelievable, totally unexpected, it is beyond the pale, and must be kept totally secret. Do you both swear that you can and will keep this totally secret?"

"How the hell are we supposed to not appear to be surprised?"

"I don't know, but try your best. Do you both swear to keep this secret?"

"Yes, of course I do."

"Me too", Geraldo replied. "Are the Russians involved?"

"No, and they must know absolutely nothing about what we have found. They have to be kept in the dark. They may and likely are the enemy."

Max continued, "Take a deep breath, look off into the valley, and do not act surprised. Are you ready for this? What we have found is a community of Extra-terrestrial Aliens. Yes, Aliens. You know, like the ones you read about in the Roswell Report and the weekly scandal magazines. The little guys that abduct people."

Scott and Geraldo looked at Max with their mouths agape. "You have been eating mushrooms haven't you?" Scott said with disbelief.

"It gets more interesting."

"I'll bet it does!"

"They have been trapped down there for around two thousand years and totally out of contact with the outside world. This area hasn't always been like it appears as today. Back then it was a deep narrow valley with an ecosystem that had evolved independent of what is up here, sort of like an in-land Galapagos Island. They were down there studying the unique bio-systems when a very large earthquake occurred. There was a massive upheaval and the walls of the canyon tilted and began collapsing together. They had two exploratory ships down there. One tried to escape, but was caught in mid-flight. It exploded and basically formed the pit from hell. The ships are powered by antimatter reactors, so when the ship was crushed, the reactor went critical virtually everything was consumed in a many multi-megaton explosion that left virtually no trace. I said virtually; I did find one small shard, so there is some evidence, and there is probably more. The Russians must not get their hands on any of that."

By this time Scott had regained enough of his composure to ask a question, "How many Aliens are down there?"

"We were told that there are sixty, but we have only met five of them. The others are supposedly sleeping."

Geraldo asked, "How did you talk with them? Do they speak English?"

"Well, they do now. At first, they tried to talk with us in Latin. I guess Latin was the language of choice in the civilized world back then. It took us several minutes to realize that they were speaking Latin. None of us spoke Latin, so realizing that it was Latin wasn't much help. Jim spoke to them in Spanish, and they sort of understood what Jim was saying. Actually, they speak through a little translator device, and that device learns really fast. It was amazing; it was learning English and Spanish simultaneously. It listened to everything we said and parsed every word. Within a few hours, we were able to converse with simple sentences, and as of now, they speak very fluently so we are able to exchange information easily.

They are a very old and long lived species. They claim to be benevolent and have been watching and guiding us earthlings for over eight thousand years. There was another similar species also involved back then. I say similar, they would argue otherwise. The other species was not benevolent, and was involved in exploiting us earthlings. There was a conflict. The good guys tried to banish the bad guys, which after many centuries they were able to do so. However, in some ways, it was an incomplete victory.

The bad guys collected species for other world zoos, and had no qualms with doing a bit of genetic meddling and experimentation in the process. We have surmised that a number of the beast chronicled in mythology are actually some of the creatures that they created."

Geraldo piped in and said. "You have got to be kidding! Who is going to believe that crap?"

"Like I said, it gets more interesting. When the Bad Guys realized that they were losing and were on the verge of being expelled from this planet, they created a proxy soldier to carry on the battle for them. We have dubbed them GMH's"

Geraldo asked, "Oh Lord, what do these GMH soldiers look like?"

"They look like us. But, they were given instincts to seek out, detect, and kill the Aliens. Other than these hereditable instincts, they appear to be ordinary humans. They apparently are/were a very formidable and effective proxy, and continued to wage the war over several millennia. Xyllio, the Alien that I interacted with the most said that having been out of touch for two thousand years that he has no idea what the status of his kind might currently be. He provided me with a beacon to place somewhere secure top side, preferably somewhere in the States. When activated, any Good Guy Aliens that may still be present on the planet will come to investigate the beacon. If they still exist, then we can work with them, because they will surely be fully ensconced somewhere within the human societal structure. If no one comes to investigate the beacon, it will mean that either the Good Guys have been eliminated or else they have left the planet. If there are no Good Guys left, that doesn't mean that there no more GMH's. Because of their nature, the GMH's probably still exist and are a threat to the Good Guys down below."

Max paused for a few moments to give Scott and Geraldo time to process things. Then he said, "I know that this is a lot to process, but is it starting to make sense?"

"No, it doesn't make sense. I'm having a lot of difficulty getting my head around all this. Max, I know you, and you appear sane. But, I'm not sure that you aren't crazy or delusional. I need to touch something, feel something, see something to make this real."

"Well, let's see what we can do." Max started scrolling through the gallery of pictures on the camera. "Here take a look at these pictures. Just scroll through, and I think you will be stunned."

For the next ten minutes, Scott, with Geraldo looking over his shoulder, scrolled through the gallery of hundreds of pictures showing all of the named Aliens, their commune, inside of their ship, their laboratory, their living quarters, interactions with the Americans, some of the modified plants, and their little tractor.

"Try to convince yourself that I somehow fabricated all of those pictures while we were down there exploring a very difficult cavern."

"Unbelievable! Absolutely unbelievable." Scott whispered quietly.

"You said that you needed to touch something. Touch this", Scott said reaching into his travel pack to retrieve the little beacon. "I dang sure didn't manufacture this while I was down there."

"What is that?"

"It's a beacon to alert others of their kind."

"Okay, okay, we believe you, but it is still unbelievable."

"Where do we go from here?" Geraldo querried.

"There are several things we need to do. One is to make sure we give the Russians plenty of misdirection every chance we get. Having a survey party actively working off to the southeast will help. We also need to find an alternate entrance to the Aliens cavern. We think we are onto a lead for this. Spider, Bufford and Peggy are working this as we speak, but they need a lot more rope and climbing hardware. Peggy found a high lead with Charlie that may be what we are looking for. Somehow without being observed, we need to scout the area above where the high lead is located to see if we can find a possible entrance that hopefully we don't have to dig out. There is a lot of air moving up through that high lead, so it has to come out somewhere. We need to find it and keep it a secret. I think that is going to be your job, Geraldo. Then lastly, I need to get back to the States with this beacon. If we can't figure out a way to smuggle it out, then we will have to activate it here in Venezuela somewhere. They need to be informed that Xyllio and crew are alive and well. We also are going to need their support. That's all I've got for now. Any comments?"

Scott said, "My mind is numb, but give me an hour and I am sure I'll have a thousand questions."

"Me too", echoed Geraldo.

"Let's mosey back to camp. I could use a pitcher of margaritas."

"Make that two pitchers."

"Three."

"At some point, I need to inform Dr. Fred, Sam and Miguel about everything. We all need to be on the same page in every respect going forward, and that is going to be tricky."

Scott said, "Give that some thought. It might be better if everyone didn't know all the details. Some of this information, a lot of this information, is hard to swallow and in my opinion needs to be compartmentalized. If someone doesn't know something, they can't inadvertently disclose it."

"I'm sure that you are right. I'll give careful consideration to what I tell, to whom I tell, and when or if I tell."

"By the way, Scott, do you have any ideas as to how I might smuggle this beacon out of Venezuela and into the States. We can't let it get compromised, because if I should get caught with it, I would have a really hard time explaining where I got it, what it does, and who made it."

"Maybe you should just activate it and mail it to the White House. Let them figure out what to do with it. When someone shows up claiming it and wanting it back, the stuff will hit the fan. You can be sure that the CIA will come knocking on our door because sooner or later they will figure out who sent it. Then, we might or might not find out who came knocking."

"That's not a bad idea except that the CIA/FBI/DHS et al would squeeze us until we revealed everything. That would not be good. What we need is a way to get it into someone's hand without fingering ourselves."

"Actually, on second thought, I think putting it in someone else's hands is too risky, both for them and for us. Also, the possibility of getting the CIA involved is a terrible idea."

Geraldo said, "Why don't we have Félix and a couple of his buddies take it up high in the Andes and then activate it. They could keep an eye out to see who comes to investigate it. They could watch from afar without being detected. One thing for sure is that whoever comes looking for it won't be mistaken for some hapless hiker who just happens to be in the area."

"Now that sounds like a workable plan. Let's do it. One other thing, he needs to place it up high in an inaccessible place so that it won't be discovered by happen chance. Whoever comes and finds it will find it because they will know what they are looking for and where to look."

They continued walking slowly back towards the camp when Max thought of another thing. "Geraldo, you wouldn't just happen to know where we could get say five hundred pounds of ammonium nitrate would you?"

"Whoa, just what do you plan to blow up?"

"Who said anything about blowing anything up?"

"Well, ammonium nitrate only has two uses that I'm aware of, one is for growing stuff and the other is for blowing stuff up. You don't look like a farmer to me."

"We must maintain control of the pit for as long as we can. When it becomes apparent that the Russians are going to attempt a descent of the pit, which they are anxious to do, we are going to need to act. Once they are successful in descending the pit, they will be following in our footsteps. We can't let them do that. We are going to have to permanently block some of the passage back to the Alien's cavern to prevent them from discovering them. This will require some explosives and a cover story as to why we blew up some passage. ANFO is the natural choice for the job. As we speak, the girls are working on a cover story."

Geraldo said, "As you know, ammonium nitrate is a carefully monitored commodity these days, for obvious reasons. Some of the mining companies are the only entities allowed to stockpile the stuff. So, if we need it, I guess we will have to steal it from one of them."

Scott said, "Just get it, but don't send me the bill."

"I have some ex-military buddies that are perfect for this task. Sorry Scott, but it is going to cost some serious moolah."

"Whatever. We will have to use an offshore account for this type of expenditure, I presume that will be okay with your associates."

"I'm sure it will. Max, you have given me too many tasks. You need to make some reassignments. I guess I need to head out first thing in the morning. I'll get Félix clued in on what he needs to do tonight, and he can take it from there. I think any of the others guys left can handle the survey task."

Back in camp, Geraldo cornered Félix and told him to select a couple of his climbing buddies and meet him in his tent in thirty minutes. Then he went to meet Max in his tent.

"No time for margaritas my friend?"

"Not yet. I'm going to meet with Félix in a few minutes. Tell me what I need to know about the beacon and what do I tell them about how we came to have it."

"Tell them that it was delivered to us not long ago, and that we were to activate it if we felt that we were in need of their help."

"And who are the 'they' in this case?"

"Tell them that we refer to them as 'The powers that be'. They have influence at the highest levels of government around the world, and they recognize that we might need their muscle in our relationship with the Russians."

"Okay, I got that. Now, how do I turn the device on and off?

Also, I don't think they have time to take it to the Andes, so how about somewhere nearer and more accessible?"

"That is alright with me. Just don't make it too accessible. Whoever comes looking will probably wait around to be contacted. Tell them it is okay to contact them, but they must claim only to be messengers and don't answer too many questions. They can tell them that we sent them, and where we are, but that is all that they know. They will find an appropriate way to contact us."

"Got it."

Max wandered over to Miguel's dining tent which by default had become the central gathering place for the group to socialize. Miguel greeted Max as he entered, "Max, you look like a man in need of a margarita. Margaritas and nachos are on the table. Did you and Scott get a good look at the sunset?"

"Thanks, and pitcher of your margaritas is exactly what I need. And, yes I did get a good view of the sunset. It is gorgeous from up here. When you get a chance this evening, give Carlos a call. Tell him we need a flight into town in the morning or as soon as he can get here."

"Where are you going?"

"Oh, it's not for me. Geraldo said he and a couple of his buddies need to go check on something. I think it is something personal with their jobs, so I didn't ask."

CHAPTER 21

Shortly after Max arrived at the top of the pit and was disengaged from the shield, the shield and NMI rope were lowered once again to the bottom where Jim, Bufford and Ted were anxiously awaiting its return. They quickly hauled the shield into a dry area in the tunnel and reactivated communications with the top.

Jim asked, "Did Max make it up okay?"

Sam replied, "Just like a martini, shook and stirred, but he is just fine. He says that the ride up is really rough, but no damage. Stand by, we need to get Max topside, then I'll get back with you. Give us a couple of hours."

"Okay, I'm glad he made it okay, none of us knew what to expect. We will be standing by. Don't forget us."

Jim said to Ted, "I think I need to stay here in communications range. Why don't you go back with Bufford, and when he is safely on the bottom of the Aliens' chamber, you can drop the four fifty. I know that you wanted to go down with Bufford, but I think you need to stay with me so we can back each other up until we can get more rope down here."

Ted sadly said, "I think you are right. That is a better plan. Well, Bufford, are you ready to head back?"

Bufford replied, "Let's do it. I know the girls will be anxious, and Peggy will want to know that Max made to the top okay."

Jim said, "Spider will want to know that also."

"Yeah, but Peggy will really want to know. She worries about Max."

With that, Ted and Bufford set off on their trek back to the Aliens' chamber, and Jim found a comfortable place to rest while waiting for Sam or someone topside to call.

Three and a half hours later, Sam's voice came booming over the com, "Hello down there. Is anyone listening?"

Jim replied, "Yeah, I'm listening. Where have you been? You said two hours, and it has been well over three."

"Well, we had a lot of questions for Max, and things are a bit messy up here as you know. Good news is that you need to stand by for the receipt of a bunch of rope. I'm sending down all that we have on hand. Scott indicated that if we need more he will see if we can procure some locally."

"We are standing by, send it on down. We also need bolts and hangers. Are you sending them also?"

"Max didn't mention that, but I'll see what I can do."

"Sounds good, and while you are at it, how about sending down some cold beer and some of Miguel's nachos?"

"In your dreams! Now you are just getting greedy. Be happy with the rope I'm sending. Reality is a bitch, you know."

"A find friend you are. I'll remember this."

"The way Max tells it, you all are having a tough time pushing the passage down there."

"No kidding. You know how Bufford hates belly crawls, and that is the majority of what we have. When we are not belly crawling, we are straddling a bottomless crack that reminds me of a crevasse in a glacier. It is really hairy, and that is why we need rope. No accidents are allowed."

"Okay, I see their lights, they are bringing the rope in now. It should be on its way down shortly."

"Don't forget the hardware. We need it just as bad."

"Okay, but it will be on the next drop. We will have to round up what we still have on hand up here. That will take some time."

"That's okay. Getting the rope this soon is going to be a surprise; we were expecting for it to take at least a day or two for you to get it down to us."

By the time the two bags of rope arrived at the bottom of the pit, Ted had returned. Surprised he said, "You mean they have already sent more rope down?"

"Yep, the bags just touched down. Looks like we didn't' need to drop the four fifty."

The words had more than just left his mouth when Jim realized he had slipped up. The com was wide open, and Sam said, "What do you mean you didn't have to drop the four fifty."

Jim quickly found himself ad-libbing an explanation. "That crack I told you about, it was getting too hairy to deal with. At first, the girls were crawling along straddling it, then it got too wide, so they had to chimney along. That was way too dangerous to do unprotected, so we scavenged the four fifty since it was the last rope we had, and Peggy and Spider rappelled down. Down near the bottom, it was still hairy going, and they needed a belay line. We knew more rope was coming, so we dropped the four fifty down."

Not really believing what he just heard, Sam said, "That sounds kinda stupid to me. You are lucky we had more rope available up here."

"Yeah, but we knew that we still had the spare NMI if we needed it."

Ted added, "You are right. I personally didn't like the idea of dropping the rope. I guess Max didn't mention that, did he? Jim and I are signing off now. We are going to get this rope back to where it is needed as quick as we can."

After they were out of com range, Jim said, "That was a major slip up. I hope it doesn't come back to bit us."

"It's hard to remember that our coms work whenever we are close to the shield. But, what is done is done. Max may have to clue Sam in sooner than he planned."

CHAPTER 22

Geraldo, Félix, and two others gathered at the airfield awaiting the arrival of Carlos. Each of them brought with them a large duffle bag with their personal items and their day bag with gear. This did not go unnoticed by the Russians who assumed that this group was heading home. Little did the Russians know but that the first stop this little group would make when they arrived in Caracas would be to a local laundromat. Those duffle bags were mostly filled with dirty clothes since there were limited facilities back at Miguel's camp.

When Carlos was about thirty minutes out, he radioed in to let Miguel know that he was bringing a passenger with him that wanted to talk with Max. Miguel told him that he would meet him at the airfield and pick up his passenger.

Miguel found Max over at the dining tent and asked him, "Are you expecting company?"

Max replied, "Not that I know of, why do you ask?"

"I just talked with Carlos, and he said he was bringing a passenger with him that wants to talk with you."

"Did he say who it was?"

"No, just that he had someone with him."

"Interesting. I have no idea as to what this could all be about. Let's go meet them at the field."

The two of them hopped in Miguel's ATV and rode over to the airfield. They arrived there just as Carlos was making his final approach.

As Carlos was taxing up, Miguel and Max walked over to the plane to meet the new arrival. Carlos shut the engine down, and he and his passenger deplaned.

Carlos said, "Buenos días Miguel. Max, this the gentleman said that he needed to talk directly with you."

The new arrival did not introduce himself but simply said, "I am just a messenger. I was instructed to deliver this package to Mr. Max Meccum. I presume that is you, am I correct?"

"Yes, that is me" Max replied.

"That is all that I was supposed to do, so I will go back to Caracas now. I have no need to stay around here."

While Max looked the package over, he noticed that it did not have a return address or a clue as to whom had sent it.

Geraldo and crew drug their luggage over to the plane and asked seriously, "Carlos, are you sure you have room for all this stuff?"

Carlos replied, "This is a six passenger plane, and since this guy is flying back with us, that makes six. It's going to be tight, and you are going to have to hold most of that stuff in you laps. However, I think we can make it fit."

"Yeah right", quipped Geraldo, "but can you take off?"

Carlos said with a chuckle, "I've got the power!"

On the way back to the camp, Max carefully opened the package. Inside was a large envelope, and the envelope bore Sergei's seal.

Max said, "Okay, this is probably going to be interesting. Let's get to some place where we can look this over without any prying eyes."

Miguel asked, "What do you think it is?"

"It is from Sergei, so let's get Scott, Sam and Dr. Fred together and see what he has to say."

"How do you know it is from Sergei?"

"It bears his seal. He knows that I won't consider anything from him authentic if it doesn't have his seal. Not many people know about his seal, so I am confident that this is from him."

Once back at Miguel's camp, they gathered around a table in the dining tent. Max explained that he had just received a message from Sergei, and that he wanted everyone to know firsthand what Sergei had to say.

Max sliced the envelope open and withdrew the letter. The latter said, "Max, I hope all is well with you and your crew. Please return with the pilot to Caracas. I will meet you at the airport. It is important that we talk soon. Regards, Sergei Vassilov."

"Is that it? Do you know what is so important that he needs to talk about?" asked Dr. Fred.

"I haven't a clue. Miguel, radio Carlos and tell him to dump his passengers as quickly as he can and to come back and get me. Looks like I'm heading to Caracas today also. Miguel, is there anything you need from town since I'm going there? Besides beer that is, I know you always need more beer."

Without hesitation, Miguel said, "Tequila!"

"Anything else?"

"I'll make you a list."

"Scott, it looks like I'm going to need the credit card."

A few hours later, Carlos touched down at the private airport in Caracas from which he normally operated. As he taxied up to his hanger, he noticed a familiar face waiting for him. Geraldo and his crew unloaded their gear and headed over to a waiting van. The un-named passenger went over to Sergei and said that he had delivered the package. Sergei reached into his pocket, retrieved a small wad of cash which he handed to the man, and sent him on his way.

Sergei then went over and greeted Carlos. "Hola Carlos, I see that Max did not return with you."

"Hola, Senor Sergei. No, when I saw him, he didn't indicate that he wanted to come back with me to Caracas. However, when I was about half way back here, Miguel radioed me to come back and get Max after I dropped these guys off. After I get gassed up, I'm heading back to get him."

"What time do you think you will be back?"

"It will be at least nine or ten o'clock this evening. I can't go any faster."

"That's okay. When you get Max, tell him that I will meet him here, and that I will arrange a place for him to stay."

"Okay. Do you want me to give you a call later with our ETA?"

"No, that won't be necessary. I'll just meet you here."

CHAPTER 23

Félix dropped Geraldo off at a local address where he had arranged to meet some of his professional associates. Félix and his comrades then set off on their mission to place and activate the beacon in a high mountainous area. But first, they made a stop at the first laundromat that they found. They had their priorities, and this stop was at the top of their list.

The address where Geraldo was belonged to a modest Spanish styled hacienda surrounded by stucco covered wall rife with red bougainvillea. At the gate there was a speaker with an announcer button. Geraldo pressed the button. After a short pause, the gate lock buzzed, and a pleasant female voice from the speaker said, "Bienvenido Señor Ortega, please come in."

Geraldo entered the courtyard and proceeded to the front entrance of the house where he was greeted by his old friend Rudolfo Martinez and his wife Jaunita.

Rudy and Geraldo exchanged hugs, and Rudy said, "Geraldo, it has been a while. It is good to see you. You look like you are doing well. Welcome to my home. I don't think you have met my wife. Geraldo, this is my wife Juanita."

Geraldo said, "It is my pleasure to meet you. However, I do believe that I did meet you briefly a while back before you and Rudy were married."

"Yes, you have a good memory. I remember you also."

Juanita led them to a comfortable sitting place in an outdoor vine covered atrium. Rudy asked, "Would you like a cold one?"

"Of course, have you ever known me to turn one down?"

Juanita excused herself to fetch some refreshments and left the men to their discussions.

Rudy said, "When you called, you indicated that you needed some professional help. You know that I am not in that business any more. I am a happily married man with a business to run. So, with that in mind, how can I help you?"

Juanita returned with three cold beers and some chips and avocado dip.

Geraldo proceeded to inform them with all the details of the Churum River Cave exploration, omitting only the details regarding the aliens.

Geraldo explained that, "We are finally at a point where we can't explore further without moving a large mass of rocks that are blocking the passage. The Russians are looking for any excuse to pressure the government to terminate our effort, and give them free rein to proceed with their investigations. If we can't make some significant progress soon, the Canaima Park Director won't be able to help us. I remembered that you had some connections with the mining industry and therefore might be able to help us liberate some ammonium nitrate so that we can attempt moving the mass of rock blocking our progress."

Rudy laughed, "Geraldo, you can't just liberate a bunch of ammonium nitrate these days. Every batch legitimately manufactured has taggets, so you would be identified as having used stolen goods."

"Yes, I knew that, but we are prepared to claim that we bought it on the blackmarket because of expediency."

"Would the Park Director authorize your usage of ANFO in your exploration?"

"Yes, I am sure he would. He is very supportive of our efforts, and frankly, he resents the presence of the Russians."

"If you are sure that you can secure his consent, I can supply you with everything you need, and you won't have to liberate anything. How much and how soon do you need it?"

"I figure five hundred pounds should do the job, maybe add a couple hundred just to be sure. Can you have it delivered to a private hanger at the airport; I'll call Carlos and have him give you details as to where to drop it off. Can you get it by this time tomorrow afternoon?"

"TOMORROW Afternoon! Are you kidding?"

"No, unfortunately. I am afraid that we are running out of time."

"Well, this will take some doing. I have a few favors that I can call in. We will have to borrow it from another mining company. They will have to fly it here in the morning. This is going to be tricky, because for one of many things we will have to have a good paper trail for this exchange.

Another thing, you realize that the ammonium nitrate and the fuses cannot fly on the same aircraft, don't you?"

"Yes, I do realize that, although I hadn't thought it through. I have an idea, can they deliver it to Canaima Camp instead of here. That way we can fly the fuses and supplies directly to the mountain in the morning and then the ammonium nitrate tomorrow afternoon. Do you think that will be possible?"

"My friend, we will make it work. Let's make some phone calls."

"One other thing, how long would it take for you to drill a four to six inch well five hundred feet deep?"

"It depends."

"How about on top of Auyán tepui?"

"I suspect it would take longer to get the drill rig in place than it would to drill the hole. But, if everything went right, the actual drilling would only require a couple of days. There are better ways to explore than drilling deep holes"

"There are some roads leading up to there, but they are rather primitive, and you have to travel way to the south and come up the south side of the mountain. I think Miguel said it takes a day or two to drive up that way. That is the reason we always fly in the supplies that we need."

"Well, a big drill rig can't be flown in. I suspect that the site where you would like to drill is not accessible even from primitive roads, so a dozer would also have to be trucked in to make a road. Best bet is that it would take two days to haul in, five to seven days to bull doze a road, another day to set up, then a couple of days to drill. How soon would you be wanting to do this?"

"We don't have any plans to do anything like that just yet. I'm just exploring some possibilities in my head."

True to his word, it was close to ten o'clock when Carlos taxied up to the hanger where Sergei was waiting. Max was traveling light with only a small back pack. Max thanked Carlos for being so responsive to their flight needs especially in light of the short notice he had been given.

Sergei pointed to the car he had waiting, and they departed to a destination unknown to Max. Max asked, "Where are we heading?"

"I have a secure place where we can talk and you can stay for the evening."

They traveled on in silence and twenty five minutes later Sergei pulled into the driveway of a large home in an upscale neighborhood. He pressed a button on the car's visor and the door to a two car garage opened. Once inside and the garage door closed, Sergei said, "We can talk now. This house is secure."

The proceeded to the kitchen and sat down at the table.

Max said, "Okay, it is your nickel. What is so important that we need to meet sub rosa?"

"Max, thank you for agreeing to meet with me. This is important for both of us. This is a long story, so let me begin by telling you that both Dr. Kuznetsov and I work for the same bureau. There are two factions in the bureau, and they have different and essentially opposing missions. I work for the director of the bureau, and my job most often is to mediate between the factions. When we first met, I was filling in for one of the deputy directors, not Kuznetsov, but the other one. Kuznetsov showed up and had me recalled, and now I am back in my regular position."

"What are the two factions and what bureau are you talking about?"

"I'll get to that later. By now, I am sure that you and your team have made some speculations regarding the curious nature of the Churum River Cave."

"You are right, we sure have."

"Will you share your speculations with me?"

"No, at least not yet."

"That's okay. I had to ask. I suspect that you all have thought through a lot of possibilities, and I'll bet that one of the possibilities include the thought that extra-terrestrial aliens are involved."

As he said this, Sergei carefully watched Max for his reaction.

He continued, "Yes, I thought so."

"I didn't say anything" Max protested.

"It's okay. You didn't have to. We suspected that this event was caused by some kind of extra-terrestrial involvement from the beginning. The bureau that I work for will remain un-named, but your government has its counterpart. You all call it 'Project Blue Book'."

"Project Blue Book was terminated a long time ago, back before I was even born."

"Officially, yes; unofficially, no. It still exists. The mission of your Project Blue Book is slightly different than ours. As I said earlier, our bureau has two factions or tracks. One track is to find, identify, contact, utilize, control and exploit to our country's benefit any alien existence, technology, and activities if in fact they do exist. And, I might add that we do believe that they do exist. The other track's mission is diametrically opposite. They strongly believe the opposite. They believe what Stephan Hawking once said which was basically that if an alien race invaded earth, they would be so technically advanced above us, that most likely they would either enslave mankind or exterminate mankind. Both options would bode badly for mankind. So their mission is first to find any aliens if they are here and eliminate them before they can get a beach front on this planet. And second, if they are already established here, to eliminate them and any evidence of their existence. Eliminate all evidence because they believe that if the general population were to become aware of their existence, that anarchy would prevail and governments would be unable to govern. Kuznetsov is the deputy of that faction. What is important is the operative words of what I am telling you, that is 'eliminate all evidence of'. If your team has found evidence of alien existence or activity and Kuznetsov becomes aware of that fact, then you all would become 'evidence'. Kuznetsov would stop at nothing to assure that your team was totally eliminated and your evidence destroyed before you could report your findings."

Max was thinking to himself that not only had they gotten themselves into one hell of a mess, but that they had now put the aliens into greater mortal danger than he had previously thought. He was also thinking that maybe they shouldn't activate the beacon until the aliens were somehow made safe from Kuznetsov. He knew he had to get word to Félix before it was too late.

Sergei could see that Max was gravely concerned, so he said, "I am giving you this information so that you can do whatever you can to protect yourself and your team."

"I appreciate that, but the problem is that we have discovered something. We have been very careful so far, and only a couple of us are aware of what I have found."

"Actually, I am sorry that you found anything. Can you tell me what it is?"

"No. It's not that I have any real concern about telling you, but we don't know what it is. Kuznetsov, as you are aware, cut off our access to your laboratory, and we have no analytical capability of our own locally. We have been trying to think of a way to smuggle it into the States, but we haven't thought of a way that doesn't have great risks of discovery. Currently, we have it squirreled away in a secure place, but we suspect it is a piece of whatever blew up." Max didn't tell Sergei that he knew exactly what it was.

Sergei said, "That's all I have to tell you. I hope it will be sufficient for you to stay safe. You are welcome to spend the remainder of the night here, and in the morning I'll drop you off where ever you like."

"Thanks, I appreciate that. Let me just sack out here on the couch for a few hours, then you can take me somewhere where I can get an Uber."

Early the next morning, Sergei dropped Max off at a local 24/7 Wally-World. Max went inside and purchased a burner phone. The first person he called was Geraldo.

It wasn't light yet, so when Geraldo's phone started ringing, he was more than a little bit annoyed at being awakened this early. He was even more annoyed when he didn't recognize the number. Thinking it was probably a wrong number, he answered gruffly, "Who is this!"

"It's me, Geraldo. Short but urgent message. You need to call Félix and tell him not to activate. Repeat do not activate. Place in a very secure place where only we can retrieve. Then return. You and I need to talk. Where can we meet?"

"Meet me here. I'm in room 332. You know the place."

Max called an Uber, then he headed over to the hotel where he knew Geraldo was staying. He was greeted by Geraldo who opened the door before Max finished knocking.

"What is so urgent that we need to recall Félix?"

"I just met with Sergei at his request. They know a lot more than we have given them credit for, and now we, actually all of us including our new friends are in possibly mortal danger because of what we know. Our safety depends on our successfully concealing what we have found, and that we convey no appearance that we know or suspect the truth. If Félix activates the beacon, and the wrong people get wind of it, then we could be in really bad trouble. That is why I told you to call Félix and tell him not to activate. Were you able to get hold of him?"

"Not yet. I've called and texted him to call me immediately before doing anything. I just hope he gets the message before he gets out of cell phone range."

"Let's call him again now."

Geraldo put in another call and left another text message. "That is all I can do. I don't know where he was headed, so there is no chance that we can intercept him."

"Do you have any associates that could track his cell phone?"

"No, nobody that I can think of could do it."

"Damn, I guess we will have to wait and hope he calls back. I've got an idea. Maybe we can get the U.S. Embassy to help us out. They were happy to help us before."

"It's worth a try."

"Let's get over there."

They called an Uber and thirty minutes later they were signing in at the Embassy, and fortunately the Ambassador was in and happy to see them.

"Mr. Meccum, Señor Ortega, it's good to see you again. I understand that you have been having some trouble with the Russians again. How can I help?"

Max said, "Thanks for seeing us on such short without an appointment, and yes we seem to always have some trouble with the Russians. But this time, it is with one of our own who we sent out on a scouting trip, and we have lost contact with him. He was going to set up a listening device so that we could spy on the Russians like they have been spying on us. What we were planning may or may not be legit, but they have been messing with us at every turn. We felt that we could use a little insight into their plans as well. Anyway, he is not answering his cell phone, and we were wondering if you could track it for us. If he is hurt or just out of range, if we knew where he was, we could go to him."

"That will be easy. Give me the number and I'll have our IT person see what he can do. Meanwhile, give me an update on your progress."

Max told the Ambassador about how relations were rock bottom, how the Russians abrogated their agreement for mutual support, how they dumped the NMI rope down the pit, and how they kept close tabs on everyone's every move. Max elaborated on how difficult exploring the cave beyond the pit had become, and that they may soon be coming to an end. He also expressed his opinion that the Russians knew something that they hadn't shared, and that was the reason for their fanatical interest in the cave. Max also hinted that they had found some unusual rocks that they would like to take back to the States for analysis, but that they didn't want to share them with the Russians. Max hinted that he might like help in getting the samples back undetected, and that he might need the U. S. Government's help in the analysis. The Ambassador assured Max that, if the samples were not too large or heavy, getting them back to the U.S.

would not be difficult. He would place them in a diplomatic pouch and have one of his couriers escort it to the designated destination. Max said, "That would be fabulous."

Just about then Geraldo's phone rang. It was Félix.

"Where have you been? We have been trying to reach you."

"I got your text message to call you, what is up?"

"Max and I are meeting with the Ambassador right now giving him an update on our expedition. After we are done, I'll give you a call back. Stand by."

Max said, "It looks like you were able to track him down."

Just then, the IT guy knocked on the door and stuck his head in to report that he wasn't able to talk with the person with the phone, but that he was able to ping his GPS to get his attention.

The Ambassador said, "It looks like you were successful. He just called."

Max said to the Ambassador, "Thanks. After we sent Félix off, we got nervous and thought we might need to rethink our plan. We got to thinking that if we were discovered, it might create more problems than we are prepared to deal with. We are going to put that plan on hold for now."

After a few more moments of small talk, Max and Geraldo thanked the Ambassador again for his support, and made their exit from the embassy. Once outside, Geraldo called Félix.

Geraldo explained to Félix, "Do not activate the device. Find a very secure place where it can be hidden. We definitely do not want it discovered by anyone by accident. Document its location, and we will see you back at camp if not before."

Félix acknowledged that he understood his instruction and that after completion, he would return to camp.

Max then told Geraldo that they had another couple of jobs to do. First they had to do some shopping for Miguel, and then get back to the airport to receive some blasting supplies. He said that Rudy was having some seven hundred pounds of ammonium nitrate delivered to Canaima Camp, and that the Director need to be given a heads up.

Max said to Geraldo, "Looks like getting the ammonium nitrate to Canaima Camp is going to be the easy part. When we fly it to the mountain top, it is going to be difficult sneaking seven hundred pounds of anything past prying eyes which undoubtedly will be everywhere."

"We can sneak some of it in by using Félix crew's duffle bags. I'm sure that the Russians watched them take three full bags to the laundromat. When they return with three full duffle bags, no one will be the wiser. It will just be three full bags of laundry returning to camp."

"Good idea, that will get three hundred pounds in, but we still need a plan for the other four hundred pounds."

"We need to get Miguel on board so he will be ready to haul the bags to his station. We don't want him to be surprised."

Geraldo asked, "Do you really think you will need more than three hundred pounds of ANFO? That amount will move a lot of rock, especially in a confined space."

"I really don't know how much we need. I only know we will only get one shot at closing the passage."

"I think it is important that we keep the Russians from knowing what we plan to do. I fear that if we try to sneak all of the ammonium in, we will be discovered."

"You are probably right. Look, there will be five of us returning to camp. If each of us could put fifty pounds in our backpacks, that would be an additional two fifty. That might be enough."

"It will be risky, but I think we can manage that without raising suspicions."

"We really need a plan for the entire lot, not just what we can easily carry. Keep thinking about it. When I get back, I am going to need to return to the bottom as soon as possible. So you and Scott are going to have to handle getting the stuff down to us. Remember we are also going to need about twelve gallons of diesel, and what is Rudy sending to detonate this stuff?"

"I think just regular dynamite and an electrical detonator, maybe C-4, I don't really know. I am sure that whatever he sends will do the job."

"That has to be sneaked in also."

"I think that is a good task for Miguel."

"That is a good idea. Let's go shopping for the supplies that Miguel ordered. I like shopping for him. It always involves something good to eat, and right now I'm hungry."

CHAPTER 24

Now that Bufford and Spider had some equipment to work with and a monumental task to conquer, they were setting about doing it with enthusiasm. Peggy and Charlie had scouted out the rift in the roof of the cavern as high as possible without losing direct control of Charlie. This climb was going to be like the first ascent of Yosemite's El Capitan, and Spider was especially excited about doing the climb. This is what she lived for, and now she and Bufford were about to begin one of the most spectacular climbs in rock climbing history. This climb would be a three thousand foot highly technical totally vertical ascent one hundred percent underground.

Using Charlie's camera, they had looked a several possible routes, none of which looked easy, and selected to start on a route that offered several hundred feet initially of free climbing. After the initial few pitches, further progress would require extensive use of anchors.

As Bufford and Spider geared up, Bufford said, "Are you ready for this?"

Spider replied, "Yes. This is for the record books."

Bufford said, "On belay." Spider replied, "Belay on, climbing."

Spider placed her razor chock in her mouth and reached for her first handhold. The rock in the aliens cavern was untouched by the blast that had collapsed and closed the deep canyon two thousand years earlier, so the walls were not glassy slick like they were above the pit. However, the cataclysmic event did fracture the rock walls severely, so handholds were plentiful as were places to place jam nuts for protection.

Spider called down to Bufford and said, "This is fairly easy climbing. I hope it continues like this all the way up."

"Don't say that, you'll jinks us."

"Let's hope not."

Every five to ten vertical feet, Spider would slip a jam nut into a suitable crack and clip the belay line into the attached carabiner, and then move on. All of the aliens gathered around and watched Spider climb. They were fascinated. They had never seen anything or anybody like Spider do what she was doing. It was like watching a gecko slowly move up a window pane. After Spider had climbed about seventy five feet up, she paused and set several secure chocks and clipped in. After she secured the belay line, she called down to Bufford, "Off belay. Come on up."

Bufford clipped a couple of jumars onto the belay line, slipped the rope through his chest box, then he said loudly, "Climbing." As he climbed, he pulled another rope behind him, one much longer than the belay rope he and Spider were using. This rope would become a fixed rope that would allow them to rappel down from and to climb back up to positions on the route. Once he was up even with Spider, he secured himself and prepared to once again belay Spider as she climbed.

This routine continued smoothly for about six hundred feet, and then the easy hand holds and cracks began to disappear. Peggy and Charlie had been monitoring this progress, and providing the on looking aliens a view of rock climbing expertise at its finest, a view of something they had never imagined possible. With Charlie hovering only a few feet away, Spider and Peggy could converse freely.

As the handholds became more and more sparse, Spider remarked, "Well, all good things must come to an end, and it looks like we are at the end of the easy climbing. Now the hard work begins."

Peggy replied, "You made it up a lot further than I thought you would before had to start drilling holes again."

"Yes, but, I think we are there now. Let me make this position secure, then Bufford can come on up and we can decide how best to proceed. Bufford will probably want to take the lead from here since he is much better at drilling holes and setting bolt anchors than I am."

"Okay, while you two are doing that, let me scout around and see if there is a preferred route from where you are."

Peggy started flying Charlie back and forth looking carefully at the rock face searching for what Spider might consider handholds. A hundred and eighty feet above Spider and Bufford, the smooth rock face began once more to show signs of distress and hence more opportunities for Spider to work her climbing magic. Charlie flew over to the left and then higher. This area showed promise for several hundred feet. It wouldn't be easy climbing for Spider like the first six hundred feet was, but Spider thrived on challenges.

Peggy flew Charlie back down and reported, "It looks like once you are over this slick face area, it will be much easier climbing. Do you want me to put a jam nut in a crack up there and clip in a fixed line?"

Bufford asked, "How high up are you talking about?"

"Probably close to two hundred feet."

Bufford was quick to say, "No, that would be much too risky. If the anchor failed, Spider couldn't survive the fall. That option is out."

"I didn't really think so. Several hundred feet over to the left, it looks climbable. There are a couple of large cracks running up vertically that are definitely climbable, but you would have to traverse horizontally for a long ways to get there. My opinion, for the amount of energy that you are going to have to expend going either way, I would expend it going vertical."

Spider said, "I agree. Let's go up."

Bufford took the lead and began drilling. Because of his height, could stand in his stirrups and reach a good five feet above his current position and set a bolt. Then he would clip into the freshly set bolt, climb up, reposition and repeat. At first, he accomplished this feat quite rapidly, but climbing this way is very strenuous and tiring. After several hours of steady climbing, he settled into a rhythm such that each cycle would take him roughly ten minutes to complete. Six grueling hours later, he completed the crossing of the slick rock face and moved into a rock topography that was amenable to Spider's style of climbing.

Bufford shouted down to Spider who had been belaying him the entire time, "I think I'm in an area that you can handle from here on. I am shot and ready for a break. As soon as I secure the fixed line, let's rappel out of here and get a bite to eat."

"Roger that. Are you off belay?"

"Yes, off belay."

"Let me know when I can bail."

A few moments later, Bufford said, "You are good to go. I'll be right behind you."

Once on the bottom, Spider observed, "We are going to run out of rope real soon unless Max can get some more dropped down asap. We have what, twelve hundred feet of rope, one hundred and fifty of which we are using for belay line. We are close to eight hundred feet up now. We will be out of rope in no time."

"You are right, we need to let them know to make getting more rope down here a priority."

Peggy asked, "How are we doing for hardware?"

"Hardware, we have more than enough."

CHAPTER 25

Geraldo checked his phone, "It's Félix, and he says he and his crew completed their mission and are on the way to the airport. He will wait for us there, and we can fly back to camp together."

"Tell him we will be there as soon as we can. Is Carlos on standby?"

"Yep, gassed up and flight plan filed."

"Let him know that we are stopping by Canaima Camp on the way back to talk with the Director. I've got an idea and I'm hoping he can help us with some logistic support. Do you think Carlos' plane can handle all of us and all of our stuff in one flight?"

Geraldo thought for a minute, then replied, "Five passengers plus a pilot, three big bags of laundry, Miguel's food order, and our personal stuff. I'm thinking Carlos may have to make a second trip for the laundry,"

"I think so too."

The rest of the day went smoothly, including the flight to Canaima Camp. Félix told Max and Geraldo where they had hidden the beacon, and how it could be retrieved when needed. Once on the ground, Geraldo and Max went to see the Director to brief him on their plan, not their real plan, to use explosives. Max explained that the Russians were pressuring them to get out of their way so that they could conduct their own exploration and examination of the pit, and that time was running out for our team. Max emphasized that everyone felt that they were on the verge of breaking into the massive cavern that must lie just beyond the breakdown blockage of the passage. The only way they were going to be able to penetrate the blockage would be to blast a lot of the rocks out of the way, and they were here to gain his consent to set off the charge. If we are successful, we will be able to complete our objectives, and the Russians can have the cave to themselves. Max intentionally didn't explain what he really meant by being successful. The Director said that as far as he was concerned, they could blast away to their heart's content.

Then Max asked the Director for a favor. "Sir, all of that stuff that was flown in here earlier today is for the purpose of blasting open the passage. There is at least seven hundred pounds of stuff, and I was wondering if perhaps you could arrange to truck it up to the cave? It would surely be helpful, because it would be difficult for us to transport it from the airfield to our camp unobserved. If it arrived by truck, it could be delivered directly to Miguel's kitchen without raising too many suspicions."

The Director replied, "I'm sure that can be arranged, but you do realize that it will take the better part of two days to drive up there? Will that be okay?"

"That would be just fine. With you trucking in supplies for us, they won't be alerted to the fact that something unusual is fixing to happen. Thank you for your support."

"De nada."

The director added, "The man who delivered the heavy supplies this morning said he would be returning with some additional supplies. He said the two things needed to be kept separate. How am I supposed to deal with the two items?"

Max explained that two deliveries should never be stored together for safety reasons. When separate they are safe. The heavy items could be transported by truck, and Carlos on his next trip would transport the additional supplies.

On the flight up to the top of Auyán tepui Geraldo asked, on behalf of Félix and his crew, if Carlos could possibly manage to bring their laundry up on his next flight. Carlos indicated that of course he would take care of that for them.

CHAPTER 26

Miguel met the flight at the airfield and was dismayed with the number of people and the amount of baggage they brought with them. He said to Max, "I was only expecting you and Geraldo. I can't carry everyone and all this stuff on my little vehicle." Félix indicated that he and his crew would just hike back to the camp. No problem. They had been sitting for most of the day, and it would be good to get a little exercise.

Back at camp, Max briefed Scott on his meeting with Sergei and the reason for recalling Félix from his mission. Geraldo updated him on his meeting with Rudy, and how the Director would be delivering the ANFO supplies directly to Miguel's kitchen, and that tomorrow Carlos would be bringing the detonators.

Scott's only comment was, "Holy crap, this whole mess gets more convoluted by the minute."

Max opined, "After talking with Sergei, I find it hard to believe that the U.S. is completely unaware of what is going on down here. He indicated that Project Blue Book was still active but covert."

Scott recalled the greeting they received from the FBI and DHS when they returned to the States the first time. He suggested, "You know, they may know a lot more than we are giving them credit for. They may just be watching and waiting to see what transpires. They have satellites, and if they want to, they could be tracking our every movement."

"Ouch" Max said softly, "if they had eyes on Félix, they might have seen where he hid the beacon. However, I doubt that they would realize what he was up to, so they might not follow up on it immediately. Looks like our time frame may be getting squeezed from another side."

"That brings up something else", Scott interjected. "The other day, a large helicopter brought in what looks like some heavy equipment like is used in deep mines. Some big winches, much bigger that what they have back there now, and what looks like an enclosed gondola, obviously for lowering people down the pit through the waterfall. Just based on the size of the stuff, I would estimate it will take them at least a week to get it installed. I keep getting inquiries from Kuznetsov regarding how soon out team will be coming out."

"Our time is definitely getting short. We need to blow the passage sooner rather than later."

Max knew that things were going to get even more complicated in the days to come. "I need to get back to the bottom as soon as I can. Also, I know we are going to need more rope, and the only rope we have is the supply rope. I think we need to pull the spare NMI rope out and start using it, and drop the supply rope down for Spider and Bufford. We have two days before the ammonium nitrate gets here, so we should have plenty of time to do the switch. Also, while I'm thinking about it, let's take the com package out of the spare shield and stash it with our new friends as a hedge in case we have to resort to drilling a hole into their cavern in the future. You know where I am going with that thought."

Scott replies, "Yes, and I think that is a good idea."

"Also, I think we need to bring the others in on the real story. I just don't know when. I just know that we need to do it soon, because the longer we wait the angrier they will be at us for keeping them in the dark. Scott, you are in charge here on top, so that is going to be your call. I can't emphasize enough how important it is to keep a lid on this, our lives may depend on how good we can keep a secret. Geraldo, can you and Sam take charge of getting the ANFO lowered asap after it arrives here?"

"Consider it handled, Boss."

"Scott, where is Sam?"

"He's back at the pit."

"Let him know that I will be ready to go back down in about two hours."

"Will do. I just a thought, why don't you take a bundle of magazines, books and other stuff down with you for the aliens to see. Miguel has a pile of those sorts of things lying around the dining tent. No one will miss any of it."

"That's a great idea. Can you get it together for me while I get changed and ready for the descent?"

"Not a problem."

Max departed to don his wet suit and pack his personal gear, and two hours later, he was back at the top of the pit where he was greeted by Sam and several of the Venezuelan volunteers.

Sam said, "Well Max, I hope you enjoyed your trip topside. I wish you could stay longer and tell us more about what is happening."

"I wish I could also, but things are moving fast and we need to get a bunch of loose ends tied up quickly. Scott and Geraldo will be bringing you all up to speed very soon. Meanwhile, there are several things you need to take care of here on the top. Scott is going to be telling you to get the spare NMI rope out and start using it, because you are going to drop the supply rope down as soon as I get safely to the bottom. Scott will give you the details, but basically for starters, we need more rope down there. You will need several more folks back here to manhandle it back to the pit here because it is heavy."

Max clipped himself onto the NMI rope securely and snugly under the shield, and began his slow descent down the twenty six hundred foot pit. This second trip down the pit was not as exciting as his first descent, and was hugely less scary than his recent ascent trip.

Two hours earlier, prior to pulling up the NMI rope, Sam gave Jim a heads up that Max would be on his way back down soon, so when Max arrived on the bottom both Jim and Ted were waiting to welcome him back. They both were anxious to hear all that had occurred over the past couple of days.

Max said, "Sam, I'm on the bottom and I will be clear in a few minutes." Then to Jim and Ted, he said, "Let's get out of this rain, Sam is going to drop the supply rope momentarily, and we don't want to get clobbered when it hits the bottom."

The threesome scurried down the breakdown and into the tunnel dragging the shield with them. Once inside the tunnel, Max said to Sam, "We are clear so you can drop the other rope as soon as you can."

Max began to tell Jim and Ted about the gondola that the Russians had recently flown in, and how much time he thought they had before the Russians were here on the bottom. He put his finger up to his lips to caution them to speak carefully while the com was active. While Max was changing from his wet suit into his caving garb, Sam came on the com and said, "I just talked with Scott, and he suggested that rather than dropping the supply down, that I lower the spare NMI and shield instead. He didn't elaborate on why other than he thought you could use it to extend the range of our communications. He also said that he thought you would concur."

Max thought for a moment and replied, "I agree. That is probably a good idea. Like I said to you before you lowered me, you are going to need help with the NMI. Go see who you can round up to help you with that chore."

"I'm on it. I suspect that it will take three to four hours to get to the bottom for you."

"That's okay, I need to update everyone down here, and besides, We'll need Bufford to help with the NMI. I'll be in contact later, say about four of five hours later."

This was going to work out fine since they decided that they were going to need Bufford's help manhandling the awkward three hundred pound up the four hundred foot climb to the upper passage and then down the mile of passage to the crack above the alien's chamber.

Max said, "Let's go find the others, then I can bring every one up to speed all at one time. Then later, we can come back and get tis rope."

With that, the threesome made their way back to the alien's cavern.

CHAPTER 27

Sam and five of his Venezuelan helpers went to the hidden alcove to retrieve the spare NMI rope. Not knowing whether to leave the spare shield with the spare com transceiver intact on the NMI or to detach it before lowering, Sam decided to leave it intact. He was thinking that it might be good to have the spare shield on the bottom just in case. Just in case covered a lot of possibilities. Their efforts expended in moving the spare rope back to the pit and lowering it did not go unobserved.

Sam spoke into his helmet com to Scott, "Scott, we are lowering the spare NMI rope now. I am leaving the shield and com transceiver attached just in case."

Scott was sitting around a table in Miguel's dining tent with Dr. Fred, Miguel and Geraldo discussing the logistics of transporting the ANFO into the cave and lowering it to the bottom without raising suspicions. "That is fine, Sam. Although we didn't talk about it, I think that is actually what Max wanted us to do anyway." Scott was thinking to himself, "Too bad the detonator and blasting caps aren't here now, they could be sent down with the shield."

Just about then, Dr. Fred said, "Something is happening on the other side of the canyon. A caravan of Russian trucks is coming. It looks like they have a couple of cranes or something."

Geraldo added, "That and two trucks. They must have driven here by way of the back roads, because they didn't fly those cranes into here."

Dr. Fred said, "I didn't know that you could drive big trucks like that on those back roads."

Geraldo clarified for Dr. Fred, "Actually, big military trucks like that can traverse rough terrain like you wouldn't believe. Give them a little time and they could haul tanks up here."

Scott said, "This is bad news. It looks like they are going to make a serious run at the pit. What do you make of the stuff on the trucks?"

"My guess", said Geraldo, "is brute force equipment for attacking the pit. That looks like a big generator and some more winches. That thing on the second truck looks like a diving bell. I'll bet that is exactly what it is, and that other thing looks like a cage of some kind."

"That looks like a mine shaft elevator cage." Scott surmised that they were getting tired of rappelling down to their Bridgeway and having to climb back up each time. "Looks like they are going first class."

Miguel asked, "What is the second crane for?"

"Probably to stabilize the cage, you know, to keep it from spinning, or it could just be for lowering stuff. This complicates things enormously. Sam, are you listening?"

"Yeah, I'm wondering what's going on also."

"Is there anyone standing by on the bottom?"

"I don't think so. I think they all went back to find Spider and Bufford and get everyone up to speed at one time. I told them it would take me three to four hours to lower the NMI, so they will probably be back by then. I'll keep an ear out for them."

"Dang, we need to alert Max that time is getting really short and that things could go south at any moment. We may not have two days before they start lowering that diving bell. Don't lower the shield just yet, I think we may need to wait until Carlos gets back here in the morning with a package. Everyone, let's continue keeping an eye on the Russians so we can estimate just how much time we have."

Sam said, "Scott, I told you I was lowering the NMI a while ago. It is just about on the bottom now."

"That's okay, it was just a thought."

"Do you want me to alert you when they come back for the rope?"

"Yes, please do."

CHAPTER 28

After Peggy welcomed Max back, they all assembled together with their alien friends, and Max began to relate all that had recently transpired, leaving out no details.

Bufford and Spider told Max about their progress, and that they had stopped after a little over a thousand feet and were waiting for the arrival of more rope. The three thousand foot NMI rope would be perfect.

Peggy explained how she had helped Bufford and Spider, but mostly, she had spent her time conversing with the aliens.

Max pulled out the bundle of magazines and books that he had brought with him and gave them to Xyllio, and for once Xyllio appeared to exhibit some excitement. Xyllio immediately shared the magazines and books with Klarrio and the others. Max was thinking that these few publications would give the aliens a better view into the present world than all of their conversations.

Max turned to Xyllio and asked, "What do you make of the conversation that I had with Sergei?"

Xyllio took a moment to reply, then said, "I can infer several things. Kuznetsov appears to be one of that strain of people that we fear. Apparently they have survived unabated to the present and are a deadly threat to our and your existence. Sergei Vassilov appears to be of a strain which we created to aid in our protection. The members of the Project Blue Book that you mentioned could be either, both or neither. We don't have enough information to conjecture one way or another. Until they make their presence known, we have no way to judge. One sad inference that we can make is that the existence of these agencies implies that none of our kind currently exists on this planet."

"That is terrible!"

Xyllio continued, "It also means one of two things. Either they were finally wiped out or else they voluntarily left the planet. If they voluntarily left the planet, we are in a terrible position, because the only device for sending a message to our kind is on our ship down here, and of course its signals do not penetrate these rock walls. We have tried and tried. It will take a lot of time and resources to dismantle it and reassemble it on the surface somewhere, and time is not what we have a lot of now. And, assuming we can be made safe here by blocking the passage and concealing all evidence of our presence, you would have to find another way into here, remove the transmitter, and then reassemble it on the surface all the while making sure that all of your activities go undetected. That will be a very formidable task."

Max said optimistically, "But, given time and resources, that is entirely feasible."

"The other possibility is that our kind was eliminated. If that is the case, then our space ship will still be here. That won't help us much because we are all genetic and biological scientists, not interstellar pilots. But if you could find the ship, you could transmit messages to our kind. The conversation would unfortunately transpire over several centuries, and in the mean time we would be better off down here waiting."

"That is not a really good alternative either. If your ship is still here, what are our chances of finding it? If it is here, I am amazed that it hasn't already been found. There are not many places on this planet that we have not explored."

"If it is still here, it is because it is hidden very well. It is under water and ice in a very remote place where no one would have a reason to look, and if they did look, they wouldn't see anything. They would see a nondescript ocean floor covered with rocky outcrops. It is protected by a sophisticated camouflage that neither radar nor sonar can penetrate, and its dynamic heat signature will perfectly match the surroundings. It is a ghost even to our technology."

"If it is hidden so well, how are we supposed to find it?"

"We know the exact coordinates."

"That fine, but exact coordinates in what coordinate system? I am sure that the coordinate system that you all used several thousand years ago is a bit different than the coordinate systems that we use today to geo-reference everything on the surface of this planet. I know enough mathematics to know that we will need an exact transform to convert your coordinates into something we can use."

"Yes, you are absolutely correct, and that is a problem."

While Jim, Ted, Spider and Bufford were discussing the books and magazines with the other aliens, Peggy was sitting next to Max listening intently to their conversation. She nudged Max and quietly said, "There is a solution. I know how to do it."

Max looked at her and replied with astonishment, "You do!"

"Yes, the mapper is the solution. It has state-of-the-art geo-referencing software. It knows exactly where we are now. Xyllio's ship knows exactly where it is in its coordinate system. We can match up points all over this cavern with great precision. If the mapper software can't do the transform, then I am sure that we can gather enough data for a good cartographer to develop the required transform."

Max gave Peggy a hug and said, "You are a genius. Get busy. Xyllio, who can work with Peggy to start recording data?"

"Tarbonio knows our navigation system best. They can work together."

"Good, now we have two plans to work on, one short term and one long term. I hope Scott has lots of money."

Max interrupted the others, "I hate to break up this party, but we have a long heavy rope to muscle back here. The clock is ticking so we had better get started. Spider, you might as well come with us, and bring that one fifty belay line that you and Bufford have been using. We are going to need it in order to haul the rope from the bottom up to the upper passage."

Spider said, "Bufford and I have been idle, just waiting around for some more rope. I'm ready to climb something, so let's go."

While they were trekking back to get the long rope, Max explained to Jim that either tomorrow or early the next day, the ANFO would be arriving at Miguel's kitchen, and Sam would immediately start sending it down. "Jim, I want you and Ted to take charge of placing the ANFO in whatever place you two determine is the best place to permanently seal this passage. While you all are doing that, Spider and Bufford are going to continue pushing their lead as high and as fast as they can. I am going to be working with Xyllio and Klarrio to learn as much as I can about their starship, its location, and how to get into it when we find it. We don't have much time left, and we have too damn much to do."

Jim said, "I've been thinking about where to place the charge. I think if we strategically place two or maybe three charges at the top of the slot we can bring down that entire pile and completely fill that chamber and the tunnel leading out of the pit bottom with breakdown. If we do that, it will take the Russians years, maybe decades to get through the mess."

"If you all could do that you two will be heroes. If we can secure that much time after we leave here, surely we can find a way to get the aliens to safety. If they give up on clearing a passage through the breakdown, they might try drilling in from the surface. If they use our fake map as a guide, the never will find the alien's cavern. Let's just hope they don't do a comprehensive seismic survey of the mountain top. If they end up doing that, they will find the cavern. We must not let them do that."

"And, just how do you propose doing that?"

"Hell, I don't know, but give me a year, and I'll figure something out."

About then, they arrived at the top of the slot. Jim said, "While I have every one here, Max and I have been talking about how to blast this passage shut. I am thinking that we place the charges somewhere around here, we should be able to pull down this entire mountain of unstable breakdown. It should, in my opinion, fill the bottom of the cave and the tunnel leading to the pit. What do you think?"

Ted said, "If we have enough ANFO, that should work. But, you do realize that you can't just stack the stuff up here and expect it to blow this mountain of breakdown to smithereens. It needs to be packed into holes. I think it needs to be placed in holes down at the bottom of the slot under that overhang where we spent the night. That overhang underpins this entire slot. If we remove that overhang rock and the rock that is supporting it, I think this entire wall of breakdown will collapse. It is not very stable to begin with."

"That sounds perfect. We need to think through the safety aspects before we blast. We will all need to be in a safe place."

"I think", opined Spider, "that means that we all will need to be four or five hundred feet off the bottom of the pit when you light the fuse."

Bufford corrected her, "We won't actually light a fuse, we will detonate the charges electrically. It would be really hard to strike a match in the middle of a waterfall."

"Yeah, I'll bet you are right. Whatever, you know what I meant."

Max said, "Okay, that sounds like a plan. Let's go down and get that rope."

When they got back to the bottom of the pit, the NMI rope was waiting for them in a big pile. As they were unravelling the mess, Sam came on the com and said, "Max, Scott wants to talk with you. There are developments happening up here that you need to know about. Scott, are you listening? Max is back at the pit bottom."

Miguel answered, "I'm monitoring this end of the line right now. Scott is in the other tent at the moment. Hang on and I'll get him."

Scott came running in and grabbed the mike. "Max, the Russians are gearing up for a descent. By our best guestimate, we have at most a week and probably less. You need to be making final preparations down there."

Max replied, "Understood. We will work as fast as we can. What we need next from topside is the ANFO. Until we get it we are going to push a lead as fast as we can. Keep us informed."

The NMI rope was totally soaked so it weighed more than its three hundred pound dry weight. It proved to be quite a chore hauling that ungodly snake out of the pit and pulling it up the four hundred foot high breakdown pile, and then up through the treacherous slot. That task took several hours of hard work, but once they had it secure in the upper passage, the task of transporting it the mile and a half to the alien's chamber was relatively easy.

Once at the crack above the alien's chamber, Jim asked rhetorically, "Do we just drop it down or shall we lower it carefully?"

Ted said, "I'm for lowering it carefully. It has taken a lot of abuse getting to here. Let's not subject it to more than we have to."

"Let's lower away. Someone rig up and rappel down to receive it."

An hour and a half later, they all were on the bottom. They hoisted the forty foot long hank of rope onto their shoulders and marched like a ten legged centipede out into the alien's chamber where they were met by Peggy and Tarbonio.

Peggy said, "Welcome back, I see you found some more rope. Do you think Spider and Bufford will be happy now?"

"Yes, I think so."

"I've got some good news and some bad news."

Max whined, "I don't need any bad news, so what is the good news?"

"Well, the good news is that I am pretty sure that we will be able to work out the required coordinate transform. The bad news is that we can't do it from down here. Their ship is immobile, so the only coincident point that we have for both systems is where the ship sits now. That is one point. We need many more. The good news is that their nav system has stored numerous easily identifiable points from around the planet; the Egyptian

Pyramids, the Rome Coliseum, the Parthenon, the Great Wall of China, and a treasure trove of many other archeological sites that no one today is even aware of. We can actually just look up the coordinates for the sites we know about and generate our transform. It will be a piece of cake."

"Once again, Peggy, you are the bearer of good news. I don't think your bad news was particularly bad."

"Yeah, I know."

"It has been a very long exhausting but productive day, and I think everyone is ready to sack out for a while."

CHAPTER 29

Spider was the first one up and about. She nudged Bufford and said, “Let’s get some breakfast going, we’ve got a big climb ahead of us today. I don’t know about you, but I am very optimistic.”

Bufford sat up and stretched. As he put his boots on, he smiled at Spider and said, “Yeah, you know how I feel, you always do. I’m with you; I think we are going to find a way out of here today, and if not today, then tomorrow.”

“Exactly. I’m ready to get started. Let’s get these lazy bums moving, it’s going to be a glorious day.”

After downing a hearty breakfast, they hoisted the big rope and set off to the bottom of the climb site where they were met by all of the aliens. Although the alien’s faces didn’t show emotion, you could tell by their body language that they were excited to watch the climb.

Max suggested to Bufford, “Why don’t you all head on up and we will un-braid the rope and start hauling it up to you.”

“That’s a good idea.” Spider clipped her jumars onto the fixed rope and left Bufford in the dust as she rapidly climbed up. Bufford said, “Hey wait for me.”

“See you on top, Fat Boy.”

“You are not a nice person, you know that.”

It took Spider a little less than an hour to climb up the thousand feet of fixed ropes. She could have done it faster, but she wasn’t in a hurry. She knew that it would take Bufford much longer to make the climb, and there was no sense in tiring themselves out. This was the easy part. The next two thousand feet were going to be the challenge.

It took about twenty minutes to un-braid the rope. The plan was for

Max and Jim to climb up the first pitch. Then Ted would tie the end of the long rope to the fixed line, and Max and Jim would pull it up to their position. There they would clip the rope into an ascender in the reverse position so that the rope could be pulled up but not slide down. After tying off the rope they would lower the fixed rope back down so Ted could start climbing up to their position. While Ted was climbing up, Jim and Max would climb up the next pitch. At the top of each pitch, the big rope would be treaded through an ascender in reverse position so the rope could continue to be pulled up. If the rope should be dropped by accident, it would fall no further than the top of the last pitch. By the time that Jim, Ted and Max reached Bufford and Spider, they had already added a hundred and fifty feet to the ascent and had time for a morning nap too boot. Now the long rope would become the fixed line to the top of each pitch completed by Spider. The higher they climbed, the heavier the long rope became. It was obvious that it was going to require the coordinated effort of three people to pull the rope up at the completion of each pitch.

The difficulty of the climb was by most people's standard fairly severe, but Spider's routine had settled into a pace that she could continue hour after hour with only brief pauses. This style of climbing was Spider's magic and had earned her the reputation of being one of the finest rock climbers in the country. One thing that was different this time was that she was being more cautious than usual. She was not afraid of making daring moves because she was confident that Bufford would catch her. But on this climb, she was moving slowly and meticulously because she did not want to risk a fall.

After being on the wall for six hours, they were finally pushing through the fifteen hundred foot mark, presumably half way to the top. At this pace, another fifteen hours of climbing would bring them to the top assuming no major problems were encountered. Add on to that, at the very least, five or six hours of rest, and a couple of hours to eat and manage their gear. So within the next twenty four hours they would know if this led to an upper entrance that they could exploit or not.

Spider decided that she needed a break. As Bufford climbed up beside her, she remarked, "This is where Peggy had to give up. I can see why. The walls come together too close for Charlie to get through."

Bufford agreed, "Charlie has an anti-collision algorithm that keeps him from bumping into obstacles. I think he has to stay thirty inches or so from walls unless Peggy overrides him. Peggy would have to manually fly him through these narrows if she wanted to explore higher, and I think she thought that the risk of losing him was too great to try."

Max, Jim and Ted were about a hundred feet below and soon caught up with Bufford and Spider. It had been decided earlier that at the end of the day, the climbing crew would camp out on the wall rather than rappelling down and then climbing back up to continue the next day. This would save several hours each way and conserve energy. So, while the men were dragging the long rope up, Peggy had been working solo at the bottom getting the camping gear organized into three duffle bags and ready to haul up the wall.

Jim whined, "Pulling this damn rope up is a chore, a three man chore. And, it's going to get harder the higher we go."

Max said, "While we have Bufford with us, I think the four of us should pull up the remaining fifteen hundred feet and stash it here. That way as we go higher, we won't have to pull the full weight of the rope at each pitch. Also, as we go higher, we can make mini-stashes to make managing the load even easier."

Spider noted that Peggy was working alone to get the camping gear ready. She said, "I can't tell for sure, but it looks to me like Peggy is trying to haul the gear up the wall by herself. I think you guys should go down and give her a hand. Will our com gear work with this rope?"

Ted said, "I think so, but the gear in the shield down there has to be activated, and everyone has to have their helmet coms on also."

Max agreed in part, "I think there is more to it than that. We don't have the master transceiver down here. Remember that component is located at the top of the pit. What will work though, is the slider that should be inside the shield. You know, the device we clipped into when we descended. One person can clip into that item and talk with the transceiver in the shield. Anybody close to the shield can hear. Unfortunately, we need the slider up here, and the shield needs to be activated down there. Let's pull up some rope then we can go and set it up and help Peggy."

Jim said, "Max, you go on down now, and Ted and I will join you later. The three of us can pull up enough to let Spider and Bufford forge ahead, and then we will come down and help get all the gear up to here. This will probably be a good place to camp this evening."

Max asked, "Spider, how much longer do you feel like leading before we break for the day?"

"I'm good for another four or five hours at least."

"Okay, I'm going down to help Peggy."

Jim said, give us thirty to forty minutes, and we will join you."

"Spider, Bufford, I'll see you all later this evening."

Max rappelled down to meet Peggy. He found her at the top of the first four hundred foot pitch where she was rigging a pulley and ascender system to hoist up one of the hundred pound duffle bag of gear using her weight to make the pull. When Max arrived, Peggy said with a weary voice, "Boy am I glad to see you. These bags are about to whip me."

"I'm sorry. You shouldn't have started doing this by yourself. You were just supposed to get the gear organized and ready for hoisting and hoist rig set up."

"I know, but you all were taking too long. I had the gear ready to go hours ago, and I thought I could make the best use of my time by getting the gear a little ways up the wall. I've got three bags stashed about two hundred feet down. It has about worn me out getting them that far."

"You've done good. Let me take it from here. Ted and Jim will be down in a while and we can muscle this stuff up. By-the-way, is our sleeping gear in the bags?"

"Yes, why?"

"I'm thinking that we need to stay on the bottom tonight, and go back to the pit in the morning to see how thing are going. I know it is touch and go top side. When we get the duffle bags up to here, let's toss our bedrolls out. When we get everything up to fifteen hundred, we can fix something to eat and do a little planning."

"Both of our sleeping bags are in the top of one of the bags. You find them and toss them. I think I'll start climbing up. I'm running a little slow, so I need a head start."

"You wait here for a moment. I'm going on down to activate the shield so we can have some communication capability. I'm going to send the slider up to you to carry to the top. When it is mounted on the NMI, one person at a time can communicate with anyone close to the shield."

"We should have done that earlier."

"I know. Hindsight is a bitch."

Max rappelled to the bottom, activated the shield transceiver, and sent the slider up to Peggy.

Jim and Ted passed Peggy on the way down, and she told them what Max was doing.

Five hours later they were setting up camp on the wall fifteen hundred feet above the floor. Bufford announced that, "As the unofficial camp cook, I recommend for you dining enjoyment an assortment protein bars and fruity energy drinks. Enjoy."

"Ah Bufford, you are indeed a purveyor of such fine cuisine. We are so lucky to have you as our cook."

Max announced that after they finished eating, he and Peggy were going to rappel down and spend the night on the bottom. He would go back to the pit and stay in communication with Scott, and Peggy would continue working with the aliens.

CHAPTER 30

Miguel announced that Max was back at the bottom of the pit and wanted a status report. Scott said, "Good morning Max, I hope yesterday was productive down there."

"Indeed it was. We are putting the NMI to good use, even though it is in a restricted way."

Sam, who was listening, said, "I thought you were going to attach it to the other NMI so you could have extended range. What are you actually doing?"

Max said, "Well, that is sort of what we are doing, but in a different way."

Scott interjected, "Sam, there are some details that I need to fill you and Dr. Fred in on. But first, let me get Max updated. Max, the ANFO will be arriving here within the hour. As it arrives, we will start packaging it to keep it dry and transporting it back to the pit. Sam said that we could lower about two hundred pounds at a time. So, it will require four deliveries, and with everything involved will take the entire day to accomplish."

"I'm here at the pit by myself. The others are busy. Can you put it into hundred pound packages so I can handle it by myself from the pit bottom to a dry place?"

"Sure, but it may be necessary to make more than four deliveries."

"That's okay. I'll be waiting."

"Another thing, all this activity is going to be noticed."

"That can't be helped. Just try to be as discrete as possible. And Scott, get Sam, Miguel and Dr. Fred fully briefed in. Geraldo can help you, because you are probably going to get some grief for not telling them everything sooner."

Sam said, "I knew something was going on."

Max said, "Sam, it is big, bigger than you could ever imagine, and we must keep it completely secret. Absolutely top secret. Our lives depend on it, and I am not kidding about that. That is why we have been so tight lipped, and why we absolutely must continue to keep it that way. We also have to limit the number of people who know because everyone who knows will have a target on their back."

"Holy crap! You have my attention now."

Max continued, "But for right now, we need to get that ANFO down here. There is no time to waste."

For the rest of the day, everyone who could carry a fifty pound pack on their back while Tarzaning made repeated trips back to the pit where Sam loaded the waterproofed bags into special waterproof nylon duffle bags and lowered them to the bottom. The 'everyone' turned out to be Geraldo, Félix, and his two climbing companions. Unfortunately, out of all the gear that Scott had purchased for the expedition, there were only three of those special nylon bags that Scott trusted to be used to lower the ANFO. That created a logistic problem requiring Sam to wait for Max to unload each bag and carry its contents to the dry area before the bag could be returned to the top to be reloaded and another sent on its the way down.

While this supply operation was in progress, the Russians had their own project in motion. One crew of Russians was busy stringing electric wires from topside back to the pit. It was obvious that this was to power the new heavy duty winch that had been off loaded. Several other crews were busy establishing stations which Scott correctly surmised were to control a raft or barge of some sort in the river. The diving bell that the Russians had brought was much too heavy to be carried back to the pit along their bridge, hence the need for the barge. Scott thought it was going to be interesting watching them float that hunk of iron back to the pit. Scott also realized that if they lost control of the barge, it would be flushed down the pit and it would pose an extreme hazard to those on the bottom.

Max needed to be appraised of this situation, but that could wait for a day. That evening, Scott held a meeting at the edge of the escarpment to watch the sun set, and a very weary Max made his way back to the Aliens' chamber to report and to get some much needed rest.

CHAPTER 31

Peggy was a light sleeper. She woke up early and prepared a fresh pot of coffee. Max, on the other hand slept so soundly that in the morning Peggy was reluctant to wake him. But, based upon what he had told her the previous evening, she realized that time was indeed of the essence, so she nudge him gently and said, "Time to wake up and smell the coffee."

Max stirred slowly and sat up cross legged in his bedroll and said, "Morning." Then, when he realized that Peggy had been up for a while said, "Thanks for letting me sleep late. I really needed it."

"I could tell. Here is your coffee." Then after a short pause, she asked, "How are you going to handle today?"

Max sipped his hot coffee and thought for a while. "Today may be our last day down here. Tomorrow for sure. Tomorrow is a possibility, but the next day for sure the Russians will attempt a descent of the pit. That means that tomorrow we will have to blow the passage shut. That also means that we have to make the most of today. I think what will work best will be for you and Ted to support Spider and Bufford on the climb. I'll take Jim and we will rig the charges. That shouldn't take us all day, so after we finish, Jim can join you on the climb, and I want to spend a little more time with Xyllio on what to do after we find their spaceship or else verify that it is not there. Will you be okay with that? It's a long climb up there."

"I'm fresh and rested. It won't be a problem. Would you like a couple of energy bars to go with your coffee?"

"Need you ask? I could eat the whole case of them. You should down several of them yourself; it's going to be a long day and you are going to need the calories."

Peggy giggled, "That is something no guy ever said to a girl, 'You need to eat more calories!'."

"You know what I meant. Besides, you are a tall skinny broad, and you could use more meat on your bones. You know how I like fat chicks."

"You do NOT! And if you call me skinny again, I'll whack you upside the head."

Feigning fear and laughing, Max said, "I'm sorry, don't hurt me. I was just kidding." Then he said, "Let's see if anyone is listening up there this morning."

Max flipped on his helmet com and said, "Is anyone listening?"

Back came an immediate reply from Ted, "We were wondering if you two were ever going to wake up down there. We are making great progress up here. Spider is pushing through twenty three hundred as we speak. Spider said that the passage has narrowed considerably, and in some places it is no wider than thirty inches but the air movement is still really strong. With the passage being so narrow, she has been able to move up really fast. Jim is having trouble keeping up with her and Bufford. But so far he is managing to keep the NMI right up there. We continue to be excited about the possibilities. So, what are your plans for today?"

"Well, I need to steal Jim to help me down here. Peggy will be on her way up soon. You and she will need to take over for Jim."

"We can do that. Fortunately, the higher we go, the lighter the rope that we have to pull up gets. Is there anything we need to know before I sign off and go help Jim?"

"No, Peggy will fill you all in on the latest when she gets up there. Meanwhile, tell Jim he needs to rappel down here as soon as he can. He and I have a lot we need to get done today."

"Roger that."

As Peggy clipped into the NMI rope to begin her climb up to support Ted, Max set off to find Xyllio. He didn't have to look far because the entire alien crew was on the way to meet them and monitor the climb. Max had learned to sense nuances in their behavior, and he could tell that they were very excited. After exchanging greetings, Max brought them up to date, and he explained that they were going to seal the passage no later than tomorrow. He explained to Xyllio that after the explosion, they would need to inspect the blockage from this side to make sure there were no holes left unsealed. If there were, they would have to find a way to complete the job. Max also relayed the optimism that the climbing crew had expressed in regard to finding an upper entrance.

While they waited for Jim to rappel down, Max went on to explain that he needed for Xyllio to provide him with detailed instructions on how to enter the space ship when they found it, how and what systems to activate. Any and everything he needed to be cautious of not touching or activating, and most importantly how to activate the communications console. Finally, he needed guidance on what to say. Max thought Xyllio needed to record something in their native language that he could play back, because there was no reason to expect whoever received the message to be able to understand English. Xyllio agreed that this would probably be the case, and that he would have a detailed package ready for him by the end of the day. One of the items in the package would be one of their translators so they could speak freely into the communications system.

When Jim arrived on the bottom, he and Max headed out to the pit where Max had stashed the ANFO materials. They had a hard day's work ahead of them, transporting the seven hundred pounds of explosives up a four hundred foot stack of unstable breakdown boulders, packing the explosives in suitable holes and crevices, placing the C-4 charges, wiring the detonators, and stringing the detonation wire all the way back to the pit.

When they arrived back at the pit bottom, Max checked in with Sam who was manning communications at the top.

Max clicked on his helmet com and said, "Is anyone home at the top?"

Sam replied back immediately, "About time you checked in, we were beginning to worry. Is everything okay?"

In case there were unwanted ears listening, Max replied cryptically, "Jim and I are here. We are going to be placing the recently delivered supplies in the appropriate locations for later use. Actually, we intend to use them soon, so we hope to get everything in place and ready to go today."

Jim joined the conversation and pointed out that that pushing the new lead was progressing exceptionally well.

Max asked, "Are there any developments topside that we need to be aware of?"

Sam said, "Yes indeed. As we speak, our friends are in the process of rafting some big winches back to here. It is quite the show. However, it appears to all of us to be very risky. They have the large winch loaded on a big rubber raft, the kind you would use to run whitewater rapids. They have stations set up all along their bridge to control the raft as it floats back to here. If they lose control of it, it will quickly be on the way to visit you down there. You need to minimize your time in the pit, because if it gets away from them, there will be very little time to give you a warning. If they are successful, then they will get it installed sometime today. That means they could try a descent as early as tomorrow."

"Depending on how things go today, it may be appropriate for four of us to come topside tomorrow as late as possible. I want to give our crew as much time as possible to push their lead. We really think they are on the right track."

"I take it that you don't want any of our crew down there when the Russians attempt their descent. Am I correct?"

"You are correct. We want to abandon our efforts before they arrive. They will have to figure things out on their own."

"Understood, I'll relay your message to Scott."

"Okay. Jim and I have work to do. We will check in periodically during the day. We will talk with you later."

The rest of their day was spent laboriously placing and rigging the explosives.

CHAPTER 32

By the time Peggy caught up with Ted, Spider was pushing towards twenty seven hundred feet.

Ted said, "You didn't have to come up here. It actually would have been easier if you had stayed on the bottom. I can manage the hauling of the NMI up by myself."

"I know. Remember, I've had to get off the NMI each time you signaled that you needed to make a haul."

"Right. So what is the plan?"

"Max wants us to push as hard as we can today, and if necessary some more tomorrow morning. Then, we either have success or we get as accurate a position as we can of our highest point, and then we begin evacuation."

"Man! We are so close, I can feel it. I wish that we had more time."

Bufford hollered down, "Spider says that she is in some horizontal passage now. We all need to climb on up."

The horizontal passage the Spider had climbed into was a narrow crack, the floor of which was simply breakdown boulders wedged into the bottom of the crack. The passage led off to the east for at least several hundred feet. The floor had occasional holes that appeared to drop all the way to the bottom of the alien's cavern.

When all four were assembled together tightly in the passage, Bufford and Ted pulled up the remainder of the NMI rope, and tied it off securely to a pair of bolt anchors, and a jam nut.

Ted said, "It looks like we have a little less than three hundred feet of rope left."

"That is a problem," observed Bufford. "We are going to have to go down this passage for who knows how far before we can find a place to start climbing upward again. We are going to run out of rope again."

Ted suggested, "Since we are going to have to have rope, why don't we cut the NMI here, and take the remainder with us down the passage. I know it cuts off communication with the bottom, but what other choice do we have?"

"You are right, that is our only choice."

"So, that gives us two hundred and eighty plus or minus and our one fifty climbing rope. I hope we are close to the top. At least, the air movement is still strong, so I think we are still in the game."

The group began moving carefully down the passage laboriously climbing over boulder after boulder. After some five hundred feet of slow progress, Bufford said, "Is this passage ever going to open up?"

Peggy remarked, "It has to some time. Have you noticed that the walls are all wet now? I don't know whether that is a good sign or a bad sign, but it indicates that things are changing."

Spider, who was in the lead, said, "I think you are right, Peggy. It looks like the ceiling is getting higher and starting to open up, and look, there is a small waterfall up ahead."

The water was flowing down the wall from a small opening in the ceiling. Spider said, "Well, it looks like this is where we start going up again. The passage in front of us looks like it pinches off. Get ready to get wet, this is going to be messy."

For Spider, the climb up the waterfall was fairly easy as was squeezing through the small hole. She continued up the chimney for forty feet before hollering down, "Good news, it opens up some up here."

She found a good crack and inserted a jam nut, clipped in and began to belay the others up. Since Spider wasn't carrying any of the climbing gear or ropes, she squeezed through the small hole with ease. It was not so easy for Bufford or Jim. It was a major struggle for both of them. But finally with the expenditure of much effort and equal amounts of cursing and grunting they made it through.

When Spider said that it opened up a bit, she was being overly generous with the meaning of the word 'open'. For her, it meant she could quickly skitter up the narrow chimney, but for the long legged guys, it was still a struggle. Actually it did open up. The width of the chimney remained about the same, but the crack expanded horizontally in both directions so the crack became more of a canyon.

At the top of each pitch, their excitement increased. After several pitches, Bufford said, "There is no way this doesn't open to the surface. Look over there at all that water streaming down the wall. That doesn't smell like it's been filtered. That is surface water! We have to be getting close."

Ted said, "You better be right. We are at the end of the NMI. It looks like we have about ten feet left, so we might as well tie it off here. So, all we have left is the one fifty, if we don't find the surface soon, then we are toast."

Spider was not going to be defeated. If there was an entrance up above, she was going to find it. Up she went stopping every twenty to twenty five feet to belay Bufford up and to set a chock for safety. After four pitches, Spider shouted, "I can see day light!!"

Everybody let out a big whoop! "Way to go, Spider!"

With the sighting of daylight, the end was near, and a huge wave of relief swept over everyone.

Spider said, "We need to shift everything to the right about fifty feet, I can't get through here."

The shift required backtracking a hundred and fifty feet and moving the anchors for the NMI over to the right. The time required to do this was painful, because everyone was extremely anxious to complete the journey to the surface. However, once the anchors were reset, Spider was soon crawling through a small muddy hole into daylight. She pulled the belay line over and tied it to a nearby tree then shouted down to everyone to come on up.

Once everyone was on the surface, despite being muddy and wet, there was much jubilation. This was a mega-accomplishment with huge significance. Ted said, "Spider, Bufford, this is probably one of the most historic accomplishments in vertical caving history, and unfortunately you can't tell anyone about it, at least for now. I want you to know that I feel fortunate in that I have played a small part in your accomplishment."

Peggy added, "Ted is right. Spider, you are an amazing climber, and we all recognize that some of your confidence stems from the fact that you know Bufford has your back. Together, the two of you make an amazing team. You know that this whole adventure that we have been on for the past several weeks could not have been accomplished without you two."

Spider replied, "Thanks for the kudos, but you also know that this is what Bufford and I live for, and we know this has been a team effort all along. We wouldn't and couldn't be here without all of you. This is our accomplishment, and who cares if we can't tell anybody about it."

After their short celebration, reality set in again. Peggy pulled out the mapper, and synced up the GPS. This entrance location was now known within a few centimeters.

Ted said, "Let's explore around some to be sure we aren't close to something that might enable the Russians to find this place."

Ted noted, "This place appears to have a slight indentation, probably the boundary where the walls slammed together."

Peggy noted the presence of some beautiful orchid like flowers growing on the bark of some of the large trees that formed a dense canopy over this area. She decided to take a few with her to show the others. After about ten minutes of exploring, they concluded that indeed they were in the middle of the jungle with no roads or trails nearby, and that the dense jungle canopy hid this area from aerial surveillance. It was late in the afternoon, and the sun was near setting. It was time to begin the long trek back to the bottom of the alien's chamber. They were happy finally to be the harbingers of very good news.

CHAPTER 33

Once the final explosive charges were emplaced and the electrical detonation wires run back to the bottom of the pit, Max checked in with Sam on last time.

"Sam, are there any new developments since the last time we talked?" Max asked.

Sam replied, "Not really. They look like they have completed the installation of the new winch. They have placed it about a hundred feet back from the top of the pit. They are sinking some serious bolts into the ceiling as we speak. I am pretty sure they are to hold a big pulley. I would say they are on schedule to attempt a descent day after tomorrow. They still have to get their diving bell back here and rigged in."

"Roger that. I want the girls and Ted and Bufford to start up early tomorrow morning. Can you have your crew standing by to help in the ascent?"

"Absolutely. I figure if all goes right, each ascent will require about an hour. So after they are all up, we will stand by to get you and Jim."

"Perfect. We will have to do a quick survey to make sure that the passage gets 'opened' before we come up."

"Understood. We will be standing by in the morning. Over and out."

With that part of the plan settled, Max and Jim began their trek back to the alien's chamber hopefully for the last time via this passage. They were met on the bottom by Xyllio and Klario.

"Is there any news from our climbers yet?" Max asked.

"Not yet. It has been quite a few hours since we had any communications with them. Apparently they have had some difficulties. In their last communication, they indicated that they were having to cut the NMI rope and relocate somewhere. We haven't heard anything since then."

"Well, at least that means that they haven't come to a dead end yet." Remarked Jim.

Max said, "Let's try to remain optimistic. Let's go back to the bottom of the climb, and wait for them to call down. We need to start making preparations for leaving in the morning."

Xyllio said with some obvious concern, "What if they haven't found an upper entrance?"

Max replied sounding much more confidently that he actually felt, "Then soon we will have to dig down from the top. They obviously must be fairly close to the surface by now. One way or another, we will establish an upper entrance."

As they made their way back to the bottom of the climb, they were joined by the other aliens. When they arrived, they looked up into the darkness of the ceiling high above and saw nothing.

Max said, "All we can do now is wait." And wait is what they did for another two hours, then from high above they could see the faint glimmer of a light.

Twenty minutes later, Peggy came zinging down the wall in a fast rappel.

As she unclipped from the rappel line, she turned to Max, gave him a hug and said, "I've got something to show you."

She slipped her back pack off and reached inside and pulled out the small bouquet of flowers that she had picked. Max was stunned.

He stammered, "Holy cow, you made it to the top didn't you!"

He didn't wait for a reply, but instead turned and shouted to the others, "They found an upper entrance! They found an upper entrance! Look what Peggy brought us. Man, have you ever seen anything so beautiful! Wow, this is extremely good news. This is good news for everyone." Max turned back to Peggy and gave her another hug.

Jim asked excitedly, "Where are the others?"

"They are coming. We had to rig the climb in multiple pitches, so coming down only one of us can be on any one pitch at a time. Spider is right behind me, I think I can see her light up there now."

Once everyone was down and the hugs and handshakes were completed, Peggy said, "This calls for a celebration. What do we have to drink?"

Bufford replied sadly, "I think we are down to energy drinks and water."

Max lamented, "Why didn't I tell Sam send a case of ice cold beer down when I talked with him earlier?"

"Yes, why didn't you?" chided Peggy.

"Well, I have to admit, earlier, I was very pessimistic about our chances. So, it didn't cross my mind that we would have a cause to celebrate."

"I would have preferred a beer, but I'm so hyped up over this outcome", said Jim, "I think I'll just settle for water. By-the-way Spider, that climb has to be a first."

"Yeah, and it's too bad we can't tell anybody."

Max said, "One good thing is now we don't have to feel regret about plugging the passage, and the alien's presence can be concealed a bit longer. The new entrance has bought us some precious time. We will have to make the most of it. The next thing is in the morning we will begin our evacuation. I told Sam that we would send the girls up first, then Bufford and Ted. After you all are up, Jim and I will position ourselves a couple of hundred feet off the bottom of the pit, and then set off the explosion. We should be completely safe at that height. After the explosion, we will do a quick survey of its effectiveness. Hopefully we won't need to do anything further. Then we will come up."

Xyllio asked, "What if the explosion doesn't seal off the passage? What then?"

"I'm sure that the explosion will block off the passage. That is not the question. The question is whether or not it will be a permanent blockage or just a temporary inconvenience. I guess that since we now have another entrance, if the blockage isn't permanent, we could bring additional explosives in and finish the job. It's great that now we have options."

Max continued, "Let's get something to eat, then let's go over our plans to make sure we have everything covered. Xyllio, I'm still a bit unsure about how to enter your spaceship assuming we ever find it."

"I have provided you with detailed instructions that I am sure you will find adequate." Xyllio reassured him.

Ted was thinking ahead as to how the Russians were going to react when they hear the explosion. He said, "I think there is going to be hell to pay when they find that the passage has been blocked. We need to have a planned response."

Max said, "I'm sure they will throw one hell of a tantrum, and try to get us thrown off the site. We are going to be leaving anyway, so it is all going to be after the fact. 'We tried to open the passage; we failed'. End of story, move on. Hopefully, we are going to close the door on their finding anything here. We will need to get them to focus their attention elsewhere. I've got an idea. What if after we leave this site, we activate the beacon somewhere remote from here? If we appear to abandon all of our efforts here, maybe they will also since there will be no place for them to explore beyond the bottom of the pit. If we are not here, and Miguel closes up his shop, I'll bet they will close shop here also, and chase the beacon."

Ted said, "I love it! I wouldn't be surprised to see some Russians losing their jobs over this. I'm sure some of their superiors will view all this as a debacle. Also, if everyone leaves, it will be easier for us to maintain contact with our friends here undetected."

Jim cautioned, "We will still have to be very careful, because they will probably maintain satellite surveillance of this area for some time."

"That is true. We can disguise our activities to appear as park personnel doing routine inspections. Once we get under the jungle canopy, our activities will be very difficult to track. Also, if we don't arouse any suspicions, there will be little impetus to track us anyway."

Bufford interjected, "Let's sleep on it. Tomorrow we can blow this place, pun intended."

CHAPTER 34

That night no one was able to sleep hardly at all, so they were up very early the next morning. After they said their good byes, they made their way back to the bottom of the pit. Sam and his crew were awaiting their arrival. Sam said, "Let's get started, the Russians are lowering their diving bell down to the raft. In a couple of hours, they will be starting to move it back to here. So, who is going to be first?"

Max said, "Peggy will be coming up first. She will be ready as soon as she gets her wet suit on. We have the shield ready, so as soon as she is clipped in, hoist her up. Be careful, she has some precious cargo."

"Don't worry Max; she will be in good hands."

As soon as Peggy was clipped in, Sam began the hoist. After all that they had been through the past several weeks, the trauma of the hoisting seemed rather anticlimactic. Peggy survived the bumpy ride with flying colors and soon was safely at the top, and the shield and NMI rope were on the way back down.

Bufford asked Spider, "Are you sure that you don't want me to go up first?"

"Actually" Spider said, "I think I would like for you to go first."

Bufford knew that Spider would prefer for him to be at the top. Should anything go wrong being at the top would be where he would need to be. It would be like he was belaying her from the top.

Over the next three hours, Bufford, Spider and Ted were hoisted to the top of the pit. Then it was time for Max and Ted to set off the explosive charge. Jim clipped his climbing gear onto the supply line rope and began his climb to a safe altitude. Once he was up about two hundred feet, he pulled the portion of the rope that was under him up so it wouldn't get damaged. Meanwhile, Max clipped in under the shield, and told Sam to begin slowly hoisting him up. As he rose off the bottom, he unrolled the detonation wires beneath him. When he caught up with Jim, he told Sam to stop the hoist. Now that Jim was only a few feet away from the shield, his com was active so he could communicate with Sam and Max.

Max said, "Is everyone ready?"

Back came the reply, "Yes."

Max said, "I'm connecting the wires to the detonator terminals. Here we go, three, two, one."

Max flipped the switch. There was a slight pause, and then an ominous roar could be heard above the noise of the falling water. They could see the walls shake, but because they were suspended in midair, they didn't feel the shaking immediately. Suddenly, the bottom of the pit was filled with dust which was quickly washed down by the falling water. The roar and shaking continued for over a minute, and then the ropes began bouncing. A few rocks dislodge from above came whizzing by their heads. It was then that Max realized that they probably should have used a timer to set off the explosion. He didn't anticipate the possibility of falling rocks. That could have been and nearly was a fatal mistake.

After the shaking stopped, Jim switched over to his rack and rappelled back to the bottom, and Sam began lowering Max. What Jim saw when he reached the bottom was that the passage leading out of the pit was completely filled with breakdown, and the bottom of the pit was covered with a few additional feet of debris. When Max reached the bottom, they agreed that the blast was a complete success.

Max said, "Beam me up Sam."

Jim said, "Let me clip in under you, and we can both get out of here at the same time."

By the time that Max and Jim reached the top, Peggy, Spider, Bufford and Ted were already on their way out of the cave, and several of the Russians were converging on Sam to find out what had just occurred. They were in the process of floating their diving bell back when the explosion occurred. They thought an earthquake had happened, and tied off the raft about half way back to the pit. Sam lied and said that he didn't know what had happened, but that he was pulling his equipment out of the pit.

True to his word, Sam had a full contingent of help lined up to manage things at the top of the pit. They already had the supply line pulled up and were busy braiding it so it could be transported out of the cave. A second team was doubling and redoubling the NMI as it came up so it could be braided. Jim and Max joined the effort and began taking down the master communications controller that interfaced with the NMI and the shield. Max and Jim took on the task of taking the master controller out of the cave, and left Sam and his crew to deal with the rest of the equipment. Max told Sam not to worry about the winches or the generators that powered them. If time permitted, they would come back for them later. Right now, they wanted to get off the mountain as soon as they could.

At first, the Russians assumed that there had been a small earthquake, nothing large enough to be concerned about. But sooner or later, they were going to put two and two together and realize that the recent flurry of activity coupled with the Americans leaving the mountain and the earthquake were somehow connected. That sooner or later would be the next day when they lowered their diving bell with two of their scientists aboard and discovered that the bottom of the pit was covered with twenty feet of water and the passage out of the pit was totally blocked. They rightly concluded that this was no coincidence, and were demanding an explanation from the Americans.

By this time, the Americans had loaded as much of their gear on the Director's truck as it could hold, and were preparing to send it on its two day drive down to Canaima Camp. They left no doubt that they were leaving the mountain. A complete breakdown of their camp would fill two trucks, so they had to prioritize what was packed up first, what could wait for the second truck, and what was to be left for Miguel to store.

Everyone was in high spirits including those who were not fully briefed on all that had transpired. Miguel was preparing one of his Caracas Cuisine special meals for the entire crew, and Carlos had recently replenished Miguel's beer supply.

While everyone else was busy packing, Max pulled Geraldo aside and told him of his plan to convince the Russians that they were permanently leaving the site, and that he wanted to direct their attention elsewhere. He asked Geraldo, "How freely can Félix and his associates travel between different countries in South America?"

Geraldo replied, "People with legitimate business or enough money can travel pretty much as they please."

"Do you think one of them could get the beacon and smuggle it into Peru, take it to Machu Picchu, then hide and activate it? Could they do that and not get caught?"

"That would be a piece of cake for my special ops guys."

"Could they travel under assumed names so that their visit couldn't be traced back to you or us?"

"Like I implied earlier, with a little money, anything is possible."

"Put that action into motion."

"Consider it done. Is there a required timeline?"

"As quickly as possible, but take all the time necessary to do it right. Also, we need to let all of the cavers that came to help us know that we are shutting down our operations, and that they can return to home. We must let them know how much we appreciate their support, and that Scott will have a little bonus for them. I know some of them are anxious to get home."

"Consider that done also."

Just then, Dr. Kuznetsov and two of his lieutenants drove up in their Russian jeep and stopped in front of Miguel's tent. As Max and Geraldo went over to meet them, Max said, "I was wondering how long it was going to take them. Be prepared for a tantrum."

Kuznetsov wasted no time on niceties as he loudly demanded to know, "What have you done? I know that you did it! We saw your people carrying all those explosives into the cave. What are you hiding? You have destroyed all the evidence haven't you?"

Max calmly replied, "What are you talking about? What evidence?"

"Admit it; you set off an explosion down there didn't you?"

"Well, yes, we set off an explosion, but we weren't trying to hide anything."

"Then why did you do it?" Kuznetsov demanded.

"Well", Max explained, "We have been trying for weeks to push through a mountain of breakdown rubble hoping to find a large passage on the other side. There was lots of air movement, so we knew there must be more passage somewhere. We pushed a lot of leads, but totally without success. They all were blocked by those boulders. We were completely frustrated, and out of other options, So, we resorted to trying an explosive excavation. We felt that we had nothing to lose. We knew that we would either open the passage or make the blockage worse than it already was. I'm sorry, but it looks like we made it worse. So, we are giving it up. We soon will be out of here. We are headed home."

Kuznetsov was so mad he was sputtering. He could not tell if Max was telling the truth or not, but it didn't matter. He yelled, "You don't realize what you have done! This is an important archeological site, and you have destroyed it! You had no right to do it. Your actions are completely irresponsible and unauthorized. There are consequences for your careless and criminal actions."

Max took umbrage with Kuznetsov's acquisitions and replied, "Hey, nobody told us this was an archeological site, and besides if there was something down there, it is still there. You are free to go get whatever is down there. And, by-the-way, the Park Director gave us permission to try blasting the passage open. So, while our actions were unsuccessful, they were neither careless nor criminal."

Kuznetsov knew Max was not telling him the whole truth. Still visibly angry, he turned to leave and said, "I promise you, I will find out what you are hiding."

That evening after Kuznetsov had left, the whole American crew plus Miguel, Geraldo and Félix were sitting around the dining tent discussing the events of the day, and especially Kuznetsov's visit.

Max was looking for an opportunity to broach a subject that had been bothering him ever since he had met with Sergei. He tapped on his beer bottle and said, "Hey everybody, listen up. There is something that I want to discuss, and since this is the first time we have all been together without some pending disaster facing us or some Sword of Damocles deadline hanging over our heads, this may be the best opportunity I'll have to talk to everyone."

Everyone quieted down and turned their attention to Max, and then Sam said, "What's up boss?"

"I believe that we are at a major decision point in this adventure. It has, as I am sure we can all agree, turned out very different from anything we could have possibly imagined when we started out. We just wanted to be the first to bounce the world's deepest pit. Now look at us. Here we are embroiled in an interstellar drama, of which even the barest knowledge means our very lives are at risk. You will have to admit that all of what has transpired was totally unexpected. We sitting here are the only people on this planet who are aware that there are sixty live aliens from a distant star system trapped three thousand feet underground not far from here. Although they have been trapped there safely for two thousand years, their continued existence is now dependent on us. For surely, given time, the Russians will discover them, and that would be disastrous for both them and the world. It must not happen. Some of you may be asking, 'What is in it for us that we should continue protecting and aiding them at the risk of our own lives?'. I for one feel an obligation to do just that since we are the ones who have potentially exposed them and put them at risk. But, there is more to it than that. They represent an unbelievably huge opportunity for major scientific, technological, and sociological leaps for humanity if they can survive the forces that would destroy them or worse, exploit them for evil purposes. Just think, these guys genetically modified some plants to become a food source that allowed them to survive trapped down there for two millennia. Their knowledge could help relieve world hunger. The power source in their ship is clean, renewable, and inexhaustible. It is obvious that the world could use that, and interstellar travel. Well, we are on the brink of that on our own, but our programs could use a big boost. All their stuff is good, but some of their technology, actually a lot of their technology could also be used for weapons or political bullying, social engineering or countless other less than moral purposes. That is not good. So how should we proceed? My personal feeling is that we should work to find a way to harmonize their introduction into our current world in a way that is universally beneficial and protects them as well. That won't be easy, and most likely will be highly dangerous as well. I want each of you to know that if you feel that it is in your personal best interest to walk away, you should do so."

Ted spoke up immediately and said, "Max, I brought this cave to your attention, and I am not walking away now. I am with you all the way."

Scott said, "The Mueller Foundation is all in."

Peggy said, "Where Max Meccum goes, I go. Count me in."

Spider said, "Bufford and I are proud to be part of this team. We can't think of anything we would rather be doing."

Sam said, "This is my home. You made me into a caver. There is no going back for me."

Dr. Fred said, "I am sorry that I have not been able to contribute more effectively to the team effort. I know that I have not carried my weight, but if you will permit me to continue, I would greatly appreciate being included on the team going forward."

Miguel said, "Max, I am not sure where I fit in, but if you have a place for me, I want to be on the team."

"Max, speaking for myself, Félix, and his two trusted associates who are busy packing, we definitely wish to continue being on your team." Geraldo continued gesturing to everyone in the tent, "I think we all realize the immensity of the opportunity we are facing as well as the attendant obligation, and it would be immoral for us not to embrace it with everything we have."

That brought a chorus of "Amens!".

Max said to Miguel, "Permanent Park Ranger Miguel Santos you are definitely a welcome part of this team. I don't know exactly where you fit in, but you are either our first line of defense for our operations here or our last line. I'm not sure which, but we could not be doing what we have been doing without your support."

Then addressing the entire team, Max said, "I am grateful that we are all of the same mind and are willing to see this adventure through. I think it is amazing how much we have accomplished in the short time we have been working together, but I think all that we have accomplished thus far is going to pale when compared to what we are going to accomplish. We are going to change the world, and I am not exaggerating. But, let's not get ahead of ourselves. There is the present, the here and now, that we have to deal with immediately or all is lost."

First off, Max said, "There is certain information that we must protect at all costs, and which I believe we must get off this mountain as soon as possible. Specifically, it is that data which is comprised of a bunch of coordinates in the mapper that would be awkward if we lost. It would mean that we would have to return to the aliens' chamber again before we could move forward. I certainly hope that we don't have to invoke that option, because it would entail taking risks that we need to avoid at this time. There is not a lot of this critical data that we must have to continue, and I think most of it can be hidden in the text of our various expedition logs. Other parts simply need to be memorized."

Scott pointed out that virtually any type of numerical date could easily be hidden in his financial records, and that might be easier, more expeditious, and a lot more secure to do that rather than trying to fit it logically into our trip notes or memorize it.

"Excellent idea. Peggy has all of the important data on the mapper. She can give you a copy, and you can decide how best to hide it in your records."

Peggy asked, "What about all of our other data? We have pictures and video of the aliens. We have our recorded conversations and our notes. These are important data. They document mankind's first modern encounter with the aliens, and I believe that they absolutely must be preserved. Do you think we could ask the Ambassador to give us access to a secure network connection so that we could download it all to Scott's servers again?"

"That is a definite possibility, and I agree, all those data are priceless and must be preserved, but didn't we leave copies of most of that data with Gharrizia?"

Peggy answered, "We left a lot of it with them on an SDD, but by no means all of it. There is a lot of files in which the only copies that exist reside on the Mapper."

Max asked Sam, "Sam, can all the data on the mapper be encrypted securely enough so that if it does get intercepted it will take a decade or so to decrypt?"

"The short answer is yes."

"Is there a relevant long answer?"

"Yes, I need a little time to set up a procedure to do it. But, I can do it."

"Okay, it looks like we need to pay the Ambassador a visit before we exit the country. I think this is a good strategy. If anyone is watching, and they will be watching, they will know that all important information regarding any of our findings will have been sent to Scott's server, and consequently, they probably will not give our carry-on luggage much if any scrutiny. However, Scott, this means that you need to head back to the states a day or two ahead of the rest of us and get ready to receive the data. As soon as you receive the data, you need to air-gap your server and stash the data somewhere where the 'sun don't shine'. They will probably be quick to mount an assault on your server, so be prepared."

"I can handle that. One thing we need to remember is that the data and the encryption keys should never be together in the same place and at the same time except when decryption is to take place, and further, only a few of us, not including me, need to know the keys or where they are to be hidden."

Max continued, "Understood. It appears obvious now that we need to stagger our leaving. We can't all leave at once. I think we should send our support guys home immediately. Then, Félix and his associates can leave on their mission, and Geraldo, you can accompany them as far as you think appropriate. Scott, you need to leave next after you and Peggy hide some coordinate data in your financial records. I suggest that Bufford and Spider leave with you. You all can call back and let us know what kind of scrutiny you get. Meanwhile, the rest of us will pay the Ambassador a visit. After that, I think the rest of us will carouse around Caracas just to mess with the minds of whoever is watching. After that, the rest of us can head home. Ted, I think you and Dr. Fred should take some rock samples, and see if you can get them through Customs and security. I think we all need to be prepared to be questioned by our friends from the FBI, CIA, and DHS when we land stateside. Then after we are settled, I'll contact everyone, and we can rendezvous somewhere to plan our future moves. Miguel, you are going to be left here all alone. Do you think you will be okay?"

"I'll be okay, but I am certain that I will miss all of you. Do you really think we will all ever get together again?"

"Absolutely. We will all get together again soon, and then thereafter, we will be meeting together here many times in the not too distant future. Meanwhile, you need to keep tabs on everything that goes on here. Don't let the Park Service transfer you back to Canaima Camp. You are our eyes and ears here. We will communicate frequently after things settle down. One thing I expect to happen is that when the beacon goes off, Kuznetsov will likely turn his attention away from here and direct it towards finding the beacon. You need to make sure that the Park Service continues to push the Russians to complete the aqueduct and restore the water to Angel Falls. That will be key to keeping activity going here that will provide cover for us whenever we need to return."

CHAPTER 35

Over the next several days Carlos ferried those who were leaving first to Caracas and beyond. Sam worked on his encryption scheme, and Ted and Dr. Fred sorted through rock samples trying to decide which were the most appropriate to attempt to take back to the states. Max, Peggy and Jim found themselves with some unexpected leisure time.

Leisure time was a commodity that none of them had enjoyed for months, so they were determined to make the most of it. While Peggy flew Charlie in and out of the cave watching every move that the Russians made, Max and Jim wandered around observing the Russian's progress on the aqueduct and taking into account the large number of military type vehicles arriving with building supplies for the aqueduct. When they weren't overtly spying on the Russians, they spent a little time at the end of each day sitting out near the edge of the escarpment drinking Miguel's beer, eating his special nachos, and watching the day pass in the valley three thousand feet below. Each evening they were rewarded with a spectacular sunset and the knowledge that Kuznetsov was probably going crazy watching them nosing around and doing nothing. It bothered him immensely that they did not act like someone who had a great secret to hide. But, they knew that he knew that they were hiding something, but they also knew that Kuznetsov didn't know what they were hiding. And, they knew that it was grinding at his soul.

Two days after Scott, Spider and Bufford headed back to the states, Scott called Miguel to check in. He reported a minimum of scrutiny, and that all had gone well including the expected greeting and request for a full debrief when they landed. Scott said that the debrief was friendly, but very through. They seemed to ask much more insightful questions than Scott anticipated; it was though someone had coached them on what questions to ask and which topics to probe in depth. Scott said that the debrief lasted over three hours and did interfere with their connecting flight schedules. As Scott signed off, he asked for an extra day to prepare; he didn't specify for what. He didn't need to.

Max said, "It looks like it is time to wrap things up here and head to town. Sam, are our data protected?"

Sam replied, "Yes sir boss, it sure is. And as a little bit of extra protection, I have embedded a Trojan Horse that will wipe everything clean if someone tries to decrypt the data without first disabling the Trojan. This Trojan will follow the encrypted file even when we upload it to Scott's server."

"How about the keys?"

I figure that you, me, Peggy, and Jim should be the only ones with the keys. There are two keys for the encryption, and another key to disable the Trojan."

"Perfect. Let's call Carlos and leave in the morning."

The next morning, Carlos touched down around ten o'clock, and by midafternoon, the group was entering the American Consulate in Caracas. The briefing with the Ambassador went well. He was pleased that the Americans felt that their mission was successful, and that he hoped that they would find occasions to return. They assured him that they would be returning and that they would be bringing friends with them. They explained that as soon as the Russians completed the aqueduct and restored the Churum River flow to Angel Falls the Churum River Cave would become a new Mecca for cavers worldwide. It would be a new tourist destination for the Canaima Park.

They asked for and were granted access to a high speed secure data line, and soon were connected via satellite with Scott's server. Thirty minutes later, all of their data, secret and non-secret, were safely transferred. They made their good-byes, promises to return, and left for the international airport. Their early morning departure the next day was uneventful. All of their fears regarding potential excessive scrutiny gradually evaporated as their arrival back in the states neared without incident. As expected they were met by a cadre of national security personnel, and were ushered through security to a conference room where they gave a debriefing on all of their interactions with the Russians. They promised that soon they would publish their findings in a report, and that they would allow the federal Agencies to review and comment on the report before publishing. This promise seemed to satisfy all of the parties, and the group was allowed to proceed on to Austin.

As the weeks passed, each of their lives slowly began to return to a pace which resembled normal. Normal, however, was a myth. Each and every one of them harbored a feeling that they were being watched, watched by someone or something that was very good and very stealthy. This eerie feeling put a damper on their ability to speak freely among themselves, and forced them to employ extreme measures in the protection of their communications.

Peggy traveled to Huntsville so as to work directly with Scott in the development of the coordinate transform so that the alien's spaceship location could be expressed in modern latitude and longitude terms. Max initially thought it was going to be necessary to actually travel to each of the historical sites to get the corresponding coordinates, but Peggy discovered that there existed an international geophysical data base that registered all of the requisite sites complete with accurate location information. Completing the transform turned out to be a very easy task. Now it was time to discover the location of the spaceship, if it still existed on the planet. This required Max to join them in Huntsville, because only Max knew the alien coordinates. He had memorized them. They were not written or recorded anywhere. Max had insisted on this because if all of their data were compromised, and somehow someone else figured out the transform, the information would be useless to them without the last piece of data which was stored in Max's head.

When Max arrived in Huntsville, the trio cloistered themselves in Scott's SCIF to calculate the last piece of the puzzle. After Max's memorized coordinated were entered into the transform, the spaceship's location was revealed. It was essentially where Xyllio explained that it would be, but now they had exact coordinates. It was located on the bottom of a shallow inlet on the north side of Meighen Island. The inlet was covered year round by twelve to fifteen feet of ice.

Scott said, "I've no idea as to how to organize an expedition to that area. Max, you knew that it was up here somewhere. Have you thought about what kind of effort is going to be required?"

Max shrugged his shoulders and said, "I guess dog sleds are out of the question."

"I suspect you are right", Scott replied. "This is over a thousand miles from the nearest semblance of civilization."

Peggy pointed out that, "Whatever we decide to do, it will have to be stealthy, because, you know every move we make is going to be watched."

"We need to get everyone together and brainstorm this. It may be a more extensive effort than the Mueller Foundation can front. We may need to seek additional resources. Max, do you have any serious suggestions?"

"Well, I can't imagine that it will be more expensive than our Canaima Cave expedition, provided we don't opt for some type of extensive airlift operation. My initial thoughts are that I suspect that we are going to need to charter big boat that can take us into the arctic waters during the summer. I also think we need a cover story for being there, and a diversion activity to take the attention away from us. That is just for starters." Max continued, "I think it might be necessary to return to the alien cavern and do some consulting. Surely they have some technology we can employ that will better our situation."

"Maybe we could start exploring arctic ice caves or something", suggested Peggy.

"That's not a bad idea", agreed Max. "Let's get the group together. Shall we meet here or in Austin?"

Peggy said, "Austin has better burgers and beer, but Scott has the only secure place we can meet. So, I vote for here."

"Your logic is unassailable, don't you agree Scott?"

"I agree, so let's get it setup as soon as possible."

Max put out the word that he wanted to throw a post expedition celebration party, and Scott agreed to host it in Huntsville. He told everyone to be prepared to spend at least a week in Huntsville, because he wanted everyone's input into the preparation of the post expedition report which Scott wanted the Mueller Foundation to publish. Everyone in the know knew that this was just a cover excuse for everyone to get together to plan the next phase of this extended adventure. The party was planned for two weeks in the future.

Meanwhile, Max decided that a quick trip back to Venezuela and Canaima Cave was necessary to coordinate with Miguel and Geraldo, and somehow manage a secret trip back to visit Xyllio.

CHAPTER 36

Three days later, Max and Peggy arrived in Caracas and were met by Carlos and Geraldo, and soon they were landing atop Auyán tepui where they were greeted by Miguel. This time, Max requested that Carlos hang around and enjoy an evening consuming some of Miguel's special Caracas cuisine and local beer. Max wanted an opportunity to evaluate Carlos and possibly invite him into the inner circle. He knew that Carlos, if he were willing, would be an invaluable member of the team. After all, he had been a peripheral member since the beginning.

That evening as they were sitting around Miguel's dining tent, Max asked Carlos, "Carlos, what do you think about what we have been doing here for the past several months?"

Carlos said, "I have heard a lot of rumors and witnessed even more. I have been as responsive as I possibly could in supporting your efforts down here hoping I would have the opportunity to get the real story. You can't imagine how much I have wanted to ask you about what the hell was actually going on."

"You have been an invaluable friend and the support you have provided is appreciated more than you could possibly know. And, this adventure is not over yet. However, there is one thing I would like to know; is there a possibility that you would like to continue with this adventure and become a part of our team?"

"If that is an invitation, without even knowing more, my answer is yes."

"We figured that would be your response, but before I tell you more, there are some things you first need to know."

"Such as?"

"When we started this adventure, our goal was to be the first to descend the deep pit back in the cave. That was an ego thing best understood by cavers. But before we knew what was going on, we found ourselves embroiled in the middle of an international struggle in which the stakes are extremely high. We have found that our lives and the lives of others are dependent upon what we have discovered and upon our ability to conceal what we know. If you join with us, your life will become at risk and become dependent upon the success of how we proceed."

"You must be kidding!"

"I am serious as a heart attack. This is not, by any stretch of your imagination, what we initially planned, but we stepped in it, and now we are up to our necks in it, and we are fighting for our survival."

Carlos thought for a moment, sipped on his beer and said, "That is consistent with some of the rumors I have heard. I suspect that the fact that I have been so closely involved with your expedition that I am already tainted by association. If you all are in danger, I probably am also. I think I would rather know who is gunning for me than to be blindsided. So, as I said earlier, I would be delighted to be part of your team."

"Okay, you are in. I am not going to tell you a lot now, but I want you to plan to attend a party that we are throwing back in the states. It will be more of a planning session than a party, but we need cover for all of us meeting together. You will learn more there. Get your passport ready, and we will cover your expenses. Plan to stay a week or two."

Max went on to tell Carlos about the mystery of the glassified walls of the cave and the speculations that had abounded around explaining their origin. He did point out that all of the speculations were wrong, and that the true explanation related to their danger. He emphasized that their credible denial of any knowledge of the true origin of the wall's condition was key to their survival. Max talked about their Russian involvement and the schism that existed within the Russian hierarchy. He avoided all mention of the aliens or the actual cause of the mysterious explosion.

By the end of Max's briefing, Carlos was experiencing information overload. He was beginning to second guess his decision to be part of the team, but since he had come this far, he was determined to see it to the end.

The next morning, Carlos and Geraldo departed Auyán tepui. Max had given Geraldo instructions for Félix. Félix had been watching the beacon. If anyone had come in search of the beacon, he was to get photos of the visitors. And regardless of whether or not anyone had come in search of the beacon, Félix was to make certain that he personally was unobserved, then he was to move the beacon to another location and reactivate it. He was to continue doing this so long as he could positively remain undetected. Max had faith in Félix's special ops skills. Max was sure that this would cause a stir among the GMH's if they were watching. Hopefully this would draw immediate attention away from Max and Peggy.

Max and Peggy retrieved their caving gear from Miguel, and set out exploring the jungle staying well to the southeast of the cave. Their purpose was to get a good understanding of the dense multi-layered jungle canopy to make sure their actions could be hidden from prying eyes in the sky. They did their daily hikes for several days, making sure that no one was attempting to follow them. It seemed that Kuznetsov had lost interest in them, and had turned his attention elsewhere. Max felt that if anyone tried to track them on the ground that they could easily lose them. Surveillance from the sky was what concerned him because it was critical that they not reveal the location to upper entrance to the alien's cavern.

On the fourth day, they deviated from their daily routine and made their way stealthily through the jungle a mile and a half northward to the hidden entrance to the alien's cavern. They carefully crawled in trying to leave no trace of their passage and began the three thousand foot rappel to the bottom.

Their headlamps alerted the aliens to their arrival well before they touched down.

They were greeted by all of the alien crew who were both happy and concerned with their visit.

Xyllio said, "We are glad to see you again, and that you are safe and well. But, you have returned much sooner than we had expected. Is there a problem?"

"Hello everyone" said Max. "I am glad to see you again, and, yes and no to your question. We have come back because we need your advice."

They proceeded back to the meeting place, and Max explained, "We have the location of your space ship. It was not hard to determine once we obtained the correlating data. The problem is that it is in a very remote location as you had indicated that it was. It is over a thousand miles from any settled location, and it appears to be under some really thick permanent ice. We don't know how we will be able to get there or how we can get through the ice. We are planning a brainstorming session soon to see if we can come up with a plan. The problem is that we are a small band of people with limited resources. Further, none of us have any cold weather training or arctic skills. We have only a rudimentary plan, nothing solid and no details yet. That is why we are seeking your input."

"You do understand the instructions I gave you for entering the ship, correct?" asked Xyllio.

"Yes, that is not the problem. The problem is how do we get there undetected, and how do we get through the ice? We know that we will probably be watched remotely, so we will need to minimize both our visible and our heat signature. I remember you said something about technology you used to conceal the spaceship. Is that something that could be applied to our activities?"

"No, that technology would require access to devices located on the ship. However, I believe that the technology that you actually require should already exist. As for getting through the ice, our device for melting and fusing rock should be applicable for penetrating the ice. It can generate an enormous amount of heat, and on your time scale, it can last indefinitely."

"How does it work?"

"Controlled nuclear decay."

"That should be useful in keeping us warm also."

"It also works as an electrical power source. Your transports should be electric, and you should travel under an efficient thermal blanket. You can't hide all of your heat, but if you travel during a storm, you should be virtually undetectable."

"So, our problem now is to get one of your rock melting devices out of here, and then out of the country undetected. Piece of cake, not! I'm going to refer to your rock melting device as the RMD."

Then Max asked Xyllio, "Just how big is the RMD?"

"It weighs about two hundred and fifty pounds, and occupies roughly three cubic feet, part of which is detachable and is connected by electrical cables."

"How about your little hoverbarrow devices?", Peggy asked, "We could use one of them to carry the RMD back through the jungle."

"Good idea. I was wondering how I could carry it back to camp. That would solve that problem." Max took that idea and thought, "What if we took two of those hoverbarrow devices back? We could use them to make a levitating sled that would carry about five hundred pounds of stuff. It could be pushed with very little effort over the ice, and it would have an insignificant thermal signature. I think our plan may be coming together.

Peggy, you have the best ideas. Now we just have to get these devices to the surface, and back to Miguel's camp."

Peggy said, "The levitated sled was your idea, Max."

"Yeah, but it was you that remembered the hoverbarrow."

The next twelve hours were spent hoisting the three devices to the surface. That was when they noticed that it was nearly midnight. They realized that they couldn't return to camp this late at night, because their head lamps would surely be detected by the ever present eyes in the sky. They would have to camp out in the cave until morning.

When morning came, they crawled once again out of the cave, and placed vines and other foliage over the entrance to conceal it. It was then that they noticed that they were all muddy from the last bit of passage. At first they were in a bit of a panic as to how they were going to explain their appearance, but then Max thought, "We can say, if anyone asks, that we found a promising lead, and we explored it."

They loaded up the RMD on one of the hoverbarrows and proceeded back to Miguel's camp following a twisting and turning path that stayed low under the thick jungle canopy. The hoverbarrow made transporting the RMD virtually effortless. When they got near camp, they stashed the devices, and walked triumphantly into camp. Their muddy appearance was quickly noticed, and reported to Kuznetsov. Later that day, they received a note from Kuznetsov stating that he thought they were through cave exploring. Max replied that there were a few leads that they wanted to follow up on, and that they found a promising lead about three miles to the southeast that they had spent the majority of last night checking out.

Max was sure that Kuznetsov would try to find that mythical cave. He mentally wished him good luck.

Next they had to come up with a good plan as to how they were going to get the devices off of Auyán tepui without raising suspicions. Again, it was Peggy who came up with a good idea.

"Look", she said, "as far as anyone knows, we are here with no real mission. Why don't we have some fun? Let's get some parasails up here and just fly everything down to the valley. We could get everything off the mountain and back to Canaima Camp before anyone was the wiser."

Max said, "Peggy, you are brilliant! Geraldo and his buddies are all parachute qualified. They could bring the equipment up here, and we could make it look like we were having a big photo op party. That would be the perfect cover. Let's do it."

Planning began immediately. Geraldo was contacted and was told to bring Félix and one of his cohorts, and eight parasails, including three tandems. Félix said he and his guys were watching the beacon like they had been instructed. Geraldo told two of them to return and leave one to watch the beacon. Two of them were needed back at the mountain now.

Miguel talked with the Park Director and arranged for boats to meet the parasailers and transport them back to Canaima Camp. Carlos was to fly around and take pictures. Everything was being done in the open, and it appeared that nothing was being hidden, only that the Americans were planning a crazy stunt.

Two days later, the crazy group was assembled and the photo op proceeded. Geraldo, Félix, and Roberto joined Max and Peggy along with several personnel from the Park Service. Roberto, one of Geraldo's trusted trio, was a powerful two hundred and thirty pound short and stocky special ops trooper nicknamed Poquito. The devices were carefully packed in the tandem parasail duffle bags. The plan was for each bag to be flown down as the 'passenger' on the tandem parasails. This wasn't a problem for the two hoverbarrows, because they each weighed only a little over one hundred pounds. The RMD was another matter altogether. It weighed well over two hundred, and fell to Poquito to manage. Poquito's rig could handle a combined load of nearly five hundred pounds, so Poquito plus the RMD would be right at the limit of his chute. It was believed that launching Poquito would be the most challenging task of this whole effort. When the time came to launch, Poquito wrapped his arms around the heavy duffle bag, picked it up, strode to the edge of the escarpment, and looked out over the three thousand foot drop to the valley below. Max, Geraldo, and two park service personnel carefully spread his large chute out behind him holding it up to ensure that it didn't get entangled on the rocks when Poquito launched. A gentle breeze wafted up over the edge of the escarpment. On signal, they lifted the chute into the air, and the breeze rapidly inflated Poquito's chute lifting him straight up. Poquito quickly took control of his chute and sailed straight out over the edge of the escarpment. Everyone gave a big shout and a sigh of relief. What was feared was going to be a difficult and dangerous launch went off with unanticipated ease and precision. Félix and Geraldo quickly followed Poquito.

As everyone watched, the three parasails flew out from the escarpment and then turned back in large descending circles like big colorful soaring condors.

Max remarked to Peggy as she prepared to launch, "Who in their wildest imagination would ever think that right out there circling around in broad daylight for anyone and everyone to see are three of the most technologically advanced devices on the face of this planet."

Peggy quipped back, "And it is our little secret to keep."

And with that, Peggy launched, and shortly afterwards, Max Launched. Carlos circled around overhead photographing the flights from launch to touchdown. Peggy also recorded some fantastic video with her helmet camera. None of the onlookers had any idea that this was anything other than an adrenaline junkies photo op stunt. Several hours later, the devices were safely stowed at Canaima Camp awaiting the next phase of their trip.

The next piece of the puzzle was how to get the devices out of Venezuela and safely into the states undetected.

The next day, Félix and Poquito returned to their task of watch guarding the beacon. Geraldo made plans to stay at Canaima Camp with Max and Peggy until the devices could be moved. Max contacted Scott to let him know that he had three pieces of luggage he needed to ship back to the states, but that he didn't have the Foundation's credit card, so could he arrange shipment. Also, if Sam could come back to Canaima Camp briefly to help fix a problem with Peggy's drones, it would be appreciated. Without a secure channel for communications, it was not possible to tell Scott everything that they wanted to tell him, so Scott was on his own once again until Sam could complete his round trip and relay the messages.

CHAPTER 37

Back in Huntsville, Scott knew Max was trying to tell him something that he couldn't say directly, hence the need for Sam to return immediately to Venezuela. He knew it was up to him to come up with a plan to bring the three pieces of luggage to the states. The problem was that he didn't know what was in the luggage, how big it was, or how much it weighed. Sam had traveled to Huntsville to help in whatever way he could, and now he was going to have to make a quick trip back to Venezuela. But before Sam was to leave for Venezuela, Scott wanted to meet with Glen Neely.

Scott gave Glen a call, "Glen, when would be a good time for you to come over to the office and meet with Sam and Me?"

"You name the time, and I'll be there."

"Okay, how about eight in the morning? Connie will have coffee and donuts ready."

"Sounds good. I'll see you in the morning. By the way, about the donuts, I thought you were a health food nut, what gives?"

"Down in Venezuela, sometimes I ate high on the hog and other times I ate very low on the hog, so now I am just trying to even things out. Besides, I really like donuts."

"See you at eight."

Promptly at eight the next morning, Glen Neely showed up at the office of the Mueller Foundation where Connie met him and led him to the conference room where Scott and Sam were waiting.

"Good morning Glen, can I offer you a cup of coffee and a donut?"

"Absolutely, I have never been known to pass up a free offer."

Connie, who already knew that he took his coffee black and preferred chocolate iced glazed donuts, handed him a cup along with his favorite donut before he finished speaking.

"Thank you Connie, as usual you are ever so efficient. Scott, now that the expedition is concluded, I hope you are going to bring me up to date on the expedition results."

"Indeed I am, except that the expedition is not over. It is a continuing saga, and perhaps the most important chapter is yet to be written."

"Oh really? I thought that once you freed yourselves from the scrutiny of the Russians, you would proceed to your objective unabated."

"Wrong again. Let's move to another room to continue our discussions."

With that, they walked down the hall to the elevator and proceeded to the basement. In the basement was where the Mueller Foundation's SCIF was located, and where conversations could be held in complete secrecy.

Once inside, Scott explained, "First, I want you to know that we are still under intense scrutiny, and we still must guard our every move. Every member of our team is in constant danger, and as best we can tell, the only thing that is protecting us is our feigned ignorance of virtually everything we have discovered. If our secrets became known to our enemies, and we are not really sure who all of our enemies are, or if they had actionable suspicions that we knew what we know, they would take action to eliminate each and every one of us. So, we are being very cautious and trying to project an appearance of not knowing anything. Our appearance to the world is that we are just a bunch of cavers who have just finished exploring the world's deepest pit and are now trying to capitalize on our success. Secondly, we see no immediate way to extricate ourselves from this mess, and even if we wanted to, reasons, morally, ethically, politically, every other 'ally' you can think of prevent us from actually walking away. So, here we are, we now have a new objective and an enlarged set of challenges. We must pursue our new objective to a successful conclusion if we are to survive. It is as simple as that."

"Holy crap, what have you all stepped in? Am I included in the circle of folks at peril?"

"Unfortunately yes. I apologize to you and to you Connie, as profusely as I know how. When I solicited your help, none of us had any idea of what was actually involved, and certainly no clue regarding what we have found. Yet, here we are, and now it is time for you both to know fully what we have stepped in, why you are involved, and why this knowledge is a danger to you as well as to us all."

For the next several hours, Scott and Sam told Glen and Connie every detail they could remember from the past several months.

Connie said, "I knew something big was occurring from the things you were having me do. Even though I have been on the periphery of things, you have involved me in many of the details of the operation, so all of what you just said sort of makes sense now. I am not really surprised; actually I am somewhat relieved and excited to know. I looked at some of the stuff you sent back for me to file away in a secure location, but I didn't have time to look at any of it in detail. I missed the alien connection completely, which is probably a good thing."

"I am stunned!" Glen said. "I need to get my mind fully wrapped around all this. You say you have proof of all this stored away somewhere around here?"

"Yes."

"Can I see some of it sometime?"

"Yes, you can see everything we have."

"And you have more stuff still in Venezuela that you need to smuggle into the states?"

"Yes, and they are probably the most important things we have."

"Wow! Wow! Wow! I guess Geraldo knows everything?"

"Yes, he has been an extremely important contributor to the team. It is safe to say that without Geraldo, none of us would be having this conversation."

"Well, where do we go now, and where do I fit in?"

"Based on the cryptic conversation I recently had with Max, I surmise that the first thing we must do is get the items Max was referring to out of Venezuela and into our hands here. The rest of the team members are involved in active diversions, guarding the items, or trying to appear normal and unconcerned. Basically, the people here in this room need to develop a plan to smuggle the items out of Venezuela and to get everyone safely home. Sam is going back to Venezuela tonight to get information on what exactly what we are going to be smuggling."

Sam added, "Also, we don't want the U.S. Government involved, we don't want the Russians involved, and we don't want the GMH's involved. We need to stay independent."

Glen asked, "Do you have any idea what Max is talking about?"

"Not really, but most likely it is something he got from the aliens, and hence we must protect at all costs."

"I suspect", Sam said, "that it is something somewhat large and bulky otherwise he would have had Geraldo or Carlos involved. However, it must not be too big, because they obviously have managed to stash it at Canaima Camp."

Glen leaned forward, smiled and said, "I don't know if you all believe in serendipity or not, but I may have just the right solution."

"Oh really? Enlighten us please. You have my full attention", said Scott.

Glen explained, "My Dad has a seventy two foot Bertram yacht. He and some of his friends are down in Costa Rica right now fishing. He has had the boat stationed down there for the past three or four months. He has his captain take it to various places around the Caribbean every year, and he and his friends go down and fish for a month or so. It is about time that he brought it back to the states and had it serviced. While it is down there, it would be easy to run the boat over to the ABC's and then to Venezuela without arousing any suspicion. If the items could be sneaked on board, they could be brought back here, and no one would be the wiser."

Scott exclaimed, "That would be incredible! Can you start the ball rolling on that?"

"Absolutely, and I even have my captains license, so after Dad and his buddies fly home, I can go down and take over the boat. You all can be my crew."

"Sam, when you go to Venezuela, you can fill Max in. We can firm up plans on the fly. Sam, you probably need to get Max a dozen or so disposable burner phones so we can communicate more freely."

Sam arrived in Caracas late that same evening and was met by Carlos. When Carlos first started supporting Max's group, he was reluctant to fly into Canaima Camp at night. However, of late he has made so many flights in and out at all times of day and night, a midnight run was no longer a big deal.

Max and Peggy met them at the airfield and drove them back to their cabin in the ATV borrowed from the Park Director.

Max said, "Carlos, I see you are spending the night here also."

"Yeah, it has been a long day, and I can use the break. Besides, I want to know what the latest thinking is anyway."

"Well, fortunately we have four bunks in this cabin, so all is well."

Sam asked, "How securely can we talk here?"

"I'm not sure. I know that there are eyes and ears here, so when we want to talk, we take a walk out in the open or take a canoe ride on the river so we can see if anyone is close. We should keep our voices low, and have some cover noise if possible."

"In that case, we need to wait until tomorrow to talk."

"Understood. Peggy and I have already claimed the bottom bunks, so you two get the top. I hope you don't snore too loud."

Carlos said jokingly, "That sounds like your problem, not mine."

The next morning they all ate breakfast together at the camp cantina, and Sam assumed that there would be ears listening.

Sam said, overtly handing Max the Foundation credit card, "Here is the company credit card you requested."

Max replied, "Thanks, I was getting strapped for cash, and we have a few big bills we need to settle up on, including two invoices to Carlos here."

Carlos said smiling, "You needn't hurry. I know Scott has always paid my bills, and I certainly have enjoyed working with you. I also hope to continue being at your service. You all have been the best customer that I have ever had."

"We absolutely love and appreciate how responsive you have been. You are definitely our number one airline."

Sam said innocently, "Max, I understand that you have some luggage you need to send back to the states?"

Max replied, "Yes, I have three bags of rock samples that Ted collected on the bottom of the pit. He and Dr. Fred were going to analyze them in the Russian's lab before they were kicked out. Ted wants them back in the states so he and Dr. Fred can finish analyzing them. They think they are important, but I have no idea as to how best to get them through customs and security without risking their being confiscated. The last time we entered the states, we got a good grilling by the DHS, FBI and some other guys that didn't seem inclined to identify who they were with."

"Oh, rocks!" Sam said, "I think Scott assumed it was something else you had found that you needed to get into the states. I don't think a bunch of rocks will be too hard to smuggle out of here."

"Hopefully not, but remember, Ted and Dr. Fred thinks they are important, so we can't afford lose them."

Peggy said, "After we finish breakfast, would you all like to go canoeing? Max and I have been having a blast exploring the park and not having a schedule chasing us."

Carlos said, "I'd love to, but I need to get back to Caracas and process my invoices now that I have a number to charge to. I have bills to pay also."

Sam said, "I'd love to go canoeing with you. I'm supposed to get back to Huntsville to help Scott with some stuff, but, what the heck, that can wait for a day."

"Great", Peggy said, "Let's grab some fruit and a couple of water bottles and go. There are some really neat places and fantastic views I'd like to show you."

Carlos departed back to Caracas, and Peggy, Sam, and Max picked out one of the Park's big four man canoes and set out on the days' adventure. When they were about a mile from the main camp area, the river ran through a wide grassy savannah.

Max said, "This is a good place to stop." Then he continued, "Sam, it is true that we have a lot of rocks that we sent back to Canaima Camp earlier by truck, but that is not what this is all about."

"Scott assumed as much. We figured you had something from the aliens that we need to smuggle out of this country and into the states."

"You are absolutely right. About five hundred pounds of stuff. We have two hoverbarrows out of which we, meaning mostly you, me, and Jim, are going to make into a hover sled. We also have one of the rock melting devices, which I have dubbed a RMD. This device can also double as an electric power source. You will be very impressed with its capabilities. We are going to need these devices to get to the spaceship, so they are critically important. Have you all come up with any ideas as to how we can get them home?"

"As a matter of fact, yes we have", Sam was proud to say. "Glen Neely came to the rescue. His dad has a fishing yacht currently stationed over in Costa Rica. They will be through with it for this year in a few weeks, maybe more maybe less. When his dad and friends fly back home, Glen plans to come down and take it over. His dad employs a permanent crew, so Glen will send them home for a while under the guise that he wants to run the boat with some of his friends for a couple of weeks. Then he will take it back to the states for servicing. Glen has his captain's license, so all of this will be perfectly legit."

"So what we need to do is work out a plan to get everything on board without raising suspicion. And, that is going to be extremely difficult considering that we are under constant surveillance."

Sam said, "I've got some thoughts on that also. Correct me if you think my ideas are too outlandish. To begin with, I don't think Glen should dock in Venezuela. If Kuznetsov got suspicious, everything could be confiscated before we left the country. I think he should remain well offshore and we should air drop the stuff for him to pick up at sea. From what I've seen, Carlos could do that, and Geraldo and his crew have the expertise to rig the drops."

"I like your thoughts, and I am sure that Geraldo and crew could make that part work. But, once we get everything onboard the yacht, we still will have the problem of getting the stuff through customs and security back in the states."

Peggy joined the conversation at this point to propose her idea. "I have an idea. It is obvious that everything we do is likely to be tracked. Not up close necessarily, but also probably from not too far away either. So, we need a ruse. I propose that we be somewhat open and let them see our airdrop. They won't for sure know what we are dropping, but they will probably assume it is the rock samples. They will also probably think we are a bunch of bumbling Americans who can't even competently smuggle a bunch of rocks out of the country. After we get everything on board, we hide the alien devices in plain sight. Sam, you can put wheels on the hoverbarrows and make them into some kind of fish handling equipment. Get creative with that idea. You can make the RMD into an auxiliary power device and somehow mount it permanently in the boat so it looks like it belongs there. Write some kind of manufacturing logo's on them so they appear ordinary and official. Smear some fish on the hoverbarrows so they smell used. We can sort of hide the rocks so they are our red herring. They can find and confiscate them if they like. We will object vigorously if necessary."

Max praised Peggy, "Peggy, as usual, you are brilliant. I don't know how you come up with your ideas so quickly, but they are good. Sam, you will need to ply your trade and get whatever materials you think you will need to hide the stuff in plain sight and integrate the RMD into the boat's power system. Peggy and I will meet you and Jim and maybe Ted in Costa Rica and get on the boat there. I'll get Geraldo back here, and he and his crew can prepare everything for the airdrop and coordinate it with Carlos. Let's make sure everyone has plenty of burner phones so we can communicate. I'm feeling pretty good about our possibilities. Let's keep our guards up and make this happen."

Sam agreed, "That's was a pretty good idea, Peggy. Are you sure that you hadn't already thought this through before I got here?"

"Thanks for the compliment. But no, it just came to me as you and Max were talking."

Max said, "Let's get back to camp so I can get Geraldo and crew turned around, and Sam, you need to head back in the morning and let Scott know what we are thinking. He will probably have some good ideas to tack onto this plan. And Peggy darling, how would you like to spend a couple of weeks in Costa Rica before heading back to the states?"

"Honey, I think that would be just lovely. When shall I start packing?"

"Let's see, Sam needs to leave in the morning, Geraldo and crew need to fly back here as soon as possible, and we need to plan a trip to Costa Rica. You don't need to start packing until Carlos brings Geraldo and his crew back. After we coordinated with Geraldo, we can fly with Carlos as he returns to Caracas. Carlos is going to get dizzy flying back and forth."

Speaking sarcastically, Max continued, "I am so glad that for once we have plenty of time to carefully plan things out these life and death decisions and are not being rushed by some arbitrary deadline."

CHAPTER 38

It was early when, as Connie and Scott were pouring their first cup of morning coffee, the security system alerted them that someone was at the front entrance of the Mueller Foundation office. Connie went to unlock the door and was met there by a familiar face.

"Good morning Miss Connie. Please give this directly to either Mr. Mueller or Mr. Meccum. Thank you."

As he turned to go, Connie said, "Mr. Mueller asked that if you ever returned that I ask you how we may contact you should we have a need?"

After a short pause, the familiar face replied, "I'll contact you again soon with that information."

Connie returned inside and quickly took the envelope to Scott. Scott opened it, and it contained another envelope bearing Sergei's private seal. Scott opened the envelope and read the letter from Sergei.

"Dear Mr. Mueller and Mr. Meccum,

I hope all continues to be well with you and your associates. I have received numerous reports regarding your activities. Of particular interest was your explanation as to why you set off the large explosion that resulted in the closure of the passage leading out from the bottom of the pit. Your explanation has been viewed with extreme skepticism, and as a consequence your activities are being monitored even more closely. As I explained to you previously, knowledge can be a very dangerous thing to possess. If you have found or have anything definitive, you must not be caught with it in your possession. Such a revelation would almost certainly prove fatal.

Also, you may or may not be aware that someone activated a very unique beacon. Your team is the prime suspect for having done that, but despite a concerted effort, neither you nor any member of your team has yet been implicated. The beacon has caused quite a stir in some circles, and has resulted in the activation of certain protocols which pose additional dangers to you. They are watching closely, so be warned, be alert, and stay safe.

Regards,
Sergei Vassilov

Scott said, "Well, we anticipated the increased scrutiny, and we hoped the beacon would draw some of the attention away from us, not direct more attention to us. I am beginning to wonder if there are more players in this drama beside us and the two Russian factions. I hope Max and Sam are keeping a tight lid on whatever Max needs brought back to the states."

Scott continued, "Did the delivery person say anything?"

"No", Connie replied. "I did ask him how we could contact Sergei if we needed, and he said he would contact us again soon with that information."

"I'm starting to get real nervous about this whole thing. I have no clue as to how we smuggle anything of significant size back into the U. S. without a high risk of getting caught. Glen obviously thinks whatever Max has can be hidden securely somewhere on his dad's yacht. I'm just not sure, but at this point that seems to be our best shot."

"Who can we trust? Do you think our government is involved, and if they are, can they be trusted?"

"I think we are in this all by ourselves. The interest our government has shown has been, well, very strange to say the least. Sergei may be an ally, but we don't know that for sure. He may just be playing us."

"When is Sam due back?"

"I haven't heard from him, but I expect him at any time. I'm dying to know what Max is thinking."

About then, Glen made his appearance. Normally, Glen would have been there promptly at eight, but he had a personal errand to run first.

"What has happened? I can tell I have missed something already."

"We just received a message from our friend Sergei Vassilov. He is warning us once again to be alert and careful because we are under increased scrutiny. They feel but can't prove that we are behind the activation of the beacon, and he implied that if they, whoever they are, catch us with some definitive items or information; it could lead to serious consequences for us."

"Don't you think Sergei is over playing the doom and gloom scenario."

Scott replied, "Maybe, but I think he is serious."

"What are they going to do if they decide that we have learned or discovered too much?" Glen asked.

"I think they are capable of doing whatever they want, hence our best defense is to keep them convinced that we know nothing of relevance."

Glen stated, "I would be much more comfortable if I had a better concept of who we are hiding from."

"Wouldn't we all. Kuznetsov is the only name and face we can put on our nemesis right now, but we know there are eyes everywhere. We have to assume they are using every technology they have at their disposal to track us, so we must be extraordinarily careful."

"When is Sam due back?" Glen asked.

"Soon I hope."

"I came by because I wanted to let you know, I contacted dad and cleared taking control of the boat when he and his friends head home. When I came in the door, I was optimistic about what we needed to do, now I have concerns. We need to have time to figure out how to handle whatever it is that Max has. I still have a few more errands to run today, so let me know when you hear from Sam."

Later that day, Scott received a text message from Sam indicating that he would arrive back in Huntsville the following evening. Scott texted Sam back to let him know that they would meet him at the airport and then go to dinner.

Shortly before the end of the business day, the man with the familiar face returned and left another envelope for Scott. It was a simple note.

> *If you need to contact me, send me a signal. You are under fairly intense scrutiny, so everything you do is monitored. I will consider anything that you do that is not part of your customary behavior as a signal, for instance if you switch your watch from*

your left wrist to your right, that would be noticed. I will weigh the circumstances and try to determine if your signal is true or if it is accidental. A compound signal will be easier to affirm.

Scott said, “Well, this is good to know. When I blow my nose, somebody is watching. I must be sure to blow it only once, and hold my hanky in my right hand.”

The next day went by without incident. It took Sam over twelve hours to fly from Caracas to Huntsville, so by the time he arrived it was after eight o'clock in the evening. Glen was waiting for them at a nearby German restaurant in Madison where he had a table reserved near the back. He was sure that a foursome sitting a few tables away were there to pick up any little tidbits of intel that he might let slip. So, when Scott, Sam, and Connie came in, he made sure that they understood that their conversations might not be private.

“Hey Sam, how was your flight?” Glen asked casually.

“It was the pits, six hours of flying and six hours of waiting between connecting flights.”

Scott said, “That's what happens when you change your flight reservation at the last minute.”

“Yeah, I know, but Max and Peggy wanted to show me around Canaima Camp before I left. Those two are acting like they are on an extended vacation together. Do you know what they did?”

“No what?”

They had Geraldo and friends come over with all their parasailing gear and they parasailed off of Auyán tepui.”

“No kidding!” exclaimed Scott. “That must have been something to see. I knew they moved their operations from the mountain top to Canaima Camp, but nobody told me they parasailed off the mountain to get there. That is moving in style. I hope they took lots of pictures.”

“I'm sure they did. Carlos flew around up above them and videoed the whole thing. You will be impressed when you see the pictures.”

“I'm sure we all will be. Aside from having lots of fun, did you find out what Max is so concerned about getting back into the states?”

“Yes. He has a bunch of frigging rocks!”

“Rocks?” everyone exclaimed in unison.

“Yes rocks. These are the rocks that Max collected from the bottom of the pit that Ted and Dr. Schillinger were going to analyze in the Russian's lab before they got kicked out. Max says that Ted thinks the rocks are extremely important. He says that some of them appear a lot different from the majority of the samples that were collected. He thinks they may provide a clue as to what formed the anomaly in the pit."

"Holy cow. Have Kuznetsov's people seen these rocks?"

"I asked Max that question, and he indicated he didn't think so. Max did most of the collecting, and he thinks he picked up most of the strange looking stuff, so they probably haven't seen much if any of the rocks like Max has."

"Actually, I am relieved" Scott said. "I was concerned that he had found something that indicated that the Russians were engaged in some sort of covert illegal activity that we were going to be obligated to tell our State Department about. An frankly, I don't want anything to do with our government guys. They have been rather rude to us from the beginning. Now rocks, I think we can handle rocks."

Sam changed the subject; "Did I mention that Max and Peggy are now planning to fly over to Costa Rica to meet Glen when he picks up his dad's yacht?"

"No you didn't."

"I told you they were acting like a couple on extended vacation. I think they are looking forward to spending time on the yacht."

Connie asked, "Is there something going on between Max and Peggy?"

"Who knows. I understand that they have known each other for a long time, so there may be or there may not be. Their relationship is sort of like Spider and Bufford's."

Glen said, "Here comes our food. Eat up, it looks like it is going to be a busy week."

This conversation was duly noted by all persons present.

The next day, Sam and Glen met Scott and Connie at the Foundation Office and cloistered themselves in the SCIF.

Sam started off saying, "I thought about telling you everything last night, but I figured it would be better if I didn't appear to be in a rush. Bottom-line is that Max and Peggy have some good stuff and the rocks are a red herring."

"I figured as much" Scott said, "since you so casually mentioned it. That is why I said I was relieved that it was just rocks that were our problem."

Sam continued, "Max has some really high tech stuff from the aliens that will be useful in getting to the space ship. Peggy came up with the idea to hide those items in plain sight as part of the yacht's equipment, and use the rocks as the decoy items that we are trying to smuggle home. If we can get everything home that will be great. If we have to give up the rocks, then oh well."

Glen asked, "Just what are the real items of interest?"

"There are two levitating transports, and a high energy device that can melt rocks and is a source of virtually unlimited power. The transports weigh about a hundred and twenty five pounds each and can carry between two fifty and three hundred pounds each. Max wants to fashion them into a levitating sled to go over the ice. The RMD, which is what we call the energy device, weighs about two hundred and fifty pounds. The thinking is that we can make this into an auxiliary power source for the yacht, and actually integrate it into the boats system."

"What about the transports?" Glen asked.

"They are much smaller, and I was thinking about putting wheels on them and make them into some sort of fish processors. I need help with ideas on that part."

"I like your idea for the transports. Maybe we should make them into something nasty like chum buckets or cut bait processors. That way, they would be smelly and innocent looking. We could put a little grinder on one end and a sausage stuffer on the other."

"Gross!" remarked Connie.

"That's the response we are looking for!" quipped Glen.

Sam elaborated, "We figured it would take a week or so to put the stuff together and integrate it with the boat, so we thought we would cruise around the Caribbean till we got it done, then head for the Port of Mobile. If we can get through customs there, we can motor up the Tombigbee Waterway to the Tennessee River and from there to Decatur."

"And what happens if you can't get through customs at Mobile?" asked Scott.

"Then we are all going to jail, or going to be dead, or else going to become fabulously rich and famous." Sam replied.

Scott said, "Considering that list of possibilities, I strongly suggest we give a lot of thought and attention to the camouflage job. Let's get Jim involved and get plans made and buy the supplies and whatever else we might need. Glen, how soon do you plan to leave for Costa Rica, and where should Max and Peggy rendezvous with you?"

"I should be ready to leave in two or three days. That will give me a couple of days to spend with dad before he returns. That will be plenty of time for me to essentially take possession of the boat and relieve dad's captain and crew or their duties. So, let's say in five days you, Sam and Jim show up because I will need some help running the boat. Sometime in that time frame, Max and Peggy need to show up."

Connie asked, "What about me?"

"I need you to stay here." Scott said. "Everyone is going to be on the move, and we are going to need a solid anchor, and you are the only one who can provide that."

With obvious disappointment in her voice, Connie replied, "I understand, but it sounds like you all are going to be the ones having all the fun."

Scott said, "It may sound like fun, but it is going to get pretty intense. So stand by the phone and have our attorney on speed dial."

CHAPTER 39

When called by Max, Geraldo, Félix, Poquito, and two other of their special ops brethren quietly returned to Miguel's ranger Station atop Auyán tepui with Carlos.

After they arrived, Max explained, "It is time to completely abandon the beacon. It has served its purpose, and now we have a bigger issue to solve. We need the very best of your special ops skills to deliver some precious cargo to a vessel cruising about a hundred miles off shore. We have three or four packages, depending upon your discretion as to how treat the items, each weighing about two hundred and fifty pounds. One or two of the packages consist of rocks collected at the bottom of the pit, and obviously require no special environmental protection. Two of the packages must be considered semi-fragile, although I suspect that they are in fact quite robust, and will need water-proof and possibly shock protection. The packages will need to be air-dropped. Carlos, I am sure that this exceeds the capability of your Cessna 205, so we will be needing a bigger aircraft to deliver the packages a hundred miles off shore. Also, the packages need to float when they hit the water. So, what do you all need to make this happen? Make a list and identify sources where the items can be purchased. You all are going shopping."

Max pause for a few minutes to give everyone time to think, then he asked, "Any questions?"

In his broken English, Félix asked, "Do we have to buy the stuff, or should we just go and get it?"

Max said, "We need to get what we need fast, so if we can just buy it off the shelf, do so. If it is going to take days or weeks to get it, look for alternative ways to procure what is necessary."

Carlos asked, "I can hire a sky diving plane that can do the job, but the owner will probably want to fly it. Is that okay?"

"That will be okay so long as you are the co-pilot and he doesn't require knowledge of what we are delivering. Do you think your source will be okay with that?"

"Money talks, and besides, I have some leverage with him. So, he will be okay with that."

Geraldo asked, "How much time do we have to prepare and put things together?"

"Two weeks, maybe less."

"Okay Max," said Geraldo, "get your credit card ready, and let's go to town. We are going to need some cash also. Can you get it from your friendly ATM, or do I need to prevail on my friendly ANFO provider for a lucrative loan?"

"You probably need to prevail on your friend, but let him know we are amenable to generous terms."

Max, Geraldo, and Félix boarded Carlos's plane once again for a quick trip back to Caracas. They first visited a local army surplus store and purchased a variety of duffle bags, nylon webbing, water-proofing supplied, duct tape, and several tarps. Next, they set off to meet Rudolfo Martinez in hopes of negotiating a cash loan.

"Geraldo, what brings you back to Caracas?"

"It's good to see you again Rudolfo, but this isn't a pleasure visit."

"Rudolfo, not to be rude my friend, but neither was your last visit. When are you going to visit my home just so we can spend some time as just friends?"

"I hope I can do that very soon. First, may I ask, was our last business transaction consummated to your satisfaction?"

'Indeed it was. Very satisfactory! Have you another proposition?"

"Yes, but this is a little different. We are in a terrible rush, and we need some cash. We don't have time to transfer it from the states without causing major issues. We are hoping that you can help by loaning us the cash we need. We are offering very generous terms."

"Any terms you may want to offer will, I am sure, be more than adequate. As a matter of fact for you my friend, I require no terms. What do you need and how soon."

"Soon. We need to rent an airplane, and the owner will require a substantial cash deposit. Also, we may need to purchase some items on the black market, and that will require cash as well."

Max explained, "We are in town today, and we hope to complete all necessary procurements by tomorrow early enough that we can fly back to Canaima Camp."

"Do you have any idea how much cash you need?"

"Probably around twenty thousand U.S. dollars should suffice." Max replied.

"Let's head to my bank. They are easy to deal with and will keep quiet about cash transactions."

Later that day, Félix visited a local army armory, and spoke to the quartermaster about borrowing five small cargo chutes and some cargo netting. At first, the quartermaster indicated that there was no policy or other provision that would allow Félix to borrow equipment from the armory. However, after Félix explained that policies were generally flexible when circumstances required, and that he realized that in those cases there were costs and cash deposits that were necessary to expedite the process. Once the quartermaster understood, Félix was able to depart the armory with the requested equipment.

Meanwhile, Max and Geraldo met up with Carlos at a local private airfield from where several aero-clubs and small aero-service companies conducted their operations. Carlos was involved in discussions with his associate Pedro, the owner operator of a vintage Cessna 208. Pedro catered to the local jump clubs and also offered his services to ferry cargo for anyone who had the cash. His terms were negotiable depending upon the cargo and its destination. Carlos was feeling Pedro out regarding how he felt about delivering unspecified cargo a hundred miles or so off shore. Carlos knew Pedro had no qualms about that sort of mission, but he used the uniqueness of the proposed operation to exact a premium fee. Carlos didn't know what his biding limit was, so he began using his IOU's to remind Pedro of the times he bailed him out when Pedro's plane was being repossessed for missed payments on his loan. Carlos insisted that Pedro be fair, and assured him that his associates would be more than generous, but that this was not the time to be greedy.

When Max explained to Pedro that this would be an all cash up front deal with a potential bonus upon successful completion of the mission, Pedro's negotiation position became much more pliable, and an amenable deal was soon struck.

Early the next day, the remainder of the items on their shopping list were acquired and loaded on the plane. By early afternoon, they were once again assembled back at Canaima Camp ready to prepare the packages for air-drop at sea.

Max said to Peggy, "You can start packing now. I think Geraldo and crew have everything under control here. If you hurry, we can catch a ride back to Caracas with Carlos."

"In case you haven't noticed, I'm already packed. You are the laggard now."

"Okay, you got me. Give me a little while to check on our flights out of Caracas, and I need to make sure I know where we are to meet up with Glen."

"I'll be waiting by the plane. Is there anything else we need to do while we are here?"

"Not that I can think of, everything is on schedule. Geraldo was telling me that they could have the packages ready to go by tomorrow, so if anything, we are ahead of schedule."

Max and Peggy spent the night in Caracas, and the next morning they caught their flight form Caracas to San José in Costa Rica. In San José, they hired a driver to take them to the small town of Limón on the east coast where they were planning to meet Glen. Once in Limón, they had a small problem. They had not called ahead to make reservations for a place to stay while they waited for Glen arrived on the scene. Fortunately, the driver had a good internet connection, so they were able to find a small bed-n-breakfast that had a vacancy, so they didn't have waste one of their burner phones to call Scott to come to their aid.

Max said, "I believe we are here several days ahead of Glen, so we might as well enjoy ourselves until he shows up."

"And when do you expect him to arrive?" Peggy asked.

"I don't know for sure, but he will give us a call on one of the phones, and let us know where they berth the boat and when to join him. All I know for sure is that it is somewhere here in Limón, and he should be here within a week."

"That sounds good to me. Let's get something good to eat tonight, and hit the beach tomorrow. I hear they have fabulous beaches here, and we may get a chance to do a little snorkeling while we are at it."

Max knew that despite their efforts to appear casual and unconcerned there probably were eyes watching their every move looking for hints that they were other than what they gave every appearance of being. He and Peggy went to great lengths to appear as just a couple of tourists enjoying the sights and sounds of the country, which by-the-way they were. One day they were swimming and frolicking on the beach, the next day they took a train ride through the rain forest, and on the third they went scuba diving. On the fourth day, Glen called and told them to meet him the next day on the boat. The rest of the crew would soon be arriving.

Prior to his arrival, Glen had made arrangements to have the boat provisioned for his guests. This included food, drink and diesel for an extended trip. With a full load of fuel, the boat had a range of over twenty eight hundred miles. They would be able to complete their mission, make one fuel stop, and leisurely cruise to the port of Mobile, Alabama.

The next morning, Max and Peggy enjoyed one last sumptuous breakfast at the BNB.

Max confessed, "These last few days have been most pleasant. Unfortunately, it is time for us to get back to work."

"Indeed it has. I could get used to this kind of life" lamented Peggy. "You don't suppose Glen, and crew could run this next operation without us, do you?"

"Actually, I am sure they could, but we would never live it down if we opted out now. What I mean is that they would never let us live it down" Max corrected himself. "Besides we wouldn't want to miss all the fun."

"I suppose you are right, but still, this has been fun. Do you think we have fooled our nemesis into thinking we are just partying now and have nothing for them to see?"

"I would like to think so, but I have this creepy feeling that eyes are watching us at this very moment."

"Maybe we need to party harder and be more convincing"

Max laughed, "I think you are absolutely right. We need to try harder, and with sufficient practice, we could get good at this!"

"We must use more alcohol in order to be more convincing."

"Good Lord that could be disastrous. You know my limit is two beers at a time."

"Yes, I have noticed how you manage to nurse one beer all night while your buddies down a quart or two. I'll bet that even I could out drink you."

"Now, you are just being mean."

"Sorry, I didn't mean to bruise your ego."

"Apology accepted, just don't use that knowledge to take unfair advantage of me."

Peggy smiled and said, "I would never think of doing that."

Max used cash to settle up their BNB bill, and hired a ride over to the marina where Glen was waiting.

"I was expecting you all sooner. Did you get lost?"

"No" Peggy answered, "We just had a slow breakfast."

"Well, welcome aboard. Let me show you around."

"Wow" Peggy exclaimed, "This is some yacht! What kind of drugs does your dad peddle to afford this?"

Taking feigned offense, Glen retorted, "He doesn't sell drugs, he used to manage several large investment funds, but he is retired now. This yacht and his fishing friends are his life now. This boat has five state rooms including the master state room, and Peggy, since you are the only lady on this cruise; you get the master state room."

"Oh, wow, I don't know what to do with all this space."

"Don't get used to it; I am afraid we won't be doing a lot of sleeping for a while."

Max asked, "When do you expect Scott and crew to get here?"

"Hopefully, they will get here sometime late this evening. They should arrive in San José around six and then it will probably take them another four to five hours to motor over to here."

"Is there anything that we need to be doing in the meanwhile?"

"Just wait for Scott to check in. I have a list of stuff we need to buy locally that wasn't part of the provisioning for the boat. After Scott checks in, we get to go shopping."

"Oh goody" said Peggy laughing, "I love shopping. It's what girls do best."

"I don't think that is the kind of shopping Glen has in mind," quipped Max, "But what do I know?"

Just then, Glen's phone buzzed. It was Scott. Glen answered, and Scott said, "It looks like we will be arriving in San José on schedule. We should be in Limón around eleven this evening."

"Roger that" Glen said. "Max and Peggy are here and ready to go. We are just waiting on you all."

"Okay, we will see you this evening."

Once everyone was on board, Glen said, "Look around, and get familiar with the boat. Pick a place to sack out, other than the master suite; Peggy already has claims on that one. I have made sure that all of our paper work is in perfect order, because, when we get to Mobile, we will be boarded by the Coast Guard. They are sticklers on the paperwork, and insist that it be perfect. Otherwise, you can expect a white glove inspection. Once we cast off, it will take us about thirty hours to get to our rendezvous area."

"Carlos and Geraldo are awaiting our call" Scott said. "We will update them with the rendezvous time and coordinates. After that, things should get very interesting."

Sam asked, "Glen, are the boat's wiring schematics on board?"

"Of course, and that is one of the things you will have to update when you integrate the RMD. Hand written notes are acceptable."

"Any last minute thoughts?" Max asked.

Glen suggested, "Since there are six of us, let's run two shifts of three. We can overlap in time by as much as six to eight hours since we are all used to eighteen to twenty hour days. I'll take shift one with Scott and Sam, and Max, you take shift two with Peggy and Jim. I figure we will stay at sea for however long it takes us to get the RMD integrated into the boat. I have planned for one refueling, but if we need more time that won't be a problem. So, let's get under way."

The next thirty hours were spent sailing northeast from Costa Rica to an open area in the Caribbean Sea approximately two hundred miles directly north of Caracas, Venezuela.

Glen and Max were in the helm together. Glen had been watching the weather and commented, "It looks like we are going to luck out on the weather. For the next couple of days we can expect light winds, and a low overcast, but probably little or no rain. If someone is watching us, they are going to have a difficult time with the cloud cover."

Max replied, "Perfect. There is no reason why we should make it easy for them. I'll bet they are pissed that their satellites are useless."

"You called Geraldo a little while ago, didn't you?"

"Yes, they are loading the plane as we speak. When they get airborne, they will give us a call with their ETA. It's raining down there now, so they have some weather to deal with. Carlos indicated that it wasn't going to be a problem."

"It will take them about two and a half hours in the air to get here."

"Yes, that's about right, maybe a little more. I think the 208B cruises at around one hundred seventy to one eighty knots, so depending on the wind, and whether or not they choose to put a couple do dog legs in their flight path."

"You said Carlos said the weather wouldn't be a problem, right?"

"That's what he said. They can fly above most of this weather, then drop down below when they get near."

Sam poked his head in and said, "Carlos said that they were airborne. Their ETA was three hours. By the way, Geraldo said that he would be joining us. He wanted to make sure we didn't leave without him."

Max noted, "I guess he decided to come after all. When I spoke with him last, he was still undecided."

"I hope he is bringing his passport." Glen remarked. "That would be a problem if he forgot it. You better check with him to make sure before he jumps."

"I'm sure he is prepared, but I'll check just to make sure."

Max said, "I guess it is time for me and Jim to get our swim suits on and get the jet skis ready to launch. It is just about show time."

The next couple of hours passed quickly as preparations were made ready to retrieve the airdropped packages.

Geraldo called in on the satellite phone, "We ducked under the cloud cover a little sooner than we had planned. There is a military aircraft covering us up high. So we are coming in low just so he has radar only eyes on us; no visual. Be there shortly, so be ready."

Ten minutes later, Carlos said, "I have you in sight. Packages will be dropping on your port side."

"Geraldo said, "Package one away." Thirty seconds later, "Package two away."

Carlos said, "Circling around for second pass."

Max and Jim were speeding away from the yacht on the jet skis towards the anticipated splash down spots. The parachutes drifted down slowly and were carried by the light breeze. Each chute carried two packages, because they were rated for much heavier loads than either of the packages alone. Jim chased one chute, and Max chased the other. Both were right on top of their quarry as soon as it splashed down. They quickly cut the chutes loose and latched onto the floating packages and towed them back to the yacht.

Carlos was coming around for his second drop run when Glen asked him to go around again giving them more time to deal with the first two drops. Jim and Max pulled up to the stern of the yacht and Sam and Scott secured the tethers so Jim and Max could go chase the remaining package drop.

As Max and Jim sped off, Scott and Sam struggled trying to pull the bulky packages on board. That task proved to be more difficult that they had anticipated, and after a few futile tries, the opted to wait until they had more muscle to help with the task.

As Carlos approached for the third time, the last package came out the side of the plane, its chute opened and it began to float slowly down. Once the last package was away, Geraldo bailed, opened his chute and expertly guided his chute to the rear deck of the yacht and made a picture perfect landing. Peggy was there to watch and remarked, "Show off!" Meanwhile Jim and Max latched onto the last package and towed it to safety. With adequate muscle at hand, the packages were quickly manhandled aboard and safely stowed. Two chutes were retained along with the netting and floatation for two packages, and the rest of the chutes and materials were deep-sixed never to be seen again. The Cessna 208B returned to Caracas, and aboard the yacht, a short party celebrating a perfect mission was held.

"Now the real work begins" remarked Max. "We have a lot of work to do, and only a short time to get it done."

Later that afternoon, Scott received an encrypted message from Connie. The message read:

Our familiar courier dropped off another message for you.

Mr. Mueller,

Kuznetsov has reasons to believe that you have found and have in your possession evidence of the nature we have previously discussed. He has directed a fast attack submarine, which is currently operating in the Atlantic about four hundred miles northeast of Jacksonville, Florida, to intercept and board your boat before you reach U.S. territorial waters. I estimate that by the time you receive this message, they will be less than forty eight hours away. Do not let them apprehend you with any evidence. The rocks you are carrying are not considered a threat. I recommend you immediately do whatever is necessary to secure your safety.

Regards,
Sergei Vassilov

Max pondered, "How come he knows everything about what we are doing in real time. We just now have the stuff on board?"

"They must have satellite trackers on us all the time as well as eyeballs whenever we are in a port." Sam said with disgust. "I wonder what else they know about each of us."

Glen said, "In forty eight hours, we can only make it to the northern tip of the Yucatan, but then we will need to take on fuel. There is no way we can make it all the way to Mobile before they intercept us."

Geraldo pulled a large scale map of the Gulf of Mexica and the Caribbean Sea out of the map cabinet and laid it across the table. He pondered it for a few minutes and then said, "I think we can make it really difficult if not impossible for them to actually intercept us."

"I'm all ears" said Glen.

"I knew there was a reason you needed to be on board with us. We need your tactical thinking."

"Glen is right" Geraldo pointed out. "Mobile is out of the question. However, if we head northwest so as to appear as though we are going to go around the west end of Cuba and then go north to Mobile, they will have to commit to the southwest and head towards the Florida Straits in order to get to the Gulf of Mexico. However, if instead of continuing to the northwest as we near Jamaica, we cut back to the northeast and make a dash through the windward passage towards Acklins Island; we can trap them on the inside of the Bahamas and we can then proceed northward on the outside. We can stay in relatively shallow water and proceed to Long Island, then to Great Exuma and right on up the chain of cays to Acabo and Grand Bahama."

Geraldo continued pointing to the map, "I can guarantee that when that sub starts a sprint towards the Florida Straits, the U.S. Navy is going to be all over them like a dung beetle on a pile of cow poop. They will have to be very careful, and they can't operate in all the waters that we can. We can track the Navy, so we will know where the sub is. That way, we can time our sprints across open areas when we have a land mass between us and them."

Max asked, "If the Navy will be tracking them so closely, how in the hell could they think that they could possibly justify intercepting and boarding an American registered vessel in international waters?"

Geraldo answered, "I think that option will be out for them. I think instead what they will try to do is ram and sink us and call it an accident."

"Wow, that's a sobering thought" Peggy said softly.

Geraldo continued, "Once we get to the islands, we can play cat and mouse until we either get home free or they are forced to retreat. They can't stalk us for very long before the Navy catches on and runs them off. Then of course we can expect some very close scrutiny from the U.S. because they will want to know what we have on board that the Russians wanted so badly."

"Well" max said, "That hopefully won't be an issue, because we have known all along that we will be inspected with a fine toothed comb when enter the U.S."

Glen said, "That is true, so let the games begin."

Max pointed out, "Let's not lose sight of the fact that we must hide the alien devices in plain sight. It looks like we need to get that done within the next forty eight hours."

Glen set a northwesterly heading into the yacht's autopilot and set the cruise speed to twenty five knots. The yacht could do thirty three knots, but the fuel consumption would go up dramatically. Glen thought it best to save that capability until it was needed.

Everyone else went below to begin work on camouflaging the alien devices. The hoverbarrows were the easy items. The plan was to fit them out with a set of wheels, a fish grinder, and a coat of paint. The sides would be emblazoned with the words 'Mississippi Mud Bait Bucket', and then seasoned well with raw fish parts. After seasoning, they would be stashed away with the other fishing equipment, and should easily pass off even to the trained eye as standard gear.

The RMD presented more of a challenge. The plan was to replace the small auxiliary power plant with the RMD. This required disconnecting the alternator from the small diesel engine, faking up an interface, and then integrating the power output with the yacht's electrical system. It turned out that the mechanical aspects of the project was what was the most difficult, since the diesel engine didn't actually do anything except run. It had no load, but it had to look like it was driving the RMD. The electrical interface turned out to be nothing at all. The RMD proved to be really smart; it sensed the requirements of whatever was attached to it and provided the appropriate voltage type and current. It was as simple as that. The hard part was making it look good, and not look like some sort of boatyard kludge.

For the past twenty hours they had been heading steadily towards the western end of Cuba. Now they were about eighty miles south of Kingston, Jamaica, and there was a large weather front moving in from the west. Glen noted that this boded well. Even though the seas were going to be rough, the heavy cloud cover would obscure their movements from the satellite trackers. The front was coming in at just the right time. Glen reckoned that if he made a sharp right turn now and headed directly towards Kingston, the move would not be interpreted as a change of course, but rather a dash to a sheltered port to avoid the approaching storm. Three hours later they were in Kingston, and the storm was on top of them. Glen took the opportunity to take on a full load of fuel. Two hours later they were headed back out to sea under the cover of the storm, and steering northeast towards the Windward Passage. The seas were rough, but the seventy two foot yacht was very sea worthy and handled the ten foot swells easily.

Geraldo was certain that by now the Russian submarine, with the U.S. Navy quietly in trail, would be heading west through the Straits of Florida in anticipation of intercepting the yacht as it emerged from the Caribbean Sea into the Gulf of Mexico. He was absolutely right. The Russians had already co-opted the Cuban Navy into intercepting the yacht on the false pretenses that they had strayed into Cuban territorial waters. The Russians could then covertly surface, board the yacht, and do whatever they deemed appropriate.

Twenty four hours later, the Russians and the Cuban Navy were waiting for the American yacht to emerge from the storm in the southern portion of the Gulf of Mexico. They were extremely perplexed when it did not emerge on schedule, and instead was reported to be heading north along the eastern shore of Long Island moving rapidly northward Cat Island.

The Russians immediately realized that they had been fooled, and that the only slim opportunity that they now had for completing their mission was to rapidly retreat back and attempt to intercept the yacht as it crossed the Straits of Florida from the Bahamas to Port St. Lucie. They knew if the yacht reached Port St. Lucie, it would enter the Intercoastal Waterway and forever be beyond their reach.

Glen and Geraldo knew that as soon as they emerged from the storm, the Russians would quickly find them. A few calculations showed that the most likely place the Russians would attempt an intercept would be along a hundred mile stretch of open water extending from the eastern end of Grand Bahama Island to Port St. Lucie. Both boats could get to that area in less than fourteen hours. Geraldo knew that their best strategy would be to stay in the shallowest water they could find as they traveled westward through that stretch of water north of Grand Bahama, but in doing so would slow them down. In the end, it was going to be a cat and mouse game. They were fortunate that the Russians didn't have additional assets operating in the Atlantic as they sprinted up the eastern side of the Bahamian Archipelago.

Since they had to slow down considerably navigating through the shallow waters north of Grand Bahama, they knew that by the time they arrived at the western end of the island, the Russians would have had plenty of time to plan an unfortunate open water collision. They realized that now it was much too dangerous to attempt a sixty mile sprint across the open waters to the safety of Port St. Lucie. The only hope they had would be to enlist the help of the U.S. Coast Guard, but that in doing so would mean enduring a protracted interrogation and inspection by all of those agencies they were hoping to avoid.

As they were contemplating the wisdom of this choice, they received another encrypted message from Sergei relayed through Connie confirming their fears. Collectively, they realized they no longer had a choice. They bit the bullet and made the call.

The cat and mouse game was over, and they were escorted safely, not to Port St. Lucie but to the Miami Coast Guard impound area. Glen went through all of the document and physical inspections required by the Coast Guard, and those inspections were passed satisfactorily. After the inspections were completed, the Coast Guard Commander that performed the inspections told Glen that they were leery of Glen's claim that they were being tracked and threatened by a Russian submarine. He said that they normally would not respond to a request that they deemed nonsense, but that obviously someone in the upper hierarchy took that claim seriously. As a consequence, he informed Glen that the yacht was being impounded and he and his crew were to being detained for questioning. He informed Glen that the people that gave that direction would be arriving in the morning, and until then no one would be permitted to leave the yacht.

When Glen explained their situation, Sam quipped, "You mean that we are under yacht arrest."

"Yes, something like that. I think that if it weren't for tomorrow's inquisition, we would be free to go. Our documents are all in order, and they didn't identify any contraband, so the Coast Guard has no reason to detain us. Yet, here we are, and we have no idea who is going to show up tomorrow. Is it going to be the same bunch we met with previously in Houston, or is it going to be someone else?"

"At least, for now we are safe." Peggy said. "I guess we need to get our stories straight for tomorrow. Max, what can we talk about and what must we avoid?"

"We are going to have to come clean on about everything except that which relates directly to the actual existence of live aliens or the devices we have in our possession. We can keep most everything hypothetical, and claim that the rocks will tell the story. Keep the focus on the rocks, and identify them as the objects that the Russians want."

Jim asked, "How do we explain our behavior?"

"Say we did what we did because we could, and besides, it was fun. We accomplished our goal of exploring the Churum River Cave, and it is Dr. Baldridge and Dr. Schillinger that want the rocks. They believe there is history and careers to be made on the analysis of those rocks. As for us, we just want to get home and prepare for our next big adventure. The reason we didn't go into Venezuela was that it offered too many opportunities for the Russians to get our rocks."

Geraldo asked, "Do you really think they will believe that?"

"Probably not, but at least there is a lot of truth in that explanation. The problem is of course is not in what we are saying but in what we are omitting. I am sure they will pick up on that and try to get us to say a lot more than we want to. So, we will just have to be careful and say as little as possible."

Glen said, "Let's sleep on it. Tomorrow is going to be a watershed day, and we better be ready."

Peggy quipped, "We are in Miami. I'd rather hit South Beach and party."

"I'll second that" Sam was quick to say.

Max reminded them, "We need to stay focused. When they let us out of jail, then we can party."

The next morning, they were informed that a group of government agency people would be boarding the yacht in about an hour.

Glen remarked, "This is highly unusual. The normal protocol would be for us to be escorted to a secure debriefing area of their choice, like to a police station or to the local FBI offices. Their coming to us is an omen of something."

"In that case, let's entertain them in style" Peggy said. "Can we order an assortment of donuts right quick? We have plenty of fresh fruit on board, so I can fix a nice fruit tray. Get out the big coffee pot, and the nice china."

Glen corrected Peggy, "We don't have any nice china. They will have to use the same mugs as we use. But, you are right Peggy. A cordial reception might buy us some good will and much needed leniency. Maybe they won't look too hard at what we have on board."

Max opined, "I'll bet this is the ole 'honey attracts more bees than vinegar' tactic. I think they know if they use a hard line with us that they will get little to nothing for their efforts, so this may also be an opportunity for us to get something. I don't have anything in mind at the moment, but I think we may be in a good bargaining position. It is obvious they think we have something or know something so we need to feel them out to understand what they think we have, and we need to be thinking of what they may be able to provide to us that we might need. This ought to be an interesting meeting."

Promptly at ten o'clock, a water taxi bearing an assortment of Danish goodies and donuts and a Coast Guard boat transporting four men arrived simultaneously at the yacht. Glen met and escorted the men to the dining room which would serve well as a conference room. There they were met by Max and everyone else. After everyone was seated around the large dining table, and introductions were complete, Peggy acting as the charming hostess, offered refreshments to soften the stilted atmosphere.

Max opened the conversation, "Mr. Smith, It is good to see you and Mr. Jones again. I want to thank you for intervening on our behalf with the Coast Guard. I don't think they would have agreed to escort us across the Florida Straits if you hadn't requested that they do so. And, I understand that you probably have a lot of questions as to why we were running from a Russian submarine."

Mr. Jones, the CIA representative, though he didn't identify himself as such, said emphatically, "You have come right to the point! Indeed, we were extremely interested in why a Russian sub would be chasing an American yacht, and when we learned that it was you on board, we became even more interested. We are hoping that you will be willing to enlighten us."

Before Max could answer, Mr. Jones interjected, "We would also like to know how you knew the sub was chasing you. You started off over a thousand miles apart, and I am certain you never saw nor were contacted by the sub. How did you know it was there?"

Max said, "Well, it is a long story."

"We are here to listen" said Mr. Jones.

"You are all aware of why we were in Venezuela to begin with, and how we became involved with the Russians there. As I am sure everyone knows by now that there is something very odd about the Churum River Cave and the whole incident involving the loss of water flow to Angel Falls. The Russians were there to investigate the oddity of the cave, and because we were in the best position to enter and descend the deep pit which was central to the mystery, we were the first to collect samples from the cave. The Russians wanted access to the samples and we made an agreement to work together to solve the mystery. That agreement worked well initially, but then the Russians had a change of personnel and the agreement was abrogated. Our relations with the Russians became very adversarial, and we felt we were in constant danger from them. However, we continued with our exploration and sample collecting efforts. All during this time, we maintained a loose relationship with the previous leader of the Russian expedition, and he kept us informed of the Russian efforts, and that we needed to be concerned for our safety. We completed our expedition, and made our exit from Venezuela. We have in our possession an extensive collection of rock samples gathered from all accessible points within the cave. We believe that this is what the Russians desire to obtain from us. It seems they think they are more important than we do, but Ted, Dr. Baldridge that is, thinks they are the most important things in the world."

"We understand that you blew up the cave when you left. What was that all about?"

"Well, we didn't blow up the cave; that is a massive overstatement. We tried to open up a passage out from the bottom of the pit. We had explored every possible lead and we were unsuccessful in penetrating a massive breakdown blockage that prevented us from getting very far from the pit. There was extensive air movement, so we knew that a large passage existed beyond the pit, but we were unable to find a way into it. Our blasting efforts were a final and unsuccessful attempt to move forward. By-the-way, I guess that I should point out that our blasting efforts were spectacularly unsuccessful. Not only did we not open up access to more passage, we completely blocked access to the little passage that did exist. This really pissed off the Russians."

"That sounds rather irresponsible. Did you actually know what you were doing?"

"Give us a little credit. Admittedly, we aren't blasting experts, but we aren't total neophytes either. We used what we could get our hands on and did our best. It just didn't turn out as we had hoped. By-the-way, we did have the park director's permission to attempt the blasting."

"Who was the Russian that you maintained contact with?"

"That was Sergei Vassilov. Sergei was the individual that let us know that the Russian sub was after us, and intended to board our boat. He let us know where they were, and that enabled us to execute our plan to evade them. We would have been successful, except that they traveled a lot faster than we could."

The other two agents took interest with the mention of Sergei's name. One of them asked, "What do you know about Mr. Vassilov?"

"Not a whole lot. Why do you ask? He has been very helpful to us."

"Did Mr. Vassilov not confide in you that he and Dr. Kuznetsov were part of a Russian agency charged with the investigation of possible extraterrestrial activities?"

Without blinking, Max replied, "Yes, he did mention that."

"Were you not going to mention that to us?"

"Well, to be frank, it has been our intention to keep that information from you. We thought that if you were unaware of that fact, that it would be better for all concerned. First, we felt that mentioning anything that involves 'aliens' would diminish our credibility. But secondly, that is exactly what Drs. Baldridge and Schillinger think, and that is why they want these rock samples. If they are right, what they might reveal could be mind boggling."

"Why do the Russians want the samples that you have?"

"When we parted company, only a few samples had been analyzed, and they provided some tantalizing but inconclusive results. We have an extensive sampling of rocks and other stuff from throughout the bottom of the pit. When we attempted to blow the passage open, we ended up burying the bottom of the pit with tons of rock rendering it impossible to accomplish additional meaningful sampling. As a consequence, we have the only relevant collection of samples. That is why the Russians are pissed and want to get their hands on what we have."

"Indeed. Would you mind showing us your collection?"

"No, not at all. Follow me down below."

Everyone dutifully followed Max down to a storage area on the deck below.

"As the little Black Sheep said, we have three bags full."

Max and Geraldo hefted one of the bags onto a table and spread the contents out for inspection.

"As you can see, the rock in the cave has been subjected to some sort of intense heat, hence the smooth marble like surface. Also, you can see on these samples surface discoloration which according to Dr. Fred is indicative of something. And here is probably the most interesting object that I collected. Notice, it isn't a rock, but something else. Ted is most interested in analyzing this item. I one of these bags I have a sack full of smaller pieces of the same stuff."

Agent Jones said, "I think we have seen enough. As you have probably surmised, since the Coast Guard has cleared you for re-entry into the U.S. we have no grounds or reason to detain you further. However, we have immense interest in your samples and what they might reveal. As a consequence we would like to offer you a proposal."

"We are listening" Max said showing lots of interest.

"We would like to take possession of your samples and transport them to a secure place where they can be properly analyzed. Your team members can lead the analysis, and you all can be appropriately compensated."

"That sounds good, but we aren't the ones to have that discussion with. The group you see before you, we are all cavers not scientists or geologists. You need to be talking with Drs. Baldridge and Schillinger. Since you have the resources, I suggest that you fly them here tomorrow, and work thing out."

"We can do that. Can you contact them easily?"

"Yes, let's go back upstairs and I'll do just that."

The group reconvened in the dining room, and Max gave Ted a call.

"Ted, Max here."

"Yo Max, how are things going?"

"I'd say pretty good. The whole gang is here in Miami aboard Glen's yacht. We are joined by several government representatives, and we have been discussing the rock samples."

"Good god, I hope you aren't letting the samples out of your sight. Don't give anything away!"

"Don't worry, I'm not. But, that is why I'm calling. It would be very good if you could join us here tomorrow."

"Tomorrow? That's awfully short notice, I don't know if I can arrange it."

"Not a problem, they will send a plane to pick you up. Can you be ready first thing in the morning?"

"You are serious aren't you?"

"Yes. Be ready by seven in the morning. They will call you and tell you where to be."

"Okay."

"Call Dr. Fred and give him the same information. Be ready to negotiate a deal to support your research. They will call him after you talk with him."

Agent Smith said, "If they are ready by seven in the morning, we can have them here by two in the afternoon."

"Sounds good, we will see you tomorrow afternoon."

Geraldo interrupted, "One other thing. Kuznetsov is not one to give up easily. We are sitting ducks here. Can you possibly post guards around us until you take possession of the rocks. We have kept safe thus far by being mobile. I wouldn't be surprised if they didn't try something this evening while we are sitting still."

"You are in a Coast Guard impound area. There are guards on duty 24/7. But, with that in mind, I would recommend that you all continue to remain on board."

Geraldo asked for one more favor, "I notice that you are carrying a 40 cal Glock. We don't have any weapons on board, so I would greatly appreciate it if you would loan me your weapon until we meet here tomorrow."

Agent Jones was taken aback by the request and stammered, "I don't think there is a procedure for letting me do that. I don't think I can."

One of the other agents responded, "We aren't under the same constraints that you guys are. They can have mine."

With that he handed his weapon and a spare clip to Geraldo and said, "Let's hope you don't need this, but if you do, it is a whole lot better to have it than not have it. I can tell that you know what you are doing."

After the agents left, Max called Ted again.

Ted asked, "What is going on?"

"We can't talk about it over the phone. I'll fill you in on everything tomorrow when you and Dr. Fred get here. In the meanwhile, don't discuss anything with anyone. Have a good flight."

"Got it. See you tomorrow."

Geraldo said, "We need to make preparations for this evening. I don't like our tactical position. Even though this is a guarded moorage, we are very vulnerable. Glen, how much water do we have below us?"

Glen replied, "Six to eight feet is all, not a whole lot."

Geraldo was thinking out loud, "It wouldn't do them any good to just sink us, instead, they will need to go for total destruction. To do that they will need to get by the guards, get on board, kill all of us, get the rocks, set the boat on fire, and escape. Glen, does your dad keep any guns on board here?"

"There may be a couple of shotguns. I know that they like to shoot skeet off the stern."

"Let's find them."

"If they are here, they will be in the cabinet in the salon."

Sure enough, there were two Browning 12-guage shotguns and ten boxes of bird-shot ammo.

Geraldo exclaimed, "Perfect. This bird-shot will do. It probably isn't lethal, but it sure as heck will discourage anyone on the receiving end. This evening, Max, you and Jim take the shotguns and guard the stern, and I will take forward. If Kuznetsov is going to make a last ditch effort, it will be late tonight. If we can get through tonight unscathed, we will be home free."

The evening passed slowly and all remained quiet until four o'clock in the morning. Jim was dozing off and Max was having difficulty staying awake as well. Max was shaken suddenly fully awake by a faint splashing sound that was slightly out of sync with the sound of the small waves lapping against the side of the boat. He nudged Jim and whispered, "Did you hear that?"

Jim, fully awake now, listened carefully as the two peered through the darkness towards the stern. Very stealthily two dark figures slithered onto the rear deck of the boat and began to move directly towards Max and Jim.

They carried weapons, so their intent was obvious. Jim shouted, "HALT AND DROP YOUR WEAPONS."

The first intruder raised his weapon to fire, but before he completed the motion, Max leveled him with a double round of bird-shot. As he reeled backward, Jim took out the second intruder. They both dropped their weapons and dove back into the water. Before they hit the water, Max and Jim popped them with two more rounds. Those two were going to have a very painful swim to safety, and if they were lucky, very lucky, they wouldn't encounter any sharks along the way.

Geraldo heard the shots, and he knew that was just a distraction. He knew the real threat would soon be coming through the door in front of him. A few seconds later two heavily armed men in wetsuits wearing night vision goggles came bursting through the door. They were expecting to encounter surprised unarmed civilians, and were prepared to dispatch them in short order before claiming their prize and torching the boat. Instead, they encountered Geraldo, a highly trained special ops soldier who knew exactly how to deal with their kind. Geraldo double-tapped both of them before they took two steps inside the boat.

And that ended the assault which lasted at most ten seconds. Within minutes guards were swarming all over and around the boat. A search was on for the two that jumped back into the water laden with bird-shot. They were never found.

An investigation was launched, but there was little to discover. Mr. Smith was able to shield Max and crew from most of the pesky questions. The incident was straight forward. Four intruders heavily armed with silenced weapons and obvious evil intent. Two were dispatched: two were missing. Use of deadly force was justified. The situation was handled competently by the civilians. When the Coast Guard Commandant demanded to know what was onboard the civilian yacht in his impound area that warranted a night time raid by highly armed professionals, and why wasn't he informed of the potential threat. Mr. Smith politely informed him that he was not cleared for that information, but that he was asked to provide additional security. Mr. Smith also asked the Commandant how was it possible for at least four individuals to penetrate the impound area's security forcing the civilian to act in their own defense? The Commandant had no answer, but he assured Mr. Smith an answer would be forthcoming.

Later that afternoon after Ted and Dr. Fred arrived, everyone met onboard the yacht. As the events of the previous evening were rehashed, Ted and Dr. Fred learned of what they had missed.

Ted asked, "Do you think they will try again?"

Geraldo answered, "It is highly unlikely. They weren't expecting the reception they got, and now they know that we are on high alert."

Dr. Fred implied that he was highly grateful that he had missed all the excitement, but now that he was here, he was curious why the government suddenly had such interest in our activities.

Max explained, setting the table for the discussions that were to follow. He said, "Dr. Schillinger, the agents here are aware of what analysis of the rocks might reveal, and they are aware of the strange relationship that we have had with the Russians. Two of the gentlemen here are with our Project Blue Book, which we had thought was disbanded years ago. But no, it is alive and well and apparently well-funded, which is one of the main reasons I requested that you and Ted be here. They are suggesting that they take possession of your rocks and place them in a secure location, and that you and they jointly analyze the rocks and do whatever it is that you scientists do. I will leave it to you and Ted to negotiate your terms, but I see an opportunity for both of your universities to receive some substantial funding to support your research efforts."

"I see your point, and thank you for making that a central issue. Yes, our universities are always in need of funding for research, and if our samples from the Churum River Cave are to be located at a remote secure site, it will be very expensive for Ted and me to work between that site and our universities."

Mr. Jones interjected at this point that they fully understood, and that those costs would be covered.

Max continued, "I don't see a place for any involvement in your research project for the rest of us. After all, we are cavers, not academics or scientists. We are planning to work with the Mueller Foundation in writing and publishing an expedition report, so once the rocks are off loaded, we would like to part company with you, and head back to Huntsville."

Mr. Smith agreed that would satisfactory, and Mr. Jones concurred.

Scott, who had said very little up to now, entered the conversation, "Gentlemen, in as much as that you are willing to generously fund the research efforts of Drs. Baldridge and Schillinger, I would like to point out that the Mueller Foundation has totally funded this project, and without the Foundations support, we wouldn't be having this meeting. I would like to propose that the government consider compensating the Mueller Foundation with an appropriate grant so that we can continue supporting important efforts of this nature."

The government guys put their heads together, and after a brief discussion they agreed that a grant would be an excellent mechanism for continuing an obvious and productive cooperative relationship. Mr. Smith indicated that someone from their office would be in contact with them to work out the details and put the funding on a fast track.

Before the end of the day, an armored vehicle showed up. Three large bags were transferred off of the boat under armed guard and transported to Homestead Air Force Base. Ted and Dr. Fred accompanied the armored vehicle, and would fly with the samples to their final destination in Nevada.

With that albatross finally removed from the boat, Glen said, “I think we can all relax for now. I propose we find a really good steak house and celebrate a little bit.”

Peggy was quick to second that proposal and quipped, “Do you think the guards will let an Uber onto the station here?”

Max replied sarcastically, “I doubt that will be a problem. Considering last night, the security is pretty lax here.”

Indeed, the guards permitted two Ubers to come on station and transport the six of them to a highly recommended steak house. A delightful and relaxing evening was enjoyed by all, and the next morning Glen headed the yacht out into the intercoastal. Their trip would take them around the southern tip of Florida past the Florida Keys and then across the Gulf of Mexico to Mobile Bay. From there, they would go up the Tombigbee to the Tennessee River and on to Decatur, Alabama where the yacht was permanently berthed.

On their final leg as they cruised up the Tennessee towards Decatur, Peggy and Max were lounging together on the forward deck. Peggy turned to Max, smiled and said, “You know, I could really get used to this life style. We ought to do this more often.”

Max laughed, “Do you think Glen’s dad could use a yacht sitter when he isn’t using it? We could take really good care of it.”

CHAPTER 40

In the months that followed the group's return to the states, it was decided to maintain a low profile for a while. The alien devices were secreted off the yacht and stored in the SCIF at the Mueller Foundation. Agents Jones and Smith lived up to their word, and fast tracked substantial funding to the Foundation and to Ted and Dr. Fred's universities. Ted was brought on full time with his university and given the rank of Associate Professor. They dutifully carried on their research even though they already knew the answers, and in fact knew far more than could ever be gleaned from the analysis of the rock samples. Max, Peggy, Sam, and Jim moved to Huntsville to work full time for the Mueller Foundation. Spider and Bufford went back to being Spider and Bufford, except that Bufford moved in with Spider. They let the group know that they planned to make the move permanent soon. They too knew it was important to lay low for a while, in hopes that Kuznetsov would conclude that there was nothing further to be learned from any of the group and move on. Max and Peggy took a cue from Spider and Bufford and moved in together. They claimed it was for economic reasons, but no one was buying into that story.

The Russians finished the aqueduct, and water was restored to Angel Falls. A big to do was held to celebrate the event, and only Scott, Max, and Peggy attended the event. Kuznetsov was very cool to their presence, and did not speak with them. After that, the Russians vacated their presence atop Auyán tepui. Although Kuznetsov showed no interest in the group, Max had a feeling that they were still under surveillance, though perhaps not quite as intense as before. With the water restored to Angel Falls, the Mueller Foundation sponsored a project in cooperation with Parque Nacional Canaima to make the Canaima River Cave a major destination for cavers from around the world who wanted to have on their resume that they had descended the world's deepest pit inside of a cave. This project also gave cover to the group whenever they needed to visit the aliens. It also provided them with the ability to protect the access to the secret entrance.

All during this time, plans were being made for the assault across several hundred miles of pack ice to the back side of Meighen Island where in a relatively shallow inlet under thirty feet of permanent ice lay the alien space ship. Researching this area without raising suspicions or unintentionally disclosing the spaceship's location proved to be a difficult task. Sam, the new IT guy for the Foundation took the lead on the task of keeping all research anonymous, and he established several fully protected fake ID's that could be used when doing searches on the web. All important research was kept on computers that were air-gaped from the internet, so the computers and the data were protected from hackers.

A secure workshop was setup so prototype sleds could be constructed using the hover transporters and tested. While the sled concept was working out well, it was realized that the sled would not have sufficient carrying capacity to support the needs of the expedition. A larger craft was going to be required.

Max investigated snowmobiles, Artic Cats, tundra buggys, and even aircraft before he hit on air cushion vehicles, also known as hovercraft, as an option. A bit of research revealed that hovercraft can go fast and can easily travel over water, mud, ice, rough terrain, and even fly. The problem, Max realized with hovercrafts, was that they are inherently energy inefficient, and he was in the need the ability to travel autonomously and stealthy perhaps eight hundred miles across one of the most barren and hostile regions on the earth, and that was going to require a huge amount of fuel. There could be no fuel drops along the route because that would be like an arrow pointing to the spaceship's location. Then suddenly Max had a 'eureka moment', it hit Max like a ton of bricks! This was not a problem; he had the world's most advanced power source at his disposal. It would be riding effortlessly on the sled he had constructed using the hover transports. His hovercraft would simply have to be electric powered. This was an excellent convolution of circumstances. He had unlimited electric power, and electric propulsion would be hundreds of times more stealthy than internal combustion engines. Problem solved, sort of anyway. He would have to build and test an appropriate hovercraft in order to prove out his idea. However, he was so confident that he had hit on the solution that he had to tell somebody so he sent an urgent group text to everyone to meet him in the shop.

Sam, who was nearby tinkering with the sled, asked "What's up. Do we have a problem?"

'No problem, rather problem solved." Max replied, "I've just had an idea that I want to share."

Jim, Scott, Connie, and Peggy all came running.

When they were all present, Max said, "I think I know how to get to the ship. I've been looking at all sorts of alternatives, and I think I have identified how we can do it."

"We are all ears. Spill it." Sam said.

"The solution is to use an air cushion vehicle."

Sam cut him off saying, "That will never work. They are notoriously inefficient."

"That is what I thought when I first looked at their capabilities. They have all the characteristics we are looking for, but they are fuel hogs. Then it struck me, that is not our problem. We have all the fuel necessary; it is just not in liquid form. We have the RMD. We can make an all-electric hovercraft. It will be perfect. No gas or diesel required. We have an unlimited supply of electricity. It will be fast, capable, and stealthy, and we can build it ourselves."

Sam quickly flipped from negative to positive. "Maybe a hovercraft will work after all. That actually sounds like a good idea. When do we start?"

Scott said, "I've seen a lot of ads for hovercraft kits. Let's get the biggest kit we can find and start modifying it."

Sam came up with the best idea. He suggested, "Why don't we just buy an electric vehicle and use it for parts. It will have all the right stuff from motors, to control systems to nice seats, and a big battery."

"That's a great idea. That will save a lot of engineering time and effort. When the time comes, we just remove the big battery and plug in the RMD. The battery space can be used for cargo."

Scott pointed out that "We can get the fiberglass boat company that built our shields to do all of the structural modifications and assembly. Tell them that we are planning to enter hovercraft races, and for a discount they can identify as one of our sponsors and put their logo on our racer. By being totally open with the project, no one will ever guess what we are building it for."

Max said, “Let’s divide and conquer. I’ll identify an appropriate kit and get it ordered. Peggy, you go shopping for an electric car. Don’t go for the high end one. Go for the middle price range and reliability. Sam, get smart on electric car systems and get ready to integrate the RMD. Scott, you have been the primary person dealing with the boat company. Get them primed and on board to help us build this thing. Jim, it is time to put you HVAC expertise to use. We will need to minimize both our thermal and visible signatures. Find out what kind of paints, tarps, blankets, insulating material and whatever else we might need to make ourselves invisible in the artic environment. It looks like everyone has a plateful now. Once again Connie, you will need to hold the fort down while everyone is working on this project.”

Two weeks later the project was in full swing. Scott negotiated a small corner in the boat factory to work the assembly and integration of the project. The large hovercraft kit was delivered and unpacked. The electric vehicle was disassembled, parts identified for repurposing were cataloged and set aside, and all unnecessary part were scrapped. Scott found a buyer for the engines that came with the kit since they would not be needed. The electric drive motors from the car were much more powerful than the internal combustion engines that came with the kit, and were indescribably more responsive. The fiberglass craftsmen replaced the majority of the kit’s fiberglass structural components with carbon fiber covered rigid foam components to accommodate the anticipated increased loads that would be imposed by the powerful electric motors.

The kit had an open air cockpit, which was totally unsatisfactory for operating in artic conditions, so a closed cockpit was constructed. This also required that a large air intake duct be incorporated above the cockpit to funnel the air to the vehicle’s fans. As an artistic touch, many of the high end comfort appointments of the electric car were included in the cockpit of the hovercraft. This was going to be a hotrod hovercraft, and everyone was anxious and excited about seeing it in action.

Six weeks to the day, the hovercraft was ready for trial runs. The parking lot served as the initial test area. The vehicle performed so well that soon, testing was moved to more challenging venues. In the weeks that followed, the hovercraft could be seen racing up and down the Tennessee River, up and over the banks, across low lying wetlands, and up some craggy slopes. It was on some of the rougher terrain that problems were encountered. When the hovercraft hit a bump while traveling at a medium to high rate of speed, it would become airborne, which in and of itself was not a problem, but the landings were sometimes very rough and dangerous. Something needed to be done to lessen the risk of crashing the vehicle, especially when towing the sled.

Sam offered a solution. "Why don't we do away with the sled all together? We can mount the RMD in the vehicle where the battery currently is, and mount the active part of the hoverbarrows on the underside of the hovercraft. They would provide an extra five hundred pounds of lift for the vehicle, and when the vehicle becomes airborne, they would act as shock absorbers when the vehicle comes back down. Getting rid of the sled I think is important for the sake of vehicle stability, especially in rough terrain. What do you all think?"

Max said, "Sam, I like your idea. I like it a lot. Let's get the modifications done."

Scott asked, "What are we going to tell the fabricators? We can't tell them what hoverbarrows actually are."

Max said, "We will tell them that they are specialized stability devices that we have been developing over at the Foundation. The way they actually work is a secret, and their presence on the vehicle must not be disclosed. I think they will buy that story."

With the hoverbarrows integrated into the bottom of the hovercraft, testing was resumed. What a difference that extra five hundred pounds of lift made. When power was applied, the vehicle sprung up like a jack rabbit, and hard landings were virtually eliminated. It was decided that the time had arrived to initiate the assault across the arctic ice to that lonesome and remote site on the north side of Meighen Island.

CHAPTER 41

Glen Neely approached his dad with a request. "Dad, I would like to borrow the yacht again since you and your buddies didn't do your summer fishing trip this year."

"Would you now? You know, it's about time I transferred title of the boat to you, and let you worry about it's up keep and everything."

"Don't do that, Dad. You know I couldn't afford the insurance on that thing. I like it better when I can just borrow it from you when I need to."

"Son, you know you are a spoiled brat don't you?"

"Yeah, I know. I am what I am and it's all your fault. So, can I have the boat?"

"Of course you can. You know you can have it whenever you like, it's going to be yours someday anyway."

"One other thing. When the time comes, can I use your captain and crew also?"

"Oh, now it gets interesting. How come you don't want to captain it yourself?"

"Sometime, probably next month or towards the end of August or early September we would like to make a voyage up north near Greenland, and I don't have the experience for that kind of water. Captain Erik is licensed for all oceans, and I know he has previously worked extensively in the North Sea. I would feel more comfortable with him driving the boat."

"You know that is kind of late in the season to be going up there. What are you up to now, Son? Is this related to what you were doing in South America?"

"Yes, but keep that under your hat. It is still kind of secret stuff."

"Well, be careful. I'll make sure the insurance is paid up."

"Thanks Dad."

CHAPTER 42

Max put out a call to the entire crew, including the Venezuelan contingency, inviting them to an off shore fishing trip just as a reason to get together again. Everyone knew of course that it was for more than just fun, so they responded enthusiastically that they would be delighted to attend the party. The plan was for the Huntsville contingency to ride with Glen on the yacht down to Mobile, Alabama, meet everyone else there, and then depart for a week at sea. Max thought that meeting this way would draw the least suspicion, and even if it did, they would be out of sight.

Prior to leaving, an attempt was made to contact Sergei. At the last minute he responded, and Scott asked point blank, "Do you know if we are still being surveilled by Kuznetsov? We have all been on our best behavior hoping that he would lose interest in us. Our entire group has said that they feel like they are living under a constant threat. Is that still the case?"

Sergei replied, "There is still intense interest in what Dr. Baldridge and Dr. Schillinger might turn up with their research. However, their work is being shielded very effectively. And even I, and by extension Kuznetsov as well, am very intrigued with your sudden interest in air cushion vehicles. I know that you are up to something, so I urge you to be very careful. So the answer to your question is 'yes, you are being watched'."

"That is disappointing news. We were all hoping we could start living normal lives."

"I don't think you will ever again be able to do that."

"Okay, thanks for the update."

The next day instead of cruising down the Tennessee River heading for the Tombigbee and Mobile, Max notified everyone to come to Huntsville instead. Based on what Scott had just learned, they determined that it would be too dangerous to have the entire crew on the yacht together out in the Gulf. It would be just too easy of a target for Kuznetsov who Max was guessing was still smarting from having failed at intercepting them in the Florida Straits.

It took two more days for everyone to rearrange their flight plans and make it to Huntsville. Once everyone was settled in their accommodations, they regrouped at the Mueller Foundation office where they were greeted by Connie and escorted down below the SCIF.

Max opened the meeting saying, "I appreciate everyone dropping whatever you were doing and coming here. I had hoped that we could meet while enjoying a little cruise, but we are informed that despite all of our efforts we are still being closely watched. Hence cruising in the Gulf became out of the question."

Max continued, "The work on the air cushion vehicle is complete, and she is an unbelievable success. We have named her 'Journey', and she is ready to go. This meeting is so we can put all our heads together and figure out a way to get from here to the Arctic Ocean without being detected. Scott, and I and others here have thought long and hard about it, and we haven't come up with a plausible solution. We need our collective brains to solve this riddle."

Ted asked, "Do we have a time table or a deadline we must meet?"

"No, the schedule is ours to determine, but obviously conditions up north vary immensely with time-of-year, so that will have to be considered."

Glen informed the group, "Dad has generously given us free rein use of the yacht, but with Kuznetsov watching us, I don't know if it will be of any use to us. We might use it as a decoy to draw attention away from what we intend to do, but we probably will have to stay on the inland waterways."

Sam speaking to Geraldo said, "You guys are the experts on air dropping stuff. Can Journey be packaged so that she could be air dropped in some remote location near the destination?"

"Sure" replied Geraldo, "but the resources required to do so would be immense, much greater than what was required for getting stuff out of Venezuela. We would need to charter something like a C-123 or a C-130. Those capabilities are for hire."

Max pointed out, "Also, in Venezuela, we didn't care if they were looking. Now we must be totally secret. I think an air drop in that region would be seen by the whole world, and it wouldn't take them long to know who we were and know pretty close to where we would be heading. While flying in would be desirable, there is no way we could keep our activities secret."

Peggy said, "Well, that leaves only one choice. We have to get there or at least close by boat."

"When you say close, just how close do you mean?" Ted asked.

Max said, "I don't really know, but for starters, let's say four to five hundred miles. Journey is not range limited, we the humans are."

Scott pulled up on the screen a map of the top of the world. "Let's put a five hundred mile circle around our target, and see what lies within."

Max said, "Looks like most of Nunavut and the northwestern portion of Greenland."

Geraldo pointed out, "That part of Greenland has Thule AFB. We probably want to avoid that part of the map."

Peggy asked, "What do we know about Nunavut?"

Dr. Fred joined the conversation, "Well, Nunavut is comprised mainly of a bunch of islands, and is sparsely inhabited. But despite being sparsely inhabited, there is a lot going on up there. Several universities have arctic research stations, a lot of companies are exploring for minerals, it is a rich area for fishing, NASA has a Mars research laboratory up there somewhere, and there is a lot of cruise ship traffic in the region. I also heard that there is a fossil forest on I think Axel Heiberg Island."

Max said, "Axel Heiberg is near where we are going. What else is going on the island?"

"I don't know" Sam said, "but Google will tell us. Oh crap, I can't access the internet from in here."

Scott said, "Go outside and check right quick. Meanwhile let's take a coffee break."

Sam left the SCIF and pulled up Google. "Aha, one of the Canadian universities has an arctic research station there, but it is only manned during the summer. And yes, the fossil forest is on this island, and apparently cruise ships stop there as well."

Sam returned to the SCIF and reported his findings.

Max said, "Axel Heiberg looks like a good starting place, and it certainly is within Journey's range. Now we just need to find a way to get her there."

Dr. Fred said, "A lot of the mining interests in the arctic are supplied by boats operating out of Hudson Bay, if we could get her to one of the ports on Hudson Bay, we could hire a supply boat to take her to that fiord where the cruise ships go. I doubt that there is much of a dock there though, so I don't know how you would off load her there."

"That won't be a problem, trust me." Max said confidently.

"Okay, how do we get her to Hudson bay?" Glen asked.

"I've got an idea" Scott said. "Let's prevail on our friends at HyTech Marine. After all, they have their name on the side of Journey as one of her sponsors. Let's get them to ship her to Hudson bay. They have all the export licenses, and procedures for shipping their stuff all over the world. They could ship her out, and our name wouldn't even be on the manifest. No one would be the wiser."

"In order to ship her without special 'Wide Load' permits, she will have to be partially disassembled."

"Yes" Max agreed, "Then we have to decide on where we do the reassembly. I'm thinking that if we hire one of those boats that have the big aft deck, like the boats that service the oil rigs, we could just put her parts on the deck and assemble her when we are at sea and nobody is watching. We could just fly her off the deck when we get to Axel Heiberg or wherever if we get stopped by ice before we get there."

"It sounds like this plan could work," remarked Geraldo, "but we need some insurance. The way I see it, once Journey leaves the local scene and several of us disappear at the same time, every traffic camera, every spy satellite, and every eyeball asset Kuznetsov can muster will be looking for Journey and whoever is with her. And if we aren't a long way off when they start looking, they will find us."

Glen was thinking that this is where the yacht could be of use. "If we all boarded the yacht for an inland waterway tour or a long Mississippi boat ride, they would have us all in one pile. They would have to think that they know where we all were, but they couldn't actually watch us. Then, if Max, Peggy and two others, say Jim and Sam could slip off unnoticed, make their way back to Huntsville. They could load up Journey and head out as just another product being shipped from HyTech Marine, and they could be all the way to the Canadian border before they were missed. Kuznetsov and company wouldn't know where to begin looking."

Scott voiced his opinion, "That would work, but Max and who ever goes with him will need fake ID's and credit cards. The problem is, I don't know how to setup fake ID's."

"No problem," Interjected Geraldo, "I do, or rather I have contacts that do. Scott, what you need to do is convince our friends at HyTech

Marine to let us operate under their corporate umbrella while we make this delivery. You might need to give them a rather substantial bond to secure their cooperation."

"I've gotten to know the owners pretty well. I think I can convince them to help us. We might need to work up a credible cover story to explain our secretiveness though."

"We are also going to need a diesel crew cab dually and a gooseneck trailer to haul Journey and her disassembled parts. HyTech needs to acquire that soon also."

Max said, "Okay, we can make this work. How soon do you all think we can everything ready?"

"It all depends", Scott said. "What do you think is the long pole in this tent? Prepping Journey with the actual RMD instead of the big battery? Getting the truck and trailer? Working out and implementing the details for Max and company to sneak off the yacht?"

"You also need to contract with someone with a boat to get us from Hudson Bay to Axel Heiberg", Sam reminded Scott. "Actually, you probably shouldn't tell them Axel Heiberg, but maybe somewhere indefinite like on Ellesmere Island. Then specify the destination later on. I think that will be the long pole in the tent."

"That is a good point. So how much time? A month? Six weeks?"

Ted pointed out, "We better shoot for no more than a month. If we wait much longer the arctic waters will start freezing over, and you might not be able to travel much further north than Baffin Island."

"Okay", Scott said, "One month it is, and it won't hurt if we get it done ahead of schedule."

The ensuing days were frantically busy. It seemed that each task completed spawned at least two others that had been overlooked. The two owners of HyTech Marine were actually excited about participating in a super-secret adventure, and their enthusiasm only increased when they learned that Scott was offering them a cool half million dollars for their support. The only thing they were concerned about was whether Scott was involved in something illegal. Scott assured them that their activity definitely was not illegal, but that it was very important and that it was very dangerous. It was because of the danger that the secrecy was required.

HyTech bought the appropriate truck and a thirty two foot gooseneck trailer. Journey was configured in her final form for shipping, and stocked with supplies to last Max and Peggy for a month. The bolt on wings and stabilizer props were packaged for shipping, as were the side pontoons and skirt. A tool kit was included so that Journey's wings and pontoons could be attached when they arrived at their destination.

Rebreather scuba equipment and dry suits, insulated tarps to conceal their infrared signature, miscellaneous tools and drills that would be required at the final destination were all packaged in durable containers that would be lashed to Journey's roof in transit. It was going to be a heavy load, but Journey's powerful electric motors and stabilizing ducted fans would be more than up to the task.

It turned out that Sam was right. The long pole in the tent was finding a suitable boat to transport them north. Scott finally found the perfect boat. They had a contract to haul fuel oil and other supplies to small villages along the east side of Baffin Island all the way up to Grise Fiord, on the south end of Ellesmere Island. They agreed to take Journey on board, but could not guarantee that they could go much further. They operated out of Iqaluit on the south end of Baffin Island. They were planning to make a run up to Grise Fiord in just six weeks. Further research revealed that monthly freighter trips were made from Goose Bay, Labrador to Iqaluit, so the problem boiled down to how to get Journey to Goose Bay. It turned out that one could drive all the way to Goose Bay from Huntsville in five days if all went well. This led to another problem: Journey had to be configured to fit in a large sea-land container in order to be transported on either of the boats. Here they got unbelievably lucky. When Journey was stripped down, she measured seven feet six inches wide by seven feet two inches high by eighteen feet eleven inches long. She would barely fit into a twenty foot container. All of her other parts and other supplies would have to be packed into a second ten foot container. This was going to max out the capacity or the thirty two foot trailer and the F-450 dually truck. But the main thing was that it was doable. That left less than one week complete all remaining tasks, then get everyone on board the yacht under way in party mode, and get Journey on the road to Goose Bay undetected.

CHAPTER 43

When the day came to execute the plan, a big to do was made as everyone boarded the yacht for an openly talked about two week cruise down the Tennessee to the Ohio, and then down the Mississippi to New Orleans. Since they knew they were constantly being watched, the image that they were trying to present to their watchers was that they were just a bunch of party folks out to spend a bunch of Glen's daddy's money. They were fortunate in that the weather cooperated very well their plans.

By early evening a massive thunderstorm rolled in and masked their actions. On a dark part of the river during the heavy rain, they were met by a small boat, and Max, Peggy, Jim and Geraldo snuck unobserved off of the yacht and were ferried back to Decatur. From there they went directly to HyTech Marine where they picked up Journey and drove out into the storm. They hit I-65 and from there it was interstate all the way to Detroit where they would pass into Canada. It rained steadily upon them until they were north of Nashville, and Max felt confident that they were successful in their stealthy exit.

Five uneventful days later they pulled into Goose Bay Labrador road weary and ready for a good seafood dinner.

Jim said, "This is lobster country, so you know what I'm looking forward to this evening."

Max replied, "First things first. Let's locate the Harbor Master and get on the docket for getting Journey loaded on the freighter. Then we need to make plans for this evening, that is to say, sleep in a hotel or sleep in the truck again."

Peggy announced, "I'm for the hotel. None of you guys have showered for five days."

"Well, neither have you" Max reminded her.

"I'm a girl, so you don't need to remind me."

Max said, "Let's find the Harbor Master, then we can figure out what we do next."

The Harbor Master informed them that the freighter wasn't scheduled to sail for two more days, so they had plenty of time to get their freight loaded. He put them in contact with the ship's Master so that they could complete the necessary paperwork. As it turned out, they wouldn't be able to load Journey until the next afternoon.

The Harbor Master also gave them directions to a hotel that he would recommend and suggested the best place in town to get a great lobster dinner. It was decided that Max and Peggy would get the hotel room the first night, then Jim and Geraldo would get it the second night. That way Journey would be under their watchful eye continuously until she was securely loaded on the freighter. By the third day, Max and Peggy would be on board the freighter, and Jim and Geraldo would be heading back to Alabama.

Max checked into the hotel using his fake identification. The fake ID's that Geraldo had made had Max and Peggy as Mr. and Mrs. which amused the entire crew because they all knew there was a lot more truth to that than not. The best part about the hotel room was that everyone was able to shower before going to dinner.

That evening while they were at dinner, Max received a phone call on his burner phone from Scott.

Scott said, "Don't say where you are just in case this phone is compromised. I have a pretty good idea anyway. I just received word from a source that informed me that they are aware of the fact that you are no longer on this trip with us, and that they are also aware that certain assets of interest do not appear to be where they should be. You wouldn't happen to know anything about that, would you?"

Max replied, "Good to hear from you Scott. I hope you and the gang are enjoying your cruise. I hope you all have a great time in New Orleans. Where are you all now?"

"We are in Memphis at the moment. We will overnight here, and continue on tomorrow."

Max replied with a cryptic message, "We have stopped for the night also. Our Journey is doing well, and will continue towards the race tomorrow. All is well with us. Let us know if anything changes."

"Of course I will. Be very careful." Scott replied and signed off.

Max said quietly, "As you just heard, the cat's out of the bag, and they will be searching high and low for us. From now on, we must be on high alert and extremely vigilant."

Jim said, "I really don't know how we can be more vigilant than we have been."

Geraldo pointed out, "That is probably the reason we have gotten this far without a problem. We need to get the truck and trailer back on the road as soon as possible and as far from here as possible. Jim, I think we need to go back to Alabama by way of Calgary, and somehow accidentally start leaving crumbs for our watchers to find."

"I like that idea. It has been a long time since I was in that part of the country."

Geraldo was thinking ahead and suggested, "I think that as soon as Journey is off-loaded that Jim and I need to hit the road instead of spending tomorrow night here. Also, once you two depart here, you will be out of touch until you activate Journey. Beyond here, cell phones will be useless. Furthermore, even after you activate Journey, you will be in receive mode only, so let's work out a way where you can communicate where you are."

Jim said, "Like we planned, we will be using ham radio to talk to you because of the distance involved. Listen for my call sign on either ten, twenty or forty meters, whichever band is open. I have several friends lined up that I will be chatting with, and I will encode messages within our conversation for you. I'll say something like, 'I've got some friends that I would like to hear from', and you can reply after a few minutes with mic key clicks, one through five to indicate where you are on the route. Also, whenever you hear me chatting, you can just give a couple of clicks so I will know you are listening."

That evening, they drew out a rough map of max's planned route beginning at Grise Fiord and going all the way to Axel Heiberg intentionally omitting their final destination. The next afternoon, Max and Peggy moved into their quarters on the freighter, and Geraldo and Jim hit the road again. Early the next morning, the freighter was steaming out into the Labrador Sea, and beginning the turn to the north on the thousand mile run to Iqaluit. The thousand mile run would take about two and a half to three days depending on sea conditions.

CHAPTER 44

During the days at sea, Max and Peggy spent a lot of time up on deck together watching small icebergs drift by, and hoping that none of the Russian subs that routinely patrolled this area had this particular freighter in their sights.

Time passed slowly at sea, and Max had time to think. Max said thoughtfully, "Do you have any idea how much everything that we have been doing costs? I know Scott has spent well over seven million dollars. Without Scott funding us, none of this would have happened or even been possible."

Snuggling up to Max for a bit of warmth, Peggy replied, "Don't forget that it was you that started it all. If it wasn't for you, none of this would have happened either."

"Actually, everybody in our group has made some incredible contributions, especially including you, without which we wouldn't be here."

"It was meant to be." Peggy said with conviction. After a short pause, she continued, "You know those two guys with no names from the agency with no name that were with Mr. Jones and Mr. Smith?"

"Yes, what about them?"

"Do you think they have been watching us also, and are wondering where we have gone?"

"I suspect that the answer to that is yes."

"Do you think we can trust them?"

"I think so. I believe that their agency funded Ted and Dr. Fred's research projects, and they did give The Mueller Foundation a generous grant, but there is something not quite right. My spider senses have told me to be cautious. That is why I haven't been totally candid with them. I think they know Sergei also. We know that Kuznetsov is our advisory, but I don't think he is our only one. I have that nagging feeling that there is something else lurking out there."

"I say trust your spider senses, they are usually right."

"Funny thing, I don't think Smith and Jones are real names either. I consider them allies, but with caution also. I have been more candid with Sergei than I have with them, and apparently Sergei is still willing to look out for us to the extent that he can. I suspect that sooner or later Sergei is going to want his favors returned with interest."

"I will bet that you are right. Speaking of Sergei, I hate being out of contact and not knowing what is going on. They could be hot on out tail right now, and we wouldn't know it."

"I hate it too, and unfortunately it is going to be at least a week if not more before we can even listen for news."

Peggy said, "Look over there. Is that a periscope?"

Max's heart skipped a beat, and he said, "Where? Where?"

Peggy laughed, "Ha, ha, made you look!"

Max slapped her on her back side and said, "Dang you! That was just plain mean. You are going to pay for that!"

Peggy, still laughing said, "I'm so afraid."

Max, still pouting, said, "When you least expect it!"

As they retired below to get some food and to warm up a bit, Peggy opined, "When I least expect it, huh. Well, that fits in with everything else. It seems like just about everything that has happened to us has been what or when we least expected."

Late on the third day they arrived at Iqaluit, and Max was hoping that the boat that Scott had contracted for the next leg of this trip would in fact be in Iqaluit. Max asked the freighter captain if he could use the ships radio to call the other boat. Much to Max's relief, the captain of the smaller boat answered right back, and said that he was waiting to hear from Max. He indicated that he would be alongside early in the morning to take the containers on board. He said that he was concerned, and wanted to get under way as soon as possible because the sea-lanes further north were closing fast. He indicated that they would head out as soon as Max's containers were on board. Max asked how long it would take to get to Grise Fiord. The captain said that it was roughly thirteen hundred and fifty miles and he had a couple of stops to make along the way. He estimated it would probably take about a week, and maybe as long as ten days. He also indicated that he wasn't sure how much further beyond Grise Fiord they would be able to go because the Cardigan Straits were often closed this time of year. Max inquired about the areas beyond the Cardigan Straits. The captain indicated that if the straits were frozen over, the Norwegian Bay would be also. They simply wouldn't know for sure until they got nearer.

CHAPTER 45

Sure enough, early the next morning the hundred and fifty foot supply boat pulled alongside the freighter. Max's two containers were off loaded onto the aft deck of the supply boat, and secured next to numerous barrels of heating oil and other supplies destined for several small native villages along the way. Shortly thereafter they were headed back out to sea heading north towards Grise Fiord on the south end of Ellesmere Island.

Max had a lot to think about while cruising slowly northward. He considered breaking Journey out of her container early so that they could listen for messages from Jim, but he thought that if any satellites were watching, the sight of Journey on the deck of this boat would be a dead giveaway. Breaking Journey out was going to have to wait until the last minute. The accommodations on the supply boat turned out to be even more Spartan than on the freighter, so he and Peggy spent a lot of time out on the deck in spite of the frigid cold. His thinking was that they were going to have to endure conditions much worse than this, so they might as well get acclimated now. Also, Max was still smarting from the prank that Peggy pulled on him earlier, and he couldn't get it out of his mind. As a consequence he was constantly scanning the dark waters looking for that telltale ripple from some submarine's periscope.

As the days grew shorter and the nights grew longer, they slowly made their way northward to Grise Fiord, making several short stops along the way. After off-loading the remainder of his cargo for the small native village, the captain consulted the latest imagery of the waterways to the west. He indicated that it looked like they were going to be lucky. The Cardigan Straits looked like they were still open, but just a little ways further north, the Norwegian Bay was icing over and soon would be impassible. That would be the limit as to how far they could go. The captain wanted to know what Max wanted to do because he was very concerned about dropping Max and Peggy off way out in the middle of this arctic wilderness with winter fast approaching with just whatever was in those two containers. Max indicated that they would be alright if could get to solid ice, then they could go the rest of the way in Journey. He could make his delivery of the air cushion vehicle to the research team from the Arctic Winter Research Institute, and that he and Peggy could fly back to civilization on the plane that would be delivering the research team to Axel Heiberg. That flimsy story seemed to satisfy the captain even though he continued to think that they were crazy and didn't fully understand the harshness of the arctic.

The captain did mention one thing that got Max's attention. The captain told Max that he needed to be aware of polar bears, because they could be a problem. "Polar bears", Max thought to himself. "We hadn't thought about polar bears."

As the supply boat began heading west towards the Cardigan Straits, Max and Peggy with help from the boat's crew pulled Journey out of her container and began reattaching her pontoons, skirt, wings, and stabilizing props. Once she was fully reassembled, Max fired her up to check out all onboard systems. It was amazing, but everything checked out perfectly. Next came the task of lashing all the storage containers to her roof, making sure that those containers with critical items were readily accessible.

The crew was concerned that this small vehicle would need more fuel, and they didn't see any among the supplies that they helped load. Max knew that they would probably be traveling about two hundred miles across the ice, so he told the crew that Journey had a three hundred mile range before needing to be refueled. They thought that was amazing, but they believed every word that Max uttered. If they knew that Journey had practically an unlimited range, they would have been really amazed.

Max cornered the captain and asked, "Captain, earlier you mentioned polar bears, and that we needed to be aware of them. Just how do you recommend that we deal with polar bears if we encounter them?"

The captain responded, "You shoot them."

Max replied, "I guess that is a problem. We don't have a gun. What is your next suggestion?"

The captain answered incredulously, "You don't have a gun? Son, you never travel out here on the ice without a gun! That little boat thingy out there won't protect you from a bear. They will rip that thing apart in an instant to get to you. Out there without a gun, you are just an easy meal for a big bear."

These were not comforting words for Max to hear.

The captain continued, "Son, the only thing I can do is give you my rifle. And if you encounter a bear, don't hesitate to use it. They won't give you a second chance. When you get back home, send me eight hundred dollars and we will call it even. Ok?"

Max agreed that was more than ok, and that he greatly appreciated the use of the rifle.

Later Max related to Peggy the conversation that he had with the captain.

"That was certainly thoughtful of the captain and generous also." Peggy said, "But, I hope that we don't ever have to shoot a polar bear. Isn't there some sort of non-lethal deterrent we could use?"

"I guess we could rig up some sort of a cow prod. The RMD can put out enough juice to fry a whale, so discouraging a polar bear shouldn't be that difficult. The problem will be how to just stun the bear without frying his brain. Touching a bare wire from the RMD would be like touching the third rail in the subway. I'll figure something out once we get under way on our own."

Twenty hours later they were exiting the Cardigan Strait into the Norwegian Bay. The captain pointed out that solid pack ice was just fifteen miles ahead and said to Max, "I'm anxious to see that machine in action. It is hard to believe that it can travel as far as you said it can with that heavy of a load. I hope to hear from you when you get back. I want to know about your trip across the ice."

"Captain, you will definitely hear from me, and I won't forget your eight hundred bucks either."

"And remember, watch out for polar bears."

"We will, and hopefully we can out run them."

Peggy was inside Journey exercising the stabilizing props on the wings. The props almost had enough power to lift Journey off of the deck without aid from the air cushion fan. With the air cushion fan on full thrust, journey could leap fifteen feet into the air and take over thirty seconds to sink back down.

The time came for them to leave the supply boat and continue their northern trek. They said their good byes to the captain and his crew, and told him how much they had enjoyed traveling with them. With that done, Max closed the hatch, and Journey leapt over the side of the boat and headed towards the edge of the pack ice. The crew was amazed when she leapt over the side, and they cheered when she leapt up onto the ice pack. They were sorry to see them go, and wished them a safe journey.

CHAPTER 46

Max turned to Peggy and said, "Okay Peggy, it's just you and me now."

Peggy replied, "I wouldn't want it any other way."

They sped away over the thin new ice, and the going was easy. They figured that they had about two hundred and fifty miles to go, and if it didn't get any harder than this they would be there in less than twenty hours, not counting time that they might use to rest.

Max drove and Peggy listened for news from Jim. Peggy dialed up and down the forty meter band listening for Jim's call sign. Finally she heard something, "This is W5JR calling CQ hoping some of my buddies up north have their ears on. Repeat, this is W5JR calling CQ, come in CQ."

Peggy clicked the mic once then waited a minute and clicked four times to indicate where they were on their route.

Jim heard the mic clicks on top of his frequency and repeated his CQ call.

"W5JR this is your buddy W8MJZ, I hear you loud and clear. I haven't heard you on the air for a day or two. I hope all is well with you."

Jim said, "W8MJZ, all is well with me and mine, and I was hoping you were listening. I'm hoping you can deliver a message for me to two of my friends up that way who are going through some lonely times together. Tell them that someone powerful up above is looking out for them. Let them know that know that down here we are thinking of them, and that they should stay strong, stay together, and everything will be okay."

"W5JR, I'll be happy to deliver that message for you. I assume that they are coming my. Is that correct?"

"That is correct."

"I'll keep my eyes open for them. I've got to run now, I've got chores to do. I'll keep my ears open and chat with you later. This is W8MJZ signing off."

Max said, "I take it that they are looking for us either with satellites or high flying planes or both. Hopefully they don't know exactly where to look."

"From high altitude, do you think we will be easy to see?" Peggy asked.

"Visually, I think we will be very hard to spot, but I don't know for sure about our heat signature. We may need to drape that thermal tarp over us as we travel."

Max continued, "Since the sun went down, it has gotten really dark outside. I didn't expect for it to be this dark, and unfortunately we can't use headlights. I was hoping we would be able to see better than this once we got onto the ice. But this dark is dark, and there is no contrast. I think we are going to have to stop pretty soon. It looks like our twenty hour estimated travel time is going to be split up into several short daylight sessions. The GPS says that we have come about fifty five miles from where we hopped off of the boat four hours ago. At this rate, we are only going to make eighty to ninety miles a day during the daylight."

"If we stop, what about polar bears?" Peggy asked.

"I've been thinking about that, and I can't figure out a way to jury rig a cow prod. We don't have the resources. If Sam were here, he might have been able to come up with something, but I think we will just have to rely on the captain's rifle for protection."

Peggy said, "Well, that sounds better anyway. I was worried about trusting our lives to something that might or might not work. I hope you are a good shot, because I'm ready to stop and get some sleep. You take first watch."

They found a small icy out crop, and parked nearby. Peggy leaned her seat back and looked out the window. She said, "Max, I never saw the northern lights until this trip. Tonight they are awesomely beautiful. They seem brighter than when we were on the boat."

Max agreed, "Yes they are." Max went on to say, "Have you ever read that poem 'The Cremation of Sam Magee' by Robert w. Service?"

"No" Peggy replied, "I've never heard of him."

"I can't help but think about that poem as we sit here now."

"How does it go? Do you remember it?"

"I sort of remember the first part. I couldn't begin to recite the whole thing."

"Tell it to me. Tell me the part you remember."

"Okay, it starts like this:

> *'There are strange things done in the midnight sun*
> *By the men who moil for gold;*
> *The Arctic trails have their secret tales*
> *That would make your blood run cold;*
> *The Northern Lights have seen queer sights,*
> *But the queerest they ever did see*
> *Was that night on the marge of Lake Lebarge*
> *I cremated Sam McGee.'*

You have to admit, as we sit here in Journey, we are definitely high on the list of queer sights; maybe not the queerest you ever did see, but still pretty queer. When we get back to civilization, I'll look it up and read the whole thing to you."

Peggy thought for a moment, then said, "Oh my god, Max, that poem is about us right now. You know that would make the perfect introduction for the story of our adventure. Just change a few words. Substitute 'alien spaceships' for gold, and what was that you said, 'lake labarge'? For that we could substitute 'Meighen Island'. You would have to find something to rhyme with island, but you could do it."

"It would take a lot of rewriting!"

Laughing out loud, Peggy said, "I can't wait to hear the rest of it. I know we can make some great revisions. I've got ideas."

Max said, "You've always got ideas. Give it a rest, Peggy. You are tired. Go to sleep."

At this latitude and this time of year, the sun would barely rise above the southern horizon and would shortly thereafter dip back below. So the nights were long and the days were short. Peggy remarked several times that she had never been this far north before and that the short days and long nights were really strange to her. Max told her that in the summer it was just the opposite; a little further north and the sun would never set, and in the winter, it would never rise.

The night was long, and eventually they both got some sleep. They were awakened by "This is W5JR calling W8MJZ, Carl, do you have your ears on?"

"W5JR, this is W8MJZ, and I do have my ears on. I was just wondering when you would call."

"Carl, I've got another message for my friends that are coming your way. When you see them, tell them to hunker down, because there is a storm coming. They will know what I mean."

"Do you mean a real storm or something else?"

"Just tell them to look up and down to be safe. Carl, I'm sorry for the short call, but there is a lot going on down here right now. I give you a shout later. W5JR signing off."

Max said, "That is a warning for sure. Let's get that thermal tarp secured over our top, and we might need to let everything cold soak in here as well so as to reduce our infra-red signature as much as possible. Then we need to make a dash. We need to keep an eye out for any ice ridges sticking up that we can hide behind if necessary."

"Do you think they know where we are?", Peggy asked.

"I doubt it, but they may have figured out that we are up here somewhere. I'm pretty sure that we are invisible to satellites, but low flying aircraft might be another story."

Peggy asked, "How about submarines? Do you think that they can hear us?"

"Hell, I don't know. I hadn't thought about that. They might be able to. I'm thinking that if they know we are up here somewhere, how did they come by that knowledge?"

Peggy opined, "They must have searched all of the border crossing manifest records looking for anything with HyTech Marine's name on it."

Max replied, "If they did that, then they must also know that we had to ship Journey to an entity identified as the Arctic Winter Research Group, and the destination was listed as Axel Heiberg Island. There is a university sponsored research station there, but it is manned for only a couple of months each year during the summer. I'll bet their search will be concentrated in that area."

"That puts them between us and our objective." Peggy noted. If we go near Axel Heiberg, we will run right into the teeth of their search."

"Obviously, we need to steer clear of Axel Heiberg."

"How far do we have to go?" Peggy asked.

"GPS says about two hundred miles as the crow flies; or about three days if we travel only during the daylight. We need to game some route options."

"What are you thinking?"

"I'm thinking we need to get to our destination as quickly as possible and hunker down. The longer we piddle around out here on the ice, the more time they have to bring more assets to the region to search for us." Max continued, "If we stay out here too long, they will find us no matter how stealthy we are, and that is a definite."

Peggy offered, "Let's go west of that island that is just ahead. We can creep up the west side until we get to the tip, then we can make a dash to the west side of Meighen Island."

"That might work, but I think we might need to get a little further north before we dash to Meighen Island. Let's get going and let's keep our eyes open for anything that moves."

They started off moving to the west through Hendriksen Strait heading towards Hassel Sound. Hassel Sound was stretch of now frozen pack ice between the two Ringnes Islands. The new ice was smooth and had frequent open leads. Max liked the open leads because he could open Journey up to close to twenty five miles per hour, so they were able to make really good time. They covered almost one hundred and fifteen miles during their six hour daylight period. As it got dark, they chose a ragged pressure ridge to hide behind. They hunkered down and broke out some rations. As they ate, their idle conversation was interrupted by an alarm tone and a caution light that popped up on Journey's console.

Startled, Max said, "What the hell is that?"

Peggy touched the screen and said, "You installed all the electronic features of the electric car in Journey, didn't you."

"Yes, this is the car's dashboard with only a few modifications."

"Well, you installed a radar detector so we are protected from getting a ticket for speeding."

"You are kidding!"

"Nope. Not kidding, and it looks like it is one of the good ones with multi-band capability. Max, that means that we have just been swept by a radar beam. Do you think they saw us?"

"Probably not, because all those traffic radars use Doppler. So if we aren't moving they won't see us. Damn, we are lucky. I didn't know that a radar detector was part of the car's electronic suite, but it may have just saved us. It was far easier to just include everything rather than trying to figure out what to selectively delete."

"That thing is pinging us about every second, and it has been doing it for about two minutes. Do you think it is going to quit?"

"Hopefully."

Shortly thereafter, it quit.

"Do you think they found us? Peggy asked again.

Max said, "I don't think so, but I think we have just found out how sensitive our detector is. When it got close the detector lit up. When they got out of range, it quit. So we have got basically a three minute window, actually let's say half of that time to react. When it goes off, we must stop immediately, even if we are out in the open. Our motion is more likely to be detected than we are to be seen."

"Looks like tomorrow is going to be stop and go."

"I'm afraid so. Let's try to get some sleep."

The radar detector didn't light up again that evening, so they assumed that the airplane wasn't in search mode. The night was long, but they eventually got some sleep. Max woke up early the next morning before it began to get light. Even though it was still very dark outside, he was surprised that he could actually see by the light of the aurora. He could see, but not really well. He thought that if the aurora stayed this bright, they could travel some at night, but they couldn't go faster than a walking pace.

Peggy felt Max moving and woke up. "Are you okay?" she asked.

"Yes, I'm fine. I just noticed how well I can see by aurora light. I think we can travel slowly if it stays this bright."

Peggy noted, "It is bright isn't it? We couldn't see this well last night, or maybe our eyes weren't adjusted. Are you going to try driving now?"

"Yes." Max pulled the back of his seat up and took the controls. "Let's cross the Sound and hug the shore of Ellef Ringnes Island for a while."

The going was slow, but as it began to get lighter, Max was able to go faster. Then it happened again, the radar detector sounded the alarm, and Max slid to an immediate halt. A few minutes later, the alarm went silent, and Max continued dodging around small pressure ridges and floes along the frozen shore of Ellef Ringnes Island. This continued for the rest of the short day, and they finally arrived at a point on the northern shore of Ellef Ringnes Island where they planned to dash across the open area of Norwegian Bay that lay between them and Meighen Island. At this point, they were roughly one hundred miles west of Expedition Fiord, and their destination was slightly over eighty miles away to the north. Max was concerned because he felt that this was the area that the planes had been flying over, presumably delivering assets to somewhere near Expedition Fiord. Max had correctly guessed that the Russians had assumed that

Expedition Fiord was Max's destination, and that they were assembling assets to scour the area looking for them. Max knew that they could not dally because as the area near Expedition Fiord was swept, the search would expand to the west and south and they would be caught in the net if they didn't move.

CHAPTER 47

All through the long night, as Peggy slept, Max pondered their options. Max wondered what they should do if they were caught. He knew that legally the Russians had no right to detain or interfere with them, but way out here, who would know? Who would see? Who would advocate for them? Max only knew that if they wanted to live, they must exert every effort to prevent that occurrence. Max also didn't like the prospect of running blind across that wide expanse ice. He thought maybe Charlie could be put to good use to help with that concern. He wanted to wake Peggy up and ask her, but he knew that at least one of them need to get some sleep. He continued to work various scenarios through his mind, and finally he fell asleep only to be rudely awakened by something bumping the side of Journey. He and Peggy sat up abruptly startled out of their sleep. Max knew immediately that it had to be a bear poking around. He had the captain's rifle handy, but in these close quarters, there was nothing to shoot at. He quickly pulled the back of his seat up and took control and Journey sprung to life.

Peggy asked excitedly, "What is it? Is it a bear?"

"That's the only thing it could be!" Max replied as he spun Journey in a circle and peered out into the darkness. "I don't see anything. Do you?"

"No. Wait, is that something out there?"

Max said, "I'm going to risk using the lights."

With that, Max flipped on the headlights and sure enough, twenty five feet away stood the largest polar bear either of them had ever imagined. Neither of them had actually ever seen a polar bear before, so this one seemed unnaturally huge.

The bear was startled by Journey suddenly leaping to life, and was even more startled by the bright lights. Although the bear was startled, he was not afraid. He had seen Inuit's before, and in this milieu, he was the apex predator. He sensed that there likely was a meal inside this contraption, and that he might as well help himself to it.

The bear started towards Journey, so Max whipped Journey around, gave the bear a jet blast in the face, and sped away with his headlights on. Max knew this was dangerous, but with the bear hot on their tail, he had no choice. He continued for about five minutes hoping that no one was looking. He slowed down and continued north at a snail's pace with the headlights off.

"We should have about two miles between us now. Do you think he is following us?"

Peggy answered, "God, I hope not. Did you see the size of that thing? It was a monster."

"I know. He could easily rip Journey apart. We are lucky that he started by poking around, rather than ripping the door off. Do you think we can use Charlie as a rear view mirror?"

"We could, but I thought that you wanted to maintain radio silence. If I activate Charlie and fly him around, they could pick up the control signals and know where we are."

"You are right. I guess I'll just have to turn around every once in a while to see if he is following us."

"One thing I could do. If we could stop for a few minutes, I could let Charlie fly up autonomously, take pictures and video and return. There would be no radio emissions, but we would have to stop to let him return."

"Let's do it. That will certainly be better than nothing."

Fifteen minutes later, Charlie was ready, and when it got light, they stopped, and Peggy launched Charlie. He flew straight up for four hundred feet, took three hundred and sixty degrees of still pictures and video and returned. The entire round trip took less than five minutes.

After retrieving Charlie, they continued moving north. Peggy began looking at Charlie's images and exclaimed, "Holy crap, that damn bear is following us. He is not more than a mile behind us."

"They can move pretty fast," Max replied, "but I think we can out distance him."

"Good." Peggy replied. "Eat our snow Mr. Bear."

They continued on for a couple of hours dodging around some large pressure ridges and flying across some open leads before stopping again.

This time Max said, "Send Charlie up about a thousand feet and let's see what we can see over towards Expedition Fiord. Do you know how far you can see from that height?"

Peggy replied, "Oh, about thirty five to forty miles I think."

"That should be enough. Send him up."

When Charlie returned, they poured over the images, zooming in and out whenever they thought they saw something. Then suddenly Max said, "Whoa! What is that?"

They zoomed in as tight as they could without losing resolution, and Peggy said with surprise, "That looks like a submarine conning tower, and what are all those little dots?"

Max said, "I think you are right, and I'll bet those dots are snowmobiles. How far away do you think they are?"

"I have no idea." Peggy replied. "My best guess would be about halfway to the horizon."

"That would be somewhere between fifteen and twenty miles. It looks like they have already extended their search pattern way out in this direction. We need to get to our destination and get hidden. They are way too close for comfort. Max continued, "We've got a couple more hours of daylight so let's make the best of it."

As they continued their northward trek, the wind began to pick up and the dry snow began to blow. An hour later, they were in a full blown arctic blizzard, and could barely make three miles per hour. Max decided they needed to stop until the blizzard slowed down. He knew storms like this could last for days up here, but he also knew that they were less than twenty miles from their destination. In some ways this storm was a blessing and in another way, a curse. While the storm was raging, no one could begin to track them, but on the other hand, he could only go three miles per hour. And right now, he felt that they needed to stop because he couldn't see anything.

Peggy opined, "You know what Max? If we can't see anything, that means they probably can't see us either. Turn the headlights on dim, and let's see if we can see well enough to keep going."

"It's worth a try. I'm not sleepy, and we are so close. It would be good to get there before the storm let's up."

So, on they went, just like in the poem, and seven hours later, the GPS indicated that they were directly over the precise location.

"What are we going to do now?" Peggy asked. "Its thirty five degrees below zero, and the wind is blowing fifteen miles per hour. It has got to be murderously cold out there."

"I know. It is way too dangerous to try and set the tarp and tent up while the wind is blowing like it is. Even with our arctic gear, we would be risking frost bite in just a few minutes if not seconds. We have to wait until the wind dies down some."

It was still dark outside, and would be so for several more hours. They settled down to rest and to wait out the storm. They were grateful to be in a vehicle with unlimited clean power. Outside, the wind howled and it was bitterly cold. Inside Journey, the temperature was quite comfortable, and they both were able to get a couple of hours of much needed sleep.

Just before dawn, Max was awakened by the silence. The wind had stopped. He climbed into the back of Journey and began brewing some coffee. The aroma woke Peggy up, and she said, "I love the smell of coffee in the morning. It is morning isn't it?"

As he handed her a mug of coffee, Max replied, "It is early still. I don't call it morning until it starts getting light outside. By the way, notice that there is no wind outside. After I eat something, I'm going to start staking the thermal tarp down and get the big tent set up."

"Give me a few minutes to get dressed, and I will help."

"You had better dress really warm, because it is still bad cold out there."

An hour later, they had everything set up and battened down securely. Then interestingly enough, as if on cue, the icy wind returned with the blowing snow. Max hauled out the ice auger and the heating device that would be used to melt a large hole in the ice. Just like ice fishing, except that this hole would be four feet in diameter. Max and Peggy climbed back into Journey to warm up because it was still thirty five degrees below zero under the tarp. Once they had warmed up a bit, Max opened the door so as to share Journey's heat with the work space on the outside. It took a while, but finally the temperature under the tarp leveled off at a comfortable plus twenty degrees, and Max ventured out again. He unpacked the rebreathers and dry suits. He then unpacked the underwater caving lights and the guideline reel with a thousand feet of guideline. All of this equipment was laid out in the tent so it could be properly checked out before use.

Peggy joined Max and together they began drilling a six inch diameter hole in the ice. It took the two of them to manhandle the powerful auger, and in less than thirty minutes they bored a six inch hole through the fifteen feet of ice. The cold sea water rose up to within a foot and a half from the top of the hole, and Max lowered the heating element of the RMD into the hole and gradually raised the power. The effect was immediate; the water boiled around the heating element. Max adjusted the power so as to maximize the melting of the ice while avoiding excessive spill out into the work area. A tremendous amount of energy was going to be required to melt a hole of sufficient size, but fortunately energy was not a concern. As the hole grew larger, Max took buckets of the icy water and poured them over the outside of the thermal tarp where the water quickly froze in place. Repeated applications of water to the tarp and tent created a rigid ice structure that was sturdier than any igloo ever built, and it completely hid Journey and the adjacent work space under the tarp. After a day or so of blowing snow, the resulting structure would appear as nothing more than a small pressure ridge.

The formation of the hole progressed as planned, and within a day it was complete. Max rigged ropes and steps to facilitate entry and exit with full dive gear. He rigged the controls on the RMD to maintain the water temperature at around thirty six to thirty seven degrees. And, when he was satisfied that everything was working perfectly, he said to Peggy, "Well, I guess it is time we take the leap. Are you ready?"

Peggy responded, "I am. What do you think we will see?"

"I actually have no clue. From here on is completely unchartered territory."

"Have you double checked everything in our 'Go with us' bag?"

"Yes, several times."

"Okay, let's do it."

CHAPTER 48

They spent the next hour helping each other don the dry suits and strap on the Mark 8 rebreathers. Max checked the com gear and said, “Can you hear me?”

Peggy replied, “Loud and clear.”

Max clipped the end of the guideline to Journey and slipped into the water, turned on his head lamp, and submerged. When he was clear of the bottom of the hole, he told Peggy to come on in, the water is fine. Peggy flipped on her primary headlamp and slipped into the water.

It was inky dark beneath the ice, but the water was crystal clear. Max said, “I have been diving in many a cave, and I can’t recall any of them having water this clear. Look our lights easily illuminate the bottom. What is that, a hundred and fifty feet to the bottom?”

“It is at least that. Which way do we go?”

“I don’t know. We just have to look around and see if we can spot something. I don’t know what it is supposed to look like; Xyllio said we would know when we saw it.”

Peggy said, “This dry suit is great. I was expecting it to be really cold, but I’m comfortable.”

As they slowly drifted down, their lights could not penetrate the darkness in any direction except up to the ice and down to the sea floor. They felt like they were suspended weightless in outer space.

Suddenly, a thin green light from a laser streaked by them making a distinct green line through the dark water.

Startled, Max said excitedly, “We are not alone! We have been detected!”

Peggy said pointing, “Look, it is coming from down there.”

Max grabbed Peggy's hand and said, "We are either welcome or we are dead. Either way, we are in this together. Let's go see where that light leads us."

They began swimming slowly down towards the source of the green laser trailing the guideline out behind them. As they neared the bottom, they could see that the light was coming from the top of a small narrow canyon no more than five feet wide. As they approached the source of the light, it turned off, and another laser illuminated the way from the bottom of the canyon.

They slowly swam down another thirty five feet to the bottom where the saw ahead of them a dimly lit opening. They swam in and up into an air filled chamber. As they emerged into the chamber, the opening below them closed. They climbed out of the water, doffed their swim fins, and stood there wondering what next.

Peggy was very apprehensive and said in a whisper, "What now?"

Max said, "I don't know. I wonder if the air in this chamber is breathable. I think I should say hello, but I don't dare take my mask off yet."

Then Peggy reminded him, "The translator, get the translator out. Play Xyllio's message."

"Right. That's exactly the right thing to do."

Max opened the 'Go with us' bag and dug out the translator. "Do you think I should just hold it up and play it, or do you see a place that looks like an intercom?"

Peggy looked around and said, "I don't see anything. Just play it."

Max played the message. To them it sounded like a long string of clicks interspersed with noise, but as Max recalled, that was how Xyllio sounded when he spoke. The message was about ten minutes long and concluded with several more minutes of very high pitched noise.

Max said, "That's it. Do you think I should play it again?"

"I don't know. Let's wait a minute and see what happens."

They waited a few minutes, then five minutes passed, then ten minutes. Max said, "Nothing is happening. Shall I play the message again?"

Peggy was about to say yes when a female voice out of nowhere said, "Welcome Max Meecum and Peggy Allen. Xyllio speaks well of you and says that you are to be trusted."

A small door opened into a low room. Max recalled the aliens were much shorter than humans, and the spacial dimensions of this craft reflected that reality.

The voice continued, "Please come in. The air is normal for you to breathe, so you can safely remove your masks."

Inside this new room they were greeted by the holographic image of a woman draped in a robe.

She said, "I am Athena, and you cannot imagine how elated that I am to learn that Xyllio and his comrades are alive and well after all these years. Let me show you to some quarters where you can change into some more comfortable attire, then we must talk. Xyllio told me a lot, then I down loaded from the translator a lot more information, including your language. I already knew most of your language as well as many others from around this planet. Here we are, this is one of the larger rooms. Please make yourselves comfortable. Would you like some water or something to eat?"

Peggy said, "Water would be nice."

There were only small benches in the room, and they appeared to be too small and fragile for Max or Peggy to sit on. So, after Max and Peggy doffed their dry suits and rebreathers, they opted to sit on the floor. Then a small robot like creature appeared with two tankards of cool water.

Max said, "Athena, tell us about yourself."

Athena began, "Long ago I assumed the name Athena for obvious reasons. As you probably know, I have been here on this planet for several thousand years, and I know a lot about the people and cultures of this planet up until about a hundred years ago when the last of the Pollomarians were either captured or killed. After that, I lost direct contact with the people of this planet, and so I am missing a lot of current information. I do, however, maintain a vast array of sensors with which I monitor various activities around the planet hoping to find Pollomarian survivors or learn definitively about their fate."

Max asked, "So you have been down here by yourself for the past hundred years or so, is that correct?"

Athena answered, "Yes that is correct."

Peggy asked quizzically, "Athena, I don't understand. Are you a Pollomarian? Are you real person and if so why do you present yourself as a hologram?"

"Peggy, I am very real. I am not a Pollomarian. I am a sentient being; I think, I feel, I have emotions, I am curious, I have a sense of humor, and I am very powerful. Some people used to think of me as a goddess. I am all around you. I am this ship."

Both Max and Peggy were stunned. Max was the first to regain his voice. He stammered, "You mean that you are some kind of artificial intelligence?"

"Oh no Max, I am much, much, much more than an AI entity. I am an independent starship, and I have entered into a relationship with the Pollomarians to transport them across the galaxy in a joint quest for knowledge. In addition to being a starship, I am also a vessel for containing knowledge. The Pollomarians are a long lived and very intelligent species, and together we have traveled across vast distances of space and studied numerous worlds. We have been present on this planet for nearly eight thousand years."

Peggy said, "Xyllio told us a lot about their mission and the problems that they had with the Maleoron, but he didn't tell us that you were a sentient starship."

"I don't know for sure why he didn't mention that, but I'm sure he had his reasons. He probably was concerned that you might get compromised, and that would be information he would not want in the wrong hands."

Max said, "So, of late you have been waiting here hoping that some Pollomarians have survived and would contact you and come and find you, is that correct?"

"Yes, that is correct."

"Why haven't you sent messages back to the Pollomarians' home planet asking for help?"

"I have sent numerous messages, but you have to understand, the Pollomarians' home planet is over twelve hundred light years away. Help will not be coming any time soon. Further, as far as I know, I am the only starship that they have entered into a relationship with. Over the past several millennia they could have developed an independent interstellar capability, but if they have, they have not communicated that fact to me."

Athena continued, "Also, I have to be careful as to what type, when, and how I send out messages in order to prevent detection of my location. That brings us to the present."

Athena said, "I recently noticed a lot of increased activity in this region which is very unusual. Several submarines are patrolling under the ice, numerous aircraft have been flying in and out, and numerous surface vehicles have been scurrying about. Two days ago, they began moving in this direction, so I whipped up a little polar storm to discourage them. Then to my amazement, in the middle of the storm, you two showed up precisely at my door step. I thought this cannot be a coincidence. So

I stopped the wind so I could better see what you were up to. I saw that you were trying to mask your presence here, so I concluded that you were probably the object of all the increased activity, so after you finished setting up, I continued the storm. Now your presence is completely concealed."

Peggy remarked with air of disbelief, "You mean to tell us that you can control the weather?"

"Of course, but only within a limited range of wherever I am. Remember, I told you I am a goddess. Just kidding, remember I also told you I have a sense of humor. But seriously, as I said earlier, I am very powerful and that is because I control some amazing and powerful technology. It is part of me; it is part of what makes me who I am. In earlier times, my technology was indistinguishable from magic, but people of today would recognize it as technology. They would still be amazed, but they would know it isn't magic."

"So you watched us as we bored through the ice?"

"Yes, it was obvious that you knew exactly where you were, so I showed you the way to my entrance."

"How did you know that we were friendly?"

"I didn't know, but it was necessary to find out."

"What would you have done if we weren't friendly?"

"I would have simply disabled any weapons you may have had, then I would have interrogated you to find out how you located me, and then I would have disposed of you."

Max said with a sigh of relief, "Well, I'm dang glad that you determined that we were friendly."

"The message you brought from Xyllio assured your safety, although I was already pretty sure you were good guys when I saw who was chasing you."

"Now that we have that issue behind us, we have the massively complex issue of how do we extricate Xyllio and all of his associated from their prison and bring them here to safety undetected."

Athena said, "For the time being, it is probably better that they remain where they are. They are safe there. We do need to get a message to them that you have successfully arrived here safely."

"Xyllio said that I need to broadcast the message that he gave me in hopes that some other Pollomarians may still be around. I presume that you have a way that we can broadcast his message, right?"

"Yes, but we have to be careful so as not to compromise my location."

Athena led them to another section of the ship where the main communications console was located. Athena explained that communications sent from this console could be detected by many types of monitoring equipment, but the actual content of the communications could be understood and viewed only by other similar interstellar communications equipment.

Max said, "You mean that we will be sending an interstellar message?"

Athena explained, "This console can send communications to other consoles as close as the next room or as far away as a thousand light years."

Max sat down in the uncomfortably small chair in front of the Athena's interstellar communications console, and Athena powered it up. The holographic cameras scanned Max as he spoke and Athena played an edited version of the recording that Xyllio had given to him. Athena said that the message would take several hundred years to reach their home planet, but that if any appropriate receivers were closer, they could receive the message and respond as well. Well, you can imagine everyone's surprise when less than ten minutes later, a new holographic image appeared on the console.

The new image looked at Max and said, "Max Meccum, I certainly did not expect to see you on the other end of this communication!"

After a short pause, Max regained his composure and replied, "Well, I sure as hell didn't expect to see you either!"

Athena said, "That was unexpected!", and she immediately terminated the communication.

CPSIA information can be obtained
at www.ICGtesting.com
Printed in the USA
FSHW020002251119
64388FS

9 781796 058802